D0386996

WRECKED

ALSO BY TRICIA FIELDS

The Territory

Scratchgravel Road

WRECKED

TRICIA FIELDS

MINOTAUR BOOKS

A Thomas Dunne Book
New York

This is a work of fiction. All of the characters, organizations, and events portrayed in this novel are either products of the author's imagination or are used fictitiously.

A THOMAS DUNNE BOOK FOR MINOTAUR BOOKS.
An imprint of St. Martin's Publishing Group.

WRECKED. Copyright © 2014 by Tricia Fields. All rights reserved. Printed in the United States of America. For information, address St. Martin's Press, 175 Fifth Avenue, New York, N.Y. 10010.

www.thomasdunnebooks.com
www.minotaurbooks.com

The Library of Congress Cataloging-in-Publication Data is available upon request.

ISBN 978-1-250-02137-3 (hardcover)
ISBN 978-1-250-02279-0 (e-book)

Minotaur books may be purchased for educational, business, or promotional use. For information on bulk purchases, please contact Macmillan Corporate and Premium Sales Department at 1-800-221-7945, extension 5442, or write specialmarkets@macmillan.com.

First Edition: March 2014

10 9 8 7 6 5 4 3 2 1

Dedicated with love to Emily Fields. *Aim High,* be safe, call your mom, and come home often!

ACKNOWLEDGMENTS

Many thanks to Linnet, Merry and Mella: the small but mighty GD3. Thanks to Dominick Abel, Todd Fields, Phyllis Driggs and Frank Disbrow for your careful reads and insight. And a special thanks to Peter Joseph and Melanie Fried for your unending patience and dedication to the work.

It is very hard to live with silence. The real silence is death and this is terrible. To approach this silence, it is necessary to journey to the desert. You do not go to the desert to find identity, but to lose it, to lose your personality, to be anonymous. You make yourself void. You *become* silence. You become more silent than the silence around you. And then something extraordinary happens: you hear silence speak.

—EDMOND JABÈS

WRECKED

ONE

Peering out her sidelight window, unnoticed by her boss, Josie tried to imagine what could possess him to visit her at home at 6:30 A.M., over an hour before her shift started. Josie checked the safety on her Beretta with her thumb and tucked the gun into the back of her uniform pants.

Mayor Steve Moss knocked again on Josie's door, looking as if he'd rather be anywhere else in the world but on her front porch.

Under normal circumstances, if Moss wanted her assistance he would have called and summoned her to his office: he would have never given up home-turf advantage. Their mutual distrust had started long before Josie's appointment to chief of police six years ago, and their animosity for each other had only grown.

"Dammit." Her bloodhound sniffed at the door and whined softly at the early morning intrusion. Josie snapped her fingers so Chester would lie down and then opened the front door. "Morning, Mayor. Come in." She pushed the screen door open and stepped back.

He cleared his throat, took off his cowboy hat, and stepped inside. The mayor would have been a couple of inches shorter than Josie, who was a trim five foot seven, but he wore custom cowboy boots with three-inch heels that put him at eye level. He was built like a bulldog, with wide shoulders and narrow hips, but Josie noticed he'd begun to add some weight around his midsection as well. *Top-heavy* was the term that came to mind.

Standing uncomfortably close to him in the small entryway, Josie motioned toward the living room.

"I know you have to get to work. Just need a minute. Off the record," he said as he took a seat on the edge of the couch.

As she pushed back the room's curtains to let in the bright morning sun, Josie knew her wariness at the early morning visit was going to be justified. She imagined *off the record* probably meant *off the books*. She was inclined to tell him they should move the conversation to the police department, but she was a firm believer in choosing one's battles, and it wasn't yet clear if this was one.

Looking around the cream-colored room, anywhere but at her, the mayor pointed to a large red and black wool rug that hung on one of the stucco walls. "That Navajo?" he asked.

Josie took a seat on the bench below the window and smiled. "No, but it's a good fake."

He nodded, his expression unchanging.

As the chief of police in a small town, Josie knew how difficult it was to approach a local officer. Family turmoil was hard enough without getting the cops involved. In the heat of a late-night domestic dispute, intimate details were often shared with the police: violence, bankruptcy filings, late child support, papers served, and on and on. Regret came the next morning like a bad hangover. As a kid, Josie had weathered the humiliation of a mother too occupied by the grief of her husband's death to worry about raising a child. Josie had watched the cops enter her home on several occasions, trying to straighten out the problems her mother had created but couldn't solve. As much as she disliked the mayor, she realized how difficult it was for him to approach her, and she stayed quiet.

The mayor leaned his forearms on his knees and stared down at his clasped hands. "I heard through a reliable source that Roxanne Spar went to Officer Cruz last night and filed a complaint."

Roxanne was a thirty-something waitress at Mickey's Bar and Grill who dressed like a hooker, but her sharp tongue and short temper typically kept potential gropers at arm's length. Roxanne had also taken on a second job this past year at Whistler's Pub in nearby Marfa, which Josie had heard through the grapevine was the mayor's weekend spot.

"About what?" Josie kept her voice level, free of judgment, though she already suspected sex was involved.

"She says I'm harassing her. Stalking her, for god's sake! The whole thing is ridiculous." His voice got louder.

In his midforties, Moss still had a thick head of brown hair, and he ran his hands through it when under stress. Josie watched him as he did it now. She hadn't remembered such deep-set wrinkles around his eyes and the corners of his mouth. His eyes were puffy and red and he looked as if he hadn't slept well in days. She wondered if his wife figured into the drama. Rumors floated around town that she was ready to take her money and move on to a more lucrative investment.

"Why don't you tell me how all of this got started?"

"It started with me trying to do the lady a favor." He sighed heavily. Josie couldn't help feeling that his reticence was part of a calculated act.

"I went to Marfa last week with some guys to celebrate Jocy Gunther's birthday," he finally went on. "You know him?"

She tilted her head. "Vaguely. I know who he is."

"There were eight of us. We went to Whistler's Pub. That old-man dive bar in downtown Marfa?"

She nodded. She had visited Whistler's to interview the bartender for an investigation about a year ago: dimly lit, sticky floor, tired waitresses, and a jaded bartender. She figured Roxanne had been hired to breathe some life into the place, and it sounded like she had.

"We got there about ten. Drank some beer. By midnight things started to get a little crazy. Some of the guys were talking to a group of women across tables. Drunk talk. Yelling back and forth."

"Friendly yelling?"

"Sure. It was friendly," he said. "We ended up taking both of the pool tables at the place. Roxanne was waitressing, but she's joking with us all night long. She's friends with some of the other women, so she's passing out free shots." He paused and gave her a look, like he didn't really want to go on with the story. "Thing is, she was hitting on me. Big time. It got awkward if you want to know the truth."

"What did she do?"

"At one point, we're playing pool. The lady leans over the top of me, her arm over mine holding the cue stick."

"By lady, you mean Roxanne?"

"Yeah, exactly. She's basically lying on top of me. So the guys start blowing me," he paused, "blowing me grief. I'd try to get her to back up. They'd laugh and egg her on some more."

"Why didn't you leave?"

"I tried to! I drove me and two other guys. Every time I talked about leaving they'd harass me. Come on, one more beer, that kind of bull."

She nodded, keeping her expression neutral. The mayor had a reputation in town as a skirt-chaser, but Josie was never sure if the reputation was deserved, or if it was his lecherous personality that got him into trouble. She couldn't imagine any woman finding him attractive, but she wasn't exactly an expert when it came to romance.

Josie glanced at the clock on the wall and saw ten minutes had passed. Dillon would just be getting out of the shower and she hoped he wouldn't come into the living room. The conversation was awkward enough as it was.

The mayor continued his story. "Finally, the bar closed at two and I told the guys I was leaving. They said they'd get a ride home with someone else. I don't know where they went after Whistler's, but they didn't ride home with me. Then, outside in the parking lot the waitress asks if I'll follow her home. Said she hated driving all the way to Artemis so late at night. Nothing between here and there if she had some kind of trouble. I actually felt sorry for her and followed her home to make sure she made it okay." He shook his head as if he couldn't believe it.

Josie nodded again, though she wondered if he really expected her to believe the story. Roxanne managed the thirty-minute drive home unescorted every other night she worked. What Josie really wanted to ask him was how long he had to wait in the parking lot for her to count her tips and close up the bar.

"So, you drove separately. And you followed her back to her apartment?"

"That's it. I did what she asked, and now she's turned on me."

"Did you get out of your car once you reached her apartment?"

He hesitated just long enough for Josie to know he was spinning damage control in his head. "She said she was scared. I got out to walk her to the door. That's it."

Chester wandered over to the mayor and tried to sniff his pants. The mayor leaned back as if the dog might soil his clothes, and Josie waved the dog away.

"Did you enter her apartment?" she asked.

"I swear, nothing happened. She wanted me to help her into her apartment, and she promised I could leave then. She said her place had been broken into. Said she was scared. She wanted me to walk around. Check out the rooms." He gave Josie an imploring look and dropped his voice. "It sounds ridiculous now. But that's what happened."

"And you only followed her home once?"

He shrugged. "A few times. I was worried about her. A woman driving home through the desert that time of the morning? Who knows what might happen. I was trying to be a nice guy. And this is what I get."

"Does Caroline know about any of this?"

He sat up and then slouched back into her couch, allowing his head to fall back against the cushion, hardly the posture of a person who usually presented himself as the man in charge.

"Are you kidding?" He laughed miserably. "She'd kick my ass all the way to Mexico. Then she'd divorce me. And she wouldn't care what the facts were."

"I'm not sure why you're telling me this," she said.

He looked at her in surprise. "I'm telling you because I expect your support! If that woman filed a report I want you to do something about it!"

"I can't control who files a report. That's her right as a citizen. And, I'm bound by law to investigate it. Honestly, I don't even know if charges have been filed."

"My marriage is hanging on by a thread." He stared at Josie as if he couldn't believe she wasn't on his side. "If Caroline finds out about some woman filing charges, my marriage is over. I want this paperwork to go away."

"I can't do that."

He sat forward, leaning toward her on the edge of the couch. "You *can* do that. You're the damned chief of police! You can do anything I tell you to do!" The mayor's face had turned red. He took a deep breath, then blew it out slowly. "Look. Roxanne is a gold digger. She's trying to ruin my marriage and my career."

"If she's a gold digger why would she want to ruin your career?"

He pointed a finger at her. "This is not a joke. You are mocking me, and I won't stand for it."

"Mayor Moss, I'm not mocking you. I'm trying to understand why you're sitting on my couch this early in the morning asking me to destroy paperwork that I haven't even seen."

"I won't be insulted like this. I came to you as one professional to another. I expect you to do the right thing." He walked to the front door, opened it, and left without another word.

Josie followed Chester to the living room window, where they watched the mayor climb into his pickup truck and back out of her driveway, spinning gravel in his wake. *Caroline will kill him,* she thought.

———

Josie turned and headed back toward the kitchen, where she found Dillon knotting his tie.

"What was that all about?" he asked. He wore pressed khakis and a starched white shirt and silk tie, the same outfit he wore every day to work, with only slight variations in color.

"The mayor's got trouble," she said.

"What kind of trouble?"

She walked up to Dillon and straightened the knot in his tie. "Police business."

"Sounded to me like he was trying to make his trouble your trouble."

Her eyebrows shot up.

"I walked into the kitchen and heard you talking to a man. It's not even seven o'clock in the morning. I was curious." He cocked an eyebrow and she noticed a nick on his otherwise smooth face. For a moment, she saw him anew, her friend and her lover.

Dillon was a clean-cut, well-dressed forty-three-year-old with neatly trimmed black hair, gray at his temples, and a wide smile he was always quick to use. Josie had been dating him for several years. He'd given up his plea for her to marry him and now appeared content with their arrangement of separate houses and frequent overnight visits. More and more often Josie wondered if one house would do. But it would be up to her to say it. He was through with pressing her.

"You didn't shave with that razor in the shower, did you?" she asked.

He leaned down and kissed her forehead. "You have time for breakfast? Preferably something other than canned fruit?"

"I don't have to be in until eight."

"Good. Come help me. You can fill me in on the mayor."

———✶———

Dillon lived in town, in a small subdivision populated by two-career families who tended to commute to larger cities to earn their rather sizeable incomes. Artemis, Texas, was a remote border town suffering the same budget cutbacks and unemployment woes as the other towns along the Tex-Mex border. Sizeable incomes were hard to earn in these towns without a commute or specialty job. As the sole accountant for fifty square miles, Dillon did quite well. He owned his own business, the Office of Abacus, located downtown. Dillon ran the office with his secretary, Christina Handley, an impeccably dressed knockout who Josie tried not to dwell on.

She watched his back as he bent inside her refrigerator to pull out eggs, peppers, mushrooms, and a pound of turkey bacon, the staples he had brought with him the night before. He opened the crisper drawer and turned to face her, holding up an orange with moldy green spots.

"Since when did you start buying fresh fruit?" He winced at the acrid smell.

"Marta gave me that last week. She claims I need Vitamin C," she said as she watched him walk to the trash can and drop the orange in with a thud.

Josie pulled a wooden cutting board from a kitchen cabinet and stood beside him at the counter. After washing and drying the peppers he swished a paring knife across a sharpening stone several times and placed it on her cutting board. "Half-inch pieces. Uniform in size."

"So how much did you overhear?" she asked.

Even though the conversation was sensitive, Josie trusted Dillon. He had worked as a pro bono consultant on quite a few cases for the department and understood the necessity of confidentiality.

He handed her the peppers and began cracking eggs over a glass bowl. "Enough. Think there's any chance the woman's on the take?"

"She could be. The mayor's got a good job and a wife who's loaded. He's a pretty easy mark," she said. "But he's also a first-rate ass with a wandering eye."

"What about his wife? I've met her a few times. She seems reasonable enough. If it isn't true, why doesn't he just tell her what happened?"

Josie grinned. "Caroline? She's reasonable in social settings. She's also a political diva." She glanced sideways at him. "I suspect she married Moss with visions of moving up the political ladder. Her dad was a four-term state senator. But after ten years as mayor, Moss can't make it out of Artemis. I hear she's pretty unhappy living out here in the middle of the desert."

"You know her very well?" he asked.

"Well enough. Several years ago I was seated beside her at a fundraising luncheon for the Red Cross. I'd only met her a few times, but she was a talker. She talked about Moss's struggles with the county council. She told me he had *difficulties* in working with a female chief."

He laughed. "That's a bit of an understatement."

"Eventually the conversation turned to relationships between men and women. Whether a woman could ever completely trust the man she is married to."

"Seriously?"

She held her knife in the air. "I'm just repeating the conversation." She watched him grab another egg and crack it against the rim of the bowl. "You aren't using the whole dozen eggs, are you?"

"Chester has to eat," he said.

Josie glanced to the floor where Chester lay stretched in front of the stove, eyeing every move Dillon made. She snapped her fingers and the dog turned his droopy eyes toward her in disbelief.

"Up, up, up. You can't lie there." Deliberately slow, one leg at a time, he pulled himself up into a standing position, but he refused to leave Dillon's side. The dog was a gentle giant, but he had an obstinate side.

"Let that poor dog alone. He's not hurting anything." Dillon slipped the dog a piece of bacon. Chester chewed it slowly, his eyes never leaving Dillon's hands. "So, does Caroline believe men are to be trusted?"

"Caroline told me that the mayor cheated on her before they were married."

"Could be she's part of the reason he can't get anywhere politically."

"It was awkward. She'd had a few mimosas at that point and she got wound up and couldn't stop. She told me she laid down the law to him. She said, 'You do this after the marriage and we're through. No tears or begging to come back. Marriage over. See you in divorce court.'"

Dillon took Josie's bowl of chopped vegetables and dumped them into the sizzling frying pan to sauté. He glanced at Josie. "More power to her."

Dillon had once been engaged to a TV news anchor in California who cheated on him in a very public way, causing him so much humiliation that he moved out of state to Artemis.

She wandered over to the coffee pot, thinking about the heartbreak and embarrassment Dillon had suffered, and poured them each a cup of strong black coffee.

"So, Caroline's verdict was clear. No man can be trusted. What's yours?"

"Depends on the man." She winked. "Fortunately, I got a good one."

TWO

After breakfast, Josie made the fifteen-minute drive into town. She took one of the few paved roads outside of downtown: the slowly curving River Road, which ran parallel to the Rio Grande. The Rio served as the two-thousand-mile border with Mexico, the most frequently crossed international border in the world. At a little before eight, Josie parked in front of the Artemis Police Department, but before she got out of her car, she dialed Dillon's cell phone number and got his voice mail.

"I forgot to remind you. We're helping Dell fix his fence line at six. You were going to come by at six thirty, after your meeting. Don't forget to bring old clothes." She paused. "Love you."

Her face flushed and she closed her eyes for a moment. She wondered if the words would ever slip off her tongue as easily as they did for Dillon—as they seemed to do for everyone else but her. Dillon had asked her one night why it was so hard for her to say the words.

"You love me, right?" he'd said.

They were walking the pasture behind Josie's home one cool evening in October, watching a deep red sunset fade to black. The sweet smell of wood smoke drifted toward them from Dell's cabin up the lane. They had been holding hands, and Josie had been thinking about how incredibly happy she was, and then he'd said *I love you.* She had squeezed his hand in return, her body tensing, but then he'd stopped walking and held on to her hand, forcing her to stop and face him.

She had smiled, embarrassed at her response, and looked away. "Of course I love you," she said. "It's just hard. I don't know why. Like a lump in my throat."

He stood nearly a foot taller, and she could feel him peering down at her as if trying to understand. She'd wanted to tell him, *This is pointless. I can't figure my feelings out for myself, so how can I explain them to you?* And then he had cradled her head in his hands and kissed her neck and the side of her face, until she had turned and kissed him back, and the question faded.

He had finally wrapped his arms around her and whispered into her hair. "You don't need to explain yourself to me. I love you for who you are."

Josie stared at the cell phone in her hand and felt the familiar burn in the center of her stomach. There were other women, young and attractive, who would be happy to slide a gold band on their finger and become the newly wedded Mrs. Dillon Reese. She knew he deserved better, and if she didn't give him better, who might take her place?

The Artemis Police Department was located in a two-story, shotgun-style brick building across the street from the courthouse. Plate-glass windows lined both sides of the entrance door, and a dark blue awning had recently been installed above them to block the afternoon sun. As Josie entered, she found city dispatcher Louise Hagerty sitting at her computer behind the long faux-wood counter that separated the dispatch station and intake area from the public.

Lou arrived at seven most mornings to relieve the night dispatcher. Despite years of that routine, anything before nine still made her grouchy, and she made no effort to hide it. She only nodded as Josie said hello and walked through the swinging access door and straight to the back of the building. She gazed at the scattered papers on the two intake desks on either side of the aisle and made a mental note to remind Otto he had a mess to clean up. The desks were used by the three officers in the department to take initial statements and fill out basic paperwork. She passed a row of filing cabinets, walked by the flagpoles that held the U.S. and Texas state flags, and up the steps to her office.

She unlocked the wooden door and flipped on the lights to her right. Several rows of fluorescent bulbs hummed to life. Josie shared a space the size of an elementary school classroom with the other two officers in the department: Otto Podowski and Marta Cruz. The office was divided into fourths, with a metal desk, trash can, and two-drawer filing cabinet taking up three of the corners and a large wooden conference table for interviews and department meetings in the remaining one. Windows covered the back wall, letting in the light and a wide view of the desert that Josie loved, as well as the radiant heat that made the room nearly impossible to cool.

Josie's desk was at the front, next to the conference table. She pitched her keys on her desk and walked to the back of the office for the coffee pot and filter basket, which she then took to the bathroom located off one of the room's back corners. She washed them out and filled the pot with water, fulfilling her first morning task. As she pulled the lid off the can of Folgers, Otto walked into the office.

"Morning."

"Morning, Otto." She watched him lay a plate covered with plastic wrap onto her desk.

"Delores made your favorite. Sticky buns. Still warm from the oven."

Josie thought about the omelet and toast, and now the sticky bun she would eat. She would need an extra evening at the fitness center that week to make up for it.

"That sounds wonderful. Make sure you tell her thanks."

Otto patted his stomach. He was at least fifty pounds heavier than the department weight limit allowed. "She tells me I have to lose weight, and then makes the most amazing sweets any man could ever ask for. What am I to do?"

"We'll order salad for lunch."

He made a dismissive snort. "I'm headed out. The high school was vandalized last night. School's out for spring break, so some kid got bored and spray-painted cuss words on the building." Otto adjusted his gun belt under his midsection. "What time is Marta on?"

Josie looked at the schedule she kept at the corner of her desk. "She comes in at three thirty."

"Good enough. I'll be back before lunch."

Marta Cruz was the third officer in the three-person department. Josie and Otto typically worked the day shift, and Marta worked seconds. They rotated nights on weekends and worked with the sheriff's department to make sure there was at least one law enforcement vehicle on the road at all times. As they operated in the most isolated county in Texas, manpower and resources were insufficient, often blurring the lines between the Arroyo County Sheriff's Department and the Artemis Police Department. Sheriff Roy Martínez's primary concern was running the jail, and he relied on the Artemis Police Department to take a good number of his calls. With a population just over twenty-five hundred, Artemis was still the largest city in the county. Given that the county had an average of only two people per square mile, taking calls on a busy night was often a difficult task.

Josie started her day drafting a memo to a group of five police chiefs who served small towns along the West Texas border. The group had been formed two years ago to address the issues that affected the citizens living along the strip of land the locals called *the territory*. It covered three hundred miles of West Texas border, from El Paso south to the end of Big Bend National Park, and was increasingly serving as a portal into the United States for drug runners. The major players in the drug wars in northern Mexico changed too frequently for local authorities to stay well informed, so the police departments in the region had banded together to share intelligence, and when necessary, resources. It was Josie's turn to compile an intel briefing, summing up the news she'd learned over the past two weeks.

After another hour finishing up a case report, she determined that Marta had been allowed the requisite eight hours of sleep, and called her for a briefing on the mayor's story about Roxanne Spar.

"The mayor came by my house this morning before work," Josie said. "Claims Roxanne Spar came by the PD and filed a report on him last night."

Marta laughed. "He is unbelievable!"

"He gave me some lame story. Then he asked me to lose the paperwork."

"There's no paperwork to lose. Roxanne didn't file charges."

"How'd the mayor find out so fast?" Josie asked.

"No idea. Didn't come from me."

"So if she didn't want to file charges, then what was her complaint?"

"She claims the mayor showed up at Whistler's a month ago, and he's been several times since. She's good with that, talks her up all night long. Big tipper. The problem is, he's followed her home several times. And it's freaking her out."

"The mayor claims Roxanne asked him to follow her home the first time. He says he did her a favor."

"Oh, no," Marta said. "That's not her story. And I really can't imagine why she'd lie about this. She said she doesn't want him to get into trouble. She doesn't want people to find out about this. She was adamant we keep this confidential."

"What did she want then?"

"She wants us to talk to him. Let him know Roxanne wants him to back off," Marta said.

"We're not a counseling service."

"I get that. She's thinking, because he's the mayor, he has a lot of pull, knows a lot of people."

"She doesn't want to lose the tips, just the jackass who's stalking her," Josie said.

"Exactly. She doesn't want him breathing down her back the whole way home at two in the morning."

"All right. Thanks for the update. I'll see you at three thirty." Josie hung up the phone. A quick conversation with Roxanne was in order.

Rather than bothering Marta again or checking with the DMV for an address, she called Junior Daggy, a local real estate agent whose propensity for gossip reached beyond Artemis into all of West Texas. He knew an amazing number of people, and delighted in scoring details he could share with his buddies. She scrolled through the contact list on her cell phone and found his number.

"Junior, this is Chief Gray. How are you today?"

"Chief! I haven't seen you in months! You visit your man friend's office, right next door to my own, and you never even stop by for a friendly chat? What's up with that?"

Josie sighed. She considered it a personal shortcoming that she had no patience for small talk, but it was a flaw she had no real desire to correct. "I'll stop by soon. I actually have a question for you."

"Let me guess. You and your man friend are looking to invest? There's some great deals right now. Real money-makers."

Josie broke in. "No, nothing like that. This is police related."

"Anything I can do to help. You know that."

"Do you know Roxanne Spar? Waitress at Mickey's?"

"Sure. Everybody knows Roxanne. She's a good gal."

"Any idea where she lives?"

"Sure. Forest Glen Apartments," he said. "Although there's no forest. No glen either." He laughed at his joke.

"You know which apartment is hers?"

"No, can't tell you that. You know, Don Carter owns those. And Don will rent to *anybody*." He drew the last word out for emphasis. "Not that I'm implying anything about Roxanne."

"Any chance you have contact information for him?"

"Sure. I can help you out." Josie listened as Junior dug around his desk, muttering to himself, until he finally came back on the line with a phone number.

After hanging up she called the number Junior gave her, and the landlord answered on the first ring.

"Mr. Carter, this is Chief of Police Josie Gray with the Artemis PD. How are you today?"

"I was doing pretty good. Rest of the day probably depends on you."

"No trouble. I just need to reach one of your tenants. I don't have a problem with her, I just need to contact her."

"All right."

"Do you have a tenant named Roxanne Spar?"

"Yes, ma'am."

"Can you tell me which apartment is hers?"

"She's in unit four at Forest Glen. And, while I got you on the phone, why don't you tell the mayor to quit hanging around my parking lot. I don't think he's campaigning after midnight, and he's making my tenants nervous."

Josie assured him that she would do her best and thanked him for the information.

Forest Glen Apartments was located on a downtown street, three blocks over from the county courthouse, with one small pine tree at the center of a grassy strip in front of the complex. The building was a one-story stucco, painted a garish bright blue, with the eight apartment doors that faced the street painted Pepto-Bismol pink.

She knocked on the door with a black plastic FOUR nailed just below the peephole, and Roxanne Spar opened the door. Josie knew her in passing, like she did many of the residents in Artemis. As chief of police, most everyone in town knew her and expected her to know them by name in return. She had a good memory for names and faces, which served her well.

Roxanne was short and full busted, with a heavy application of dark eye makeup. She wore a tight-fitting T-shirt with a roaring lion emblazoned across her chest, and white capri pants with high-heeled shoes that crisscrossed up her leg. In the bright sunlight, Josie figured Roxanne was in her late forties, but in a dark bar Josie was sure Roxanne could pass for early thirties.

Josie showed her badge and introduced herself. The woman eyed Josie for a moment; not unfriendly, but with a look that said she'd seen plenty of cops in her lifetime and had learned to reserve judgment.

"Morning, Roxanne. Would you mind if I came inside for a minute? I just have a few questions."

The woman whistled. "I am headed out the door right this minute. Got to meet somebody and I'm already late."

"I'll walk you to your car then," Josie said.

Roxanne hesitated. "Well, then, hang on." She shut the door and came back outside a minute later carrying her purse and a leather cigarette case. She pointed toward a red Chevy Malibu parked in the lot and they started toward it.

"This about last night? I told Marta, I don't want to make a big fuss."

"I just want to follow up with a few questions."

She squinted in Josie's direction, into the glare of the late morning sun, her expression weary.

"I talked with Officer Cruz this morning. She said the mayor has been following you home. Has he threatened you, tried to force his way into your apartment?"

Roxanne was taking tiny, careful steps across the grass, as if she might trip. She looked up for a moment and frowned at Josie. "I don't know about threaten. I just want him to back off."

"You realize, without filing charges, there isn't much the police can do?"

When they reached her car, she stopped and placed her hand on her hip. "Look. Some men think if they lay the money down on the table, they're entitled to something outside the bar. Usually all those men need is a wake-up call and they get the picture. The bartender at Mickey's takes care of guys like that. Whistler's though? Jimmy's a hundred years old. He's not scaring anybody into anything. So I came to you guys. This'll probably do the trick. See what I mean?"

Josie nodded. "Understood. Just don't let him get away with a crime just because he's the mayor."

Roxanne looked at her watch. "I gotta go before my old man has a coronary."

Driving back to the office Josie thought about the mayor. He didn't like her; he'd made that much clear over the years. When Otto had retired as chief and encouraged Josie to run, the mayor had stopped her one evening and told her to take her name out of the running. She'd been so shocked by his arrogance that she had not responded. She still remembered his exact words. "Don't take it personal. A woman just isn't suited for this job."

The chief of police was jointly appointed by the city council and the mayor. After the mayor's comment, Josie was surprised when the job had been offered to her. She had never learned which members of city council had voted against the mayor's wishes, but she preferred to keep it that way. The mayor, however, conducted her performance evaluation each year, and with the support of the city council, could fire her at will. She didn't allow it to cloud her judgment, but it was a fact the mayor waved around in front of her like a pocket knife: a minor threat, but still a threat.

By six that evening Josie was at Dell's in jeans and an old T-shirt, dragging tree limbs away from his fence line. A massive oak had fallen directly across the fence, and it needed to be repaired before the cows figured out a way around the branches. As Dell worked the chain saw, the sweet smell of wood chips and sawdust filled the air.

Chester lay beside the cooler as if protecting their dinner. Dell had smoked a brisket all afternoon and made a citrus barbecue sauce for dipping. He had decided they would wait on supper until Dillon arrived, although Josie was starved. She thought about snatching a piece of the brisket while Dell had his back to her, but instead walked back to the pile of wood on the ground and grabbed another load. Between the two of them they had already made an impressive stack of wood.

She continued to stack the logs onto the flatbed wagon hooked to the back of Dell's tractor and stopped to take in the evening. It was perfect in every way. Temperatures in the low seventies, a blue sky, no humidity, a soft breeze, and a relaxing night that would be spent with Dell and Dillon, two of the three men in her life that mattered most.

Dell stopped the chain saw and walked over to the wagon. His stained blue jeans were so old they looked as if they might disintegrate during their next trip through the washing machine. Wood chips stuck to his Carhartt sweatshirt and mixed in with his thin silvery hair.

She watched as he set the chain saw on the back of the wagon and opened a small container of bar and chain oil to fill the reservoir.

"This new blade cuts through that wood like butter," he said, as much to himself as to her.

Josie smiled as she watched her friend wipe down the bar with a greasy old T-shirt. She realized it was the simplicity of his life that she appreciated. Life was black-and-white with Dell, and that's how Josie preferred it.

THREE

Dillon logged off his computer and replayed the message Josie had left on his cell phone that morning. He grinned at her hesitation, and then her quick *love you*. He had quit trying to figure her out: she was the most complicated woman he had ever dated, and he loved her more than he thought possible. Josie was the woman he would spend the rest of his life with, but he knew she had to realize that on her own terms.

He slipped his phone into his breast pocket. He had a meeting at six, and Josie wanted him at Dell's place at six thirty. That would give him twenty minutes to introduce himself to the potential client and schedule a proper meeting at the office.

Dillon took the new-client packet that Christina had left for him at the corner of her desk and walked out of the office. She had scheduled the appointment with the client's secretary, who had told her that the client had just moved to the area from Argentina and asked if Dillon would mind meeting at his new home. Dillon had thought the request was a bit odd, but from what Christina had told him, there was potential for a lucrative business deal, as the man intended to set up a tax shelter in Texas for his American business holdings. He had found that he could learn quite a bit about a client from a home visit, but he typically only visited established clients, not strangers. He hoped the payoff would be worth it.

Dillon drove several miles on River Road before turning right onto Driftriver Drive, and into the small housing development west of town. He drove past several homes on the front side of the sub-division, and then around the oval-shaped road past a half-dozen empty lots. On the back side of the development, two houses sat side by side, exiled from the rest of the neighborhood. Slowing his convertible in front of the first house, he squinted at the address on the mailbox. He picked up the Post-it note off the passenger seat and glanced at the number again. 5657 Driftriver Drive. The numbers matched, but the windows had no curtains, revealing what looked to be an empty house.

The only sign of life was a white cargo van parked on the left side of the driveway. Dillon considered calling the phone number Christina had written on the Post-it but, assuming a moving crew was getting the house settled, instead pulled in beside the van and turned off the car.

As he slammed his car door shut, the van's side door opened. Two men with white stocking masks and coveralls jumped out of the van, and a third man in the passenger seat opened his door and swung the butt of a rifle directly into Dillon's face, gouging his forehead. Too stunned to respond, he felt his knees give out and his vision blur. Two of the men grabbed his arms and pulled him into the van, headfirst, knocking his shins against the doorframe as he was dragged inside.

Terrified now, he knew that escape was his best chance at survival. Josie's words sounded in his head. *Never let them get you in their car.* He yelled and threw his weight to his left and tried to twist free, but their fingers dug into his arms, and his feet slipped on the metal floor. Dillon struggled to remain on his knees, but the men forced him toward a narrow bench seat at the back of the van. He caught a glimpse of the driver, who was wearing a black baseball cap, before the others shoved him and he fell to his stomach. The last things he saw were a toolbox and a pile of burlap sacks before a pillowcase was pulled over his head and his hands were tied together behind his back with rope.

As the sliding door slammed shut, Dillon felt hands grab his clothes and flip him onto his back. He then felt a man's knees come down hard onto his chest. He lurched forward, trying to resist, but was punched in the gut. He wheezed, his lungs straining for air against the weight. Two pairs of hands forced his legs out straight, and one shoved a hand into his front pants pocket and pulled out his keys. Catching his breath, he tried to resist by flailing his arms and legs, but he was rolled onto his side anyway and his wallet was pulled from his back pocket. For a moment Dillon had a glimmer of hope that this was a mugging, an armed robbery, a carjacking; he prayed for anything but a kidnapping.

He listened to his car start, the engine revving, and then pull away. Moments later the van lurched backward out of the driveway. And then he realized with sudden clarity that it was all a mistake.

"You took the wrong man! I don't live there!" he yelled.

Without a word, the man on his left kicked his shoulder.

"I'm an accountant! I'm not who you want. I don't live here!"

A brutal kick to his kidney caused bile to rise to his throat. He said nothing, breathing slowly through his nose, hoping they would look at his license, confirm that he wasn't the man they were looking for, and drop him on the side of the road.

He could see Josie's face as if it were before him, the sun lighting up her eyes as she turned her head up to kiss him good-bye that morning. What had she told him in the past? He tried to focus. Remember the details. People don't pay attention to the moment. They're too busy focusing on what is to come, she had said. Details. Mentally, he forced his thoughts to slow and realized that he had no idea what direction the van was heading. He tried to concentrate on his breathing, on estimating how many minutes they had been in the van, but the driver was making frequent turns, and he couldn't hold his thoughts together. He was lying flat on his stomach, facing the back of the van, his head turned to the right, his sense of direction gone. He could feel blood seeping from the gash on his forehead and one of the men sitting on the bench pressed the heel of his boot into Dillon's back each time he attempted to move. He strained to listen for conversation but he had not heard a word from any of them.

When he felt a vibration against his chest, for a moment he thought it was coming from underneath the van. But the vibration stopped and started again and he realized it was the cell phone in his breast pocket. The phone rumbled against the metal floor and he panicked that the man sitting behind him would realize it was still in his possession. He attempted to hunch his back so that the phone wouldn't be heard above the engine noise, but the heel of the boot ground into his spine and forced him back against the floor.

———•———

Josie called Dillon at seven to check on him, but he didn't answer his cell phone. She sent him a text, still no answer. She called his office at eight and got the answering machine. With each call her level of concern rose considerably. She imagined his car destroyed on one of the back gravel roads, his body unresponsive. Speed was his vice. He drove a two-seater Audi sports car that he loved to open up on a well-paved road in the desert. Trouble was, 90 percent of the roads in Artemis were gravel, and loose gravel could lead to disaster.

At eight thirty she called his pretty secretary, Christina Handley, both on her cell phone and home phone. No answer.

Dell had shut down the chain saw and was pulling the food out of the cooler. They had decided to eat without Dillon. Dell passed Josie a plastic cup filled with tea brewed in the sun earlier in the day, and a plate piled high with smoked brisket and sauce. Dell never served sandwich bread that might disguise the taste of the meat. He then took his seat next to her on the end of the wagon where she had been piling the cut wood. Josie tried to use dinner as a distraction, but her mind was stuck on Dillon.

Finally, at eight forty-five, he sent a brief text back. *Can't make it*.

She read the message and looked at Dell, perplexed.

"What's that look for?" he asked.

She told him what the message said and he shrugged. "Guess he can't make it."

"It doesn't sound like him. I can't believe he wouldn't at least call."

Dell continued eating.

After several minutes she said, "You suppose I should run by his office? Make sure something isn't wrong?"

"Maybe the pencil pusher and the secretary are together," he said. He turned his head to face her, then apparently realized how his comment had sounded. "On business. Maybe they had work to do. Had to work over."

Josie ate the rest of her dinner in silence, worried about Dillon, as well as the plausibility of Dell's remark. She tried to focus her thoughts elsewhere as she packed up the cooler after dinner. "You splitting all this wood tomorrow?" she asked.

"Need to let it dry first. I'll stack it outside the barn."

She nodded.

"This old man's going home to bed. You worked me too hard. Do yourself a favor. Go drive by his house and his office. You won't sleep tonight if you don't."

They packed the equipment onto the end of the wagon and Dell drove his tractor back to the barn. Josie and Chester walked the half mile back home in the dark. She checked her phone again for a message, trying to decide if she was being an overbearing mother hen, a jealous girlfriend, or just plain irresponsible for not dropping everything to check on Dillon. By the time she reached her house a variety of scenarios had played out in her mind, but the one she kept coming back to was a scene in Dillon's home. Josie would walk down the dimly lit hallway to his bedroom, where soft voices and laughter would filter toward her. Josie would push the door open and find Dillon and Christina. It made her physically ill to even imagine. When she finally reached her house she fed Chester a bone and went to bed, disgusted that she was unable to bear the risk of putting her insecurities to the test.

Dillon's head pounded. Sweat stung his eyes and the wound on his forehead. The van had stopped for at least an hour, maybe two, but the men had sat in the van in silence. Finally, the engine had started and the van began moving again. After another five to ten minutes the van slowed again to a crawl and began inching its way over rough rocks and small boulders. When he pressed his ear against the metal floor of the van, he could make out the sound of rushing water. They moved slowly forward, bouncing heavily, and he soon heard the rhythmic sound of slatted boards that Dillon assumed was a makeshift bridge. Once the van was over the bridge it stopped again. He closed his eyes and felt every bit of hope drain from his body. He was certain they had just illegally crossed the Rio Grande and entered Mexico, where he would be taken to a stash house and held for ransom.

As the van continued over rough, bumpy terrain, he tried to force the hysteria from his thoughts. An acquaintance of his, a businessman in Houston, had been kidnapped and held for six months, and then released after a million-dollar ransom had been negotiated, his family and friends extorted for everything they had. The government and police intervention had been ineffective: a rare case in this region, but certainly not isolated. The photograph in the paper had shown a man severely dehydrated and suffering from malnutrition. Dillon fought to force the vision from his mind.

The van eased onto a paved road, stopping shortly after. The side door slid open and a man yelled in English with a heavy Spanish accent, "Get up. On your knees!"

Dillon rolled to his side and struggled to push off with his shoulder into an upright position without the use of his hands, which were bound behind his back. As he turned, he felt the phone slip from his breast pocket and drop, then slide across the metal floor. One of the men hollered something in Spanish. Dillon heard the palm-slap of someone catching it just outside the van. His last link to the outside world now lost.

With no chance to think, he felt hands grab his upper arms and pull him out of the van and into the night. He was then dragged forward, forced to walk through gravel for a hundred feet.

The group stopped and a man shouted, "Hold this." He felt the hard steel of guns on either side of him jabbing into his ribs, then a piece of paper pushed against his chest, his hands forced to hold it up. He saw several flashes of bright light.

The man who spoke English pulled open the pillowcase gathered around Dillon's neck so that he could see out the bottom. "See this?" Dillon looked down to see the barrel of a gun pointed directly at his heart, the beam of a flashlight shining on the barrel. "I'm going to take your blinder off your head. If you look up, try to see who we are, or where you are? You die. Understand?"

Dillon nodded.

The man turned Dillon and walked him several feet forward. "Keep your head down. I take the pillowcase off, you step down the ladder. Get to the bottom, keep your head down until we get the case back on. Nod your head if you understand."

He did as he was told. The man pushed down Dillon's head, then took the bag off. He felt a moment of panic as a beam of light from one of several flashlights shone on the surrounding men's blue jeans and cowboy boots. Keeping his head down as instructed, he saw a rope ladder that led into a dark concrete hole. Dillon assumed it was an old cistern, used to hold water during the rainy season.

The man forced the blade of a knife between Dillon's wrists and sawed back and forth several times until the rope broke and his hands were freed.

"Do not look up when you reach the bottom."

Keeping his chin to his chest, Dillon walked toward the ladder and turned his body to step over the edge. Damp with sweat, his hands slid down the rope. With each step down the swaying ladder he imagined plummeting to the floor from a bullet through his head.

He could see the beam of a flashlight below him. At least two men were already down there, yelling at him in Spanish as he reached the bottom. As soon as his feet touched the ground his arms were grabbed from behind and the pillowcase pulled over his head.

One of the men began ripping at his shirt, the other man pulling at the legs of his pants. Sweating even more now, terrified at what lay ahead, Dillon removed his shirt, shoes and socks, and dress pants. One of the men began laughing as the other man shouted, yanking at Dillon's underwear until he was completely naked.

The men pushed him from all directions, shoving him off balance and yelling. Then suddenly it all stopped and he heard them climbing up the ladder. He listened as the wood slats clinked against the concrete as the rope ladder was pulled up and out of the hole. There was a final loud thump and he ripped off the pillowcase, but there was absolutely no light from the entrance hole above. The trapdoor sealed him from everything.

Trying to keep from hyperventilating, Dillon bent over at the waist and placed his hands on his knees, forcing himself to take slow, deep breaths. He closed his eyes and counted to one hundred, slowly, concentrating on his breathing. After several minutes he stood, but vertigo overcame him. The floor seemed to tilt, and with nothing to focus his sight on, it was impossible to get his bearings. He shut his eyes again and tried to keep from swaying. He was now focused on one thought: *I am going to die.*

FOUR

After a sleepless night of checking her alarm clock and then her cell phone, Josie got out of bed an hour early and showered. She was worried. The text message wasn't like Dillon, and it wasn't like him not to call. She should have driven over to his house and office last night to check on him. He would have done the same for her, but foolish insecurities had kept her from acting on her fears.

She put on her blue and gray Artemis PD uniform and then drove straight to Dillon's house. The garage door was shut. The mail was still in the box beside the road. She slipped on latex gloves as she jogged up the walkway to his front door and found it locked. Using the key he had given her, she unlocked the door and pushed it open. The foyer and living room were cool and quiet. Everything was as neat and orderly as normal.

She walked down the hallway and found his bed made. The bathroom door was ajar, the light off, but she opened the shower door to be sure and found it dry. The spicy smell of his shampoo and shaving cream caught in her throat and she forced back panic, trying to convince herself there were still rational explanations for his absence. At the other end of the house she opened the door into the garage and found the bay where he parked his car empty.

Back in her car, speeding into town, she thought of three possibilities: he was at the office after a night spent working (almost too difficult to imagine because he would have called her), he had stayed the night at Christina's (even more unlikely), or something had gone terribly wrong. With no cars coming toward the crossroads, Josie slowed, then breezed through the red light and pulled up to the Office of Abacus. She could see the nose of Christina's car parked in the alleyway behind the building, a troubling sign because she never arrived at work before 9:00 A.M. and it was just 7:00. Josie parked and walked quickly up to the front door, scanning her surroundings for anything out of the ordinary.

Two large plate-glass windows faced the street with a glass entrance door between them. The building itself was brick, painted dark gray with cream trim around the windows. As she approached the entrance she saw the dark outline of Christina sitting in her chair. Her desk sat about fifteen feet back from the front door and off to the right another ten feet. It was difficult to see from outside in the bright early morning light. Christina's chair was to the left of the desk, as if she had rolled away from it. Her legs were stretched straight out in front of her toward the side of the desk, and her body was leaned back in her chair. As Josie reached for the door handle, her thoughts changed from thinking Christina's posture was odd to knowing it was wrong. Josie jerked her hand back and found the latex gloves in her back pocket and pulled them on. The door was locked. She banged on the window but Christina didn't move.

Josie pulled her radio out of her gun belt. She called the station's night dispatcher, Brian Moore, as she ran to the back of the building to check for forced entry. The back door was locked and intact.

"I'm at Dillon Reese's office. I believe there is a seriously injured female inside. I'm going to force entry. The doors and windows are secured. Request backup and emergency medical personnel."

"Ten-four."

She ran back to her jeep to get her tire iron and then back to the front door. She turned her face away from the door and rammed the heavy iron against the window three times before the tempered glass finally cracked. Using her foot she kicked out the center of the window and hundreds of small pieces of glass fell to the floor. Throughout her break-in Christina still did not move.

Time slowed. The senses in Josie's body picked up details in tandem: scattered files on the floor, the dimly lit room, the faint patchouli scent of a candle, the sound of her footsteps crunching over the glass then onto the hardwood floor as she walked toward Christina. Josie noticed that Christina was dressed in a skirt and blouse and stifled a scream when she saw the crimson stain down the center of her blouse. From Josie's position, Christina's head was in profile, facing the side of her desk, her eyes open and staring upward.

As Josie got closer she saw that blood had soaked the skirt's brown tweed fabric. Josie covered her mouth with her hand and closed her eyes for a moment, struggling to process what she was looking at. She had a sudden vision of Dillon sitting at his own desk and she moaned at the thought.

She ran down the hallway to his office. His desk chair was knocked over on its side. All four sets of filing cabinets were open and files were scattered across the floor. She ran behind his desk to make sure he wasn't on the floor, then did a quick search of the bathroom and the two closets in the building. Her relief was short-lived: if Dillon wasn't here, where was he?

As she ran to the back entrance she heard a siren approaching the front. She snapped a picture of the back door, with the deadbolt secured, and used her gloved hand to twist the lock and push the door open. Christina's was the only car in the alley, and a cursory look through its windows showed nothing suspicious.

She heard Otto call her name and she ran back into the building. He was standing in the front room staring at Christina.

"Where's Dillon?" he said.

"He's not in his office or out back. Her car is the only vehicle in the alley." She turned away from Christina's body. She could feel her heart pounding against her chest and knew that she had to lower her heart rate. She was suddenly hot and the periphery of her vision grew black and fuzzy. Guilt washed through her body like a poison. She had ignored her instincts and allowed petty insecurities to keep her from checking on Dillon last night.

Otto grabbed her arm and led her over to a wooden chair backed against a window. He gently pushed her down into the seat.

Two other sheriff cars pulled up outside the office and a moment later Sheriff Roy Martínez entered the building, dressed in the brown sheriff's uniform. He was a burly ex-marine with a thick head of black hair and a bushy mustache.

He glanced at the body in front of the computer and said, "You have a perimeter set up outside?"

"I just got here a minute ago," Otto said. "Nothing's been done."

Roy turned and gave brief instructions to Deputy Scott Jones, who had arrived at the same time. Roy told him to cordon off the street and run crime-scene tape around the building and the realty office next door. All officers were to remain outside until further notice to keep contamination of the office as minimal as possible during the early investigation.

"Tell me what you know," Otto said. He kneeled down on the floor to be eye to eye with Josie.

With her thoughts a scattered mess, she struggled to keep his face in focus. She was afraid she might be sick.

He put a hand on her arm and squeezed gently. "What happened here, Josie?"

She took a deep breath and exhaled slowly, forcing the lump in her throat to settle. Roy came back inside and stood beside them.

She stared at Otto's hand on her arm and told the two men about her plans with Dillon the night before. She explained that Dillon had not shown up at Dell's or answered his phone all evening.

"When was the last time you had contact with him?" Otto asked.

"Yesterday morning at about seven forty-five. He left my place. I called him just before eight A.M. and left him a message, reminding him to stop at Dell's to help out." She pulled her cell phone out of her uniform shirt pocket. "He never showed up. After a dozen phone calls and messages and texts from me last night, he finally left this text at eight fifty P.M."

Otto took the phone and read the text aloud to Roy. "Can't make it." Otto frowned. "That's pretty abrupt. Does that read like a typical text from him?"

She shook her head, too ashamed to admit she had second-guessed herself the night before.

"You didn't talk to Dillon or Christina at any time yesterday after that morning phone call?" Roy asked.

"No. He had a full day. He was going to meet this client at six for a quick meeting, then come out to Dell's to help with the fence by six thirty. I remember him saying the meeting was at the client's house, on Driftriver Drive. It was on the way, out to my place."

"Is that customary? For him to meet a client at their house?" Roy asked.

Josie gave him an uncertain look. "I don't really know."

"Do you have the address of the meeting?" Otto asked.

She shook her head.

"We need to get someone out there to look for his car."

Otto walked away and called Lou Hagerty, the daytime dispatcher who'd just come on duty, and gave her a summary of what they'd found. "Call Marta at home and brief her. Ask her to scout out Driftriver Drive for Dillon's car, then report here. And let me know how soon the coroner can get here." Once he finished, Otto returned and laid his hand on Josie's back. "We need to get the lead investigator set."

The thought hadn't even crossed her mind yet. She was still trying to process what she was seeing.

"It's your call to make," Otto said.

Josie took a deep breath, summoning up a resolve she didn't feel. She knew Otto was asking her to make the correct ethical and tactical decision, but it was a decision that would effectively take her out of the command role in terms of the investigation into Christina's murder and Dillon's disappearance. She would not be making the key decisions. But she had to admit that it would be almost impossible for her to remain impartial, to ask the tough questions required in a murder investigation.

"You're lead," she said, looking at Otto.

Otto nodded once. "You're doing the right thing."

Josie felt the energy drain from her body. "I may be a pain in the ass to deal with."

"I expect that's true."

"Okay, then," she said.

"You have to trust me, Josie. I'm going to run this investigation like a cop. Not like a friend."

"Understood," she said. In her four years as chief of police she had never relinquished control of an investigation.

Roy's eyes were focused on Josie. She knew where the conversation was about to head, and the thought of it made her want to walk out of the building.

Otto cleared his throat and smoothed his hair over his balding head. "Let's get this established. Until we find additional information, Dillon Reese is a suspect. As far as we currently know, he was the last person to be seen with Christina, and he is missing. The knowledge that he is missing will be kept internal until further notice. No need to share that with the public just yet."

Josie looked away from Otto. "It's obviously a murder and a missing persons case."

"We don't know that. Dillon could have shot Christina and taken computers to hide any number of things," Otto said. He raised a hand to acknowledge the look on her face. "Josie, you know the drill. Probable or not, it's our job to investigate all possibilities."

She could feel the anger building. "It makes *no* sense, Otto. It's absurd and you know it." She pointed to Christina's body. "Dillon Reese is not capable of that, and you know it as well as I do!" She looked from Otto to Roy, who both stared back in silence. "This is a clear-cut kidnapping."

"What makes you so certain?" Otto asked.

Josie gritted her teeth and breathed in through her nose. Otto was in cop mode. This is how it would be. She sat for a moment and collected her thoughts.

"Dillon deals with clients who are millionaires. He has access to more sensitive information than anyone else I know. Bank accounts, investments, overseas accounts. And if someone came wanting that information, and he wouldn't give it to them?" She shrugged.

Roy said, "The argument's a moot point. Dillon is top priority. He has to be found." He looked behind him toward Christina. "Any guess on how long ago she was shot?"

Josie shook her head, trying to get her anger back in check. "Not too recently. Looking at the blood, I'd say late last night."

Otto looked at Roy, then at Josie, weighing his words. "We need you to walk through the office with us. Tell us everything you can about the space. What was taken. What's out of place. We'll take a careful look at the files that appear to be missing. But I'd like your first impressions before we touch anything."

She nodded and stood. The inner anger she felt toward Otto at that moment was clearly misplaced; he was doing his job. Still, she resented the underling role she had been placed in, as well as the way he was framing the case. She had agreed to the arrangement, and she knew it was right, but her fear for Dillon's safety would cause her to second-guess every decision Otto made.

———

Josie took the next few minutes to relay exactly what she had seen when she drove up to the building: the locked doors, Christina's still body, breaking the glass to enter. As she talked, Otto opened his evidence kit and took out his 35 mm camera to snap pictures.

Deputy Jones hollered through the shattered front door, "Sheriff, Junior Daggy wants to know what's going on. Says he saw something last night."

The sheriff turned toward the door. "I'm on my way. Sit him down in a patrol car and let's get a statement." Roy promised to keep Josie and Otto informed and followed the deputy outside.

Josie forced herself to look at Christina. She looked posed, as if she were on display, and Josie wanted to cover her body with a blanket out of respect. "Who would do this? She had no enemies. She was just a nice person. I can't get my head wrapped around it."

Otto laid his hand on Josie's shoulder until she looked at him. "We'll get whoever did this. You count on that." He paused, understanding the unstated fear she had for Dillon's whereabouts.

Otto's cell phone rang. As he walked away to take the call, Josie took a long breath and concentrated her attention on the objects around Christina. She kneeled on the floor and studied the file folders without touching anything, trying to get a feel for the organization of the office. Dillon had never explained the daily operations; she now wished she had asked for details.

When Otto came back he said, "That was Lou. The coroner will be here in ten minutes. Two state troopers are on their way from Presidio. Be about thirty minutes." He nodded toward the folders on the floor. "Can you make any sense of them?"

"They look like files that Christina would take care of," Josie said. "Billing files. One of these is labeled 'Warranty Papers.' Another says 'Office Maintenance.'" She pointed to the bottom drawer on the left side of Christina's desk. "It's open and the middle section of the drawer is empty. Notice the files all over the floor beneath the drawer. It appears someone took the files and scattered them. Hard to tell what's missing."

Josie made a list of the files on the floor as Otto read them off. When they finished the task, Otto pushed away from the desk and asked, "Any ideas on the location of the chair?"

Josie stared at the position of Christina's body.

"It looks like someone pulled the chair away from the desk after she was shot, maybe to have easier access to the files," Josie said.

Otto nodded in agreement. "Her legs stretched out in front of her, toes pointed up, would support that."

Josie stepped behind Christina and pointed toward the wall about three feet to her left. "Look at the wall, though. See the red flecks?" She leaned in closer, her finger inches from the wall. "There's blood splatter here, so this is where she was shot. Which means they pulled her away from the desk, and then shot her?"

"Doesn't make sense. There doesn't appear to be any struggle." Otto gestured the length of her body. "She's still in dress clothes and high-heeled shoes. So we can assume she was still working when the gunman came into her office. What time does she leave work in the evenings?"

"She and Dillon both leave at five most nights. She might have stayed until six last night since he worked late." Josie looked out the front window of the office, wishing Roy would check in with them.

Josie had a sudden image of Dillon with a gun to his head, watching Christina being shot, the bullet ripping into her chest. She imagined masked men dragging him out of the office at gunpoint. She turned her back on Otto and walked away. He came to stand beside her and laid a hand on her back. She crossed her arms at her chest and closed her eyes, forcing the tears back. "I have to keep it together, Otto. I can't lose it. Not here." Tears were in her eyes and she felt an overwhelming urge to find a corner and let go.

"Take a deep breath. You're the best chance Dillon has at getting help right now. Shut down your emotions. You can fall apart later." He gave her a rough pat on the back. "Right?"

Josie stared at the ceiling, blinking away tears.

"You're a tough one. You can do this."

She nodded and took a deep breath. "I'm fine."

Roy walked back into the building. "I talked with Junior. He says he walked out of his office at five last night with Christina. They usually park in the back lot. Dillon's car was still there."

Josie nodded. "His meeting wasn't until six."

"Junior says he and his wife drove back into town last night. Went to Presidio to do some shopping and eat dinner. As they drove back through town at about ten o'clock he noticed Christina's car and an SUV. Both were parked in the lot behind the office."

"Was Dillon's car here?" she asked.

"No."

"Were the lights on?" Otto asked.

"Junior said he drove by on Seminole Street." Roy made a T with his hands to indicate that Daggy didn't drive in front of the office, but rather the street that runs perpendicular to it. "He said the lights were on in the front of the building, but he saw Christina's car and didn't think much about it. He's pretty torn up about it now, blaming himself for not stopping to check on her."

"Can you get an officer over to Christina's house?" Otto asked.

Roy nodded.

"See if she ever made it home," said Otto. "Ask if neighbors noticed any cars last night."

"And another officer to canvass downtown? A two-block radius of the office," Josie said.

"I've got two deputies available today," the sheriff said. "Jones is the one with Junior Daggy right now. Dave Phillips is on at eight. I'll get him to come out now. I'll call the jail and let the intake officer know what's going on. Maria will have to handle the jail while we get a jump on this."

Josie nodded. Roy walked away from them to talk with his deputy by phone.

Josie turned again to finish examining Christina's desk. "Her calendar's gone. She has a large desk calendar that she writes all of her appointments on in one color, Dillon's meetings in another color. It looks like someone lifted the calendar and sent the rest of her desk supplies flying."

Otto was taking notes as Josie thought out loud.

"Anything else missing?"

Josie looked over the area again. "Her computer tower is gone, but not the monitor. They obviously wanted the information stored on the computer. They weren't stealing it to hock it later." Josie stepped carefully around the body and looked underneath her desk. "She also has a computer bag with a spare laptop that she stores under her desk. It's gone." Josie used the pen in her pocket to pull open all three desk drawers. She found a purse in the bottom desk drawer with the contents dumped beneath it.

After inventorying the contents Josie said, "Aside from a wallet, what's the main thing someone carries in their purse or pants pockets?"

Otto frowned and then nodded. "Where are her keys? Car keys, keys to the office?"

"So, someone stands in the front of the office, shoots her from the side, with apparently no struggle from Christina, and then the shooter takes the time to find her keys and lock up the building on the way out?"

"I don't know, Josie. The scene makes no sense."

After finishing their review of the front room they walked back to Dillon's office. He didn't wear cologne, but she thought she could smell lingering traces of his shaving cream. She imagined him sitting in his desk chair, leaning back and smiling as she entered the office, lacing his hands behind his head. Instead, there were file folders strewn across the right side of the room where his cabinets had all been opened.

"His computer tower is gone too." She pointed behind the desk. "It sits here, on the floor." She leaned over the desk and looked around for the small brown pottery bowl where he kept flash drives. She and Dillon had purchased the bowl together on a trip to Mexico several years before. Both the bowl and the storage devices were gone.

Dillon's eyes ached from the strain of searching for a sliver of light or shadow in the black room. His sight was completely shut down, but his sense of touch had so intensified that the muscles in his body seized up, his bare skin alert to the lightest touch: the whisper-soft stroke of an insect across his ankle caused spasms up his legs, and he clenched his eyes shut in pain, brushing away what he couldn't see.

When bats had come loose from their perch in the hole sometime in the night, the frenzied slap of wings had terrified him. He had imagined them becoming entangled in his hair. He had lain down on his stomach and pressed his side up against the wall, covering his head with his hands; each time he heard them somewhere up by the ceiling he flattened his body against the dirt floor, motionless. He thought he had distinguished at least three bats circling the room in endless laps, emitting high-pitched noises. He knew bats roosted in caves and would use an underground cistern with an opening for shelter, but with the hatch now shut, they had no exit, no way out for food, and he had no idea how that might affect their behavior.

Sitting up again, fearing unseen insects and small rodents on the floor around him, he brushed at his legs obsessively. He drew them up against his chest and wrapped his arms around them, attempting to fold his six-foot body into as small a shape as possible. Dillon had not been able to see beyond the rope ladder he had climbed down and thus had no idea how large the room was, nor what else was inside it. He was completely naked and vulnerable. He couldn't remember a time when he had experienced such absolute darkness.

At some point during the night he jerked awake, but it was impossible to tell what time it was or how long he had dozed. He knew that Josie would be frantic by now. He forced himself to get up from the floor, even though the thought of waking the bats above made him cringe. He took deep breaths, slowing his bodily functions and thoughts. He tried to orient himself in the room and thought that he was directly under the hatch where the ladder had been removed. He began running through every detail he could remember.

He started with his trip down the ladder. He imagined that he took approximately fifteen steps down it and assumed the cistern was about ten feet deep. He turned and felt for the wall. Running his hands along the concrete he discovered rough seams that indicated mortar. He ran his fingertips along the grooves and distinguished individual cement blocks. Leading with his left foot, then his left hand, he inched around the room, counting blocks as he went. He found nothing on the floor or the perimeter of the room against the walls. No shelves or furniture.

He walked along the perimeter of the room, estimating it to be about eight feet in length and width. It was a square shape and he began to doubt that the room was a water cistern, but rather a cell used to hold victims out of sight. His stomach seized up and he felt along the wall to the opposite side of where he thought the ladder had been dropped, and dry heaved in the corner. Exhausted, he felt his way back around the room and pressed his back against the cold block wall where he thought he had originally positioned himself.

His body was slowly recovering from shock. His breathing was returning to normal, but he was cold. The muscles in his stomach and intestines ached and his body involuntarily shivered. He knew that caves were cold year-round, even in the desert. He was certain that his core temperature was dropping and he began to worry about hypothermia. More so, he worried that the confusion he would experience as a result of hypothermia, combined with his extreme anxiety, might cause a mental breakdown if he was kept underground. It was becoming increasingly difficult to focus on anything other than death.

FIVE

Coroner Mitchell Cowan walked the two blocks to the crime scene with his medical bag in one hand and his evidence kit in the other. City police and sheriff's department cars, an EMT unit, and the Trauma Center ambulance were all massed around the crime-scene tape that held the local media and curiosity seekers at bay. It was only ten o'clock in the morning and he was already hot and imagining a cool shower at the end of the day. One of the deputies lifted the tape for Cowan to enter the crime scene and mercifully didn't require him to struggle over the top of it in front of his colleagues.

One month away from his fiftieth birthday, he was feeling slow and weighed down by his considerable midsection. He'd conducted enough autopsies over the past ten years to know what fat did to a person's innards. The inside of his body would not be pretty, and while that bothered him a great deal, his sugar cravings throttled his willpower every damned day.

Once inside the office he found a corner to drop his bags and catch his breath. He wore the same style of Haggar pants and button-down dress shirt that he'd been wearing for twenty years. He felt as if his life as a small-town coroner dawdled along comfortably while everyone else in the world seemed desperate for excitement. Cowan opened his bag and arranged his supplies, thinking to himself that his life may not be exciting, but it was fulfilling. He often made this small assessment before the encounter with the body of someone whose life was over. This case, however, would be especially troubling. Josie Gray was one of the finest officers he had ever worked with, and he could not imagine the stress she was enduring over the disappearance of a loved one and the death of a friend. When the dispatcher had called to tell him the news he could hardly believe it.

Cowan turned and surveyed the scene before moving on to the body. The room basically had two spaces. The area on the left was a waiting room with comfortable couches in earthy shades of brown and red and yellow. The other side of the room was the secretary's area, now cluttered with file folders and other materials. Maple furniture complemented the old redbrick walls, and framed black-and-white Japanese etchings were clustered on end tables around the waiting room and hung in small groupings on the walls.

Cowan sighed and turned his attention to the body. It had taken on the awkward pose of death, with the stiff unnatural angle to the limbs. He felt eyes on him and looked up to find Josie staring at him intently from across the room.

Josie stood on the edge of a conversation between Otto and Roy. They were a fine group of officers, competent and friendly enough, but conversation had never been easy for Cowan.

He approached Josie and extended his hand. "I'm terribly sorry about all this."

She shook his hand and thanked him.

"Any indication what happened?"

"No sign of a break-in. It looks as if the office was closed between five and six o'clock. Sometime before ten o'clock Christina came back to the office."

Josie turned and they walked toward the front of the desk so that Cowan could get a better look.

"Okay, take me through your observations," he said.

"We pulled her body forward slightly," Josie said. "The bullet, or bullets, did not exit her body. It looks as if she was shot while sitting in the chair. The blood splatter on the wall to her left makes it look as if someone shot her from over there." Josie pointed toward the front door.

"So she was shot from the side, not from the front. Either a lucky shot to the heart, or a damned good one."

"My guess is lucky," she said. "I can't imagine a skilled shooter taking a chance with this shot. Too much room for error."

He turned to Josie. "When Lou called, she filled me in on Dillon's disappearance. Any word yet?"

"Nothing." She started to say something else and then stopped, unable to continue.

"That'll be all for now then. Thank you for the help." He paused, struggling for the right words. "I'm sorry about all this. I'll do everything I can."

Josie found Otto and Martínez in Dillon's office, both on their hands and knees, looking at the mess of file folders on the floor. They both looked up when she entered.

"You find anything?" she asked.

"We're getting the files in alphabetical order. We'll know more in a few minutes. Cowan here?"

She nodded. "He just got started on the preliminary."

"Good." He nodded and smoothed the hair down over his head. "Marta's outside. She drove through the Driftriver Drive neighborhood and found no sign of Dillon's car. I was hoping to find the exact location for the meeting somewhere in the office."

"We don't have the address," Josie said. "The desk calendars are gone, so are the computers."

"All right. Why don't you ride with Marta, interview everyone in the neighborhood." He paused and considered her for a moment. "Do you have keys to Dillon's house?"

"Yes." She patted her front pants pocket. "I have them with me. I walked through his house this morning on my way in to work."

Josie and Otto exchanged a look. In hindsight, she regretted entering the house, which was now part of the investigation, but she could have never predicted what they were dealing with.

"I'll do an initial sweep of the house. If anything's out of place, I'll go back with a search warrant."

Josie nodded.

"I'll get prints on the exterior doors." He paused and she picked up the unease in his expression. "I don't want you back at his house. If this case ends up at trial, the last thing we want is you spending time in his house alone."

He kept his eyes on her, waiting for a reply. All she could manage was a nod. There was also a spare key hidden underneath a rock in Dillon's backyard, but she said nothing.

"Call me when you're finished on Driftriver. I need you and Marta back at the PD pulling records. First thing, ask Marta to see if they can ping that cell phone text. See what tower the message was sent from. Hopefully we'll get a general area where Dillon was located when the text was sent last night."

"All right."

"I'd like Marta to focus on Dillon's information. You take Christina's. Pull credit cards, bank accounts, cell phone activity, anything you can get access to," he said. "We need to keep this clean, for your sake as well as mine."

Josie hesitated and pulled Dillon's house key out of her pocket and placed it in Otto's hand. For a beat too long Otto stared at her, and Josie wondered if he was weighing his role as the lead investigator against their friendship. A look passed between them, and Josie was certain that Otto's role as investigator would remain the priority: their friendship would no doubt be tested.

───

Outside the office, Josie saw sheriff's deputies Jones and Phillips talking with the EMT driver across the street. They tipped their heads at Josie, but said nothing. She was living a cop's worst nightmare.

Half a block down the street, she saw Officer Marta Cruz standing guard beside her patrol car, her thumbs hooked through her belt loops. When Josie reached her, the concern in her face was obvious, and Josie was suddenly glad to be leaving the scene.

"I'll drive," Marta said.

As they drove, the vivid image of Dillon knotting his tie in Josie's kitchen doorway the morning before came to her. It was as if she could reach out and touch his oxford cloth shirt and feel the smooth texture of his silk tie. The reality of what was happening once again hit her like an iron ball to the chest as she heard Marta say, "Everything that is humanly possible."

Josie nodded, trying to focus. She felt Marta's eyes on her as they drove toward River Road. "Did you find an address?" she asked, her voice gentle.

"Dillon said his meeting was on Driftriver Drive at six with a potential client. That's all we have."

Marta nodded. "We'll drive through the neighborhood, see if you catch anything I missed. Then we can split the houses up and question." She drove for a moment in silence. "You remember last year when Teresa ran away? You put yourself at risk, risked your life even, for my daughter. And you brought her home."

Josie stared out at the road flying by them.

"It's my turn to return the favor, Josie. And I'm not the only one. This community appreciates what you've given through the years. We'll find who did this, and we'll find Dillon. He's an innocent man. We all know that."

Josie listened to the passion in Marta's voice and tried to find hope, something more than the numbness in her fingers and the white noise in her brain.

She quietly thanked Marta and checked her cell phone for messages, again. Nothing.

Driftriver Drive was an oval-shaped neighborhood with six homes facing the center of the development: four houses on the front side of the circle, and two houses on the back. In the center was a small field of brown grass that had originally been intended as a park. The neighborhood was less than half developed, halted by a flagging economy.

A quick drive around the block showed again that Dillon's car wasn't in the area. Marta pulled up in front of the four side-by-side homes at the front of the development. "You take the two on the right? I'll take these two?"

The first home Josie approached was a one-story mauve-colored adobe with arched windows and doors. White rock and a few gnarled cactuses were interspersed between two cottonwood trees in front. An older-model Toyota Camry was parked outside of the garage. Josie could see the outline of someone standing inside the house, looking out what she assumed was the living room window.

Josie rang the doorbell and a thin man in his late twenties answered the door in spandex biking shorts and a bright yellow T-shirt. Josie recognized the man as the owner of a new fitness club downtown, yet another business struggling to keep its doors open.

After Josie showed her badge and introduced herself as the chief of police with the Artemis Police Department, he invited her inside to a small foyer where a young woman joined them, also wearing bike shorts, along with a sports bra. Her short black hair was wet and her cheeks bright red from exertion. Half of the living room was filled with exercise equipment, and the house had the distinct odor of sweat that she associated with a gym.

Josie questioned the couple about their neighbors and whether they'd seen Dillon or had any knowledge of a meeting taking place in the subdivision. Neither of them knew Dillon other than as a local businessman, nor were they aware of any new people moving into the neighborhood. Both looked perplexed at the line of questioning.

Josie finally summarized the investigation. "A young woman was murdered at the Office of Abacus, last night. The owner of the business, Dillon Reese, is missing."

The couple looked at each other with shocked expressions.

"Mr. Reese was scheduled to meet with a new client yesterday evening at six. The house was located somewhere in the Driftriver Drive development."

"Which house?" the man asked.

"We don't know that."

"The only people living out here are in these four homes." The woman pointed with her thumb behind her back. "The two houses on the back side of the block are empty. I just talked to Junior Daggy a few days ago. He said he didn't know of anyone looking to buy a house out here."

"We hope they get sold before the property gets run-down," the man said.

"Did you notice any unfamiliar vehicles in the area yesterday?" Josie asked.

Again, nothing.

Josie left her business card and asked them to call if they thought of anything, or discovered any details that might pertain to the investigation.

She walked across the front yard to a house with a similar shape but khaki in color. No cars were parked out front but she could hear a TV inside. When she reached the front porch she heard the TV noise stop. She rang the bell and a moment later a woman in her seventies, carrying a Siamese cat, answered the door. She had silver-white hair in a stylish short cut, and wore trendy black rectangular glasses and a ring on her thumb. She motioned Josie inside as she introduced herself.

"I know who you are," the woman said. "I see you and Otto at the Hot Tamale all the time. I'm Janet Knight. Friends with Delores."

Josie smiled and nodded. "That's right. I thought you looked familiar."

They sat in a small but comfortable living room where Josie declined iced tea and coffee. They talked for a moment about Delores and Otto, and then Josie asked the woman the same series of questions she had asked her neighbors.

"Did you see anything yesterday, notice any vehicles that were new to the neighborhood?"

She nodded. "I did see a white van. About the same time you're talking about, too. It was about suppertime. I remember looking out the window and seeing it drive on past the house. I thought maybe it was a van setting up cable or something for the two houses behind us. They're both still empty."

"Did you see the van leave?"

"No. That was it. I sat down with my dinner on the couch and forgot about it." She looked upset, and pulled the cat closer to her chest.

"Did you notice a small sports car at any time yesterday?"

"No. I believe that van was the only car I saw. And I didn't go anywhere yesterday. I left the house early this morning for about an hour, but didn't see anyone then either. Just waved hello to the Andersons next door."

"Can you describe the van?"

"It was just a white van. Not like a minivan."

"A cargo van?"

"Yes, that's it. I thought maybe it was a cable van, but there weren't any words painted on it. But it was the same shape and size as the cable and satellite TV vans."

Josie finally filled the woman in on the purpose of the visit and she moaned softly at the news of Christina's death and tears welled in her eyes. She stroked her cat's back and the cat purred loudly, oblivious to the woman's distress.

"I just don't feel safe anywhere anymore. When I left the city to move to the desert my husband convinced me we wouldn't even have to lock our doors. He passed away ten years ago. He'd be shocked if he knew how things have changed."

They finished talking and Josie stood to leave. "I appreciate your time. Your information gives us something to start on."

The woman stopped Josie at the door. "Do you think I need a security system? Living out here on my own?"

"I don't think you should panic, but I think a security system is never a bad idea. You call the office tomorrow and ask for Lou. She can recommend a few companies for you to talk with."

———•——

Josie found Marta already in the police jeep and told her about the cargo van. Marta had talked with two married couples, both with kids, and neither family had noticed anyone new or strange in the neighborhood the day before.

Marta drove around the block to the two homes at the back of the oval. Both homes were obviously empty with no curtains in the windows, and the landscaping was minimal, with rocks and cactus in lieu of a lawn. Marta and Josie got out of the car and walked around the homes but found nothing out of the ordinary.

Back in the car, Josie called Otto and gave him a summary. "The van, the empty houses, the fact that none of the residents had an appointment with an accountant. This is a probable kidnapping."

Otto said, "That makes sense with what we're seeing. I don't think Dillon was taken from his office. There was no indication of a fight there. The chair was overturned but it looks like it was done for effect. Nothing on the desk was knocked over, as it would have been if there was a disturbance. The only thing out of place appears to be the files and the overturned chair."

"What about the files?"

"We can't find any files for letters A through G. From the way the files are lying on the floor it looks as if a section of folders bearing last names that start with those letters was removed from the cabinets. Then, it looks as if additional files were just pulled and thrown to the floor. Maybe to mislead. Hard to tell."

"How about a client list? Something to figure out who the missing files belong to?"

"Not yet." Otto talked with someone in the background for several minutes, then finally returned with an apology. "We've put out a description of Dillon's car to law enforcement agencies, including in Mexico."

"Has Lou tracked down Christina's parents' phone number yet?" Josie asked.

"I talked with them just after you left. I tracked down an officer in St. Louis who went to their house while I informed them by phone. They were devastated, of course. They couldn't imagine anyone wanting to hurt her. She had no enemies, loved working for Dillon. They're flying into Odessa tomorrow to retrieve her body." Otto paused. "I'll call Dillon's parents now. Tell them what we know."

"I need to call them, Otto. This is my responsibility."

Marta stepped out of the jeep, understanding Josie would need privacy. Josie closed her eyes for a moment, trying to gather up the courage she needed to make the call, to sound strong and confident for this couple who would be shattered. She had met Dillon's parents on several occasions. Both in their late fifties, they were a sweet couple, entirely devoted to one another. Dillon's dad, Steve, had owned a printing store in St. Louis and his mother, Eva, had worked as an elementary school secretary until they both retired just last year. They were incredibly proud of their only son, doting on him to the point of embarrassment. They were a close family, and Dillon thought the world of them.

Josie dialed their home number and pictured Dillon's mom, a trim woman who dressed in the conservative Midwestern clothing that one would expect of a school secretary: slacks and shirts.

"Hello?"

"Hi, Eva, this is Josie."

"Josie! Good to hear from you!"

"It's good to talk with you too. I'm afraid I'm calling with some bad news though."

"What's wrong?" Her tone was instantly guarded.

"Is Steve there with you?"

"He's here by my side. Oh, no. What's happened?"

"Have you heard from Dillon either yesterday or today?"

"No. It's been about a week since we talked. Is he okay?" Josie listened as Eva whispered to Steve, "It's about Dillon."

"He didn't show up to work today. And, he's not answered my phone calls or messages."

"I don't understand. You think he's left? Gone somewhere?"

Josie closed her eyes, imagining the look of confusion and concern on Eva's face, and the terror that was soon to come. "We're not sure yet. I'm afraid the news gets worse.

"Dillon's secretary, Christina, was murdered. We found her body this morning in the office."

"Murdered?" she whispered the word.

Steve came on the line. "Josie? What's going on?" His voice seemed frightened, too loud for the phone.

Josie repeated the details for Dillon's father. He suggested they fly immediately to Texas, but Josie encouraged them to stay home by the phone until they knew more information. She promised to call them the moment she heard any news about Christina, or Dillon's whereabouts.

SIX

After talking with Josie, Otto walked through the details of the case with two state troopers from the Texas Department of Public Safety. The officers left the scene to take fingerprints at Christina's apartment and Dillon's home, and then to canvass the neighborhood and take statements. The extra support was a huge relief.

At that point, the investigation had two priorities: analyzing the physical details of the crime scene, and searching records—phone transactions, credit card usage, bank account information, billing statements. TV cop shows portrayed retrieving online information as a simple phone call, but the reality included red tape, subpoenas, and waiting.

At this point, a trial was a distant thought, but Otto knew that what might seem like an inconsequential detail early in an investigation could turn into a time bomb in court. He had seen plenty of high-profile cases that made police officers look like bungling idiots. The general public didn't realize that the details the attorneys spent six months dissecting under a microscope were sometimes processed by an officer in a matter of minutes. It made his blood burn thinking about it.

Worse yet, this investigation was shaping up to have all the characteristics of a big publicity trial: murder, possible kidnapping, sex, and money. Josie wasn't thinking of herself as a sexual link to the case, but Otto knew that a defense attorney would scrutinize her relationship with Dillon. Any action Josie performed would be perverted by a defense attorney if there was even a slight chance of a not-guilty verdict for the accused.

Sheriff Roy Martínez opened the front door of Dillon's office building and pulled Otto from his thoughts. Roy had just provided an initial statement to the local media. Once word got out to those outlets, it would spread to the larger news agencies, but Otto would put off dealing with them until he had something more tangible to work with.

"That'll suffice for a while. I said you'd provide an update tomorrow morning," Roy said. He glanced at his watch. "It's almost noon. Still no leads on Dillon?"

"Nothing. His car is missing. I've got officers taking prints at his place and Christina's. Josie and Marta are interviewing neighbors where Dillon's meeting was supposed to have taken place." Otto frowned and rubbed his neck, frustrated they didn't have something solid at this point.

"Where are we in here?"

"We've just made one pass over the outer office area and Dillon's office. I want to go back over everything now, more closely," Otto said. "I'll take Christina's desk area, you take the waiting area, then we'll move back to Dillon's office."

Roy nodded and pulled a pair of plastic gloves from his back pocket. Otto walked over to Christina's desk. Mitchell Cowan had just left with Christina Handley's body to perform the autopsy. A local company had arrived to begin installing a new pane of glass for the front door to secure the building, but the bloodstained secretary's chair and the blood splatter on the wall were vivid reminders of what had taken place.

Otto opened his evidence kit and removed a large round magnifying glass that he used to scan the top of Christina's desk, and then her chair. In bigger police departments there were evidence techs to take care of these details, but he never minded the job. The minor details could fry an officer in a trial, but they also solved cases. On her chair he collected a fiber sample, hairs that most likely belonged to her, as well as several shorter, darker-colored hairs that most likely belonged to Dillon.

"Look at this."

Otto stood up straight and saw Roy inspecting something in his hands, holding it under a lamp to get a better look.

"I've seen these around. The smiling skulls with the roses. Any idea what the significance is?" Roy asked. He passed Otto the round metal pendant. The skull and torso of a skeleton were carved in black. The hooded skull smiled demonically, a burning cigarette hanging from her mouth, a rose in one hand, a gun in the other.

Otto handed the pendant back to Roy, careful not to smudge with his gloves what might hold a partial fingerprint. "I think it has something to do with the Catholics. Some bizarre splinter group."

"Phillips is Catholic." Roy stepped around the two men installing the new piece of glass and yelled down the street to Deputy Dave Phillips, who was patrolling the perimeter.

"I need you a minute!"

Phillips said hello to the men working in the entryway as he walked inside. He wore the standard sheriff's department uniform: beige pants with a brown stripe down the side of the leg, and a brown shirt with a silver sheriff's star over his breast pocket. His hair was cut in a buzz so short that his sunburnt scalp was visible. He was a clean-shaven kid of about twenty-five, trim with an athletic build. Otto hitched his gun belt up and wondered how many weeks of pastries he would have to deny himself to look like that.

"What's up, Sheriff?"

He even sounded young, thought Otto.

Roy said, "What do you know about this?" He held the pendant under the floor lamp that stood between the couches.

Phillips took a look and pulled back. "That's Santa Muerte."

Roy gave him a skeptical look.

"She's supposed to be some kind of saint, but the Catholics don't like her."

"A saint with a gun and a cigarette?" Otto said. "What's the significance?"

"No clue," Phillips said.

"How hard would it be to track down something like this? To find out where someone might buy it?"

Phillips grimaced and shook his head. "They're all over the place. My wife's family lives in Mexico City. There's stores called *botanicas*. They sell little . . ." He stopped, trying to think of the English translation. "Like herbal stuff and religious trinkets. Alternative medicine and folk remedies. They carry Catholic stuff, rosary beads and holy water. Some of them carry Santa Muerte jewelry and statues. She's a big deal in Mexico."

Roy pulled a hand down his long bushy mustache, frowning at Phillips. "In other words, this won't help us narrow down our killer."

Phillips shrugged. "The only Santa Muerte followers around here that I know of is that group outside of town."

"That little ranch house over by the mud flats?" Otto asked.

"Yeah, that's it. Don't know much about them. Just rumors," Phillips said.

Otto nodded. "That's good. We'll check it out."

By the time he and Roy finished with the crime scene and the paperwork, it was going on seven o'clock. Otto drove back to the police department to check in with Josie.

After canvassing the Driftriver neighborhood, Josie and Marta had returned to the police station to run account information on Christina and Dillon. Josie started with the cell phone company, West Texas Mobile. Josie knew Christina used the company because Dillon had secured a small-business package deal for them. Josie had a contact there who had provided her confidential information in the past. The employee could have been fired for divulging the information without a subpoena, but she had been genuinely intent on aiding the police. Josie figured she either had a family link to someone who worked in law enforcement, maybe a husband who was a cop, or she just liked the diversion, the thrill of doing something behind the boss's back. Regardless of the reason, Josie had been thankful for her help.

Josie dialed the company's number and asked for the woman by name.

Several seconds later she picked up. "This is Arlene. How may I help you?"

"Arlene, this is Chief Josie Gray with the Artemis Police. How are you today?"

"Oh, I'm good! How are you, Chief?"

"I'm not so good. We had a tragedy this morning, and I'm desperate for information."

She lowered her voice. "My husband called me about the murder and the missing man. He heard it at the press conference the sheriff gave. Is that the case?"

"Yes, ma'am."

"I knew you'd be calling. I already pulled both their records."

Josie sighed into the phone. "You are a godsend. This will go no further. I'll get the records subpoenaed if it looks at all necessary."

"I know you will. I'm not worried. I've got an Excel file pulled for the Office of Abacus, and for Mr. Reese and Ms. Handley for the past two weeks." She paused for a second. "Just please destroy the file once you've taken an initial glance?"

"Absolutely," she said before hanging up.

A few minutes later the file appeared in her e-mail and Josie sent a copy to Marta's work account so she could examine Dillon's calls. Josie scrolled through Christina's personal cell phone record for the previous day and discovered she had received a three-minute phone call at 8:45 P.M. from an unknown caller. It was a received call, so Josie was fairly certain Christina was still alive at that point, unless the killer had answered her phone.

Josie glanced at the clock at the bottom of her computer screen and realized Dillon had officially been missing for twenty-four hours. She had been scouring records and studying call logs for the past three hours. Her cell phone lay beside her desk phone, and every time either phone rang her heart raced in hope and fear of what might be demanded.

Two years ago, one of Mexico's most prominent drug cartels, the Medranos, had begun using Artemis as an illegal port of entry into the United States. Artemis was a convenient entry point because of its isolated location and easy access across a low point in the Rio Grande. The battle with the cartel had ended with several high-ranking members arrested and several others killed, including the Medranos' patriarch. Josie now feared that her involvement in the killing of cartel members may have led to Dillon's abduction. The cartel may have decided they could also get access to the records of Dillon's wealthy clients. It would be a double score: easy money and revenge against Josie at the same time. The thought of Dillon bound and gagged, tossed into a stash house, fearing for his life, was torture. Worse yet was the fear that no call would ever come, that Dillon had already been killed to show Josie that the Medranos' power was greater than her own.

Otto entered the office with the same stoic expression Josie had left him with earlier in the day.

"Anything?" he asked.

"We've narrowed down the time for Christina's killing. We've got a few minor leads," Josie said.

He pointed to the conference table and Josie and Marta took a seat with him. "Roy and I took a few good prints from the office. Some hair and fiber samples."

Josie noted that his voice sounded weary, not the tone of a man convinced he had a lead.

"What about the files?" Marta asked.

Otto explained that files with client names starting with the letters A through G, and L and T were missing, assuming he had clients whose names ended in all those letters. "We have one piece of information that supports Josie's theory of a kidnapping." He described Junior Daggy's description of a dark-colored SUV found behind the building.

"It was parked behind Christina's car last night around ten P.M.," he said.

"Were the lights on in the building?" Josie asked.

"He said he saw lights on in the front of the building."

"When I arrived at seven this morning the lights were off," Josie said. "So we have the cargo van in the Driftriver neighborhood around six, and the SUV at the office at ten. I confirmed a cell phone call, off the record, for Christina last night at eight forty-five."

Otto flipped through the pages of his notes and found the entry he was searching for. "One of the state troopers talked to Christina's landlord, Debby Williams. Debby confirmed she saw Christina arrive home sometime between five and six, but she didn't notice her car after that. None of the other neighbors remember seeing her car last night, but it's a quiet neighborhood. People keep to themselves."

"Anyone other than Junior see anything around the office last night?"

Otto shook his head. "Nothing."

"Then we can establish her time of death between eight forty-five P.M. and seven this morning when I arrived." Josie rubbed at her temples. "It doesn't make sense that Dillon was taken at six."

Otto finished her thought. "And they waited to kill Christina until after eight. The kidnappers should have been long gone by that point."

Marta said, "I'm waiting on the cell phone company to tell us what tower Dillon's text message was sent from last night. That should help narrow the area, but that information takes longer to track down."

"Why kill Christina? Why kidnap Dillon? What's the motive?" Josie asked.

Otto sighed in frustration. "The only experience I have with kidnapping cases involved a ransom, not information. If they kidnapped Dillon for banking information, then we may not receive contact from them. No phone calls or letters to help us find him."

Josie listened to Otto and knew she had been right to relinquish command of the investigation. Working a typical case in the early stages was exciting on some level; determining how best to pull the seemingly unrelated pieces together into a coherent whole was a challenge. But now she felt none of that. She felt heavy and exhausted, like her limbs were operating underwater.

"Something else to consider. We rule this a kidnapping and the feds come in and take over," Otto said.

"I still have a gut feeling the Medranos are involved in this," Josie said.

Otto shook his head. "I'm not so certain. Cowan called and confirmed the gunshot came from the right side of Christina's body. One .38 caliber bullet. He said the shot nicked the heart, the ascending aorta. With the angle of the shot, Cowan said she stood a chance of surviving if she'd received medical attention. She just bled out. The cartel wouldn't lure her to the office with the intent to kill her, and then take a potshot."

Marta nodded in agreement. "She'd have been full of bullets if it were a cartel job."

Josie said nothing. Her face flushed red with shame and guilt. Christina bled out. If Josie had followed her instincts, checked the office like Dell had encouraged her to do, Christina might be alive right now. And, they might have gotten information from her to save Dillon.

"But if she wasn't dead when she was first shot, why doesn't it look like she tried to move, to fight for herself?" Marta asked.

"Cowan said it was a debilitating shot. The shock and loss of blood would have caused her to lose consciousness, but it probably wasn't instant death," he said.

"It's as if someone was in the middle of ransacking the office, stealing files, and then got caught," Marta said. "Or, they saw a light outside, something spooked them, and they shot Christina because she'd seen too much."

"But if they were ransacking the office and got spooked, they wouldn't take the time to shoot her and then lock the door behind them if they left in a hurry," Otto said.

"What do you mean?"

"Well, they'd just leave. They aren't going to take the time to lock up behind them if they think someone is about ready to catch them."

"Unless there were multiple people in the office. Which supports the cartel theory," Josie said.

"Maybe Christina tried to leave. She was going to make a run for it and they took off a quick shot," Marta said.

"That's the odd piece to this. It was a bad shot, but Cowan said she was sitting in her chair when she was killed. She wasn't in the process of standing up, trying to escape, and then got shot and fell back into the seat. Her back and bottom were firmly planted in the chair. And the blood splatter on her clothing, the chair, desk, and wall, all indicate that she wasn't moved after the shot." Otto paused and picked up his notebook from the conference table, flipping back to notes from the crime scene. "We also found a pendant across the room, lying on the floor by the front window. And a silver necklace under her desk. Doesn't look like her style. Looks like a man's necklace that got ripped off."

"So you're saying there was a struggle after all? A tussle between Christina and her attackers?" Josie asked.

Marta gave Josie a skeptical look. "Christina fought with her attackers. Then she sat down in her office chair, and calmly allowed someone to take a quick shot at her?"

"There was a struggle," Otto declared. "For whatever reason she sat back down in her seat. Most likely at gunpoint. Then, the gunman is startled, maybe sees a car drive by outside the office window. He panics. Christina knows too much, so he takes a quick shot, but he doesn't have time to make sure she's dead and instead runs for the back door."

"But the lights were off when I came to the office the next morning," Josie said.

"So he hit the lights before he left to keep from drawing attention."

"And got Christina's keys out of her desk drawer and locked up after he panicked and took a potshot? Doesn't make sense," she said.

"Did someone take prints on the back door?" Marta asked.

"I checked myself. Nothing." Otto paused and stared out the windows in the back of the office for quite some time. He finally said, "I just don't want us to jump on the cartel angle too quickly. To me, it looks more like an abduction for client accounts. You know Dillon. If someone tried to get confidential information out of him, what would he do?"

"He would resist," Josie said.

"And someone who was trying to gain account information about a wealthy client could have taken him somewhere to access the information by force."

They sat for a while longer, trying to fit the details together. Josie tried to concentrate on Christina's murder as it might have happened, but random images of Dillon derailed every coherent train of thought.

Eventually Otto scooted his chair back and stood. "It's time to go home. Get a good night's sleep so you're clearheaded in the morning."

"Why not her style?" Josie suddenly asked. "You said the pendant you found couldn't be hers because it wasn't her style."

"Ever heard of Santa Muerte?" he asked.

"Sounds familiar."

"Saint Death," Marta said. "It's a bastardization of the Catholic faith. A way for criminals to excuse their crimes in the name of God."

Marta's hand moved to her throat, grasping for the silver cross she wore every day around her neck, a gesture Josie had seen her perform a hundred times. Josie wished she had something in her life that gave her the security and comfort that Marta obviously drew from her religion. To Josie, religion was a mystery. She wasn't brought up in the church, had never learned the Bible stories that other kids learned in Sunday school. She had no sense of her place in a spiritual world.

Still standing at the conference table, Otto repeated himself. "We've reached a point where it's time to stop for the day. Let's be ready for tomorrow with clear heads."

Josie got up and straightened the stack of folders in front of her. She said, "Dillon's parents called again just before you got here.

Checking in, wondering if we'd heard from him. His mother said she called his ex-girlfriend from back in California to see if she knew anything. She also checked with several friends to see if he'd called."

Otto raised his eyebrows.

"No, nothing. No one has heard from him." Josie felt pressure in her chest and a tremor in her hands.

"Tomorrow we focus on his clients. Go home now. Try to get some sleep."

Josie knew there was nothing more she could do that night. She shut down her computer, and as she reached the door, Otto called to her. "It goes without saying that our house is always open. If it's too much, staying by yourself."

Josie drove home in a fog, struggling to make sense of the day. She called Dell from her cell phone and filled him in. She asked him to keep watch, and to let her know if there were any suspicious cars or people around the property. He offered to come down, but she declined. She needed to get some sleep, though they both knew that would not happen.

Chester greeted her on the porch: tail wagging, whimpering and barking, body swaying, anxious for a bone. Josie entered the house and gave everything a cursory once-over to make sure no messages had been left. Then she went through the motions: changing out of her uniform, feeding the dog, opening a can of soup, dumping its contents into a bowl and putting it in the microwave, and finally, reaching for the bottle of bourbon in the cabinet beside the refrigerator. She poured a juice glass full. Josie did not drink socially. She drank to forget, to feel numb, to quiet the demons.

In the living room she put on an old Johnny Cash CD and collapsed onto the couch, where she forced down the glass of bourbon, her eyes watering from the burn. She scooted up to the edge of the couch and cleaned off the coffee table, a musty steamer trunk that she'd purchased at a flea market. She moved a stack of magazines to the floor, along with the wooden box of aggie marbles she had been collecting since she was a kid. Inside the trunk she stored family photos and trinkets from a childhood she typically chose not to think about.

The happiest but most painful memories of her childhood involved her father. She searched for the photo album he had given her as a gift for her eighth birthday. Six months later he was killed in a line-of-duty accident. All these years, and those were the words she associated with her father's service as a police officer. *A line-of-duty accident*: as if those words answered all of her questions and defined him in some way. Her mom refused to talk about his death. A car accident was all she would ever say, but Josie had heard stories that her father had been shot during a routine traffic stop. Her mother's avoidance of the truth was one of the many reasons she and Josie rarely spoke.

Josie lifted out a pile of high school yearbooks that she had not opened since graduation, smiled at a stash of high school softball medals, and found a framed picture of her grandma. Leaning back on the couch, she studied the picture, looking for signs of her father. It was one of her favorite family photos, the portrait of a woman with a head full of frizzy gray pin curls, wrinkles framing her eyes, and a smile that lit up the picture. It was the smile that got Josie, made her laugh every time she looked at it.

Josie felt the hard edges blur as the bourbon worked its magic. She closed her eyes for a moment, then sat up to put the photograph away. Buried between the folds of a quilt her grandma had sewn, Josie found the photo album she had been searching for. The word *Memories* was inscribed in gold across the front. She opened to a page almost halfway through the book, and found her father, sitting in a porch swing at the front of their house, smiling at her. His fine black hair was combed to the side, and he wore shorts and no shirt, his bare chest narrow and hairless. He sat in the middle of the swing, his arms stretched out across the back of it as if he owned the world.

Josie got up and walked to her bedroom, where she pulled a

framed picture of Dillon from her bedside table. Wrapping herself in her grandma's quilt, she sat back on the couch and held the photograph of Dillon next to her father's photo and recognized the quality she had known they shared but had never been able to identify: the genuinely happy smile.

SEVEN

Just before her alarm went off the next morning, Josie woke with a start. She had been dreaming about Dillon. He was sitting at her kitchen table, working on her computer, staring at the screen but not speaking. She had been across from him, angry that he wouldn't look at her, wouldn't talk to her. As the dream filtered from her memory, something clicked. It wasn't an unfamiliar image, Dillon at her laptop, working from her house using her wireless Internet connection rather than driving to the office. She sat up suddenly, ignoring the nausea and the throb in her temples, and ran to open the junk drawer in the kitchen. She rooted around its contents until she remembered tacking the paper onto the corkboard inside the pantry. Opening the door, she saw the paper she had been searching for.

———————

Josie arrived at work an hour early and found Otto at the coffee-maker.

He turned and smiled. "Coffee's on. Delores sent apple dumplings for breakfast. She's convinced that you'll forget to eat. I suspect she's right."

Josie remembered the soup she had put in the microwave the

night before but forgot about. She realized suddenly how hungry she was, but felt guilty eating.

"You going hungry won't help his situation in the least."

She turned her computer on. "I have good news," she said, and walked to the conference table. There she found an apple dumpling and fork on a glass plate covered with plastic wrap. She unwrapped it and took a bite, glancing back at her computer, waiting impatiently for it to load.

Otto sat down with two mugs of black coffee and slid her cup across the table.

"I don't know why this didn't occur to me until this morning. Dillon stores his files on the Internet. He logs in to some program and can access his files from anywhere."

"His work files?"

"I've seen him access them at my house. On my laptop."

"Let's hope you find a list of clients somewhere," he said. "I spent last night going through Christina's file folders. More files were taken than we'd thought. I was searching for a client list, some kind of billing statements, but couldn't find anything."

When her computer was finally ready, Josie stood and carried her breakfast over to it. She pulled the piece of paper out of her shirt pocket and sat down. "Dillon kept his log-in information on a piece of paper at my place so he could access everything. There's a list of Web sites here, log-ins and passwords. I'm just not sure which one of these will give us access to his work files."

Josie took the list over to the copy machine and made Otto a copy. Of the seven Web sites, Josie took the first four and gave the other three to Otto. The first accessed a Web hosting application for his business Web site, but she found nothing out of the ordinary. She found what she was searching for on the third site.

"Take a look, Otto. It's called Sky Drop. I think he just saves all of his files to the online Sky Drop folder. Then he can get to them anywhere."

Otto pulled up his chair and looked over her shoulder as she logged in to Dillon's account. She clicked "Open Sky Drop Folder," and a list of about fifty file folders appeared in a desktop window.

Otto patted her on the back. "Good work. Open up the file folder titled 'Clients.'"

Josie double-clicked and found a client database. She opened it to find a number of files, each one listing information for a different client. The first file was for James Aiken and contained information such as address, employer, money market, etc.

"Click through those files," Otto said. "See if each one contains the same basic data."

Josie found the same template for a total of thirty-nine clients.

"Does that sound about right? Thirty-nine clients?"

She shrugged. "Probably. He's never said."

Over the next two hours Josie and Otto read through Dillon's work files. From this information they made a list of current clients whose physical file folders were missing.

"I'll check each name with NCIC for an arrest record or a warrant," Josie said.

"Assuming the records were entered," Otto said.

They both knew the National Crime Information Center was only as good as the reporting agencies that fed them information. If small-town departments didn't keep up with entering cases, criminals slipped through the system undetected.

As they continued to examine files, Josie came across a name that she recognized. "Dillon doesn't talk work much when he's away from the office. But I remember this name."

Otto looked over his computer at Josie.

"You recognize the name Julian Beckwith?" she asked.

"Isn't he the financier? The guy that owns all the property in El Paso?"

"That's him. The twenty-something super genius with millions in the stock market."

"The kind of kid you want to take out back and beat the snot out of."

Josie nodded. "Worse than that. He's had death threats. He provokes and taunts people. Enjoys bilking stupid rich people out of their money. Then brags about it. Another twisted Robin Hood."

"Dillon is that kid's accountant?"

"I don't think he's the accountant, but he represents some part of his business," she said. "Now that we have actual client names, let's go back to Dillon's office."

Josie took the list she had assembled and photocopied it for Otto as he took a phone call. She found two plastic crates for carrying the files back to the department once they were finished at Dillon's. Otto hung up his phone, his expression guarded.

"What is it?"

"That was Showalter Funeral Home. They've arranged a memorial service for Christina tomorrow afternoon at one o'clock. Her family is flying in tonight to be there."

Josie listened to the noise in her head, like a windstorm, knocking out the power. What would she say to these grieving parents when she was still grieving herself, and terrified of more bad news that might come?

It was another pretty spring day, the kind of day that would cause Dillon to start making plans for the weekend. Pack an overnight bag, throw the tent in the back of Josie's jeep, and drive to Big Bend National Park to hike and kayak the canyons. Josie would buy the groceries and Dillon would cook over a fire. He hated to grocery shop, and she hated to cook. Now, as she watched Otto remove the yellow crime-scene tape and unlock the newly repaired door, panic welled up inside her as reality hit her all over again. She could only hope they would make such a trip again.

The office was cool and the shattered glass had been swept away. Christina's chair had been removed and taken to the police station as evidence. It didn't change the horror of what had happened, but it was a relief not to have to look at the bloodstained chair anymore.

Josie checked each of the phones' voice mails and listened to several new messages, jotting down the callers in her notebook. Otto carried a ladder-back chair from the waiting area over to Christina's desk and laid out Dillon's list of clients.

"How do you want to do this?" he asked.

Josie knew he was asking how involved she wanted to be. "I'm fine. It makes more sense for me to work in his office since I know somewhat how he operates."

Otto stared at her for a moment, then nodded and sat down to begin working. Josie walked down the dark hallway to Dillon's office. The wood-slatted blinds were drawn against the early morning sun and the office was gloomy. She turned on the overhead light and sat down in his office chair. She scanned the objects on his desk, looking for anything missing that she hadn't caught the day before. She then switched places and sat in the client's seat, the chair she often sat in when she stopped by to visit. She observed the room for quite a while and, finding nothing, moved to the set of three lateral filing cabinets against the wall to the right of Dillon's desk.

Two of the file drawers had been open when she entered his office the morning before. She started with the drawer on the left, which was filled with legal and policy guides. The next drawer contained client files, surprisingly thin. Although it appeared the majority of his information was scanned and stored online, she did find the names of twenty-one clients who weren't in his mail merge file or the client database. She collected those folders and packed them into the plastic crate.

The last file drawer seemed to contain files specifically for current clients. They would focus first on the missing clients from that group.

After spending another fifteen minutes checking through desk drawers and searching closets, they were ready to go back to the department to begin sifting through documents. Before they left, Josie found the key to Dillon's post office box in his desk drawer and took it with her. She occasionally picked up his mail for him and knew that his box was number 246.

Josie locked up the office and Otto drove to the post office, where she retrieved the mail with no issue. Seated in the car again, Josie flipped through the pile of bills and came across a letter addressed to Dillon from the United States Attorney for the Western District of Texas.

"This looks like a summons for federal court," she said.

He glanced at the envelope. "Better open it."

Josie quickly read through the letter and said, "Dillon received a summons for the district court in El Paso. The case is against a Walter Frank Follet."

"Wally Follet," Otto said. "That's one of Dillon's clients. I remember seeing the name in the database."

"He runs the salvage yard. Wally's Folly."

Otto nodded and glanced at Josie. "I know who Wally is. I've never had a run-in with him, but I can't imagine him ever winning businessman of the year."

Josie turned in her seat and looked at him. "A federal indictment? Motive for a murder and kidnapping?"

"If a guy like Wally thought it would keep him out of jail? Absolutely."

Back at the police department, Josie logged on to the Internet to find the number for the district attorney prosecuting the Follet case.

She reached a secretary first and introduced herself, explaining that she might have information regarding the Follet case. A minute later a man came on the line.

"So, you know Wally Follet?" he asked. His tone was congenial, almost joking. She was caught off guard by his candor. She had expected an attorney to be more reserved.

"Actually, I'm calling about a case that may be related. I'm the chief of police in Artemis, Texas. I'm investigating a murder and the probable kidnapping of Dillon Reese. I found the court summons for Mr. Reese in his mail."

There was silence on the other end for a moment. "Well, there's a bombshell. I can be there in about four hours. That work for you?"

Josie raised her eyebrows at Otto and said back into the phone, "See you then."

Five hours later, Josie and Otto shook hands with Gary Hardner, assistant DA with the District Court of West Texas. In his midthirties, he wore a gray suit that was at least a size too large for his slender build, a red tie, black shades, and sported a trendy haircut with just the right amount of hair product.

"How ya'll doing? Appreciate you taking me in on short notice," he said as he took off his sunglasses and tucked them into his suit coat pocket.

"We're glad you came down," Josie said. "We've got a terrible case we hope you can shed some light on."

Hardner followed Josie and Otto up the stairs to the office and declined coffee. As they sat at the conference table Josie noted that he had not brought any files or a briefcase with him. *Not a good sign,* she thought.

"Tell me what you have," he said.

Josie nodded to Otto.

"The body of Mr. Reese's secretary, Christina Handley, was found in her desk chair at the office yesterday morning by Chief Gray. Ms. Handley was shot once in the chest. The shot was from a side angle. We think either by someone firing off a quick shot, or by someone who didn't know what they were doing with the gun. All of the computers in the office are gone, as well as the desktop calendars and some file folders. Mr. Reese has not been heard from since about eight in the morning, the day before yesterday. There was one text message sent yesterday evening, although we're concerned the text wasn't sent by him. Our fear is that he's been kidnapped."

Hardner gave Otto a skeptical look, as if he had been listening to an amateur's account of the case.

"Sounds to me like a domestic gone wrong. Nice-looking secretary, jealous boss, she gets shot. He takes off with the company secrets, and sets up a new life in the Cayman Islands."

"I think that's highly unlikely," Otto said.

"See it all the time," Hardner said.

His demeanor pissed Josie off.

Otto glanced at her, probably gauging her reaction, and then turned back to Hardner. "How much do you know about Dillon Reese?"

Hardner gave a dismissive tilt of the head. "He's the accountant for the accused. We're after his records, and the phone communications he's had with Wally."

Josie understood that he didn't know the Artemis PD, or even their reputation, but she expected to at least be treated with respect. He was the kind of person who dismissed others' questions as if they weren't important, thus keeping his own information safe. In return he would expect full disclosure. Meanwhile, the Artemis PD was facing a horrendous crime and getting no help in what could be a critical lead.

Otto said, "Since you have limited background on Mr. Reese I can tell you he's a respected member of the community. We have no reason to suspect him of wrongdoing. He is in a committed relationship—"

Hardner interrupted, "With Chief Gray, no less."

Otto continued without pause, "—and we have circumstantial evidence piling up that points to a kidnapping."

Unable to remain quiet any longer, Josie pitched her pencil onto the conference table. "I don't care for your condescending attitude, Mr. Hardner. I called you as a professional courtesy. I would expect the same of you. If your purpose was to come here and treat me like a witness, raise my ire, see if you could trick me into sharing something important, then I'll save you the time. We have virtually nothing to go on." She paused, dialed her temper down a notch. "A murder has been committed and a man has most likely been kidnapped from our community. Both of these victims deserve every resource that we can give them."

He stared at Josie, obviously weighing his response.

"I hope you'll share information from your indictment and allow us to talk as professionals. I hope our two offices can work together to share what could be vital information to both of us," she said.

He pursed his lips and cocked his head as if properly chastised. "Never intended to get off on the wrong foot here. I will certainly provide what I can, as long as you understand the absolute necessity for confidentiality."

"That's understood."

"Here's what I don't want to happen. I don't want you conducting an investigation into Wally Follet's business that will jeopardize a case that goes to the grand jury in a month. We've spent six months investigating and I plan to nail the bastard."

Otto said, "Our case involves a murder and a missing person. We'll respect your time, and we'll do nothing to interfere with your indictment. However, if you have something that will help us understand why Dillon Reese is missing and his secretary is dead . . . ?" Otto shrugged and left the obvious unsaid.

Hardner held a hand in the air as if surrendering. "It's a fairly cut-and-dried indictment. A junkyard operator buys totaled cars from insurance companies and sells them across the border to Mexican buyers. These companies rebuild the cars and sell them off with a clean title. Granted, he wasn't fabricating the titles, but he was part of the business operation that was. Wally was getting by until we discovered he's also selling stolen cars across the border, where they switch out the VINs and titles and send back a car with a clean history."

"So, it's a federal crime because he's selling the cars to Mexico, correct?" Otto asked.

"You got it. He's sold stolen cars across state lines and the national border." He smiled. "That's why my office was graced with the likes of Wally Follet."

"Is he reselling the so-called clean cars in the U.S.?" Josie asked.

"We don't have anything concrete, but I believe so. He appears to buy wrecked cars and sells to buyers in Mexico."

"So, the indictment is for selling stolen cars across the border. And that's it?"

Hardner tipped his head slightly and smiled. "We've also tried to find a connection to guns or drugs. He's either really slick, or he's just what he says he is—a used car dealer."

"A stolen car dealer," Josie said.

Hardner ignored her comment. "That's really about it. No more complicated than that. We have proof Wally took possession of stolen cars. We know he worked with an outside shipper, but we haven't been able to track down the company yet. At this point, I'll settle for Wally. And Mr. Reese's accounting records can make all of this cleaner for the jury. Transaction amounts and key dates will seal the case for us."

"Were you planning on involving local law enforcement at some point?" Josie asked.

"No, ma'am." Hardner gave her a condescending smile. "We already believe someone tipped Wally off about the indictment and he took off. My experience has been the fewer people involved, the better."

"How did that work out for you?" she asked.

Otto quickly cut off the exchange. "And you're going ahead with the indictment?"

"Absolutely. We'll try him in absentia."

"Who's taking care of the business while he's away?" she said.

"Left his eighteen-year-old son to run the business and deal with the feds. Follet's a real sweetheart."

"I take it you don't think much of Mr. Follet," Otto said.

"He's a greasy wise guy who fits every stereotype in the book. You want a Ford? He'll sell you a Chevy just to prove he can." He narrowed his eyes and pointed a finger at Otto. "The truth? He thinks he's a brilliant negotiator, but he makes terrible decisions."

"Are there others involved in his business? Partners?" Josie asked.

"We've looked but can't find partners. Just his boy. I don't think the kid's smart enough to steal a pack of bubble gum though. It's a one-man operation as far as we can tell."

He stood and leaned over the table to shake Josie's hand, and then turned to Otto. Josie and Otto stood as well. "It's been a pleasure. Obviously we'll want the records from Mr. Reese's office as soon as you have things cleaned up here. We'll get the subpoena together." He paused and offered a solemn frown that came across to Josie as insincere. "And, be assured, if I hear anything that could help in clearing up your cases you'll get the call from me immediately."

"Thank you, Mr. Hardner," Otto said.

He smiled curtly. "Now, I've a long drive. I should make my way back up north."

Josie showed him out, wished him safe travels, then made her way back up to the office, where she found Otto on his computer.

"Wouldn't want to be his paralegal," Josie said.

"A tad condescending, wasn't he?" Otto turned his chair toward her.

"What did you think about his theory of jealous boss shoots his pretty secretary?" Josie asked.

"I was afraid you might come out of your seat," he said.

"Actually, it was just the reference to the good-looking secretary that got to me. How would Hardner know that Christina was pretty? He played it off like Dillon was a small part of the investigation. And Dillon never mentioned anything to me about an assistant district attorney interviewing him. I feel certain that Dillon would have told me. That's not a typical day in the life of an accountant."

"What are you getting at?"

"He tried to play off Dillon's involvement as minor. But I wonder if he's holding back information. I think he knows quite a bit about Dillon. He couldn't resist the jab at me—letting me know that he knew we were romantically involved. So why would he want to downplay Dillon's involvement in the case?"

"Downplaying isn't Mr. Hardner's strength," he said, and pointed to his computer screen. "Check this out. Wally Follet's Web site. Not much more than contact information."

Josie checked her watch. "It's five thirty. You have time to run over there tonight?"

"You bet. Let's go visit the kid who can't steal a pack of gum."

———

Wally's Folly was located on the north end of Arroyo County. Josie offered to drive to distract herself from the situation. Otto did his own part by providing a running commentary on his family's current state of affairs: his daughter's pregnancy, his wife's local drama at the Homemaker's Club, and the state of his goat herd. He pointed out the trees turning lime green with new growth and the swaths of bluebonnets and neon yellow broomweed fields on either side of the road, but Josie still struggled to connect with anything beyond her own bleak thoughts.

They followed River Road a mile upstream to the Rio Camp and Kayak, a local vacation spot. The salvage yard faced River Road, with the backside of the property sloping down into the Rio Grande. The lot was dusty with a smattering of driveway rock here and there. A Rottweiler was tethered to a chain under a shade tree beside the office. He was already on his haunches with his teeth bared as Josie drove toward him.

Trees lined the east side of the yard and the other two sides were enclosed by an eight-foot-high wooden fence. There were ten to fifteen rows of cars and trucks and various other vehicles in pieces, from stripped-down bare-metal frames to piles of tires and a collection of several hundred steering wheels hanging from the side of a large hay barn. It was hard to imagine that any vehicle in the several-acre lot was actually worth anything. The skeletons of the rusted cars and rows of parts and pieces gave Josie the impression of an auto graveyard patrolled by a murderous dog.

She parked in front of the mobile home office and read the weathered, hand-painted sign: WALLY'S FOLLY: WRECKS AND REBUILTS. DAILY 9:00–5:00.

"I believe the kid who can't steal gum is staring out the office window at us," Otto said.

"Let's go have a chat." Josie got out of the car and the Rottweiler leaped toward her, the chain straining at his neck as he barked and growled. She hoped the chain would hold but placed a hand on the butt of her gun just in case.

She knocked and the kid opened a dented, flimsy metal door.

"Can I help you?" he said.

His hair was in need of a cut, and his lanky body gave the impression that his muscles hadn't kept pace with a recent growth spurt. He wore blue jeans and a Chicago Cubs T-shirt. She noted several fading bruises on his forearms and a split lip that was healing.

Josie held her badge out and introduced herself. "We'd like to talk with you a few minutes about your business."

"Sure." The kid walked down the steps and Josie noticed how painfully thin and pale he was. It appeared as if he hadn't stepped out of the trailer in months. He turned toward the dog and snapped his fingers, telling him to lie down.

When the dog finally settled Josie looked back to the boy. "What's your name?"

"Hector Follet. People call me Hec for short."

Josie and Otto both shook his hand. She said, "Is this your place?"

"You mean, like, my business? Or my home?"

"Either one."

"Sure, both I guess. My dad owns the business. I stay here at the shop."

"Your dad here?" she asked.

"No, ma'am."

"When will he be back?"

He lifted one corner of his mouth, an expression that indicated he wasn't sure how to answer. "You don't already know?"

She tipped her head. "We heard some officers from El Paso were looking for him."

He nodded. "So why are you here now?" There was no malice or disrespect in his question.

"There's a crime that took place in town. In Artemis. A man is missing that worked with your dad. His name is Dillon Reese. You recognize the name?"

"Yeah." His expression had grown wary. "What do you mean missing?"

"We're not sure yet. How do you know Mr. Reese?" Josie asked.

"He does our books."

"He was your accountant?" she asked.

"Yes."

"Did you ever meet him?"

"No, I just know his name."

"Did you know Mr. Reese's secretary, Christina Handley?"

He shook his head.

"Do you understand the charges against your dad?"

He shrugged, turned his head away from them, and looked around the salvage yard. "I guess. He was selling cars across the border. The police say some of them were stolen. I don't know how they know that. My dad didn't know they were stolen."

Josie noted that he had avoided eye contact with her.

"How long has your dad been gone?"

He didn't hesitate. "Nine days."

She nodded, imagining the stress the kid must be under. "So how does your business work here? You buy wrecked cars?"

"Mostly insurance settlements. Somebody wrecks a car and insurance totals it out. We buy the wrecked car for a cheap price, then we sell it to an auto body shop in Mexico. They rebuild it and sell it."

"With a clean title?" she asked.

"I don't know."

Josie pointed to his arms. "How'd you get those bruises?"

He narrowed his eyes and looked closely at Josie, taking several seconds to respond. "Playing with the dog. He likes to roughhouse."

She nodded, studying him in return, but his expression remained neutral. "You mind if we take a look around the yard?" she asked.

He shrugged. "Not much to see. Just a bunch of junk cars."

"It's okay. We'll just get a better sense of what you do here." It was a bogus response. Josie just wanted to see how he would react to having the police walk around the grounds.

He looked away, avoiding eye contact, and shoved his hands in his jeans pockets. "If you want."

"Thanks. We'll just be a minute."

A driving lane split the rows of vehicles and parts into two main sections. Josie and Otto took off walking down it. When she glanced over her shoulder she saw the boy walking back into the office, probably to watch them from the window.

"That kid's a nervous mess," Otto said.

"I feel sorry for him. Living his life based on his dad's lousy decisions."

They reached the last row and saw it was mostly filled with vans and travel trailers in serious disrepair. They turned left down the last row and heard Hec yell their names.

"I got something!" he yelled.

They glanced at each other and rushed back to the office. When they reached Hector he was holding a paper out to them.

"I thought you might need this. It's the name and address of my dad's attorney. He could probably answer all your questions about the case."

Josie took it and read the kid's hurried cursive writing on a piece of spiral notebook paper.

"Thanks, Hec. I appreciate the information and your time today," she said.

Otto reached out and shook the boy's hand.

Josie said, "Hec, we're not here because of what happened to your dad. We're trying to figure out why Mr. Reese is missing. It might not have anything to do with your dad's case, so I don't want to worry you. But, if there's anything that's bothering you, if you're scared, or worried about something that has to do with the case, will you call me?"

He was staring intently at her, as if trying to figure out if she was just throwing him a line, or if she was sincere.

"Have you had anyone bother you out here since your dad was taken away?" she asked.

He looked away. "No, not really."

Josie pulled her business card out of her pocket and handed it to him. "You get police protection just like anyone else. If someone is bothering you, you call nine-one-one, or you call me directly using that card. I'm sure this whole thing has been pretty stressful."

"Yes, ma'am." He pulled his billfold out of the back of his jeans pocket and slipped the card in.

EIGHT

After interviewing Hec, Josie drove back to the office and tried to organize her notes and write a summary of the information they had collected. When she left work at 8:00 P.M. she felt as if she had little to show for the day. Too much time was passing with too few leads. The police had received no tips from anyone about Dillon's disappearance. Otto had said rumors were beginning to surface around town that Dillon had stolen money and absconded. Josie could imagine the stories being swapped at the Hot Tamale, the diner that specialized in local gossip. She hated to think what her reaction might be when some insensitive idiot approached her with the rumor.

Before stopping at home, Josie drove up to Dell's to give him a quick update and to collect Chester. When Josie left for work each morning, Chester made a beeline for Dell's, where the dog spent the day on the front porch, or followed Dell around the ranch, napping in the sun as Dell did his chores.

Dell was in his barn with the front leg of a horse, bent at the knee, leaning against his thigh as he dug something out of the horseshoe. When she walked into the barn he let the horse's leg back down to the ground and faced Josie, his expression troubled.

"Any news yet?"

"Not enough to make a difference. No contact from Dillon or the kidnappers."

"All's quiet around here. A few cars drove by on Schenck Road, but no one stopped. I been outside all day."

"All right. Thanks, Dell."

She didn't have the energy to talk, and Dell no doubt understood. Josie opened the back door of her jeep and Chester climbed inside. She drove home and checked the mailbox for communication concerning Dillon, but it was empty.

Chester jumped out of the jeep and ran to the house, his nose to the ground. He reached the front door, whining and then barking, sniffing at the jamb. Typically he was excited to be the first one through the door, but now he barked and whined as if he'd picked up a strange scent; his anxiety was obvious and she was immediately on edge.

She pulled her Beretta out of her gun belt and held it in her left hand, safety off, while she unlocked the door. She carried a Beretta PX4 Storm Compact, a 9 mm that fit her hand perfectly. She snapped her fingers and ordered Chester to sit. She switched her gun to her right hand and held Chester's collar with her left. She bumped the front door with her knee, and as it swung open slowly, the living room came into view. Since Dillon's disappearance she had been keeping the house closed up and the curtains pulled. The living room was dimly lit by a table lamp that turned on automatically at dusk. Everything appeared to be in order.

She stepped inside, holding Chester back by the collar. Barking, he strained toward the kitchen. She yelled his name to get him to stop but it was no use. He lunged forward and broke free as they reached the kitchen door. He frantically sniffed around the kitchen, his nose to the floor. Josie held her gun in the ready position, checked the kitchen, and, standing to the side of the pantry doorframe, opened the pantry door. Once she was certain the front part of the house was clear she crept down the dark hallway.

She moved quickly through the bedroom doorway, backed into the nearest corner to scan the room, then moved to the bathroom, and followed the same procedure on into the spare bedroom. She flipped on the room's light and found the alarm control box lying on the floor. It had been ripped out of the wall. She cursed and went back to the kitchen, where she found the back door closed but unlocked, and a six-inch, round piece of glass in the window to the right of the door removed. The sight of it made her face burn with rage. Someone had cut the piece of glass out of the sidelight beside the door, reached their hand inside, unlocked the door, and entered her house.

Chester stood at the entrance to the pantry, pawing at the wall where Josie hung her gun belt each night after work. Ignoring him, she pulled her cell phone out of her pocket and called in a breaking and entering to the night dispatcher, Brian Moore. Within seconds he was back on the line to tell her Marta was on her way.

Staring at the back door now, with the glass removed, she called the security company's number that she had saved in her phone. When she received a recorded response she left an angry message about the failure of their system and demanded a call back that night. She hung up and walked over to the pantry, where Chester was still whining and pawing. When she stepped inside she gasped, pulling back in shock. There was a small, gray mesh bag that she had never seen before hanging from the hook where she hung her gun belt. The idea that someone knew where she hung her gun each night made her feel physically ill.

Unable to wait for Marta, she called Otto.

"What's up?" he said.

"Someone broke into my house. They disabled the alarm and broke in through the window."

"Are you safe? Are you in the house now?"

"I've checked the house. Based on the way the dog's reacting, I figure they stopped at the front door to see if it was locked, then cut the window out of the back door and did a quick dash through the house to disable the alarm system. They spent time in the kitchen and the pantry. Beyond that I'm not sure."

"You call this in yet?"

"Marta's on her way." Josie had grabbed a pair of tongs from the kitchen drawer and was carrying the mesh bag over to the kitchen counter. "They hung a bag inside my pantry where I keep my gun belt. There's a cell phone inside the bag."

"Hang on! Those phones can be used as detonators! Don't open that until we get someone over there from the bomb squad."

"Otto. This is from the kidnappers. I know it is. They don't want to blow up the person they're communicating with." She clicked the speaker button on her phone and laid it on the kitchen counter. "I'm putting my gloves on now. I want you on the phone with me when I open this."

She could hear him exhale. The phone in the bag was a cheap flip model. Holding the edges, she opened it and clicked the menu button to look at the sent/received calls. There were none. She used the tip of a pencil eraser to scroll down to text messages and clicked "open."

"Jesus, Otto. There's three messages." She clicked the first and a photograph of Dillon appeared. She drew her breath at the sight of him.

"What?"

"The first message is a JPEG. It's Dillon." She choked back a sob. "Jesus, Otto, there's a bag over his head. It's just him from the waist up. It's a bad picture so I can't see details. I know it's him though." Tears welled up in her eyes and she forced herself to continue. "He's wearing the shirt and tie he had on that morning."

"I'm getting in my car right now, Josie. Give me five minutes. Just wait to open the rest until someone gets there with you."

Josie wiped the tears from her eyes and took several jagged breaths, trying to calm herself enough to see the screen. Josie clicked the second message and it was a picture of someone holding a piece of paper. She squinted at the small picture, but the image was too small. "I think the next might be a ransom note, but I can't read it. I'm forwarding this photo to my e-mail account."

"Use your work e-mail, Josie. We want this done right."

She said nothing as she sent the photos. She carried the phone with her to the kitchen table, where she plugged in her laptop, willing herself to remain calm.

"Does it look as if anything has been taken from your house?" he asked.

"Not that I can see. The only visible signs are the busted alarm, the window and back door, and the bag hanging in the pantry." She heard the sirens from Marta's jeep approaching outside. "Marta's here. I'll open these photos in my account. They'll be loaded by the time you get here."

Josie started her computer and walked to the front door to unlock it and let Marta inside. She explained everything that had happened.

"They've got him, Marta. I have no doubt this is Medrano. Someone has been watching me. They know where I store my damn gun belt." Anger welled up inside her to the point where she felt like screaming. She turned away from Marta, balling up her fists and pressing them against her forehead. "They have Dillon. They have access to my house. They have shut me down."

From behind her, she felt Marta's hand on her shoulder. Her voice was quiet, calm. "Josie. Show me where they entered."

Josie took a deep breath and pointed to the back door and the glass that had been cut out of the window.

"Don't you have an alarm system?" Marta asked.

Marta followed Josie down the hallway and into the spare bedroom, where the alarm control box lay on the floor. Dangling from the wall was the phone cord that should have made the automatic call to the alarm company when a security breach was detected.

"How long is your entry delay before the alarm goes off?" Marta asked.

"Thirty seconds." Josie shook her head. Looking at the aftermath, she felt foolish. Thirty seconds gave them plenty of time to enter the house and rip the panel off the wall, disabling the alarm and the intruder call. Josie was furious that something so critical could be so easily destroyed. Back in the kitchen she sat down at her computer and opened her e-mail account while Marta went outside to check for other signs of entry.

A moment later the full-sized photograph of Dillon appeared on the screen. Josie cried out and placed her hand over her mouth. It was a grainy picture of Dillon with a gray bag covering his head and tied shut at the neck. He was flanked on either side by shorter men carrying machine guns, the barrels of both guns pushed into his chest. Both men wore camouflage jackets and white ski masks. She stared at the photo, trying to imagine the terror Dillon must have felt at that moment, and she wondered where he was now.

Josie heard Otto pull up in her driveway. He walked into her kitchen wearing a plaid short-sleeved shirt with blue jeans and farm boots. His face was red and his hair tousled, as if he'd just finished doing chores in the pasture. His eyes were wide, his expression panicked.

"What's happening?" he asked as he walked toward the table and bent over her shoulder to examine the picture. "Are you certain that it's Dillon?"

"Without a doubt," she said.

Josie opened the second photo. The sides of Dillon's shirt were visible just behind his fingers, which were holding a piece of paper up to his chest. In Dillon's handwriting were the words, *$9 million paid in full gets me back. $50,000 by tomorrow 5:00 PM or I lose my arm.*

Unable to speak, she opened the third message and found a photograph of notebook paper with directions for wiring the money into an account.

She placed her head in her hands and cried.

She heard the kitchen door open and knew Otto had gone to get Marta.

The door opened again and Marta soon stood behind Josie, placing both her hands on her shoulders. "At least you've had contact. You know he's alive," she said. She squeezed Josie's shoulders and bent down to talk closer to her ear. "We can move forward with a plan."

Josie grabbed a napkin from the holder on the table and pressed it against her eyes. She had never in her life been so terrified. She finally turned to face Marta and Otto, who both stood behind her.

"Fifty thousand dollars? Or he loses an arm? They're sadistic psychopaths. Human life means nothing." Josie's throat was tight with emotion, her voice barely audible.

"We'll call the FBI tonight," Otto said. "We have no choice." He leaned against her kitchen cabinets looking old and tired.

"We lose the investigation," Marta said quietly, echoing Josie's own thoughts.

"We gain their resources, their investigators," he continued. "Kidnappings within Mexico take place daily. Kidnappings along the Texas border are still rare. The last thing the government wants is a mass panic. The governor will want this taken care of immediately. We need their support."

"And they need ours!" Josie blurted out, her fear from moments ago now turning to anger.

"How do we convince the bastards we have something important to offer? How can we be certain they won't take over the case?" Marta asked.

Otto gave Marta a frustrated look. "That's a stereotype. We've worked with arrogant bastards, and others who weren't. Same as any other agency. Don't judge them before we even meet them."

Josie lost the thread of the conversation, unable to keep her attention on anything but the newfound knowledge that Dillon was being held captive. She clicked the Back button on her computer to stare at the photo of Dillon. What was he doing now? Were they feeding him and allowing his basic needs to be met? Had he given up hope? Did he believe in her ability to get him home safely? She knew that for years to come that picture would haunt her.

NINE

By eleven o'clock that night a sedan carrying two FBI agents had arrived at Josie's home. Agent Josh Haskins looked to be in his late twenties, with a new-recruit buzz cut, clean-shaven face, and tasteful suit. He appeared smart, well-spoken and tactful, and interested in the details of the case. His partner was Bob Omstead, a fiftyish bald man who seemed to be all business, all of the time, a trait Josie was fine with as long as he didn't shut her out. Omstead wore a lightweight FBI windbreaker over a button-down shirt and black trousers. His badge was clipped to his gun belt, and a 9 mm was holstered just inside his jacket but still visible.

They had listened attentively from the couch as Josie told them about finding Christina's body, the timeline they had put together for the murder and kidnapping, and the new ransom demands. Otto sat in a chair beside the TV, and Josie sat on the bench under the window directly facing the agents. Marta had been called out an hour prior for a motorist stranded down by the river.

At the end of the briefing, Agent Omstead faced Josie. "You mentioned that Officer Podowski is the lead. As the chief of police, why aren't you the lead investigator on this case?"

Josie glanced at Otto before she responded.

"Mr. Reese and I have been in a serious relationship for four years. I didn't think it wise for me to retain the role of lead investigator. I assigned the job to Officer Podowski."

"Serious relationship?" he asked.

"We are romantically involved." She felt the flush in her cheeks.

Omstead let it drop and switched the subject. "Can you talk more about why you believe the kidnapping is linked to the Medrano cartel? I get your connection, but it seems early in the investigation to limit your focus."

Josie leaned forward and rested her arms on her thighs. She was mentally and physically exhausted and angry at no one and everyone. She knew the questions were necessary, but she wanted everyone out of her home. She was a private person, and discussing intimate details of her life with strangers bothered her immensely.

She took a long breath and finally said, "Two years ago, the Medrano cartel and La Bestia cartel were battling for drug routes and territory in Piedra Labrada, our sister city just across the border from us in Mexico."

Haskins nodded. "Sure, I've been there."

"The leader of the Medrano cartel was brought here for medical treatment after he was shot at a nightclub in Mexico. He was dying and needed immediate attention. The Mexican authorities knew the rival cartel would finish the job if he was taken to a Mexican hospital, so they brought him to the Trauma Center in Artemis."

"How could they bring him here if he's a Mexican citizen?" Omstead said.

"He had dual citizenship. He owned several hundred acres of ranch land in Texas."

Haskins shook his head, smiling in disbelief. "I remember this now. You guys had a gun battle in your Trauma Center. The rival gang came in and blew the Medrano leader to bits."

Josie nodded. "Then all hell broke loose."

Otto broke in, unable to keep quiet. "The Bishop, the Medrano family's second in command, blamed Josie for his father's death.

Cartel members broke into Josie's home and shot up her bedroom in the middle of the night. They've accessed her home in the past."

"It would take someone with a lot of knowledge about my house and my habits to know that I hang my gun belt on the hook in the pantry," she said. "That's where I go when I come home each night from work. The first thing I do is hang my gun belt on the same hook that the kidnappers placed the phone."

"So, members from the Medrano cartel have been in your home before. And now they've shown you they still have access. Still have control," Haskins said.

Josie forced herself to keep her gaze on Haskins. "Mr. Reese was with me the night they entered my home. He was with me as they attacked my house, shot up my bedroom with automatic weapons."

Haskins shook his head again. "No one was hurt?"

"No, but they sent a clear message. They didn't want me interfering in cartel business."

"So you think the cartel may be after you as retribution?" Haskins said.

Omstead shook his head, his expression doubtful. "It doesn't work for me. You have family money?"

"No."

"Any rich friends able to chip in on a multimillion-dollar ransom?" he said.

"No." Josie thought of Macon Drench, a local millionaire and personal friend, but he made no sense. If someone wanted Drench's money, they would go through his wife or a family member, not the police chief. She chose not to mention him for now, to keep the investigation from derailing.

"Then the nine-million-dollar ransom doesn't make sense," Omstead said. "Obviously the Medrano cartel knows personal things about you. They would know that you don't have access to that kind of money. They wouldn't set a nine-million-dollar ransom without good reason. If it's unattainable, you won't pay up. You can't—so you give up the fight. That's the last thing they want. It wastes their time and resources."

Both agents stared at Josie as if she ought to have some answer. As if she were protecting some rich family member from view. It struck her suddenly—*This is what it feels like. To be innocent on every level, but to be made to feel like a criminal at your very core.* She stared back at them both silently.

Haskins, the younger of the two agents, finally broke the tension by asking to see the phone the kidnappers had left. Josie showed him the messages while Omstead went out to the car and brought back a large plastic case. Josie took the agents into the dining room, where Omstead unpacked an assortment of recording devices and cords. He explained that they were setting up a wireless mobile phone recording device that would allow them to record all incoming and outgoing calls from the phone and would transmit them wirelessly to the FBI.

When they had finished, Haskins said, "Okay. Let's break this up for the night. Agent Omstead and I have a great deal of information to start working with in the morning. I'll be your primary contact. You'll be keeping the phone left by the kidnappers. Keep it with you at all times. If you are contacted, call me immediately afterwards." He passed Josie a business card. "Any new information, any contact from the kidnappers, anything you can think of, you call my direct number."

"We'll be in touch tomorrow," Haskins continued. "We need to get this information into the system and start pulling together intelligence. We have an agent in Mexico we'll contact for information as well."

Josie suddenly felt panicked. They hadn't even discussed the ransom demands and they were getting up to leave. "They disabled my security system, broke into my home, left me pictures of Dillon with a bag over his head. They said that Dillon will lose an arm tomorrow if I don't come up with fifty thousand dollars. Every minute puts me closer to five o'clock, and we haven't even discussed a plan! What the hell am I supposed to do?"

Agent Omstead broke in. "Don't do anything. We've got an extensive database we'll be tapping into. We'll narrow by geography, by ransom, by every factor we can deduce. If you think of anything else tonight, call us. We'll make use of it. For now, we need to get to work. Sit tight and we'll update you as soon as we can."

"We appreciate your cooperation," Haskins said. He stood, but made no move toward the door. He looked at Otto, then Josie, his gaze sincere, but Josie felt like he was just saying that to mollify her. "Chief Gray, when we're asked into an investigation we're often met with reluctance, with the worry that we're coming in to take over, to close you out. That is not our intent. We're here to work as partners. We just need time to get things rolling on our end."

After they left, Josie and Otto stood at her living room window and watched the sedan drive down the road. "Think that was legitimate? Wanting to partner with us?" Josie asked.

Otto turned toward her, ignoring her question. "Why don't you pack a bag? Stay with us tonight? We've got a spare bed."

Josie smiled. "You're a good friend, Otto. I already called Dell and told him that Chester and I would crash on his couch tonight."

He raised a hand and walked to the front door. "That's good. Just didn't want you here with no lock on that back door." Before he stepped out, he turned to her again. "You want to pack a bag and I'll wait on you? I can drive you and the hound dog up to Dell's place."

Josie gestured at the door. "I'm fine. Go home and get some sleep. I'll see you in the morning."

Josie changed into sweatpants and a large *Just Do It* Nike T-shirt that belonged to Dillon, one of several favorite items that had been mixed in with her laundry and made their way into her own drawer. She brushed her teeth and washed her face, then slipped into her boots and barn coat to shield her from the cold night air. She grabbed her bed pillow, cell phone, the Beretta and both magazines from her gun belt, and then she and Chester started the quarter-mile walk down the lane to Dell's cabin. She wasn't too worried about her safety walking down the lane; whoever had kidnapped Dillon wanted her money at this point, not her life.

As they walked, the cold air felt good against Josie's face, and she forced her mind to settle and let the sound of the wind whistling through the cedar trees hush her thoughts. The deep porch on the front of Dell's cedar-planked house soon came into view. Walking there at night it looked more like a sprawling ranch house than a cabin, but inside it was a one-bedroom home with a large living room, modest-sized kitchen, and dining area. The cabin had high ceilings with exposed beams and rafters. A stone fireplace dominated one end of the cabin with a hearth that stretched across the end of the room as bench seating. By day, large windows on either side of the fireplace offered a beautiful view of Dell's Hereford cattle grazing in the foothills of the Chinati Mountains.

She breathed in the sweet smell of the wood smoke drifting down the valley, and smiled to see the soft light from a reading lamp that lit up the back bedroom of Dell's cabin. She was certain he would be up reading with the door closed to give her privacy but waiting on her in case she needed anything.

She and Chester clomped up the wooden stairs and across the porch to the front door. A lamp on the table beside the couch had been left on for her. Sheets had been tucked into the couch and blankets piled onto the coffee table. She opened the door and Chester made his way straight to the rug beside Dell's recliner. It was hours past the dog's bedtime; he would be asleep within minutes. She turned and set the deadbolt on the door, something Dell never did.

She positioned her pillow on the couch and took off her coat, draping it over Dell's recliner. As she approached the fireplace she could feel heat radiating from the stones and she placed her hands over them to warm her fingers. She pulled two more pieces of wood from the small arched opening beside the fireplace and arranged them on top of the smoldering coals. She used the poker to jab at the logs, letting air underneath the coals to get the fire burning again, and then sat on the hearth with her back to the fire, letting the heat soak through her shirt and into her skin.

TEN

Josie awoke at five the next morning with a clear head and, more importantly, a plan. She folded the sheets and blankets and left Dell a quick thank-you note on his kitchen table. Once she got home, she started with an Internet search on her laptop and then a phone conversation with Sergio Pando, an officer with the Mexican Federal Police—the Federales. Sergio was both a friend and a respected law enforcement contact. By seven o'clock Josie was pulling out of her driveway to investigate further, determined to keep an emotional distance from the horror she was facing.

She parked in front of the Artemis PD and poked her head in the door to tell Brian her plans. He was in his late twenties with the athletic build of a basketball player and the most even-tempered disposition she'd ever encountered. Brian never got shaken up; even while studying all hours trying to pass the bar exam for the third time, he still kept his chin up. His dream was to be an attorney in Artemis, but Josie worried he'd never make enough money to pay his massive college debt.

"Mayor sent me a text," Josie said. "He wants me in his office at seven fifteen. I'm headed there now. Otto check in yet?"

"No, ma'am," Brian said.

"Good enough. Tell him where I am."

Typical of most courthouse squares, most of the buildings facing each side of the courthouse were connected. The Artemis City Office was attached to the east side of the police department, and also faced the Arroyo County courthouse across the street. The mayor's office, located at the far end of the long narrow building, was still decorated with 1970s wood paneling and beige shag carpet. Cigar smoke permeated everything, sometimes creating a haze at the end of the nonsmoking building. It was a dreary place, and it surprised Josie that Caroline hadn't hired someone to redecorate her husband's office.

Josie pushed open the glass entrance door and said hello to the mayor's secretary, Helen, who wore a navy blue pantsuit with reading glasses that matched her outfit. She pulled off the glasses and let them dangle from the beaded necklace that hung around her neck. She was a hefty woman in her fifties who took her role as secretary to the mayor very seriously. A person did not reach him unless they first passed muster with Helen.

"Tell me you've come here with good news. Tell me you've caught the person who killed that poor girl."

"I'm afraid not, but we're doing everything we can."

"Any word on what's happened to Dillon?"

Josie could see the genuine anguish in the woman's eyes and appreciated her concern. "Nothing concrete yet."

"If it happens here, what's the rest of the world coming to?"

"I don't know, Helen. I have a lot of unanswered questions right now." Josie could hear the weariness in her own voice.

Helen picked up the phone and called the mayor to announce Josie's presence.

Halfway down the empty hallway that led to the mayor's office, Josie stopped and leaned against the wall. She tipped her head back and breathed deeply, closing her eyes, mentally clearing her head, forcing the thoughts of Dillon to stop. The loss of focus was unprofessional and would help no one. She took one more deep breath and exhaled slowly, then walked into his office.

Josie could tell he was angry. The man used body language like a weapon. He was red-faced and looked puffed full of steroids. She noticed a box of NoDoz lying beside an energy drink on his desk. Before Josie had time to sit down in the seat across from him he started in on her.

"I went to talk to Roxanne Spar." He stared at her for a moment. "Surprised to hear that? Didn't think I'd follow up with her, did you? Guess what she tells me? She says you went and told her she should file charges! What the hell is wrong with you? Are you trying to get yourself fired?"

Josie took a breath and exhaled. "Mayor, I've got bigger issues we need to deal with this morning."

"I'm not done with you yet! Why would you tell her to file charges after I came to you in confidence? I trusted you with sensitive information."

"Two things, Mayor. I didn't tell her to file charges. And you came to my house and asked me to destroy paperwork."

"Bullshit! You had no business talking with her. There wasn't even a case drawn. So why did you go see her, unless it was to put my ass in a sling?"

Josie said nothing.

"I'll tell you why! You saw this as your chance to screw me over. You tried to convince her that she needs to file charges on me!"

"That's not true," Josie said, her voice calm and rational. "All she wants is for you to leave her alone. Don't go to her apartment anymore. Don't visit her. Don't go to the bar. She doesn't want to file charges, she wants you to leave her alone."

He set his elbow on the top of his desk and pointed his finger directly at her. "You'd sure as hell better hope she doesn't press charges. It'll be your job if she does."

"I didn't come here today to talk about your issues. I received a message from the kidnappers last night," she said. She felt the muscles in her neck and shoulders tense as she brought up the kidnapping. "They didn't identify themselves. They demanded fifty thousand dollars today by five o'clock as earnest money. And nine million in ransom for Dillon's return."

The mayor looked stunned.

"Otto and I called the FBI last night once we received the ransom notice," she said.

The mayor said nothing for a moment, obviously shocked by the news. "What do you mean 'earnest money'?"

"It's like a down payment. Tells the kidnappers I'm working on getting the full amount."

"Why wasn't I called?"

"It was too late. The FBI didn't arrive at my house until after eleven."

"I don't care what time it was! When a member of my community is a confirmed kidnapped victim I expect to be called. Common sense has to kick in somewhere, Chief. Understood?"

"Absolutely."

Josie struggled to keep her tone calm and professional as she finished filling him in on the rest of the details, then she left with no further mention of Roxanne Spar. Josie was curious what his conversation had actually been with Roxanne, but she would not call the woman. Roxanne would have to make the next move.

Josie was in a horrible mood by the time she reached the police department. She decided to talk with Otto first thing, to get the conversation over with. She had lain awake on Dell's couch for most of the night, weighing her options. Should she pay the earnest money, wrangling up every cent she could get from the bank and begging friends for loans? Or should she wait, and hope that the kidnappers already knew that she didn't have that kind of money? She hadn't found a direct solution, but she had come up with a plan that might help her arrive at one, a plan she knew Otto wouldn't like.

She asked him to sit down at the conference table with her. They reviewed the conversation they'd had with the FBI agents the night before.

Josie finally asked, "What can the FBI do for us?"

"They have resources we don't have. They match up key characteristics of the kidnapping in their database. They'll narrow down a list of possibilities. Give us a place to start looking."

Josie felt herself growing impatient, and her words were becoming clipped. "Kidnapping is an industry in Mexico. There are rules and expectations that we don't understand." Josie paused, looking at Otto across the table from her. "I want to work with a negotiator. Someone from Mexico."

Otto frowned. "That's just not done. You don't sneak around behind the feds' backs."

"We don't negotiate with kidnappers or terrorists in this country. In Mexico it's a given," she said. "If we approach this from an American perspective we may lose Dillon."

"Josie, you're getting in way over your head. We don't know anything about negotiating with kidnappers," Otto said.

"That's my point! They said Dillon would lose his arm if I don't deliver fifty thousand dollars by this evening. How the hell am I supposed to respond to that? Trust those two agents to have the answers? Did you listen to them? They don't know any more than we do."

"How do you know they don't have answers? You think they don't have access to Medrano? Don't be so naïve," he said.

She sighed, frustrated by his response even though she had anticipated it. Otto was straight as an arrow, by the book. In another profession he would have been called a company man.

"Remember the senator in Arizona several years ago who was kidnapped, held for several months, and then finally released?" she asked.

He nodded.

"Sergio gave me the contact information for the negotiator. Nobody thought that senator would come back alive. Nick Santos saved that man's life. I have his contact information."

Leaning back in his seat now, Otto rubbed his eyes. "It's not professional," he said.

"I don't really give a damn whether it's professional or not. I want Dillon home, safe, before his life is destroyed. If that means tugging on someone's ego, then I'll do it."

"He's not an investigator, he's a kidnapping negotiator. What he does could very well be in complete conflict with the FBI's investigation." He pointed at her, suddenly angry. "Don't pretend like you don't know that, Josie."

"So what if it's in complete conflict? If this Santos can get him back any sooner, then I say go for it."

"He could compromise the investigation that the agents have put together. It goes both ways. As a cop, you've been on the losing end of another agency meddling in your business," he said.

"The bastards broke into my home. They have kidnapped one person and killed another. They operate with a different set of rules that we don't understand. I want to at least talk to Santos about the earnest money. I need advice, Otto. I don't know where else to go with this, and your support would mean a great deal to me."

Otto caved and finally nodded. "All right. Make the call."

Josie dialed the number and was surprised when the call was answered. After the Arizona senator's release Santos's reputation as a first-rate negotiator had spread all along the border. Josie had assumed he would be hard to track down.

"Santos."

She felt hot with anxiety and beads of sweat broke out on her forehead. "My name is Josie Gray. I'd like to talk to you about a kidnapping."

"Where you from?"

His dialect surprised her. Expecting a Spanish accent, she instead heard New York City, the voice of a tough-talking street cop.

"I'm the chief of police in Artemis, Texas. Across the border from Piedra Labrada."

"Who was kidnapped?"

"A community member. An accountant named Dillon Reese."

"Is he family?"

She hesitated. At thirty-four she could hardly call him a boyfriend. "He's a . . . close friend."

"Your lover?"

She hesitated.

"It matters," he said.

"Yes. We've been seeing each other for several years."

"You married?"

"No."

"So, you're a small-town cop making minimal. He's an accountant, but you aren't married, so you have no legal access to his money?"

Josie was caught off guard by his pace. "I don't have access to his money, but I don't think he—"

"I've been negotiating for ten years. I'm good. And I'm expensive. I'm sorry to say this, but a cop's paycheck won't cover my expenses."

"Just talk with me about the case. Give me an estimate. I'll find the money."

He laughed. "You don't *find* money, not during a negotiation. The money is there, or it isn't."

"Give me thirty minutes."

He hesitated and she could feel him giving in.

"Who's working the case?"

"Local police. We just brought in the FBI last night."

"You talk to anybody in Mexico yet?"

"Sergio Pando. He's a Federal and a personal friend. He's the only one. What city do you work out of?" she asked.

"Wherever the case is."

"Are you close to Piedra Labrada?"

He cursed under his breath. "My location isn't really the issue."

"I live in Artemis. Just across the border from Piedra." She paused, trying desperately to come up with the hook that would get him to talk with her. "It's the Medrano cartel. I'm sure of it. I have a history with them. I just need some preliminary advice."

He cursed and took a moment to respond. Finally he said, "Tonight at seven. Preferably your home so I can see the setup, but I want you by yourself," he said.

"I received communication from them last night. It's a nine-million-dollar ransom, and they want fifty thousand tonight by five o'clock." She felt the panic in her throat as she looked at her watch. "I don't know what to do."

He whistled. "You got money."

"What do you mean?"

"They don't start at nine million for a cop. Unless they know there's money somewhere. Family money, friends."

"I don't have money. Anywhere. My bigger concern is the fifty thousand they want today. Or Dillon is—"

"Look. You give them what they want on the first round, they know they got a money cow. Next demand they double it. Negotiate."

"What do I say if they contact me? 'Sorry, I can only give you a thousand out of my savings account'?"

"Shit. I been back home two days," he said. He was silent for a moment, as if reconsidering. "Fine. I'll be there at four, but we meet at your place. How'd they contact you?"

She told him about the phone that had been left in her home, as well as the pictures of Dillon and the ransom letter.

"Text me directions to your house. See you at four o'clock."

Otto looked intently at her over the top of his reading glasses. "Well?" he said.

"He's meeting me at my house at four. He's not agreed to take on the case. He knows I don't have any money. But he's at least agreed to talk with me tonight."

"And how do you plan on breaking this to our FBI partners?"

"I don't. I would like to keep this confidential. Just for now, until I can talk with him."

The door to the office suddenly swung open and Marta walked in, wearing blue jeans and a white polo shirt. It was only nine in the morning and her shift didn't start until noon.

She pulled out a chair and sat down next to Josie at the conference table. "Just wanted to check in. Anything new?"

Josie had called Marta after the FBI agents had left the night before and filled her in on the situation.

She looked over at Marta. "I haven't briefed Otto yet on the credit card information you found yesterday."

Marta turned toward Otto. "Josie gave me access to Dillon's log-ins and passwords that you used for the Sky Drop account. I found credit card information saved in his files. I checked both his Master-Card and Discover Card. He hasn't made a purchase on either one in over a week."

"If he was kidnapped for money, wouldn't the kidnappers have tapped out the cards?" Otto said.

"They're playing it safe. They don't want any trace back to them," Josie said.

"I also called Wally's attorney using the contact information you took from Hector. No surprise he wouldn't give me anything," Marta continued. "And I called the bank. Wally banks here at Texas Trust. I talked with the bank manager and she wouldn't give me specifics, but there were no red flags. I took that to mean no withdrawals. No need for a subpoena at this point. She also promised to monitor his account daily for us."

"Good," Otto said. "What about Christina's accounts. Anything?"

Josie shook her head. "I talked with her parents again yesterday. They didn't have any information about finances for her. We need to get into her apartment."

"The judge approved the search warrant last night," Otto replied. "That's first on my list today. I'll get her bank files, bring the paperwork back, and we'll dissect it here."

Otto paused a moment, seeming to collect his thoughts. "We have the ransom demand, but we have big issues yet to settle. Until I see compelling evidence, we continue to search all leads. Someone believes Josie has access to millions. At this point, I see three distinct possibilities. Medrano has the most obvious connection to Josie and thus Dillon, but Medrano knows Josie doesn't have access to that kind of money. Beckwith makes sense as a client with access to millions of dollars, but there is a weak connection to Dillon and Josie. Then there's Wally, who disappeared and has a clear connection to Dillon, and thus to Josie. His criminal enterprise is definitely worth examining."

The three officers sat for a moment, thinking through Otto's assessment.

"If we're all in agreement, then Josie, I'd like you to follow up on the indictment," Otto said. "Go back out and put some pressure on Hector. I think he knows more than he's saying, and he's terrified."

Josie nodded. She agreed with Otto, but it was still difficult to suddenly begin taking orders.

He turned to Marta. "I've left the names of three of Dillon's highest-grossing clients. See what you can find, but don't contact them directly yet. Let's talk before you do that. I'll work on Julian Beckwith today. He's the big-money client. I'll also follow up on the Santa Muerte pendant today, too."

Marta nodded.

"That's good. We have a plan," Otto said, folding his hands on the table in front of him, and taking a moment before continuing. "I'd like us to attend the memorial service this afternoon as a group. Brian said he'd fill in dispatch and Lou will come with us. We'll leave here at twelve thirty. I'll drive."

Marta began discussing the dress uniform they would wear, and Josie felt her attention fade. She thought of meeting Christina's family, paying last respects, and her heart swelled with pain.

ELEVEN

By 12:40 P.M., the parking lot by the Showalter Funeral Home was packed, and cars were parallel parked around the neighborhood for blocks. Otto pulled into the lot and took one of the spots reserved for police cars near the back entrance of the building. The three officers and Lou were all wearing their formal dress uniforms and black armbands. It took them forty minutes to make their way through the receiving line to Christina's parents. Several of Christina's close friends stood next to the Handleys to offer support to them. Josie listened as Otto and Marta made small talk with other people in line. Josie remained silent and instead focused on the butterfly print on the jacket of the woman in front of them, not allowing her thoughts to drift from making it through the moment.

Mrs. Handley bore a striking resemblance to her daughter, with the same impeccable style and petite features. Mr. Handley looked the part of the all-American father of a beautiful daughter and lovely wife. In addition to their beauty, the family appeared in every respect to be kind, good people. That had been Dillon's description of Christina. "She's good people."

When Josie reached Mrs. Handley and introduced herself, the woman grasped Josie's hand and patted it, rubbing her palm over Josie's hand.

"I'm praying for you," she said. "I'm praying that you find Dillon, and that he comes back home to you safely." She pursed her lips, tears welling up again in her red eyes. "And I am praying you find the monster that did this to my daughter, and you put him in jail forever."

Josie walked out of the funeral home heavy with the knowledge that this family was relying on her to provide justice for their daughter's death. While the gravity of her job was with her in every case she worked, she had never felt so overwhelmed by the responsibility.

After the memorial service, Josie drove back to the department and changed into her regular duty uniform. Lucy Ramone, owner of the Hot Tamale, was standing in the front office talking with Otto and Marta when Josie came downstairs. Unable to face anyone outside of the department just yet, she left through the back door and walked around the block to enter her car unnoticed.

On the drive to the junkyard, Josie called her friend, and local philanthropist, Macon Drench and arranged to meet with him at his house late that afternoon. It was a conversation she dreaded, but she saw no way around it.

Next, she called the security company to check on the time frame for fixing her system and finally reached the manager. Josie tried to keep her cool as she explained the break-in at her home. The man apologized and described the malfunction as a "crash and smash," as if naming it would excuse the system breakdown. He promised to have someone there in forty-eight hours to reassess and provide their best upgrade. She demanded a faster time frame but he said they were booked with installations that week. He assured her that he would send someone to review the outside of the house and e-mail her an estimate.

She had no idea how much the new system might cost, but a bank loan was worth the peace of mind she hoped to gain. Thoughts of loans and credit card debt ran through her head as she calculated just how much money she might be able to pull together.

It didn't take long before her thoughts snapped back to the ransom. To Dillon. She wondered if he could see the sun. Criminal investigations and true-crime stories involving kidnap victims often described them locked away in closets and boxes, and she tried to block the persistent image of his body lying contorted in a small, airless place, or kneeling before a man with a gun. She imagined him praying that she would come through with the money that would save him from losing his arm. Instead all she could manage was a visit to a junkyard to talk with an eighteen-year-old kid? She had not felt so lost and alone since her father died over twenty years ago. The grief filling her head signified the loss of control, of everything she cared about, and she could do nothing to stop the pain.

As she reached the opening in the junkyard fence, she realized she had virtually no memory of the drive. She turned off the engine and sat with her hands on the steering wheel, staring at the dashboard, struggling to remember why she had driven all the way out there. She couldn't remember what questions she had planned to ask, and had to open her steno book that lay in the passenger seat. But she had to focus. She needed to be a cop now, not a civilian. Dillon needed her to use her skill, not have some damned breakdown. After a few minutes of reading through her notes she took a deep breath. She got out of the car, walked up to the door, and knocked.

Hector Follet pushed open the door and walked down the front steps to meet Josie. She felt a rush of cold air from the dark trailer and could hear music playing from somewhere inside.

"Yes, ma'am? What can I do for you?"

"I'd just like to talk with you a few minutes. I hope you can help me answer some questions I have."

He looked wide-awake and earnest. He looked like a kid who wanted to help, to belong, but with no resources to make that happen, his life stunted by a father who cared more about making a buck than raising his kid.

"Do you want to come inside?" he asked. "I could get you some iced tea."

"That would be great."

Inside, the trailer was tidy, uncluttered, and, surprising to her, decorated and comfortable. John Wayne memorabilia hung on the walls, from signed photographs and movie posters to items that seemed to have been collected from old Western movie sets.

Josie noticed a Lee Marvin poster hanging behind the TV stand and smiled. "I used to watch his movies with my dad."

"Who's your favorite Western actor?"

"Clint Eastwood, no doubt."

"He's good all right, but Alan Ladd was best. You ever see *Shane*? Best movie ever made." He smiled and turned to the refrigerator, pulling out a glass pitcher half-filled with tea. "It's fresh. I brew a pitcher every day."

He washed his hands and dried them on a towel hanging over the handle of the oven door, then removed a tray of ice from the freezer and put three cubes in each glass.

"Sugar?" he asked.

Josie smiled. "No, thanks." There was something about the kid that broke her heart. He had mastered the art of blending in, of appearing insignificant, staying out of trouble. It was a skill lousy parents everywhere taught their kids so that attention was diverted from whatever criminal activity the parent was involved in.

She followed him to the living room, where he sat on the couch and she sat on the love seat opposite him. They discussed movies for a while longer, and he brought out a collection of arrowheads that had supposedly been collected by one of the gunfighters on the set of the John Wayne movie *True Grit*.

Finally Josie said, "I have to know more about your dad, Hec." She was surprised that he didn't appear nervous or resistant this time. He just bobbed his head like a compliant kid.

"I haven't heard from him since he left. His lawyer called once and told me he was in Houston. I don't know if that's true."

"You can't call him?"

"No phone."

"You don't have a phone here?"

Hec pointed to the beige wall phone hanging in the kitchen. "I got a phone, but Dad doesn't. We don't have cell phones. Dad don't like them."

"Nobody else has talked to him?"

He shrugged. "My family's all from Georgia. He'd never go there. My grandma calls and asks about him. Nobody knows anything."

"What do you know about the Medrano cartel?"

He looked startled but said nothing.

"I think that might be who kidnapped Mr. Reese. We suspect they killed his secretary. Christina Handley? They shot her in the heart. I didn't tell you the other day because I didn't want to scare you, but I think you need to know. If your dad was mixed up with the Medranos then you could be in pretty serious danger."

He blinked, then swallowed, but he wasn't giving away anything.

"Just give it some thought. Give me a call if you want to talk about it." She laid her business card on the coffee table between them and decided to change tactics. "Can we take a walk?"

He asked skeptically, "A walk?"

"Sure. I can't sit for long. Let's take a walk around the yard. You can tell me how the business works."

Hec shrugged. "A junkyard's all it is."

Josie stood. "I don't know anything about the business. I'm just curious."

He carried their glasses into the kitchen and rinsed them out under the faucet. She wondered if he was buying time.

They walked outside without talking. He seemed to be contemplating where to take her, so Josie took the lead and headed down the center aisle, toward the back of the lot where she and Otto had been when Hec had called their names the day before.

As they continued down the center aisle, Hec pointed out several cars and described the process of purchasing them from the insurance company.

"You wouldn't believe what they total out these days. Used to be flipping houses was the big thing. Now it's flipping cars."

"What do you mean, totaled out?"

"That means they won't fix the car. The insurance company figures it would cost them more to fix the car than it would to send the guy who wrecked it a check to buy a new car."

"Do they sell them cheap?" she asked.

He laughed. "You wouldn't believe some of them. Practically nothing wrong but some body work, and we get 'em next to nothing."

"So what's your part in this?"

"Dad buys the parts. I got a good eye for body work. I get the wrecks in decent shape, then Dad sells them."

She noticed his pace slowed considerably as they approached the back of the lot. He led her to the right.

Josie pointed to her left and began walking that way. "So a car like this, an old VW station wagon. You would buy this from an insurance company?"

He gave her a doubtful look. "Maybe. I think some guy brought that in and sold it outright." She noticed fresh dirt on the ground behind the car and looked around to see if she saw signs of excavation elsewhere.

"What's up with the dirt?" she asked.

"The dirt?"

"Sure. I see the backhoe parked over there." She pointed to the yellow machine parked in the far corner of the lot.

He stammered, and then was silent for a second. "We move cars around the lot. Take them over to the car crusher. We sell the cars for scrap metal. Make decent money on scrap."

Josie gestured down beyond the edge of the row to the bank that sloped into the Rio Grande. Trees bordered the river on either side, but a twenty- to thirty-foot opening had been cut through both sides of the bank, leading directly into the water. "Looks like some fresh tracks headed toward the river."

"One of the cops who came looking for my dad tried to say we were shipping cars across the river illegally."

"How would you get the cars across the water?" she asked. The river was at least twenty feet wide at this point, and it wasn't the rainy season.

"I know! That's what I said. He tried to say we had a temporary bridge we crossed. Even if we had a bridge, we couldn't get that truck and trailer across it. It was stupid."

Facing the river, Josie looked to the west side of the yard where

Hec had pointed. A large pickup truck and trailer with a hitch sat along the edge of the fence.

"I know it's my dad, but I still don't think their case is very strong," he said.

As they walked around the rest of the lot, Hec kept up a running commentary. When they finally made their way back around to where Josie had parked in front of the office, she bluntly laid it all out.

"Here's the deal. I'm worried that there's more to your dad's indictment than a couple of stolen cars getting shipped across the border. I'm worried that your problems may be linked to a kidnapping and a murder. I want you to think all this over. I know the police department is the last place you want to go for help, but I think you need us. You can't fix this by yourself."

Hec watched the cop pull out of the yard and turned back to the trailer. Before entering he scanned the yard, searching for movement. Once inside, he walked to the back of the trailer and touched the door that led to his dad's bedroom, then turned and took the familiar twelve steps back to the front. He counted as he took each step, tapping the window at the front of the trailer before turning back again, twelve more steps. He had worn a path into the carpet but he no longer cared. He balled his fists in fury every time he thought of his dad. Hec imagined him entering the trailer, taking one look at Hec, and asking what the hell was wrong with him, pacing like a caged animal. Hec stood motionless in the middle of the kitchen. The room tilted like he'd been spinning around and around and had suddenly stopped.

The anger he felt toward his dad at that moment made him want to sit on the floor and cry like a baby. He missed him. His dad was his best friend, the funniest person he'd ever met, the one who took care of him after his mom left them ten years before. His dad never complained about a single thing he had to do for Hec. He took him to the doctor, bought his school clothes, got him up for school every day. He knew parents who treated their kids like crap.

Hec knew what some people thought about his dad, but it wasn't true. He just liked to deal, beat the system. That was his thing. But when he started messing with the cartel, he pushed it too far. And when Hec refused to leave with him, his dad had fought and yelled and even cried one night when he got lit on whiskey. Hec had told him that he didn't want to live his life like a lie. So his dad finally left. No phone. No plan. No word on where he was going. Hec figured Canada, but that was just a guess.

He walked to the window that faced the back side of the property that ended in the river. Hec knew that men were watching him. They didn't try to hide. When other people showed up, like the cops, the men took off, but as soon as the cops left, they came right back. Watching and waiting.

They'd already taken him once. Kidney punches and kicks to his gut so no one could tell he'd been beaten. He ran his tongue along the dried crack in his lip where he'd been punched for not answering a question.

Hec was a quiet kid and stayed out of trouble. He'd never been in a fistfight, not once all the way through high school. He didn't even know how to duck when the men came at him, kicking their cowboy boots into his stomach until he thought he was going to die, right there in the dirt, down by the river. Finally, one of the men yelled and the others stopped. Two guys picked Hec up by his armpits and dragged him to a rowboat. They threw him in it and rowed across to Mexico. They held him at some house for a week, locked inside an empty bedroom. They asked him questions day and night, but Hec had nothing to say. He told the men the truth: his dad had told him nothing.

One of the men who spoke English finally pulled him off the floor and sat him in a chair. "We're sending you home. You don't leave the junkyard until your dad comes home. Your dad's the only person who can set you free. We watch you day and night. You try to leave?" The man made a face and shrugged like it was no big deal. "We kill you." He hadn't left since.

Christina Handley's apartment was located in Debby Williams's renovated garage. Debby was the local middle school principal and caretaker for all who needed a break. She typically boarded teachers who were new to the area, with no family or friends to stay with while they found their own place. Debby had known that to entice a young person to accept a job located just outside two ghost towns in far West Texas, there had to be some extra incentive—support. In an effort to convince talented new teachers that Artemis was a worthy place to call home, Debby and her husband had renovated their detached garage, turning it into a one-bedroom efficiency apartment designed to accommodate a young person until he or she found permanent housing.

Otto pulled into the driveway of Debby's two-story home, just a half block from Dillon's home, and shut the jeep off. The house was made of chunky tan stone and had a red barrel-tile roof and brown shutters that surrounded long narrow windows. Otto wasn't an expert on home styles, but the house reminded him of what one might see in the French countryside. It was a tasteful home that he and Delores had always admired.

Debby walked outside to greet him. They shook hands and then hugged. Debby was almost a foot shorter than Otto. She wore her hair short and carried herself as a professional, compassionate, and caring, but always in control.

"This is awful, Otto. I never would have imagined this could happen here."

"It's a scary time. When life means no more to these mercenaries than this." He glanced back behind the Williams's home to the garage apartment. "Twenty-four years old. Hadn't even had time to make her mark on the world yet."

"No time to be loved," she said. She looked away, overcome with grief.

After a moment, Otto said, "I talked with her parents today at the memorial service. They want to go through her things. I explained that I need to check the apartment this afternoon. I may be able to allow them in tomorrow. They plan on flying her body home the day after tomorrow."

"What do you need with the apartment?"

"I need to examine her records, her financial statements and so on. I have a search warrant."

She gave him a startled look. "A search warrant?"

"It's standard procedure. We can't go barging into a deceased person's home until a judge makes it legal."

"Murders and search warrants. Kidnappings? This isn't supposed to happen here," she said.

Otto unfolded the search warrant and tried to hand it to her, but she merely glanced at it and waved it off.

"Any more information on Dillon?"

"I'm afraid not," he said.

"I don't know how Josie is holding herself together right now."

"She's running on adrenaline, but that only lasts for so long."

"You know if there is anything John or I can do . . ." She dabbed at the corners of her eyes with her fingertip, trying to hold back tears.

"I appreciate that."

Debby nodded and pointed toward the garage. "I have the keys in my pocket. Come on back, and I'll let you in."

A stone pathway meandered around the side of the house and led to a courtyard covered with a large pergola shielding the paved patio against the intense Texas sun. Several tables and chairs were arranged around the patio. It was a comfortable space designed for a couple who enjoyed entertaining.

The stone path continued from the patio to the back of the small yard, where the garage was located. Two large carriage-style doors were positioned on the east side of the building, while the door to the apartment was on the south end and was flanked by two small windows. Debby used her key to open the door and then turned away, tears welling up in her eyes. She sniffed and pulled a tissue from her pocket.

"There's no need for you to stay."

"Did you know her?" she asked.

"I knew her through Josie and Dillon."

"She was a sweetheart, Otto. A genuinely nice person." She began crying openly and turned from him, toward the house.

"I'll let you know when I've gotten what I need."

She nodded and walked away.

———————

Otto entered the apartment wearing gloves as a precaution, even though two state troopers had fingerprinted the apartment the day Christina was found murdered. He found a light switch just inside the door and flipped it on. The apartment was the size of a typical two-car garage, approximately twenty-five by twenty-five feet. It was an open floor plan with the living room located to the right of the entrance door, and the connected efficiency kitchen and dining room off to the left. A door located where the kitchen and dining room areas met was open and led to what looked to be a messy bedroom.

The living room consisted of a couch upholstered in a small floral print and a matching chair—typical starter furniture, nothing fancy. The apartment seemed neat and well ordered until he stepped into the bedroom. The closet doors were open, revealing a bar that looked as if it might break under the considerable weight of the clothes hanging from it. More clothes were folded and piled high on the shelf above the bar, and boxes of shoes filled the bottom of the closet. Clothes covered a small chair in the corner of the room and the top of the dresser. Jackets hung off the corners of the mirror attached to the back of the dresser.

After thirty years in law enforcement he was good at being detached, but the sight of the clothes, the awareness of her love of fashion, the memory of her blood-soaked skirt almost made him weep. He took a deep breath and quickly searched the drawers, the piles of clothing, and the bedside table for any notes or paperwork that might have information about the final days of her life.

Inside the small bathroom off her bedroom he found a collection of makeup and beauty supplies. The drawers and cabinets were packed with bottles and tubes and spray cans. He found a prescription bottle half filled with antibiotics from two years ago, but he found no birth control or other paraphernalia that might suggest she was in a relationship of any kind.

The dining room contained a table large enough for four, and an old wooden teacher's desk located in the corner behind the table. The desk appeared about as unorganized as her clothes closet, with piles of opened bills and paperwork crowding it. Otto found three months' worth of bills lying on the table but with their actual notices removed and the return envelopes gone. It looked as if she had written out the bills but hadn't filed away the paperwork. He also discovered two credit card statements with charges from Macy's, J. Crew, Anthropologie, and several other stores. All appeared to be online purchases. Seeing no desktop computer, he looked around and noticed a laptop lying on the couch across the room.

There was one phone in the apartment, a landline with no answering machine attached to it, located on the corner of the desk. Hoping the phone had been activated with the two credit card accounts, he dialed both companies and, after providing the account number on the statements, was given the current balance and recent transactions for both cards. No purchases had been made on either card since two days before her death. As had been the case with Dillon, her credit cards didn't appear to have been compromised. He was surprised that neither Christina nor Dillon's personal finances had been tampered with since the kidnapping. It had become fairly obvious to him that they weren't dealing with petty thieves.

Otto had already been monitoring the messages left on her cell phone. He had discovered it inside her purse, which had been kept inside a coat closet at the office. The only messages she had received over the past few days were from a phone number in St. Louis that he had tracked down to be Christina's mother. The first two calls from her mother were confusing to Otto, as at that point she had known full well what had happened to her daughter. Earlier that morning Mrs. Handley had called again, just before her daughter's memorial service. He had listened to the voice mail and heard the woman sobbing on the other end. Using the number listed on her phone bill, Otto called Christina's number from his own phone and heard her pleasant voice stating that she couldn't be reached, but would call back as soon as she could. "Have a great day!" she said.

After finishing at Christina's apartment, Otto drove to Artemis, intent on getting Josie to take a thirty-minute break from the case and sit down with him to eat lunch. He reached Josie on her cell phone as she was driving back into town after meeting with Hec.

"It's well after lunchtime. Let's meet at the Tamale. My treat," he said, attempting a lighthearted cheer that sounded flat in his ears.

"You go ahead," Josie said. "I'll meet you back at the station."

"I'll wait."

"No, go on. I'm not hungry."

Otto sighed. "The *Big Bend Sentinel* called. I've got a meeting with one of their reporters, along with Dave from Marfa Public Radio this evening to brief them on the investigation. I'm ready to go public that we suspect this is a kidnapping but aren't ready to release details at this time. Agreed?"

"Absolutely." Josie saw no benefit at this point to keeping the local citizens in the dark.

"I was going to fill you in on the FBI update at lunch too. Agent Haskins checked in. Asked if you'd had any additional contact."

"Did he have any new information?" she asked.

"We're dealing with a highly organized, well-established group. Most likely a cartel."

"Are you kidding?"

"Josie. He's as frustrated as we are."

"Doubtful."

He sighed heavily now, aggravated by her. "You have to eat."

"Not at the Tamale. I can't take the gossip," she said. "I have a stop I need to make. I'll try and make it back into the office before I go home. My meeting with the negotiator is at four and it's already after one."

Otto neglected to tell her that the two agents had stopped by the office to question him about Josie's possible role in Dillon's disappearance and Christina's death. It had been a difficult conversation. They had grilled Otto on Josie's relationship with Dillon and Christina, her alibi, her reputation as chief, her ability to respond objectively throughout the kidnapping negotiation, her relationship with various members of the community, and so on. Otto presented the facts openly and honestly. They cleared her as a suspect, but the conversation was mentally exhausting. It saddened him, the idea that his friend who valued integrity and loyalty to the point of putting her own life in harm's way could be considered, even for a moment, a murderer.

TWELVE

True individualists like Macon Drench were hard to come by. In 1976, after he and his wife had made their fortune in the oil business in Houston, Drench had purchased Artemis, then a ghost town, and sunk twenty million into its infrastructure. Artemis had once been an army settlement built to protect a now defunct weapons factory on the outskirts of the county. Two thousand factory workers were carted in each day by train, so when the cold war ended and the plant shut down, the town basically shut down as well, until Macon revived it. Josie had always imagined the building process must have felt a little like playing Monopoly on a grand scale.

Josie considered herself fortunate to have gotten to know Macon over the past few years. When his old childhood friend Red Goff was killed, Josie had interviewed Macon on several occasions and had since been to his house for a few social functions. He and his wife now spent their money on charitable projects. There was no doubt Drench had money, but everyone with a problem knew it. Josie never imagined she would be the one knocking on his door, but she had no other options. He was the only friend she knew with enough money to play hardball with the cartel. The visit shamed her, but she had no other choice.

Josie's aversion to asking for help was rooted in her childhood experiences. Before her father died, they had lived in the suburbs on a block with fifty other nearly identical ranch homes. At impromptu block parties on the weekends, the men grilled, the women mixed cocktails and side dishes, and the kids played outside until the party broke up around midnight. It had been an ideal childhood, Josie's mom would say a perfect marriage, up until the day her father died.

Within six months of her father's death, her mother had sold the house and moved into an apartment. Her mother never explained the finances, and Josie had never asked about them. She was certain there had been insurance money: her mom had never worked. Josie often wondered if she had sold the house to keep from having to work. It wasn't long after the move that other men entered their lives, usually short term, some to solve a financial need or fix whatever problem she encountered: a leaky faucet, a clogged drain, a piece of furniture that needed moving. Josie had watched her mother "turn on the charm" to get what she needed, what she wanted. As a child, without the maturity to understand her mother's motives, she had seen it as pure manipulation. Josie remembered telling her girlfriends in high school, *I will never ask a man to solve my problems. I don't care what happens. I will take care of myself.* It was a core value she had shaped her life around. Now, as she pulled down the lane to Drench's ranch, she felt as if she were selling her soul.

———◆———

The Drench ranch was located north of town, beyond the mud flats, a dried-up lake bed that filled with rain during the fall monsoon season for a short time, then drained into a muddy pit that eventually drew four-wheeled vehicles into an annual unregulated teenage party in the mud that inevitably led to police calls and a few trips to the emergency room. Beyond the flats was the Chinati Mountain range. Drench's place nestled into a stretch of the range that he had named Big Rig after the oil platform that raked in his millions. The home was made of three glass-and-steel boxes stacked atop each other at odd angles and tucked into the jagged coffee-colored edges of the mountain. As monstrous as the home was, it somehow naturally blended in with its surroundings.

Josie pulled into a small paved parking area surrounded by pine trees. Pine needles and cones littered the pavement, and the pungent smell of sap that usually intoxicated her was now suppressed by her dread. She glanced at her watch. It was 2:00 P.M. She wanted to be home by 3:30 to prepare for Nick Santos.

———————

Macon stepped out onto the flagstone patio in front of the house with a coffee cup and waved. He stood beside a rectangular reflecting pool surrounded by black granite that reflected the afternoon sunlight. Half-ton boulders around the patio looked as if they had fallen naturally down the mountain during a rockslide. The temperature was balmy, a novelty in the desert, and a light breeze rustled through the pine trees, sounding like a whisk broom on pavement. A thin strip of cirrus clouds streaked an otherwise perfect blue sky.

"How do, Chief?" He held out his hand to shake Josie's. He was an imposing man, over six feet tall, and his cowboy boots and cowboy hat gave him an extra foot. His angular body and deeply lined face matched the rough exterior of the mountains behind him.

"Such a pretty day, thought we'd sit outside and chat, if that's okay with you?"

They sat on rattan chairs by the reflecting pool. A carafe of coffee and a tray of flavorings and creams were already laid out. Macon took a cup from the tray. "Black, right?"

"Yes, thank you."

"So, what's the word on the kidnapping? Any news on Dillon?" he said as he filled her cup.

Josie appreciated him bypassing the small talk. "That's actually why I asked to meet with you today."

"I suspected as much."

"We've confirmed it is a kidnapping. The kidnappers broke into my home yesterday. They left a phone with pictures of Dillon, wearing a pillowcase over his head and holding a ransom note asking for nine million dollars. They want fifty thousand by five o'clock this evening or Dillon will lose an arm."

"Son of a bitch." He stared at Josie, his dark eyes unblinking and his expression grim. He finally scooted his chair back from the table and crossed one ankle over his other leg as if preparing to make a business deal. "Okay, one piece at a time. First. You say they broke into your home? What have you done about increased security for yourself?"

"I called One Life, out of Odessa. They said they'll try and get something installed in the next two days."

"Not good enough. You let me take care of that." He pointed over his shoulder. "The best security system you can buy, installed right here." He picked his cell phone up off the table and searched for something. Eventually he placed the phone to his ear and spoke with a man named Chet. Macon briefly explained the murder and kidnapping, and Josie's relationship to the victims. He then handed Josie the phone and she spoke with Chet for several minutes about the layout of her home and the acreage around her house. He took her address and promised to have someone at her home before seven o'clock that night.

Once the call was over, and before she had a chance to thank him, Macon moved on.

"Next, tell me who's working the case."

She explained the progress they had made locally, the recent call to the FBI, and her meeting at four with Nick Santos.

Macon narrowed his eyes at Josie and rubbed at the stubble on his chin. "Do you have any idea how much a professional negotiator costs?"

"I'm not going to worry about it. I'll take out a loan from the bank. I can mortgage the house. I have some options."

"You're probably looking at four to five thousand per day, plus living expenses."

Josie looked at him in shock. She knew the cost would be high, but never dreamt that much. Kidnappings could last for months, occasionally even years. Even with the house mortgaged she could never afford that kind of money, not even for a month.

"What was his name again?" Macon asked.

"Nick Santos. He lives in Mexico but wouldn't say which city. He seemed familiar with this area. He has a good name with law enforcement in both Mexico and the U.S."

Macon didn't respond and instead tapped at his cell phone again. He then held it up to his ear and walked into the house. For close to ten minutes he was gone. Josie felt some of the tension release from her shoulders. The security system was a huge relief for her, but she had yet to approach him about the real reason for her visit.

Macon walked outside with an attractive young woman wearing dark jeans and a black button-down Western-style shirt with pearl snap buttons. She set a plate of cookies and cheese and crackers on the table.

"Josie, this is Sherry Sail, our assistant."

Josie stood and shook her hand. "It's good to meet you."

"Nice to meet you as well," she said. "Can I get you anything other than coffee? That's all Macon ever drinks. He thinks the rest of the world is as obsessed with it as he is." The girl put her hands on her hips and smiled at Josie as she squinted into the sunlight.

"No, I'm fine, thanks. The coffee is great."

"You must simply accept that I know what I'm talking about," he told the girl, his tone friendly.

She rolled her eyes and walked away, ignoring his comment. "Just yell if you need anything."

Macon smiled and watched her walk away for a moment before turning back to Josie. "You've done your homework. I talked with an associate who said Santos is one of the top negotiators in Mexico. I'm surprised you were able to connect with him. I'll come with you and we can negotiate the price. We'll contract for one month and reevaluate."

Josie frowned. How could she tell him no when he was offering to front the cost?

"He said I had to meet with him alone. I'm sorry, I don't know why."

He put a hand up to stop her. "Give him my name. Explain the situation. Tell him to call me." He reached into his billfold and handed Josie a business card to give Santos. "Did he give you any insight about the ransom? Who might be involved?"

"I'm certain it's the Medranos. I'd bet my career on it. All Santos said was that I had to have money somewhere for them to set the ransom so high."

The expression on Macon's face darkened and he gestured back toward the house. "Gladys watches cop shows. Obsessively, if you ask me. She's talked about kidnappings nonstop since we heard the news about Dillon. She's afraid they'll find out we've got money and ransom me off too."

"Kidnappings are still rare, even along the border, but there's always the risk. Obviously it can happen." Josie wasn't sure how to proceed. Had he just cut her off before she could mention meeting the ransom demand? She sipped her coffee, trying to think of how she could ask for his help, knowing that his wife already feared the cartels would target their family.

He pursed his lips and studied her for a moment, giving away nothing in his expression. Josie felt as if she were sitting in front of a chessboard, staring at the pieces, with no understanding of the rules or the strategy involved, but aware that it was her turn to move.

"I'm just out of my league, Macon," she continued. "They're asking for money from me that I have no way of getting. And they've tied Dillon's life to my response. So I came here to discuss things with you. To talk about the ransom." Josie stopped. She could feel her face redden as she stumbled over her words with embarrassment.

He finally said, "You're here to ask for my help. With the ransom demand."

She cleared her throat, and forced herself to not look away from him in shame. "I'm sorry to do this to you. To bring you into this evil mess, but I don't know where else to go."

"No apologies. If someone took Gladys I'd move heaven and earth until I got her back. I suspect you'd do the same for Dillon."

She nodded, no longer able to speak.

"Let's talk about a few things first. Assuming I help, we do things a certain way. First, no one knows I'm involved except you and Nick. I need your guarantee on that or I can't help you. I won't tell Gladys. If she thought I was involved with a cartel negotiation she'd have bodyguards on us by supper." He paused and considered his words. "That's just a worry she doesn't need."

"I understand." She nodded again, noting the acid burn starting in her stomach.

"Second, you make sure money is the best route. Nick will coach you there, but I'm not so sure it is."

She was relieved to finally be laying it out on the table, and thankful that Macon had broached the subject that was tearing her up. "The fifty thousand dollars," she said, "I'm making myself crazy. If I pay it they'll want more. They could even keep Dillon longer if they think more money is available. But if I don't pay it, and Dillon loses his arm, or his life?"

"What did Nick say?"

"He said no, not on the first request. He said the request would double if I paid that quick."

"Makes sense."

"But what if they shoot Dillon? If they take his arm and want more?" Her throat constricted and she couldn't go on. Macon had not offered the money. She couldn't make herself bring up the fifty thousand again, but she wanted it. She wanted to put it in a suitcase and deliver it herself, anything to buy Dillon at least a day of safety and her some more time.

"Talk to the negotiator. You and I sitting here trying to plan a response is pointless. Neither one of us knows the first thing about ransom negotiation. That's why he gets paid the big bucks."

"But what if he's wrong? In the end, it's my decision. And what if I choose wrong?"

"Santos will help you make a calculated decision based on past practice. If you need money, and it's the right thing to do for Dillon, you can have it. I'll write the check today. But I want to know it's not out of desperation."

At two o'clock Otto walked down the block from the office to the Hot Tamale for a bologna sandwich and a bag of chips. The front door of the diner opened up into a seating area with about fifteen tables and a slew of chairs that were in constant flux. Customers came in and moved tables and chairs to fit whatever setup they needed. Otto took his customary table next to the window facing the courthouse at the front of the diner, but then sat with his back to the room and shoved the chair opposite him over to another empty table, making what he thought to be quite a clear signal that he wasn't interested in conversation. However, the owner, Lucy Ramone, wasn't always keen on social cues. She was a short woman in her late forties with long black hair and a bossy personality. She special-ordered Polish kraut and quality bologna for Otto in exchange for what she called "preferential treatment," which to her meant getting the gossip before everyone else. Lucy knew as well as Otto that she never received such treatment, but Otto allowed the farce to go on, if only for the grilled bologna and kraut.

Lucy now placed his meal before him and without another word dragged a chair over to Otto's table. She hurried away and came back a minute later with a soft drink for herself, dropping into the chair with a huff. "What a day. Hurry, hurry all morning long, then lunch slammed us." Otto took a few big bites, hoping to ease his hunger before Lucy demanded conversation.

"You know we love you, Otto. But you police need to do a better job informing the citizens. We're not New York City. We don't have news conferences and briefings about big cases. Any progress on Christina's murder? And what's happened to Dillon? Any word from him? We heard it's a kidnapping, but who knows what's rumor and what isn't?"

Otto placed his sandwich on his plate and wiped his mouth. As he laid his napkin back in his lap he noticed the place had grown quiet. He looked to the back of the diner and saw three customers and two waitresses staring at him, apparently waiting for a response.

He sighed, glared at Lucy, who smiled in return, and rose from his chair to face the room.

"I apologize. I'm making a statement tonight to the paper and radio. I'll tell you what I can, now."

The two waitresses walked closer to hear him better.

"We believe Dillon Reese was kidnapped. Chief Gray received a ransom demand of nine million dollars. At this point, we're assuming Christina's death was linked to the kidnapping but that has not been confirmed. We're working with the FBI and trying to establish the location of the kidnappers. At this point all we have is speculation."

"Was it a cartel kidnapping?" Lucy asked.

Otto turned to face her. Lucy's forehead was creased with worry lines and her hands were clasped in front of her on the table. He realized how incredibly on edge the community must have been. "I'm sorry, Lucy, we can't confirm that yet."

One of the waitresses took a step forward and then stopped. "Why Christina and Dillon? That's what no one can figure out. Two of the nicest people you could ever meet. And it's not like they were rich. Who could possibly want to hurt them?"

After lunch Otto paid his bill and walked down the street to the Curiosity Shop, an odds and ends store that sold flea-market finds from estate sales and cheap items imported from Mexico. A maze of bookshelves and tables, the store was packed from floor to ceiling, most items covered in a layer of dust.

"Enter at your own peril!"

Otto smiled at the voice, which, separated from him by a thousand knickknacks, sounded far away. Owner Simon George lived at the rear of the store. He had once invited Otto back there to see his pet ferret, curled up in the middle of his twin bed. That was several years ago. Now the ferret had free rein in the store and could often be seen curled up on a pillow in the front window, soaking up the afternoon sunshine.

Otto wound his way around two bookshelves and found Simon at the back, wiping his hands on a dish towel as he emerged from behind the curtain that separated his home from his business. The shopkeeper wore a flannel shirt and baggy blue jeans held aloft with suspenders. Bald on top with a fringe that had grown down to his shoulders, he looked like an old hippie farmer. He smiled and bowed.

"Come in, come in. Watch for Brownie. He's underfoot. Just about gave a woman a heart attack yesterday. Some out-of-towner who'd never seen or heard of a ferret. Screamed like a banshee, stomped her feet. Tried to crush him like a spider! Brownie scampered up on top of the bookshelf, his nose pointed down at the old woman, hissing. She's holding her head screaming about a rat in her hair." Simon laughed. "Damndest thing you ever saw. Poor old Brownie's still traumatized."

Otto laughed and joined Simon around a table full of used paperback books for sale. "Never heard of a ferret, huh?"

Simon shook his head, still smiling.

Otto pulled a small clear plastic bag from his uniform shirt pocket. "I'd like you to take a look at something. And please don't mention this to anyone. It's evidence in the Christina Handley murder."

"Not a word. What can I do for you?"

"I wonder what you know about this."

Simon pulled a pair of reading glasses from his shirt pocket and slipped them on. He looked closely at the pendant in the bag, turning it over several times and murmuring to himself. "Santa Muerte. Saint of Death. She's a miracle worker, some believe, who saves sinners. A narco saint."

"Connected to the cartels?"

"She's widespread now. There's Santa Muerte followers in the U.S. too. Even here in Artemis. She can save you from death, or bring death to your enemies." Simon raised a shoulder in consideration. "You think about it, she's a pretty convenient saint."

"This Santa Muerte, is it a separate religion from the Catholics?" Otto asked.

"No, her followers still consider themselves Catholics, but the

Catholic Church doesn't recognize the saint, and condemns the cult around it." Simon stood and came back with a magnifying glass. He studied the pendant in his hand for a minute and then looked up at Otto. "You understand where they're coming from. People believe praying to the saint will keep them safe. Protect them from the cartels, from the government, the police. Whatever violence they have to live with every day."

"So, if she's a saint like any other, why would the Catholic Church not recognize her?"

He smiled. "Because the Catholic Church never canonized Santa Muerte. She's a cigarette-smoking Mexican folk saint worshiped by the cartels to keep them safe. Her appeal has spread beyond the cartels, but she's still basically the go-to saint for criminals. The Pope certainly would never endorse her glorification of violence."

Otto gestured back to the pendant. "So you recognize it? Looks to be a nice piece."

"I do." He turned the baggie over and pointed to the back of the pendant. "The initials CC on the back refer to an artist living in Presidio named Celeste Chesnick. Rumor is she works for the cartels." He handed it back to Otto.

"You mentioned local followers?" Otto said, slipping the baggie back into his shirt pocket.

Simon nodded. "People come in here occasionally and buy cheap Santa Muerte trinkets. I sell them, just nothing from CC." He led Otto through the store to where the cash register stood on a glass case by the front door. Simon opened a sliding door beneath the case and pulled out a tray of what appeared to be charms and small dolls, all bearing the smiling skull.

"Usually it's kids who buy them. They like the skull." After Otto examined several of the trinkets, Simon slid the case back under the counter and locked the door. "You know the Conroys out by the mud flats? Live out by Sauly Magson?"

Otto nodded.

"If you want more information go talk to them. They're followers."

"How do you know?"

Simon smirked and shook his head in disgust. "I used to go to church with them at St. Anne's. The whole family came. You ever see the old Ma and Pa Kettle movies from back in the fifties?"

Otto laughed. "You're even older than I thought! I know Ma Kettle. Had a herd of goats and a passel of kids."

"Well, that's who Bea Conroy reminds me of. Except her kids aren't just ornery. They're downright mean."

THIRTEEN

Josie called Otto on her way home to tell him she didn't have time to go back into the office before her meeting with Nick Santos. She could tell he was frustrated with her, probably more worried than anything, but her sole focus was currently the negotiator. Everything depended on this stranger.

As she drove down Schenck Road toward her house she began scanning the desert, stretching beyond both sides of the road, looking for anything that appeared out of place. She had called Dell twice earlier in the day and he'd assured her the dog was fine, and that no one was prowling around outside.

She pulled down the lane toward Dell's house and Chester loped out of the barn to greet her. Dell followed, wiping his hands on a grease rag. Josie tried again to convince him that he needed a security system, but he assured her that he didn't want any part of whatever she was having installed. He wasn't turning over his safety to a computer and some woman sitting in India taking response calls. Thanks, but no.

Josie and Chester walked the perimeter of her house and then checked each room inside before she set him up with a bone and then changed into jeans and an Artemis PD T-shirt. She paced the house and tried to find something to occupy her time until Santos showed up. She washed the countertop in the kitchen and realized she hadn't cooked a meal there since Dillon left. It was those odd moments of recognition that made her feel like her heart was being ripped out.

She checked her watch again. 3:55 P.M. She checked the cell phone the kidnappers had left for the hundredth time that day. Nothing.

The doorbell rang and Chester rushed to the sidelight, the hair on his back raised. The dog was aware things weren't right. Josie looked out the same window to find a middle-aged man with shoulders like a linebacker walking up to her door. He had the aggravated grimace of a commuter about to miss the next train home.

She opened the door and they shook hands. His hands were dry but his handshake gentle, as if he was purposely holding back.

"This like cop purgatory?" he asked, looking back out through the front door.

She laughed in spite of herself. "No. I live here by choice."

"How do you buy groceries? Go to the movies?" He gave her a serious look but she could tell he had a sense of humor.

She led him to the kitchen. "I have coffee or water. Or I can make some iced tea."

He walked to her refrigerator and put his hand on the handle. "May I?" He glanced back at her for her response.

She nodded, surprised.

He opened the door and mumbled something about a grocery run. "Water's fine."

Josie filled two glasses with ice and tap water, and they both took seats at the kitchen table.

"Okay. Give me everything you know. Start with the first moment you knew something wasn't right."

Josie gave him the details, from the missed date cutting wood at Dell's, to the odd text message, to the following morning when she found Christina murdered at the office. As she talked his expression changed from indifferent to fascinated. She found his excitement disconcerting, but encouraging: she hoped it meant he would take on the case.

When she finished he said, "Who'd you piss off in Mexico?"

She took a sip of water, wondering how much detail she should provide.

"It was almost two years ago, the Medrano and La Bestia cartels were fighting over routes through the territory."

"You're talking about the land on either side of the border?"

She nodded. "Around here, the territory represents about three hundred miles on either side of the border."

"Okay."

"There was a fight in a nightclub one night that turned deadly. Hector Medrano was shot, and they determined it was too risky to take him to a hospital in Mexico," she said.

"So they took him to the U.S." He finished the story for her, an incredulous grin on his face. "You're the lady cop that killed the Bishop's father. I can't believe it took me so long to make the connection."

"I didn't kill him. He was killed by a rival cartel member, but it took place on my watch, in my hospital."

"And now they want revenge?" he asked.

She shrugged. "I've had threats on my life since then, but it's been bravado. Friends in Mexico, other cops have told me that the Medranos have issued a death threat against me, but so far it's just been talk. Killing cops in the U.S. isn't something the cartels have taken on. Yet."

He narrowed his eyes and gave her a skeptical look. "It doesn't feel right. If they wanted revenge, you'd be dead. They'd kidnap and torture you, not someone associated with you. Even if he is your lover."

"But why Dillon?" She held up the cell phone. "This is what was left in my pantry. They broke into my house yesterday while I was at work and left it hanging on the hook where I hang my gun belt each night after work."

He rolled his neck and shook his shoulders several times as if trying to loosen up, but said nothing.

She passed him copies of the pictures that were sent on the cell phone. She had printed the photographs for the FBI agents and had made copies for herself.

He read the ransom demand in the second photo several times. "Strictly money," he muttered to himself.

"What about Dillon's secretary? Why kill her?" Josie asked earnestly. "We're fairly certain Dillon was abducted while supposedly meeting with a new client in a deserted neighborhood. It was a setup. And Christina wasn't killed until several hours later."

"The killing was a warning. They couldn't have sent you a clearer message. They are not screwing around. They used to do it with dogs, or horses, or by torturing someone. But it's all the same to them, and a life is more effective." He looked at his watch, and Josie glanced at the clock on her stove. 4:39 P.M. "You need to prepare yourself. Most likely, they'll injure Dillon on camera and send it to you. They will hurt him so you can watch him scream. The goal is to scare the shit out of you so you do what they want."

Josie got up and walked to the kitchen sink. She stared out the window above it; the anger she felt was so strong her vision was blurring. This was not what she'd expected to hear. She wanted a plan of action, something she could finally do that would make a difference.

Nick remained at the table, his tone still firm. "They can't afford to injure him severely. He's worth too much money. They don't have the medical staff to deal with infection and it's not worth their time. I can almost guarantee it won't be a gunshot. There's too much risk, too great a chance the bullet will miss the mark. You'll probably see a knife. A surface wound. A lot of blood."

Josie rested her hands and her head on the edge of the sink for a minute to think. How the hell was she supposed to deal with this?

"You need to prepare for the phone call. They can't know I'm involved. Again, that would tell them you have money. Come sit down."

She closed her eyes for a moment and tried to shut down her anger. It was like a fever raging through her. She returned to the table, silent.

Nick leaned forward. His eyes were black with dark circles beneath them. He looked directly at her, forcing her to return his stare. "I've negotiated over a hundred cases. I get your anger, and I already know all the other shitty emotions you're about to move through. I can write it all down on a piece of paper. Shrinks have all this shit written in books about what victims can expect. It doesn't make any difference. You just have to get your head around the fact that your life will be hell until this is resolved. Anger is okay. It's a hell of a lot better than guilt and tears, which get you nowhere. But you can't let the anger take over."

Josie stared at him, allowing his message to sink in. She finally nodded.

"All right then. Let's get busy."

———

As Josie was talking with Nick Santos, Otto was skimming through Dillon Reese's Sky Drop account, searching for any files involving Julian Beckwith and Wally Follet, two potential links to Dillon's kidnapping who couldn't be more different. Even though they suspected the Medrano cartel was behind Dillon's kidnapping, the Medranos had not been specifically identified and the motive for the kidnapping was still unclear. While Agents Omstead and Haskins were focusing on the cartel angle, Otto firmly believed the PD needed to continue pursuing other leads. After thirty years of police work, he'd seen too many investigations derail after an officer let a hunch overrun the facts. It was a danger Otto would not allow.

While examining Dillon's e-mail and work records, Otto had checked the dates on each file to learn which had last been modified. He discovered that Julian Beckwith's account was the last one Dillon had worked on the day he was kidnapped. Dillon had sent four e-mails to Blake Smith, an employee at a Redford, Texas, oil company named Black Gold Drilling, over the two-day period before his disappearance. From what Otto could tell, the company was going under and Beckwith was attempting to buy it out. Dillon appeared to be the middleman, e-mailing Blake for tax information, although his involvement beyond that wasn't clear.

Otto also found notes that Dillon had typed in response to his first meeting with Beckwith over a year ago. *Unbelievably young, wealthy, and arrogant. Must be constantly stroked. Discuss his home—2 million. Youngest millionaire in Houston. Calls himself the most hated millionaire in Houston. Proud of it.* From what Otto could tell, Dillon apparently completed this standard report after every client meeting. He figured that Dillon reviewed the notes before every subsequent meeting in order to appear tuned in to the client's specific needs.

Otto's office phone buzzed. "Agent Haskins is on line one for you," Lou said.

Otto thanked her and picked up line one. "This is Otto. Can I help you?"

"Yes, sir, this is Agent Haskins calling with an update on the Reese kidnapping. Any contact from the kidnappers today?"

"No, sir. Five o'clock is the deadline. She's not heard anything today."

"The cell phone is monitored. We should get a ping off a cell tower to at least confirm the general location of where the message is coming from. If it's the same location as Mr. Reese's iPhone location when that text was sent, it should narrow down even more."

"I didn't realize you'd picked up his phone," Otto said. "What's the location?"

"I'll ask you to keep this within your department."

"Of course."

"We picked up a GPS signal in Piedra Labrada, but since then the signal disappeared. I'm sure they've destroyed the phone at this point."

Otto sighed, discouraged to hear confirmation that Dillon was being held in Mexico. He could only hope that they wouldn't take him farther south of the border region.

———————

Still sitting across from each other at Josie's kitchen table, at 5:30 P.M. they received contact. She picked the phone up and looked up at Nick. He nodded and she opened it to find two messages.

The first text read, *You don't follow directions. See what happens to your friend.*

She then opened the second text, which said, *Check your e-mail.*

She passed the phone to Nick, who said nothing as he reached out and slid Josie's laptop in front of him. He clicked on the e-mail icon and opened the attached video clip. Josie watched Nick's face, which was calm and expressionless. From across the table she couldn't see the video. Nick had prepared her for several different scenarios, but she hadn't been prepared to hear Dillon's voice.

"Why didn't you send money? They're going to kill me. Don't you love me? I'm wrecked unless you do something." And then came the horrifying scream. Josie gripped the seat of her chair and listened until the clip stopped, her heart pounding in her chest.

Nick looked up at her, reached across the table, and squeezed her hand. "Just what I said. A knife wound. They'll stitch him up, put some antibiotic on it. He'll be fine by tomorrow."

She nodded and gritted her teeth, unable to speak.

"This was strictly for you. To set the parameters, let you know they mean what they say. Got it?"

"Can I?" She hesitantly nodded toward the laptop.

"You don't need to see this. Not yet."

Chester suddenly began barking in the living room.

They both stood and Josie stepped into the pantry to pull her firearm from her gun belt. Nick put a hand up for her to follow him. She bristled at the idea of following someone else's lead through her own home but complied. As they walked into the living room she saw the tail end of a white cargo van parked outside.

She whispered to Nick, "There was a white van that a witness described in the neighborhood where we believe Dillon was abducted. But I also have a security team coming from Stinson Security to set up the house with an alarm system. The company sent me a text to confirm installation and said the installer would be Becka Houser."

Nick approached the door and looked out the sidelight window. "The side of the van says Stinson." He put his left arm out to the side and motioned her back behind him.

Josie bent down and pulled Chester against her to get him to quit barking. The woman approached the door and Nick yelled,

"Place your company ID and your driver's license up against the window so I can see them."

The woman did as instructed. Both IDs read *Rebecka Houser*.

Nick opened the door and Becka walked inside, nodding hello to both of them. She seemed calm, not at all surprised by the request for ID and the barking dog. She was a short, stout woman with a no-nonsense appearance, wearing cargo pants and a navy blue T-shirt with STINSON SECURITIES embroidered across the pocket, beige work boots, and a tool belt that clanked with gear every time she moved.

After introductions were made, and Josie explained the break-in and her fears about vulnerabilities in her home, they all walked around the perimeter of the house, poking around its windows and doors and locks and latches.

"You're actually in a good place, wide open like this. The places we worry most about are tucked into woods with a thousand hiding places for someone to observe you unnoticed. You don't have that here," the woman said. Then she smiled. "I guess you know that, being a police officer."

Josie tilted her head in return. "Everything feels a little off center when you're talking about your own home."

FOURTEEN

Dillon woke to blinding light from above and the voices of men yelling in Spanish, shouting instructions that he couldn't understand. Curled into the corner of his cell where he had staked out to avoid the circling bats, he heard the wooden rope ladder tumble to the dirt floor. He shielded his eyes from the light above, squinting up to watch a man climbing down the rungs, an automatic rifle banging off his leg as he descended.

"*Vámonos, vámonos!*"

Dillon forced his bent legs into an upright position, wincing at the pain in his joints as he stood. He had been out of the cell only once since entering, and that had been what he thought to be earlier that same day, when they had forced him to read from a script that was obviously written for Josie or his parents as they slashed his arm. Dillon had finally stopped asking himself questions. They had still provided no reason for the kidnapping, and no indication of how long he would be held.

The cut came with no warning. He thought at first he had been shot before realizing there had been no sound to indicate a gun had gone off. He had screamed and looked down at the blood dripping down his arm. He assumed his captors had filmed the slashing and that the film was likely being sent to Josie or to his parents. The thought of their fear made him burn with anger. Now, he worried that the stabbing was the first act of violence and that the torture would increase every day. He fought to keep from obsessing over what they would do to him next.

Two meals had been dropped through the hole above since he had been locked away. They'd thrown a sack containing a combination of tortillas and shredded greasy chicken wrapped inside foil, and a pasty glob of rice held in a plastic bag. A small amount of water was also sent down via a used plastic milk jug that was lowered from a rope. Someone would yell, "Untie!" and he had to crawl to the jug and untie the rope, pulling on it to indicate the jug was free. He had quickly drunk every drop and yelled for more, but he heard nothing in return. His thirst had become unbearable; his lips were already cracked and bleeding.

Now, the man pressed the barrel of his rifle to the back of Dillon's neck, forcing him to look at the ground. The guard shoved the pillowcase into Dillon's hands, and he knew to slip it down over his head. He was shoved in the direction of the ladder and put his hands out, feeling in the dark for the rope, afraid his cramped muscles and injured arm wouldn't allow him to make the climb.

Ashamed of his current state, he took the rungs slowly, hunched over, his left arm burning and throbbing from the makeshift stitches. Eventually, reaching the top of the hole, he felt around with one hand at the sand and gravel above him. Two pairs of hands grabbed his upper arms, paying no attention to his injury. He moaned in pain as his feet left the ladder and he was pulled up the final few feet of the hole to solid ground. Through the bottom of the pillowcase, he could tell that it was dark outside. The light he had seen in the hole had come from flashlights. He assumed he had been in captivity somewhere between a few days and a week, but with no light seeping into the hole to signal sunrise and sunset, his sense of time was gone. When he slept, he never knew for how long, and he always woke disoriented, panicked, the sickening new knowledge of his captivity smacking him in the face.

His arms were then pushed into the sleeves of a robe and a belt was cinched around his waist. He heard the rolling track of a van door being opened and then was forced inside, onto what he thought was the same metal floor as before. After what he guessed was about a thirty-minute drive, he was dragged from the van and into a room with concrete floors. Footsteps echoed and voices carried, making him think it was a large room, perhaps a warehouse or commercial garage with an empty open area.

He was stopped and then pushed by the shoulders into a wooden chair. After being told to close his eyes the pillowcase was replaced with a blindfold, presumably so the kidnappers could see his face. Since his captivity his emotions had soared from despair to hope to fury. When the men left the room, he prayed for strength and vowed that his captors would not break him.

After what seemed like hours a door opened and the footsteps of several men echoed off the walls as they approached him. Dillon could feel their eyes on him as they whispered to each other in Spanish.

Finally, a man said, "Dillon Reese, accountant. Ms. Josie Gray's lover. Correct?"

Dillon said nothing and received a powerful blow to the stomach. He gasped for air as the man continued to talk, his English excellent. "I don't play games. When I ask, I expect an answer. If you don't provide what I want you will pay a heavy price.

"So I ask the question again. Are you Josie Gray's lover?"

Dillon nodded once. He could hear voices at a distance talking quietly and the noises of people moving. There was obviously something else going on in the room, but he couldn't distinguish the sounds.

"Nine million dollars. That's your worth to me. She brings me cash in exchange for you."

Dillon's head fell back at the absurdity of it. It was the first time he had heard the ransom amount.

"You don't think your Ms. Gray can handle that?" He laughed with the arrogance of a man accustomed to getting what he wants.

Dillon didn't speak and received another blow to the stomach. He doubled over, wheezing.

"I thought you understood how this worked, Mr. Accountant. Aren't you a money man?"

Dillon struggled to understand the amount of money he had just heard. Surely they realized he wasn't a wealthy man. And why would they ask this of Josie? How could they possibly think that she could provide that kind of ransom?

———

After Josie had forwarded the kidnappers' messages to both Otto and Agent Haskins, she walked outside to where Nick stood behind Becka as she examined the deadbolt on the kitchen door.

"You haven't slept here since the break-in, have you?" Becka asked.

Josie shook her head. "I stayed up the lane, at a friend's house."

"Mr. Drench has put a rush on this job. If you can give us tonight and tomorrow to work, we'll have you locked up tight by the time you get home from work in the evening."

The tense muscles in Josie's shoulders loosened somewhat at the news. She was surprised at the amount of relief she felt. "I appreciate it. That's great news. I can stay up the lane again tonight."

Becka gestured toward Dell's house. "Does he have security?"

"No, and he refuses to get it."

She winced. "Me personally? I wouldn't stay out here without it."

Josie smiled. "Dell has his own form of security."

While Becka walked back to her truck to call in help and order equipment, Nick and Josie went inside to iron out details before he returned to Mexico. As they walked through the kitchen door, he said, "Security team will be here all day. I'll come back tomorrow at four. We'll talk then about ground rules."

She gave him a wary glance. "For what?"

"You got a spare bedroom. I'll take that for my personal space, but we need an incident room. Somewhere I can work. Probably take over your dining room table."

"For what?"

"I can't run this operation from Mexico. I'm moving in."

"Oh, really?" she said, trying to keep the shock from her voice. She had not expected this and wondered suddenly what other surprises awaited her. She sat down across from him and folded her arms against her chest, processing the idea that she would have someone living with her. Two years ago she had turned down her own mother's request to move in, although the reasons for her decline were far more complex than space and freedom. She and Dillon had separate houses because of Josie's reluctance to give up her independence. Now, this stranger had invited himself to stay in her spare bedroom. She noticed him staring at her and realized that a response was required of her.

"For how long?" she asked.

"Until we get Mr. Reese home. Or until your Mr. Drench pulls the plug. Now, back to the case."

Her eyebrows arched in reply.

"You've had time to recover since you listened to the ransom contact. You ready to watch the video with me? We need to dissect it. There's some wordplay that bothered me."

She got up and took the seat next to him, their arms almost touching as they leaned in toward the laptop.

"You watch this with two sets of eyes. One as the girlfriend, one as a cop. What is he telling you? Any body language that's off? Anything that might signal something to you?"

He clicked the Play button, and they watched the grainy image that filled the fifteen-inch computer screen. The video showed only his naked body from the waist up. He was facing forward wearing a black headband over his eyes. After several seconds she heard his voice.

"Why didn't you send money? They're going to kill me. Don't you love me? I'm wrecked unless you do something."

He paused after each sentence.

Josie said, "Play it again. I'm not hearing it right."

She listened again and the significance of his words stunned her. "Does he say, *I'm wrecked*?"

"That's what bothered me."

She stared at Nick intently, desperate to find meaning in Dillon's words. "It's just not something he would say. Why not, *I'm desperate*? Wouldn't that make more sense?" she said. "Or, even, *I'm frantic*?"

"Notice the break between sentences."

She nodded, trying to understand.

"Why *wrecked*?" he said. "Why would he use that word?"

Suddenly the hair stood up on her arms. She scooted her chair back so that she could turn and face Nick. "The day after Dillon was kidnapped he received a summons to federal court in El Paso for the indictment of Wally Follet. Guess what Wally does?"

"What?"

"He was indicted for selling wrecked cars across the border to Mexico."

"What do you mean wrecked? Totaled cars?"

"Exactly. The sign in front of the business says *wrecks and rebuilds*. Wally buys the cars from insurance settlements for cheap, and then either rebuilds them or sells them to dealers across the border for a profit."

Nick nodded slowly, thinking for a moment before responding. "Is there a confirmed connection between Wally Follet and the Medranos?" he asked.

"We've just started to focus on Follet. His son, Hector Follet, is staying in a trailer at the salvage yard. He's basically hunkered down. His dad took off over a week ago, leaving no word about where he was headed. No phone. The kid knows more than he's telling us, but he doesn't trust the police. We're working on him."

Nick glanced at his watch and seemed to notice how late it was. He got up from the table. "You hear anything more tonight, you call me immediately. My cell phone is never off."

After Nick left, Josie sat at her kitchen table with a pencil and a sheet of lined paper, trying to sort fact from theory. She'd drawn nothing but a series of empty square boxes stacked atop each other. Her mind was racing so fast she wasn't able to hang on to anything that came to her. When her department-issued cell phone buzzed on the table she stifled a scream. She recognized Otto's number.

"This is Josie."

"Is Nick still there?"

"No, he just left. I'm getting ready to pack a bag for Dell's house. The security team is getting set up outside. They'll work through the night on the new system."

"What's Nick's take on Dillon's message?"

"He didn't really commit. I think he'd like to see a clearer connection between Wally and the Medranos. I think we'll find it."

"Same here. The agents agreed. They can't trace the actual text message but they're hoping to ping the tower." Otto paused and Josie could sense his hesitation.

"What is it?"

"Agent Haskins said they traced Dillon's cell phone to a tower in Piedra Labrada. They've lost the signal, but that was where the text he sent you on the night he was kidnapped originated."

Josie felt her body sigh. She had still been hanging on to the hope that he was being kept in the United States, where law enforcement could at least operate with authority. A confirmed kidnapping in Mexico made their job exponentially harder.

"If the texts you're receiving from the kidnappers match the same tower in Piedra Labrada, we'll at least have a location, Josie. That's good news."

Josie said nothing, unable to see the bright side.

"What kind of information did Nick give you?" he asked.

"He's moving in with me. Tomorrow. He went home to settle his things and pack his gear."

"You think that's wise?"

Josie laughed, but there was no joy in her voice. "Who the hell knows what's wise when every move is a gamble?"

Otto paused, evidently deciding not to quiz her further. "I made an appointment for you to talk with Julian Beckwith at his office in El Paso tomorrow morning."

Josie closed her eyes and pressed the cell phone against her ear, clenching her jaws for a moment. "I thought you were taking that one?" she finally asked.

"The kid's a smartass. He'll take one look at me, some over-the-hill fat cop, and dismiss us. I think he'll deal better with you. Young and female."

"We've got a better lead with Wally Follet. I'd planned on working that angle tomorrow."

"Josie, the statement from Dillon is compelling, but—"

"Compelling? It's a hell of a lot more than that! Have you ever in your life heard Dillon use the phrase *I'm wrecked*? Come on!"

"As I said, it's a compelling lead, but so is Beckwith." She started to speak but he cut her off. "Josie. Hear me out. I've been working on Dillon's activity for the week before he was taken. The last phone call Dillon made from work? To Beckwith's office. Dillon was gathering financial data on an oil company in Redford for Beckwith. It's a family-owned oil company being bought out by this smartass kid, and Dillon's in the middle. To my knowledge, Beckwith is the only person associated with Dillon who has that kind of money at his disposal."

"Why would Beckwith work with an accountant in Artemis?"

"Dillon's the only accountant for fifty miles. If Beckwith wanted a local connection, Dillon would be the one to choose."

"Let's send Marta."

"Come on, Josie. She's not the right person for this any more than I am. Get your head on straight and approach this as a cop."

"You're really pissing me off right now."

"Look at the evidence," he continued. "The files that were taken? A through G. Beckwith is also in those files. We can't base an entire case on one phrase."

"That's ridiculous and you know it. That phrase clearly connects Dillon to Wally Follet. Maybe Follet is the middleman. Maybe they took Dillon hoping he could lead the kidnappers to Follet." She paused and sighed heavily. "Come on, Otto. Give me tomorrow to work on him. One day."

"I won't budge on this, Josie. Beckwith rescheduled his appointments to get us in so quickly. Go talk with him. If he has nothing to offer, then at least we'll know."

Josie hung up and stormed off to pack a bag to take to Dell's for the night. By the time she finished, the security crew was already drilling holes through the ceiling in her living room, and two men were setting up a wireless alarm system in the pantry. When she had called Dell to confirm she could stay at his place another night, he had offered to fix them both a late dinner. She gladly accepted.

By seven o'clock Josie stood on Dell's front porch with Chester and her overnight bag. The dog pushed inside before her and skidded across the plank wood floors, toenails clicking, until he slid into Dell, who was taking a casserole dish out of the oven. Dell laughed, removed his oven mitts, and bent down to scratch the dog's ears, dodging his attempts to lick Dell's face.

She couldn't help but smile at the interaction. Dell had infinite patience with the dog, but claimed he had no patience with people. He had chosen a life of desert solitude over one that involved interaction with people, but Josie had never seen anything from Dell but kindness and compassion, at least toward people who gave a shit. She often wondered what had brought him to Artemis twenty years ago: never married, no kids, no close friends besides Josie. She had hinted at the question, but he'd never elaborated and she respected his silence. She had enough silence of her own to justify.

Josie watched Dell return to the casserole, which he cut into squares with a spatula. He wore his standard worn-out Levi's and a threadbare plaid flannel shirt. She wondered where he bought his clothes. He refused to get a computer, so there was no online shopping, but she couldn't imagine him in a store, searching for the perfect shirt, trying on clothes.

"Tuna casserole. Made from the same recipe my mama used sixty years ago. Basic. That's the key. If it comes in a box, don't buy it."

"Can I help with anything?"

"Tea's on the counter. Grab that and we're ready."

Josie carried the pitcher of tea to the table, which was set with two plates and napkins, a small garden salad in the middle of each plate. Dell never touched salad. She was touched by the gesture, at the trouble he had gone to.

Conversation throughout dinner focused on a sick heifer over which Dell had been battling with the veterinarian for the past week, as well as the beautiful weather and the high price of gas. Finally, once dishes were washed and they had settled onto the couch in the living room, Dell asked for the full report.

Josie wasn't sure where to start. "We're moving too slow. We don't have enough to show for three full days of work."

"So tell me what you have."

Josie rubbed her temples as a wave of weariness settled into her bones. She felt sluggish and frustrated. "The evening you and I were waiting on Dillon to come cut wood, he drove to his new client meeting on Driftriver Drive. It was most likely located in one of the empty homes in the back of the subdivision. I think he was lured out of his car, abducted, and his car was stolen."

Dell stood and walked to the kitchen as Josie talked, bringing back two Dos Equis. Josie was surprised; she hadn't seen Dell drink anything in years. He had given up drinking, not for a physical or moral reason, just because he got tired of it. She accepted the beer gratefully and took a long pull, resting the cold bottle on her thigh.

Josie continued, "They most likely drove him straight to Mexico, where he's being kept in a stash house. Later that night, about two hours after Dillon was kidnapped, Christina Handley received a cell phone call and drove from her home back to the office." Josie took a long drink and considered how to explain her theory to Dell.

"This is where it gets sketchy. We're assuming someone lured her to the office because they wanted information about one of Dillon's clients. It appears Christina struggled with someone. A necklace was found, presumably flung across the room during an argument. But then it also looks as if Christina just sat in her office chair, maybe at gunpoint. The perpetrator then walked to the front of the office, about three to five feet directly in front of the front door, and fired a shot at Christina, who was sitting in her chair, a few feet to the side of her desk. It's a contradiction we can't reconcile. If there was a struggle at one point, why wouldn't she have attempted to flee before she was shot?"

"How many times was she shot?" he asked.

"That's the most bizarre part of this. One time. From the side. The coroner said the shot nicked her heart, but it wasn't a particularly good shot. She bled out, but it wasn't instant death." Josie stopped, staring at Dell, unable to keep the guilt from her expression. Dell met her gaze, unflinching.

"Don't go there. Her death had nothing to do with you. She was murdered. You called her phone and you called Dillon and you called the office to check on him. End of story."

She nodded absently; her thoughts were broken into pieces by the frequent recollection that she had not listened to her instincts. And it most likely cost a woman her life.

"They steal anything from the office?" he asked.

She nodded, drank down half the beer, and set the bottle on the table, hard. Chester raised his head off the floor, his eyes wide in concern.

"File folders. A through G, and I, and T appear to be missing. Computers and flash drives."

"What's your best guess?"

"The Medranos. The size of the ransom is huge. Nine million. Nick, the kidnapping negotiator, said ransoms don't go that high, not unless a cartel is involved and the victim has big money."

Dell raised his eyebrows and smirked. "You not telling me something about Dillon?"

She attempted a smile. "He's no millionaire."

"So who has the money?"

"Maybe one of Dillon's clients. Maybe Dillon has access to a client's accounts that the Medranos want access to. Honestly, Dell, none of it makes sense anymore. Who would pay nine million dollars for their accountant?" Josie shuddered involuntarily, the sound of Dillon's scream still fresh in her mind. She took a deep breath. "On top of the original messages, I received a video clip from the kidnappers today. Dillon was cut, his arm sliced open. He was forced to talk on camera, ask me why I didn't love him. Said they were going to kill him if I didn't come up with the money."

Dell shook his head in disbelief, his eyes narrowed in concern. "Jesus. I'm sorry. Sorry you have to do this."

Josie looked away, not able to meet his eyes. "I went to Macon Drench today. Begging for money." She shook her head and picked at the label on the beer bottle. "After the way my mom manipulated people for money when I was growing up, I swore I would never put my hand out, no matter how bad things got in my life. Now, here I am. It's like God's trying to teach me a lesson. Telling me, don't be so self-righteous. Have a little humility in your life. And Dillon's paying the price."

"This isn't your fault." His voice was low, measured. "You're a cop. You know the drill. The bad guys commit the crimes. And somehow the victims feel the guilt. They blame themselves for not doing something to stop the crime, for things going wrong. You only have so much energy. Do not waste it on worthless guilt."

※

Officer Marta Cruz logged on for third shift at eight o'clock, several hours later than her usual shift. Otto and Josie had asked her to stake out Wally's Folly for several nights to check for any action after dark. Josie had hoped Wally was visiting his son at night, sneaking in to take care of business.

Marta parked her car outside the main office of the Rio Camp and Kayak, a mile down the road from the salvage yard. At that time of year the business didn't have much traffic. The owners' home sat just east of the office. It was a modest cedar plank with two additions onto the back that gave it a slapdash feel. The extra rooms were bedrooms to accommodate the kids, five girls under the age of eighteen. Marta made the sign of the cross on her chest at the thought of raising five girls. One was quite enough for her.

She knocked on the front door and heard two girls, one screaming, the other laughing. The youngest girl yanked the front door open, still laughing. She saw Marta and the girl's face fell in disappointment. The older girl, the same age and friends with Marta's own daughter, sighed and shoved her younger sister out of the way.

Marta smiled. "She's not trying to harass you, is she?"

Ella sighed dramatically. "Every time my boyfriend comes over she spends the entire time trying to tell him lies about me. I don't care what she says, but it's so incredibly annoying. Teresa's lucky she's an only child."

Marta tipped her head. "That means all the attention is on her. She would tell you that's not so good either."

The girl pushed the door open to allow Marta inside. "You want Mom or Dad?"

"Either one. I just have a question for one of them."

Ella left Marta standing in a large living room cluttered with enough toys and books to make her feel claustrophobic. Three of the girls lay on their bellies in pajamas, their heads turned up to the TV in front of them. Watching a Disney movie, they were oblivious to everything else around them. Marta heard glass clanking in the kitchen and assumed dishes were being washed.

Lisa Rankin stepped through the doorway and flung a dish towel back over her shoulder, smiling at Marta.

"Hello! What are you doing out so late?" Her expression quickly turned to one of concern. "I hope something's not wrong."

"It's fine. I just have a favor to ask."

"Sure. Let's step out onto the front porch where I can hear myself think." She turned to the girls. "Turn that TV down! Everyone in the house doesn't need to hear that."

They walked outside, both certain that the volume would remain exactly where it was.

Marta said, "Are you aware that Wally Follet has taken off?"

Her eyebrows knitted together in confusion. "What do you mean taken off?"

"He's left home."

"No! Is Hec down there by himself?"

Marta nodded. "Wally's got into some trouble with the feds. Evidently he found out he was facing an indictment and he took off."

Lisa crossed her arms over her chest and drew them in against the cold night air. "That poor kid. His dad's such a sleazebag. David and I have said for years we'd like to bring Hec home with us and raise him with our own. He's such a good kid."

"His dad sure didn't do him any favors," Marta said. "I'd like to observe the junkyard for the next couple nights, just to make sure Wally isn't sneaking back home. Would you mind if I parked my car here and walked down to the salvage yard? I don't want to draw attention to my car down there."

"Sure. Leave your car where it is. We can get around it if we need to."

———

Marta carried a black duffle bag packed with a thermos of coffee to keep her warm and awake, a small foldable stool, and snacks for the long night ahead, down the empty road to Wally's Folly. The front gate had been closed and padlocked shut. The fence shielded the front of the business from the street, but the east side of the yard was bordered with nothing more than a line of thick mesquite bushes and trees. Marta pushed herself through the narrow break between the eight-foot-tall corrugated metal fence and the bushes to her left, wincing at the loud scratch of the branches against her nylon coat. She was wearing her navy blue Artemis PD coat with a flap that covered the POLICE identification on the back. If need be, she could quickly pull apart the Velcro patches fastening the flap to her shoulders, and the neon yellow reflective ID would announce her presence.

Once in the yard she stood motionless for several minutes, scanning between the rows of cars and piles of vehicle parts. Josie had warned her about the chained Rottweiler beside the house, but she saw nothing and assumed the dog had been taken into the trailer with Hec for the night. Marta walked silently along the edge of the trees, thankful for light cloud cover.

Halfway down the fence line she stopped and pulled her foldable stool out of the duffle bag. She'd intentionally kept the bag unzipped to keep from causing excess noise. She'd settled on her stool alongside the bushes to listen and take in the area again before deciding on a place from which to observe for the night. She was wearing long underwear under her blue jeans and insulated boots to keep her feet warm, but she was still cold. The stool was about twelve inches tall with a seat barely wide enough to hold her rear end. She huddled down low over her lap, already dreading the long night.

After just a few minutes of silence she heard small branches snap, the sounds of people walking in the distance, and then the laugh of what seemed like several men. Her head turned toward the direction of the sounds, down by the river. As she listened, she wondered if the stolen car ring was still hard at work, possibly still buying from Wally Follet. Marta picked up her stool and backed into the undergrowth.

She listened to the noises for almost twenty minutes and saw a flashlight turn on for some time, and then eventually go off, confirming that the men were across the river in Mexico. The voices settled into quiet conversation and she felt certain they were either waiting for Wally to show up, or they were watching the junkyard, the same as she was doing.

She needed to get closer to them, but it was too dangerous to go alone; she'd have to get backup. She stood to put away the seat and head back down the road to the Rio Camp and Kayak.

Just as she stepped away from the tree line she noticed movement. A figure dressed in black walked slowly down the trailer steps, barely moving. Marta stood perfectly still, her vantage point offering a clear view without leaving her exposed. She was fairly certain the tall thin person in black was Hector, based on Josie's description of him, but Marta had never actually met him. With the sky somewhat overcast it was difficult to follow his movement. She saw him run quietly across the yard to the center aisle, but then she lost him. She wondered if Hec was meeting up with his father and the men down by the river. Marta hunkered down with her phone and texted Josie. *Wait for further. Men by the river. Hec is outside. Don't send cars. Stay quiet until I know more.*

The only way Marta could move toward the back of the yard without making noise was to leave the underbrush, leaving her exposed to other unknown dangers. The rows of cars ran perpendicular to the river. She walked along the outer edge of the line of cars closest to her until she reached the end of the row. She edged up the next row of cars, then down again, searching for the figure that she thought to be Hec. She stood still for a long time, searching the dark for the black-clad slim figure. Then she heard the light creak of metal and saw a pale face. He was in the next row over from her, at the end closest to the river, bent down, inside the empty frame of what appeared to be an old station wagon. He was squatting, watching the men watch him.

FIFTEEN

At three o'clock that morning Josie left Chester sleeping on the floor
of Dell's house and walked home to find the security crew running
wires above the ceiling in her hallway. Drywall was in piles on the
floor, doors off their hinges, but she was thankful for all of it. She
said hello and excused herself to take a shower and get ready for
work. By four she was on the road to El Paso to meet with Julian
Beckwith. She had begrudgingly agreed to conduct the interview at
eight in the morning, which would hopefully put her back in Artemis by one that afternoon so she could work on Hector.

Sometime before midnight, Josie had received a text from Marta
stating that there was movement by the river. After several texts over
a tense hour, Marta had deduced that two men were sitting beside a
pickup on the Mexican side of the Rio, apparently watching the
salvage yard. She had gotten down next to the bank of the river,
within thirty feet of them, and could hear them talking quietly,
speaking Spanish. Marta said it appeared the men had been there
before; they seemed relaxed and were paying little attention to their
surroundings.

At some point, someone had left the salvage yard trailer and
snuck outside to watch the men. Marta was certain that it had been
Hector. She had been expecting to see Wally Follet show up, but she

knew Wally, and she said she would have recognized him. He was still nowhere to be found. Josie told Marta to hold off doing anything that night, to stake out again the following night but to try and find a way to capture conversation between the men, hopefully via a recorder. Josie thought the distance across the water might be too great to pick up any clear conversation, but it was worth the effort.

The list of questions had grown considerably overnight: Why were the men watching Hector? And why was Hector watching them? What was Wally's role? And, most importantly, was any of it connected to Dillon's disappearance and Christina's death? Dillon was Wally's accountant. Was the indictment, Wally's disappearance, the odd behavior down by the river, the kidnapping, the murder, all of it coincidental? Josie had a hard time believing that.

The long, quiet drive to El Paso at least gave her the chance to think. When a breakthrough in a troubling case happened, it was usually upon waking, as sleep generally settled her thoughts. The problem was she hadn't slept well since Dillon's disappearance.

———•———

Josie drove the I-10 west and arrived in El Paso at seven thirty along with another thousand cars. She glanced at drivers in suits and dresses, women with hair fixed and makeup carefully applied, and she wondered how many of those grim-faced people were happy pushing their way through the day, trying to impress, to get noticed, to get ahead. For some reason she could never explain, the city always depressed the hell out of her.

She took the Downtown El Paso exit, fought the traffic to the Wells Fargo Plaza, and pulled into the parking garage across the street. After several laps up the ramp she finally found an empty spot and parked. She called in her location to Lou, then checked the safety on her Beretta and her ankle backup. Taking one last swig of cold coffee, she grabbed her steno pad and got out of the car, locking it behind her.

Beckwith's office was located in the twenty-one-story Wells

Fargo building, the tallest in El Paso. After calling up at the security desk, Josie rode the elevator to Beckwith's floor with two older men in suits. The doors opened into a spacious reception area with a marquee that directed her down a short hallway to an office with BECKWITH INDUSTRIES painted in gold across its large glass entry door. Behind a curved ebony desk sat a young woman receptionist in a light-pink business suit. She greeted Josie with a smile, and then tried not to stare at her badge and the name plate on her uniform.

"Can I help you?" The woman asked the question as if Josie might be lost.

"I'm Josie Gray. I have an eight o'clock appointment with Mr. Beckwith."

"Yes. Ms. Gray. Please follow me."

Josie followed the woman down a hallway, past a glass-walled conference room dominated by a table and at least twenty leather swivel chairs. A woman in a catering uniform was placing pitchers of ice water and glasses on the table from a rolling cart. Just beyond the conference room was a closed office door. The name plate on the door read JULIAN BECKWITH CEO.

The woman knocked and then turned to Josie. "One moment, please." She turned back to the door and opened it slowly, as if not sure what she might find. Evidently satisfied with what she saw, she pushed the door open further and said, "Ms. Gray is here to see you."

The woman gave Josie what looked to be an apologetic smile and stepped back to allow her entrance.

The corner office had a stunning view of the business district, which stretched across El Paso and up into the Juarez Mountains into Mexico. It also had a bar and a media center with two camel-colored leather couches.

Beckwith was sitting at his desk. A phone headset was wrapped around his ear and he talked while studying information on two different monitors and absently scrolling through a cell phone with his thumb. He wore a tasteful shirt and sweater vest that fit his slim build perfectly. His brown hair was neatly combed and parted to the side, his face smooth and shiny. She stood in front of his desk beside two guest chairs and waited to be acknowledged. He gave Josie the impression of a well-groomed boarding school student who hadn't quite mastered the social norms of adulthood.

He held up a paper Starbucks cup to Josie as if toasting her. Using his pinkie finger, he pushed the headset microphone down and slightly away from his mouth and said, "Sit down. You can help me rip these morons a new arse." He gave her a thumbs-up and smiled conspiratorially. She was surprised at his British accent and wondered what would motivate a British twenty-something financial genius to settle in West Texas. "It's the curse of the intelligent, listening to the incompetent," he whispered. He didn't actually appear angry despite his harsh words. *A game player,* she thought.

Josie sat down in one of the chairs and listened to Beckwith complain to someone on the other end about the poor judgment of someone named Edgewood. He finally hung up and flung his headset onto the desk. He turned to face Josie.

"Good morning, Mr. Beckwith. I'm Josie Gray, chief of police in Artemis."

He shoved his chair away from his desk with a flourish and stood, looking out the window. "I know who you are. Population two thousand four hundred and ninety-seven at last count. You operate a three-officer department. And, most importantly, you are Dillon Reese's girlfriend."

Josie reached into her pocket to retrieve her identification card, uncomfortable with his description of her. She felt too old to be just a girlfriend, but what else was there to describe her relation to Dillon? She held the card out for him to view. He stared at it for a moment, then finally walked to her and took it from her.

"I appreciate you talking with me on such short notice. I assume you've heard what happened to your accountant, Mr. Reese."

"One of my accountants. Plural."

Josie cocked her head, acknowledging his correction. "Mr. Reese has been kidnapped and his secretary was murdered." Beckwith's expression did not change. He simply nodded once. "The kidnappers have demanded a nine-million-dollar ransom."

"From whom?"

"They contacted me."

"Why you?"

"We don't know the reason. We have very little information from the kidnappers other than the ransom demand. One working theory is that he was kidnapped for information. The kidnappers stole the computers in the office. Dillon has access to your accounts. Possibly the kidnappers took him for access to you. Is that a possibility?"

"I own a private equity fund. I have access to millions. But he couldn't get to my money without my consent. He's an advisor of sorts—smart, honest, or he wouldn't be mine. But no one touches my money. No one."

"Is that typical?" Josie asked.

"I've no doubt there are people who turn their fortunes over to their brokers and want nothing to do with it. Speedy way to lose the millions, I think."

"Have you received contact from anyone in the past few weeks that's concerned you?"

He laughed openly "I'm an investor. I buy up trash and spin it into gold. Right?"

She nodded once.

"When you buy up shit companies you have to get rid of the shit. Right? Flush it down the Rio. People get fired. Sometimes lots of people. *El Paso Times* referred to me, fondly I think, as the most hated man in Texas." He smiled and raised an eyebrow. "Also the most eligible bachelor. A nice combo, don't you think?" He raised his left hand and wiggled his fingers. "And yet, here I remain. Working my arse off with no time to collect the benefits."

"I'm not sure what your answer has to do with my question."

"More to the point then, almost everyone I work with concerns me at some point. I buy up businesses that are falling apart. People are vulnerable and angry and they see me as both savior and saboteur."

"They think you sabotage their business so that you can then buy them for a profit?"

"Inevitably, there are people who are losing their jobs who see it that way."

"Is it true?" she asked.

"I don't need to sabotage their businesses. Their alternative is bankruptcy."

"What can you tell me about Black Gold Drilling?"

He nodded once, acknowledging the abrupt change in the conversation. "I buy businesses all over the southwest, so many that I have to rely on local accountants like Dillon Reese." He paused and cocked his head thoughtfully. "Have you ever been to Redford?"

She nodded.

"It's hours from here, in the middle of nowhere. No cell phone reception, no stores, no gas stations. Just a few ranches. I needed someone close to Redford who could work with the family, gather data, and monitor progress. I certainly wasn't going to make that drive."

Josie acknowledged his point. West Texas was one of the most remote areas of the United States, and Redford was one of the most remote border towns in West Texas. The closest Walmart was a three-hour drive, located in Fort Stockton.

"The last case Dillon worked on the day he was kidnapped was Black Gold Drilling. Employees were refusing to cooperate. It looked as if things weren't going smoothly."

Beckwith smirked. "You're not here because you think his kidnapping could be linked to Black Gold, are you?"

"Could it?"

His phone buzzed and he picked it up, spoke to someone, and asked them to wait.

He faced her, his expression sober. "Mr. Reese represented a West Texas venture in Redford for me. That's it. I can't see any reason someone would kidnap him for access to a drilling company in Redford. It's actually a fairly lame takeover. Maybe a half million at stake. They were so far under they were begging for someone to keep them all from drowning." He stood. "I have a meeting. Sorry I can't help you."

He walked toward the door and she followed, but said nothing. She shook his hand and thanked him. He walked ahead of her down the hallway and entered the glass conference room, where a table full of people seemed to be waiting for him. She couldn't believe his callous response to a woman's death and a man's kidnapping.

In what sounded like a childish afterthought, Beckwith popped his head back into the hallway and called after her. "Hope things go better for Mr. Reese."

The flat stretch of asphalt, the miles of eighteen wheelers, truck stops, and desert flatland, flowed along in a monotonous progression, allowing Josie time to dwell on the disaster that she was living. The investigation was barely limping along. Otto and Marta had already talked to twelve other clients and gotten nowhere. As far as she was concerned, the Beckwith and Black Gold Drilling connection was unlikely. She could understand abducting Dillon, trying to force information from him to gain access to a wealthy client's investments, but the ransom didn't connect. If the kidnapper was after client information, why ransom Dillon for nine million dollars? And, especially, why send the message through her? What could a kidnapper possibly gain by demanding a ransom from her, someone who didn't have the money?

Once again, Josie was drawn back to the revenge angle. She could imagine the sadistic bastard, the leader of the Medranos known as the Bishop, playing with their lives and enjoying every minute of it. But Nick was adamant that the Medranos wouldn't put this much money into play without expecting a big payoff in the end. He claimed money was the driving force for the Medranos. So then, what about Hector Follet, creeping around his own backyard, spying on a group of men sitting across the river in Mexico as they spied on his house at night? What the hell did that mean? Were they all looking for Wally? It seemed clear to Josie that Wally hadn't fled town because of the indictment alone. He most likely left because he screwed one too many people over. And his son was now paying the price, as well as Christina and Dillon.

She stared at the yellow lane divider, rolling out in front of her, mile after mile, and she allowed the thought that she had been avoiding since Dillon's disappearance. If Dillon didn't return, then her constant struggle to maintain her independence would suddenly be replaced by heartbreaking loneliness.

SIXTEEN

Josie was back in the office by one that afternoon, typing up a few notes from the Beckwith interview, when she heard Otto's uneven footsteps coming up the stairs. She dreaded the day he would walk into the office and announce the physical demands were too much and he was handing in his badge. Delores wanted him to set a retirement date but so far he'd refused to do so. Josie hoped this case wasn't the one that pushed him into a retirement he wasn't ready to take. He may have been slowing down physically, but mentally he was a first-rate cop whom the department could not afford to lose.

"Any word?" he asked as he entered the room.

"Nothing."

"Anything come up with Beckwith?"

"He's worth a fortune and hated by all. But he claims no one has access to his money but himself." Josie explained that the Black Gold Drilling buyout was no different from any other buyout. It was worth a half million, and at this point, not worth exploring further. She was mildly surprised when he accepted her verdict with little argument, but she could tell he was preoccupied with something else.

"What's up?" she finally asked.

"You assigned me as the lead investigator, Josie." He paused, letting that statement settle between them. "I have to tell you, I'm not very happy about what took place last night."

Josie was taken aback. She started to speak, to say that she didn't understand what he meant, and then her conversation with Marta came back to her. Her indignation quickly faded and she slumped back into her chair.

"That was a major development last night. Why wouldn't you call me? We needed to talk that through. There was an argument to be made for going in last night, catching Hec off guard, bringing him in and interrogating him. But I wasn't privy to that information. You decided for me. I had to find out from a report written by Marta, left on my desk, when I came to work this morning."

"I'm sorry, Otto."

"Apologies are useless in a murder investigation."

Otto stood by the windows in the back of the office, hands shoved into his uniform pockets, his eyes on her, a disappointed look on his face. Josie was not one to let down a friend, especially not Otto.

She said nothing and looked away from him. He was right.

"Are we clear on this?" he said.

"We are."

Otto kept his distance from her, allowing his anger to cool. Josie had worked with him long enough to know his anger was short-lived. He didn't hold a grudge. She sat quietly at her desk, waiting for him to move on. He finally said, "I talked with Agent Omstead at length last night. He said the agent they have in Mexico said the Medranos aren't kidnapping these days. Their drug business is so lucrative they don't need to go that route. Their focus is money laundering and the drug trade."

Josie blew air out in frustration. "So who kidnapped Dillon? Where's the motive? Nothing makes sense. Nothing!"

Otto poured a cup of coffee and sat down in front of his desk. Ignoring her outburst, he turned his chair to face Josie. "So fill me in on Marta's visit to the salvage yard."

Josie described the stakeout, and her desire for Marta to move in closer to the men located on the Mexican side of the river. Otto leaned his forearm across his stomach, propping up his other arm to rest his chin on his fist.

"What's your best guess?" he asked.

"Wally's business partners are watching the salvage yard, waiting for Wally to sneak home one night. And maybe his business partner just happens to be the Medranos. He's screwed them over, probably taken off with their money, and they want it back," she said.

"Do you see a connection to Dillon and Christina?"

She frowned. "Nothing other than the accounting connection and the indictment. We need to know more about Wally's business. It may look like a sleaze operation from the outside, but he could have a million-dollar business set up for all we know."

Otto pressed his fingers into his eyelids. "The feds have been investigating Follet for six months. All they can find on him is some stolen cars getting shipped to Mexico."

Josie got up to stare out the back window. At times, it felt to her as if she and Otto were an old, bickering married couple.

"Here's what I don't get," Otto continued. "If the cartel is after Wally, why not kidnap his son? Why Dillon?"

She turned back to Otto. "It goes back to your theory. Dillon is Wally's accountant. He has access to Wally's accounts."

"Wouldn't Wally be more inclined to come home if his kid was in jeopardy than his accountant?" Otto frowned at his own question and then answered it. "Probably not."

"He'd never win father of the year," Josie responded. "He's a crook, and he left his kid to fend for himself. But part of me thinks he's not such a complete failure. Maybe he left thinking it was in Hec's best interest."

"Are you seriously taking up for Wally Follet?"

"Not taking up for him." She looked away, trying to gather her thoughts. "I think it was the trailer that got to me. It was in such good shape. Decorated and clean. It wasn't the house of someone who doesn't care. And Hec. He's seems like a good kid. Well-mannered. He gave me iced tea. After we drank it he took our dishes to the sink and washed them out. That's a learned behavior. His dad did something right along the way, at least with his son."

Otto narrowed his eyes at her. "So, what's your point here?"

"I think someone knows Wally will come back for his son. Hec is the bait. That's why they didn't kidnap Hec. The big question is why is Wally so important to them? Does he have a load of stolen cars hidden away somewhere that he didn't deliver?"

Otto nodded. "We need a link to the Medranos. So far we have nothing but a ransom request that technically could have come from anyone."

The phone on Josie's desk buzzed. "Chief Gray?" Lou asked.

"Yes?"

"Roxanne Spar is here. She'd like to talk with you."

Josie took her finger off the conference button. "Shit." She looked at Otto and he shrugged, implying that the mayor wasn't his problem.

Otto motioned to get up and said, "I'm headed out. I'm going to take the Santa Muerte pendant to Presidio. Ask the artist if she recognizes it. See if we can narrow down the owner."

Josie sighed and buzzed Lou. "Thanks. Send her on up."

Otto adjusted his gun belt and left.

Josie heard Roxanne and Otto mutter a polite hello on the stairs.

Roxanne entered the office wearing a pair of tight white pants tucked into black suede boots with fur wrapped around the top. She wore a red shirt with drawstrings at the neck that ended in tiny white pom-poms, which bounced against her chest as she walked. The outfit looked out of place on a woman with wrinkles around her mouth and eyes and across her forehead. Josie flashed to an image of her mother the day she arrived in Artemis two years ago in a miniskirt and skintight top, and she felt a moment of sadness wash over her, and then the crazy urge to call her mother. One more attempt to make things right.

Roxanne closed the door behind her and Josie gestured to the conference table, where they took a seat across from each other.

"What can I do for you, Ms. Spar?"

"I guess you talked to the mayor. Well, it backfired." She wrinkled her nose in disgust.

"What do you mean, backfired?"

"I figured you'd talk to him and he'd lay off. Instead, he's come to see me twice. Asking why I'm trying to set him up. Why I don't trust him. If you want the truth, he's a grown man acting like a juvenile."

"If he's harassing you, then file charges. Don't let his position keep you from doing the right thing."

She leaned her head back and laughed. "And what do you think the knucklehead men of Artemis would do to me when they found their crony strung up over stalking charges filed by a barmaid? You think they got my back?"

"This isn't about the men in Artemis. It's about your rights."

"Let me remind you, I make my tips off the men in Artemis. They think I turned on one of their buddies, what happens to my tips?"

"I understand that. But you shouldn't have to worry about walking from your car to your apartment at the end of your shift."

"I just want him to leave me alone. Quit driving by my place. Quit creeping on me, and I forget the whole thing."

"So he can harass someone else?"

Roxanne dropped her chin to her chest in frustration. When she lifted her head she gave a look that showed she was worn out by the conversation. "Let's be honest. I'm not a save-the-planet kind of lady. You want someone to string up the mayor then get somebody else. Got nothing to do with me. Just let him know, I've read up on the stalker laws, and he's getting mighty close to crossing the line."

Otto felt a twinge of guilt leaving Josie to deal with Roxanne. Josie had filled him in, and the situation had the makings of a political drama that he hoped she could derail.

He drove thirty minutes to Presidio to find the artist known in West Texas as CC, or Celeste Chesnick. Her studio was in her home, located in a tree-lined neighborhood south of town. Otto had called ahead and the woman said she would be in all morning.

Her small clapboard-style house was surrounded by similar homes, but the property was distinguished by emerald glass balls hanging from its trees, colorful pots of bonsai pine trees, and a multicolored picket fence. It gave the chipped paint on the house a hip flair, especially compared to the old and unkempt homes in the block. He parked in the gravel driveway under a shade tree and met CC on the front porch. She was wearing a red gauzy dress that drifted around her thin body, faded cowboy boots, and a floppy-brimmed leather hat that all together signaled her vocation as an avant-garde artist. Her skin was a creamy chocolate brown. Dozens of beaded cornrows clicked against each other as she moved.

"Welcome!" She smiled warmly and held her hand out to Otto, who introduced himself.

"Please call me CC. It's good to meet you, Otto." He held his hand out as if to shake, but she grasped it in hers, holding it as if they were high school sweethearts, and led him inside her home. She waved her other hand around her living room–turned-gallery with a flourish.

"Welcome to CC's world. Take a moment to look around while I get us drinks. Iced tea good for you?"

"Sure. That would be great." He watched her glide out of the room, her dress wafting behind her and leaving the scent of lavender and lemons. He couldn't place her accent, but it was soft and friendly, he guessed Caribbean.

After Simon had said that he refused to sell CC's jewelry in his secondhand shop, Otto had imagined a devil-worshiping hag, not a pretty waif offering iced tea. The artwork in her gallery was a mix of colors and textures, but it all came together against whitewashed plank walls. Certainly no satanic signs or gang symbols were present.

CC entered the room carrying a wooden tray with a pitcher and two giant margarita glasses filled with iced tea and a decorative umbrella. Otto thanked her and they sat down on high-backed chairs that flanked a fireplace.

After a brief discussion of her art and gallery openings Otto pulled the small plastic baggie out of his shirt pocket and handed it to her.

Her eyebrows rose in recognition. "Yes, this is my piece. Is there a problem?"

"This necklace was found at the scene of a murder."

She drew in a sharp breath, her expression concerned, and made the sign of the cross over her chest.

"The secretary that was killed? Are you familiar with the story from the news?"

"Of course. It was terrible. And a man kidnapped?"

He nodded. "The murderer hasn't been found, but we think he may have been wearing this necklace."

She shuddered.

"Can you tell me about the necklace?"

She looked at the necklace through the baggie. "Can I take it out?"

"It's evidence. You'll have to look through the bag."

She ran her middle finger lightly over the pendant through the plastic.

"Santa Muerte. Yes, this is definitely mine."

"Explain what you mean by Santa Muerte."

"Señora de la Noche, Lady of the Night." She studied the piece for a moment and seemed to be lost in her own thoughts. "Some believe she protects those who work at night—police officers, taxi drivers, prostitutes. She's a saint. People pray to her for favors and miracles. She protects the truly faithful from death."

"But I thought she was a saint used by criminals. Basically, murderers who want her to protect them from other murderers." Otto was becoming frustrated that this so-called saint apparently had multiple purposes depending on the needs of the believer. He had hoped for a clear path to the Medranos.

She tilted her head in thought. "Criminals request miracles from God just like policemen, correct? God doesn't only allow prayers from policemen."

"As a Catholic, doesn't it bother you making art that goes against your beliefs?"

"That's a bit presumptuous, don't you think?"

Otto felt his face redden in embarrassment. It had been an inappropriate question.

She continued. "Does an author who writes about murder fret because she doesn't condone murder?"

"I can't answer that," he said. He worried he was losing control of the interview, and he needed to get to the point of his visit.

"Like it or not, death is part of the human experience," she said. "And that is what art strives to represent. Life in its most basic forms."

"CC, I need to ask you a question that is key to our investigation." He looked at her until she nodded once. "Is it true that you create jewelry for the Medrano cartel?"

Her neck and chest turned a deep red and her lips turned down in a disapproving frown. "I don't quiz my patrons about their vocation or their religion. What they do with the art that I make for them is none of my business."

He held a hand up. "I've offended you and I'm sorry for that. I'm not being judgmental. I'm trying to track down the person who wore this necklace. Santa Muerte followers are not that common, at least not around here. If you can look at this pendant and tell me who purchased it, that would be a huge break for the murder case, CC."

She considered Otto for quite some time, and then turned her attention back to the piece of jewelry. "This pendant is one of a series I created about two years ago. I've sold probably thirty necklaces from that series. But I can't give you names of my customers. I don't keep that kind of information."

He said nothing and she finally sighed, her shoulders slouching forward as if the conversation had weighed down her good spirits.

"Will you keep this confidential?"

Otto nodded.

"I'm certain that cartel members have purchased jewelry from me." She raised her hands as if to say, *What can I do?* "But so have others who follow Santa Muerte who are perfectly good people. People hoping for protection from the violence they face each day."

Otto said nothing, wondering how many perfectly good people actually worshiped the saint.

She scowled, seeming to have picked up on Otto's train of thought. "My cousin who lives in Mexico City has a shrine to Santa Muerte. He says life is so dangerous here on earth that people have to rely on her for protection. He's a good man. He just wants to keep his family safe from harm." She shrugged as if to indicate it wasn't her job to judge a person's beliefs. Then her expression changed suddenly. "You have a family in Artemis who's purchased several Santa Muerte pieces over the past several years."

"Who's that?"

"Do you know the Conroys?"

This was the second time that the Conroys had come up in reference to Santa Muerte. Otto knew them, a dysfunctional family who'd been living on the margins of the law for years. But the family had a white sheep among the black: Dave Conroy, the local elementary school principal, was one of the Conroy sons. Otto was up and moving, thanking CC as he walked out the door. Dead saints, praying crooks, smiling skulls. Hopefully the Conroys would provide some path from the bizarre necklace to its wearer.

SEVENTEEN

On his way back into town Otto stopped by the Artemis Elementary School to talk to Dave Conroy. The school was a one-story L-shaped building with a flat roof that made it look squashed. It was located on a patch of land surrounded by miles of wide-open desert and mile-high blue skies. A few short trees dotted a playground that was filled with bright red swing sets and playground equipment and enclosed by a chain-link fence.

Otto parked in the circle drive in front of the school and was buzzed into the building. A young woman in a pale blue button-down sweater and slacks looked up and offered a pleasant hello upon recognizing him. He asked if Dave was available and she leaned back in her chair toward his office to make sure he wasn't on the phone. She motioned Otto into Dave's office, just behind her desk.

The secretary, Otto thought, always the first line of defense. A lump rose in his throat. Maybe in big cities a cop could grow a thick skin, could talk about the "victim." But Christina Handley had been part of his small community. He hoped he could remember her life. He hoped he could learn not to associate her only with her death.

Dave smiled when Otto entered.

"Good to see you, Otto! What brings you by for a visit?" He stood and leaned over his desk to shake Otto's hand.

As principal, Dave worked closely with the local police to handle truancy cases, severe discipline problems, and parental neglect issues. Otto had been disturbed to find such problems had been affecting younger and younger children.

Dave was in his late thirties. He wore rimless glasses, khaki pants, and a trim-fitting navy polo shirt with the words ARTEMIS ELEMENTARY SCHOOL embroidered over the breast pocket. He looked like a department store advertisement for casual work wear. Otto wished he could feel comfortable in something other than uniform pants, a button-down, and a shoulder holster.

"I have a few questions. You mind?" Otto gestured to the door behind him and Dave nodded.

Otto shut the door and sat down at a small round table, where Dave joined him.

"The information relates to Christina Handley's murder."

Dave looked dumbfounded. "How can something like this happen in Artemis?"

"I don't know, Dave. It's a terrible tragedy. And the investigation isn't moving fast enough. We're checking every possible lead we have."

Dave nodded, obviously confused about what any of this had to do with the elementary school.

"We found a necklace at the murder scene with a pendant of Santa Muerte. I was told that you or someone in your family is a follower."

Dave sighed and shut his eyes for a moment. "It's not me. I have nothing to do with it. And I have no idea where my parents' interest in Santa Muerte came from. It's something I choose not to discuss with them." He paused briefly, his eyebrows pulling together in worry. "You aren't suggesting—"

Otto raised a hand in response. "Don't misinterpret. I'm not here because I suspect your family is involved. I'm just trying to understand who might have been wearing the pendant, and where we might find them. It's a stretch, but sometimes it's the smallest detail that breaks the case."

Dave stared at Otto, silent.

Otto gave Dave an uncomfortable look. "I'm sorry to drag you into this."

"Look, I've never denied my family. It is what it is. I even use it with some of the kids I work with as an example. You don't have to deny your family, but you also don't have to live their life. I didn't." He stood from his desk. "Come on. I'll drive you out there. They aren't fond of the police. If I take you out, they should at least talk to you."

They walked out of the office and Dave stopped at his secretary's desk. "I'm going to make a quick home visit. I'll be back by dismissal. Any problems, call me on my cell. Okay?"

She glanced at Otto, then back at Dave. "Sure. We'll be fine." She lowered her voice. "Is everything okay?"

"It's all good. I'm going to help Officer Podowski with something."

As they walked to the parking lot Dave said, "That woman is the glue that holds the school together." He pointed to a small navy blue pickup truck. "Are you okay with me driving?"

"Absolutely."

Dave's family—his parents and several of his siblings and their significant others—lived on a dusty road in an area of the county with very few homes. The land was hardpan, like concrete, with very little vegetation. Bare desert punctuated by boulders and rock and not much else. Solitary confinement is what came to mind when Otto drove through this section of Arroyo County.

The house was a sprawling adobe in a U shape with a large courtyard in the middle. The courtyard could have been a serene place to congregate as a family, but instead it was a dumping ground for items that were either being collected for one reason or another, or had been removed from the house but not yet made it to the landfill. In one corner, an old couch and mattress were propped up against a leafless oak tree that looked to have been dead for years.

A flagstone pathway led to sliding glass doors located on the opposite side of the courtyard. When they reached the door Dave rang the bell, turned and raised his eyebrows to Otto as if preparing him for what was to come, and walked on inside.

Dave led him into a living room that once must have been nicely decorated, but was now covered in a layer of debris that would take a pickup truck to haul away. Toys were strewn amid piles of papers and magazines, soft drink cans, ashtrays, and used paper plates. The stale smell of old food and cigarette smoke was nauseating. A scowling young woman sat curled up into a corner of the couch with an afghan pulled up around her chin, struggling to open her eyes after being awakened by the doorbell.

She recognized Dave and lifted her head. "You need to tell your dad to turn that stupid air conditioner off. It's March and he has the freaking air-conditioning on," she said.

"Good to see you, Brittany."

Otto stepped around a trail of toys and followed Dave to the kitchen. The girl laid her head back down on the arm of the couch, but her eyes followed Otto as he walked by.

"Tell me you're not here because of the boys? 'Cause I really can't deal with it today," she said.

Dave said over his shoulder, "The boys are at school. They're just fine."

A woman in her sixties was sitting at a large kitchen table in the middle of the brightly lit kitchen.

"Mom, this is Otto Podowski."

She looked up from her magazine and wrapped her lips around the straw of a large soft-drink cup that said *Monster Size It* on the side. She sipped from the cup, staring at her guest. She was a hefty woman wearing a loose cotton shirt and shorts, her hair tied in a messy wad at the base of her neck.

"Otto, this is Bea Conroy."

"It's good to meet you, Mrs. Conroy."

She finally pushed the cup back, eyeing Otto suspiciously, but said nothing.

Dave then pointed to a gaunt man in his early thirties who sat at the same table playing solitaire on the vinyl tablecloth. "And this is my brother, Tim."

Tim looked up momentarily and gave Otto a wide-eyed, vacant look. "How's it going?" he said flatly.

He wore a white undershirt and flannel shorts that looked like boxers. Otto could see the resemblance with Dave, the same full mouth and deep-set eyes. It was the level of engagement that Dave had with others that his family did not share.

An old man shuffled into the kitchen tethered to an oxygen tank on wheels. He didn't acknowledge anyone in the room as he pulled a chair out and sat down at the table. The oxygen tank clicked with each breath as he leaned across the table to point at a red jack and then at an open black queen.

Tim looked up at the man and made an angry growling sound. "I know. I see it. Will you quit telling me already?"

The old man just grinned.

Dave pulled a chair out from the table for Otto. "Dad, this is Otto Podowski."

The old man looked up and stared at the badge on Otto's uniform. He nodded once and then looked back at the solitaire game.

"Pleased to meet you too, Mr. Conroy."

From the back of the house two small kids screamed "Daddy" at the same time.

The younger man slapped his hand on the table. "Damn it." He pointed a finger at his father as he got up from the table. "Don't let Mom take off with my cigarettes. I just bought them this morning."

Bea turned in her chair and swatted him on the butt with her magazine as he walked by.

"Otto has some questions for you, Mom. He was asking me about Santa Muerte. I told him you're a believer, and you'd talk to him about who she is."

The death glare that Bea Conroy then gave Dave was something only a mother could give a son.

"You know who she is. You didn't need to drag him all the way out here to ask that question."

"Otto's investigating the murder of that young woman in town, and the man who was kidnapped. I told Otto, once you found out this was to help find that girl's murderer, that you'd be happy to help."

Dave had said no such thing, but Otto noticed a change in the woman's expression. He hoped she was warming up to him.

"What do you want to know?" she asked.

"How is worshiping Santa Muerte different than worshiping like a traditional Catholic?" Otto could tell instantly that he'd gotten off to a bad start. When Otto asked his question her face pinched with anger, and she sat up straight in her chair, crossing her arms over her chest like an angry child.

Dave intervened quickly. "This is why I brought Otto here. So you could explain to him. So he doesn't have bad information."

"I'm a God-fearing Catholic just like anybody else. Santa Muerte is a saint, just like any other saint. If you know anything about Catholics, you know our saints do jobs for us. Santa Muerte's job is to keep you safe. You say prayers for safety." She jerked her head in the direction of the back of the house where her son was now yelling at the toddlers. "Timmy prays to her to keep him from getting sick like his old man. Santa Muerte keeps the kids safe when they go off to school. All kinds of bad things happen in life. You need some extra help in life to make it through to another day."

The oxygen tank clicked and hissed and Otto noticed the man staring intently at his wife as she talked.

"Is she a saint that you could learn about here in Artemis, at St. Anne's?"

She made a face and swatted at a fly buzzing slowly around the table. "Bunch of snobs. If you don't pack the coffers each Sunday, they don't want nothing to do with you."

"Is there a church where you can go and worship Santa Muerte?"

She gave him an exasperated look. "She ain't a religion. She's a saint. Just like any other saint."

Except the Catholic Church refuses to recognize her, he thought.

"Do you know of any other followers in Artemis?"

She puffed air from her lips, obviously irritated by the questions, and her eyes wandered over to the solitaire game her son had been playing.

To keep her attention, Otto pulled the baggie out of his shirt pocket and held it up to Bea.

"What's that?"

"An artist named CC makes these necklaces. Do you recognize this one?"

"Do I look like the kind to buy jewelry?" she said.

"Any chance you or your family know someone who might wear this kind of necklace?"

She laughed and looked at Otto as if he had a third eye. "My boys don't wear jewelry. You're barking up the wrong tree."

Otto gave up. He thanked the Conroys for their time and he and Dave left.

On the drive back to the elementary school Dave was quiet.

"I appreciate you taking me to your parents' home," Otto said.

Dave glanced away from the road at Otto, and offered a sad smile. "Were you close to your parents?" he asked.

"I don't know about close. Even as a young boy my parents were distant to me. I'm afraid I was a disappointment to them."

"How so?"

"I was raised in a small village in Poland. My parents wanted me to come to America to become a doctor. I tried but it just wasn't in me." Otto shrugged, the old melancholy never far away. "Delores and I went back home but," he paused, searching for the words that would describe his homeland, his family. "Home was never the same. I could see it in my parents' eyes. So Delores and I moved back here to raise our own family. We became citizens and left Poland for good. It was a heart-wrenching decision, but the right one for us."

Dave nodded at Otto, acknowledging the story. Dave was a man with a perpetual positive attitude, and Otto was surprised at the sadness now in his eyes.

"For reasons I'll never completely understand, I'm a disappointment as well. I never fit in with my family," Dave said. "I'm like that old kids' story. The ugly duckling. When I was in elementary school, I fantasized about switched-at-birth scenarios. I imagined doctors in white coats knocking at our door and explaining it had all been a mistake, that I actually belonged to a different family. And they'd drive me to a house in the suburbs. My new mom would bake cookies and my dad would pitch a baseball to me in the backyard." He glanced at Otto again. "Pretty sick, huh?"

"I don't think that fantasy is sick at all. It's called coping. By the time you get to be my age you realize there aren't good or bad families. They're pretty much all screwed up in one way or another."

EIGHTEEN

Josie arrived at Wally's Folly at a little after three in the afternoon with an agenda. It was important that Hec trust her, but it was even more important for him to understand the danger he was in. Having no kids of her own, she could only guess at his mental state, and she hoped he would realize her intention was to help.

She pulled up in front and warily got out of her car, watching the chain press into the growling Rottweiler's neck as it strained to reach her. The chain looked securely wrapped around a metal laundry pole, but just in case, she placed a hand on the Beretta in her belt and slammed her car door.

Josie peered to the back of the salvage yard. The Rio flowed far enough down the bank that she couldn't see whether anyone was on the other side of the river keeping tabs on Hec. She walked up the stairs to the trailer door and knocked.

Hec opened the flimsy metal door, but left the screen door latched. Josie knew it would take little more than a strong kick to gain entrance. It seemed such inadequate protection against the danger he was facing. Hec squinted at her as if the sun hurt his eyes. Josie thought he looked even more pale than the last time she saw him. He said nothing.

"How's it going?" she asked.

He lifted a shoulder and tilted his head in response.

"I need to talk with you, Hec. Can you come outside a minute?"

He unlatched the screen and pulled both doors closed behind him, setting off the dog again. At the bottom of the steps Hec turned toward the Rottweiler, straining on his leash and whining for Hec's attention. The doghouse was located under a tree at one end of the trailer, but the chain kept the dog about fifteen feet from the front door.

"Is he friendly?"

"He's never snapped at me. People say they're mean dogs, but he's got a good nature about him." Hec kneeled in the dirt and buried his head in the dog's neck. "Come here, Buck. Come here. That's a good dog." He finally stood and noticed that Josie was watching him.

"My dad's still not here."

"I know, Hec."

"So why are you here again?"

"I think it's time you made some choices. I think you're in a really bad place, and you need help. I know I'm a cop, probably the last person you want to trust, but I'm here to try and make things better."

"Why?"

"Why do you need help?" she said.

"No. I mean, why do you want to help me?"

"I'm a cop, Hec. It's my job to help people when they're in trouble. It's not all handcuffs and tickets and mug shots. What I want is to help you sort out things. And I'm afraid if you don't let me, there'll be bad trouble. Real trouble, not just threats. I'm not here to screw you over, but I'm afraid other people might be."

Hec didn't respond. Josie noticed a bead of sweat rolling down his temple and continued. "I'm going to tell you what I know, and I hope you'll do the same," she said. "Maybe between the two of us we can figure out a solution. Is that a deal?"

He studied her. "Maybe."

She nodded slowly. "Okay. That's fair enough."

Josie pointed to a picnic table under the tree that also provided shade for the dog. The table was located on the other side of the doghouse, just a few feet out of the dog's reach. He was lying down and quiet now, but his eyes still tracked Josie's movements.

"Mind if we sit down?"

Hec glanced toward the river before walking to the table and taking a seat. He was probably worried someone would see the police car in his driveway. The rows of cars and parts and the sloping riverbank kept Josie from seeing the water. She wondered if the Mexican men Marta had watched were watching them now. The thought made her uneasy.

Josie noted that he hadn't offered her a drink this time. Something had changed. She laid out everything she knew, starting with Christina's death, Dillon's kidnapping, the indictment from the federal court. Hec's attention became more focused the longer she talked. His expression became animated as she described in detail what she found when she walked into Dillon's office, including the missing business files for Wally Follet. When she went on to describe the summons to federal court, Hec asked her what that meant. She finally had his attention.

"The court sent Dillon a letter stating that he was required to attend your dad's trial. He was required to bring the files for your business to the trial as evidence."

"But my dad's gone. They can't have a trial without him."

"They can. It's called 'in absentia.' That means, even though your dad isn't here, the district attorney will still prosecute him, still go ahead with the trial."

"So, if they find him guilty, then when they find him, he'll automatically go to jail?"

She nodded.

"Is that why Dillon was kidnapped? To keep the files away from the prosecutor?"

His question caught her off guard. She had dropped that theory after talking with Assistant DA Gary Hardner. He had assured her the files were a minor component of the case; Wally Follet would be convicted with or without them. Could Dillon have been kidnapped to keep him from testifying? Could the ransom be a foil, something to sidetrack the investigation?

And then she remembered Hardner's description of Hec, as someone who wasn't smart enough to steal a pack of bubble gum. Hardner had misjudged this kid by a long shot. What if Hardner was wrong about the importance of the files as well?

"Do you think there are files that the kidnapper wouldn't have wanted the prosecutor to see?" she asked.

Hec became very still, like a rabbit caught in a trap. "I don't think so. No."

He was lying; she could feel it in his slow reaction time.

"Hec, we know that there are men camping out, just over the river, watching you."

He sat hunched over the table motionless and looking down, his arms crossed in front of him, his jaw rigid.

"Those men are after something. Is it your dad they want?"

Nothing. He looked at the table, but behind the stare Josie could sense his mind was racing.

She slapped her hand down on the wooden table and the noise startled him. "I'm trying to help you!" Josie dropped her voice, but her tone was angry. "The men across the river? They won't let this go until they get what they want."

Her phone buzzed in her pocket. Hec remained hunched over the table, running a fingernail through the grooves in the wood as Josie flipped the phone open and walked away from the table, frustrated at the interruption.

"Chief Gray."

"Just checking in." Otto's voice came through the phone.

Josie huffed in response. "I'm with Hec at the salvage yard. The kid's driving me crazy. He's so sure we're out to screw him or his dad over that he won't budge. He's terrified, but he won't give me anything."

"We need to get him out of there. Maybe he'd open up."

Josie looked back over her shoulder and saw Hec sitting on the ground, his dog's two front paws on his lap, licking the side of his face.

"Your place?" she asked.

"I was thinking the exact same thing. I'll call Delores. See what you can do."

Delores waited for the second ring of the phone. It was an old habit she'd learned from her mother; a person never wanted to appear too eager.

"Delores?"

It was Otto. He always first asked her name when he called, as if there was some question as to who might be on the other end of the line. They had been married forty years. Their only child, Mina, had left home almost twenty years ago. She always wondered who else he expected to answer their phone.

"Hello, Otto. How's your day so far?"

"I have a favor. The Follet boy I mentioned, Hector Follet?"

"Yes, I remember."

"He's got big trouble. I'd like to bring him to the house for dinner. Along with Josie. We need to get him away from that salvage yard. There are men sitting across the river in Mexico watching him, breathing down the kid's back like vultures."

"You tell me when, and I'll have supper waiting."

"I'll call you."

Delores hung up the phone and stood in the kitchen, running through a mental inventory of the cuts of meat in the freezer and the vegetables she could pair with them. If Otto said two people were coming to dinner it often meant six. She always fixed extra as a precaution.

The garlic and onions were fresh, and she had a bag of potatoes in the pantry, so in the end she decided on a standing rib roast. As she pulled the roasting pan from the bottom shelf of the pantry she thought about Mina. She and Mike and their two kids lived in Odessa, too far away for a quick visit or Sunday dinners. A visit had to be an overnight thing, harder to make time for. Delores missed cooking for the family. Growing up in a Polish household with nine kids, she had spent many hours in front of the kitchen stove with her mother. Poor Otto paid the price now. She knew he had little will-power, but she couldn't resist baking the cakes and conjuring up the dumplings and stews of her childhood.

Delores plopped the five-pound bag of potatoes on the counter and began washing and peeling. Her thoughts drifted to Hector Follet. Delores knew the boy's father, Wally. He'd actually once dated, if you could call it that, the daughter of Delores's friend. Sheila Gordon was a nice girl but clearly had no common sense when it came to men. She had been smitten, and it had just about sent her mother to an early grave.

Delores had told Sheila's mother, Maggie, "It's probably the boy Sheila's fond of. She probably feels sorry for him, and wants to give him a good home." Delores would never forget the appalled look on Maggie's face. "It's not the boy. It's him. That man! Sheila says she's in love. I didn't raise her this way. The man is a degenerate. He sleeps around with any woman who will have him. He neglects that boy. He's practically let the boy raise himself." Maggie had lowered her voice to barely above a whisper, as if too humiliated to hear the words spoken aloud. "He stays all night at Sheila's house and lets his son stay home alone. What kind of father does that? And my daughter? Allowing it!?"

This had been two years ago. Hector had been in high school then. Delores wondered if Sheila had ever gotten herself straightened out. In the notepad on the counter by the kitchen phone she scribbled, *Call Maggie*.

When Josie returned to the picnic table, Hector came back to join her. He'd lost the smile he'd had when petting the dog. He looked miserable again. He looked ill.

"Okay. Here's what I'd like to do," Josie said. "I'd like to get you away from this place for the evening. I suspect you haven't left the yard since your dad left."

"I can't leave."

"Because of the men at the river?"

He closed his eyes and nodded once.

Josie was shocked. It was the first time he'd actually admitted the men were down there. "Do you know how many men?"

"There's usually two."

"Can you see them from here, at the trailer?"

He glanced toward the river and shook his head. "When some-one pulls up they disappear. As soon as your car leaves they'll park their pickup truck right across the river where I can see it."

"I have an idea. Come with me."

He stood, looking at her in surprise, and followed her to the jeep. She got a plastic bag containing something from the gun shop out of her backseat. "Can we go inside your trailer?"

Josie followed him inside and dumped the contents of the bag onto his coffee table. She wanted to ask him to open a few windows. The living room was still neat, but it smelled like sour milk. It smelled like the house of someone who lived in fear, too afraid even to open the doors for fresh air.

"I bought these yesterday for my own house," she said. "They're timer switches that connect to lamps. You program them to turn on and off at various times so that it looks as if you're home."

Hec grinned. "That's pretty slick."

"We can install these on a couple of your lamps, and you're free for a night." She could see the question beginning to form in his eyes. "You don't need to drive. You ride with me. I was talking to a friend of mine on the phone a minute ago. His wife, Delores? She's the best cook I've ever met. She wants to make dinner for all of us. She knows your situation. She wants to make you dinner, give you a little vacation. What do you say?"

The words caught in her throat. Josie guessed it had been a long time since Hector had been treated that way. Otto had told her that Hec's mom had left when he was in the third grade; about the same age that Josie had been when her dad was killed. It made her sud-denly very sad for him, knowing how much her own loss had cost her growing up.

Josie could see in his face that he was conflicted: leave and face the possible wrath of the men across the river? Leave and possibly miss his father's phone call or visit? Or stay and spend one more night suffocating between the walls of the trailer?

"You'll bring me home tonight?"

"Whatever time you want. We can park down at the Rio Camp and Kayak and you can walk back to your trailer so you don't have cars showing up late at night. I'll walk with you to make sure you get home safe."

With his eyebrows still knitted together in worry, he finally agreed.

———

After installing the timers, Hec backed out of the front of the trailer, positioning a small rubber ball just inside the door so that when he arrived home, he could tell if anyone had opened the door. Josie wondered who he thought might enter his home while he was gone: his dad, maybe a business partner his dad had screwed over, the men by the river, or the cartel coming back to finish what they had started?

Josie dropped off Hec at the police station and Otto drove him home to Delores to spend the afternoon there until dinner. Josie worked at the office for an hour, checking e-mails and returning phone calls, both dreading and yearning for contact from the kidnappers. She carried her personal cell phone and the cell phone from the kidnappers at all times, checking them both obsessively throughout the day, but she'd heard nothing since the video of Dillon's slashed arm.

At five o'clock she pulled into her driveway and parked behind Nick Santos, who was unloading suitcases and boxes onto her front porch. The idea of him living in her home for an undetermined time still made her uncomfortable, but she had no doubt it was the correct move to make.

Josie got out of her car and said hello as he made his way by her and back to his shiny black Lexus SUV. She followed behind him to help carry his bags. He wore stylish jeans and an untucked button-down shirt that strained the seams around his bulky shoulders. His hair was cut short, neatly trimmed, and his face looked freshly shaved. She could smell the faint trace of a spicy cologne.

"You'll find I'm prompt. When I say five, I'll be here at five. That's just the kind of guy I am."

"I respect that. You should also know that prompt isn't always possible for a police officer," she said.

"So I hear. That's why you guys have such a high divorce rate. Too many pissed-off spouses waiting on dinner for hours on end."

She smiled and considered saying there was no divorce rate for negotiators because they couldn't find a spouse willing to put up with the stresses of the job, but she said nothing.

When they reached the porch Josie asked if he had any news.

"I'm working some leads. Nothing definite yet."

She took the duffle bag he handed her, already suspecting he would be slim on the details unless he had something concrete to provide.

"I received a call from Becka at the security company earlier today. They're completely finished with the house." Josie knocked on the new front door and could hear the density of the steel. It still looked like the wood door that had been replaced, but bullets couldn't penetrate this one. Using the pad to the right of the door, she keyed in the three-digit code Becka had given her and pressed her thumb to a fingerprint reader. She heard the whisk of locking mechanisms releasing and the door popped opened several inches. She raised her eyebrows at Nick, who cocked an eyebrow back at her. "Impressive. Keep Mr. Drench on your good side."

"She showed me how to set you up. We'll get your fingerprint entered and a code so you have access to the house."

Josie walked into the living room, and aside from the smell of fresh paint, she couldn't even tell the security crew had been in her home, let alone running wires through every room in the house and installing doors, locks, and bolts Becka assured would protect her from Armageddon if need be. Josie couldn't imagine how much the job had cost Macon Drench.

Nick left his things in a pile in the living room and pointed at it. "I try to be as invisible as I can. All of my private belongings stay in the bedroom you assign to me. I'm no slob, so you don't need to worry there." He looked slowly around her living room. "Okay. Show me the lay of the house. I want to see all doors and windows."

Josie glanced at her watch and knew she needed to get to Otto's to meet with Hec.

She picked up the duffle bag and carried it down the hallway to the spare bedroom on the left. She gestured toward the open door. "This is where you'll be staying. There's fresh towels and linens on the bureau."

"I brought my own. You'll find I'm very self-sufficient. What about a bathroom?"

"There's a guest half-bath next to your room." She pointed back down the hallway to the left. "There's only one shower though. The access is through my bedroom." She gave him a look, daring him to make the wrong comment.

"When do you leave for work in the morning?" he asked.

"Usually seven to seven thirty."

"That's fine. I'll wait until you've gone for the day."

Relieved they wouldn't be struggling with the same morning schedule, she pointed across the hall to her bedroom. He followed her inside and looked out both bedroom windows, one facing pastureland and the other the driveway back to Dell's.

"That's the old man back there?"

"Dell Seapus. He keeps a good eye on things. He's got his opinions though."

"I got a few myself."

I bet you do, she thought.

Josie pointed into her bathroom. "This is where the shower is." She stood awkwardly back, feeling as if she was exposing herself to a complete stranger.

As they walked back down the hallway she said, "I'm sorry, but I've got to go. We're interviewing a kid whose dad may be connected in some way to the Medranos. We're hoping this may lead to a connection to the kidnappers. It's a long shot, but it's all we've got right now."

"I'd like to come."

Back in the living room, Josie stood over his remaining luggage and turned to face him. She hadn't considered his involvement in the police investigation, and she imagined Otto would not be happy.

"I'll be honest. My partner isn't convinced that working with a negotiator is a good idea."

"You've heard about full-immersion language learning? I'm full-immersion negotiation. I want to meet everyone. Immediately. Dillon's been gone five days now. You've been investigating four with scant leads. We've had two contacts from the kidnappers. I want to be prepared when the third hit comes."

Nick's demeanor was unnerving: eyes so dark the pupils weren't visible, and bicep and pectoral muscles defined well enough to show through his shirt. He was born for law enforcement.

"Okay. That's good, then. I'll call Otto and let him know."

"I'll get acquainted with the house while you make arrangements."

Josie pulled her cell phone out of her pocket and expected resistance from Otto when she explained that Nick would like to tag along.

"I talked with Senator Abilene from Arizona earlier today," Otto said in response. "The senator that Santos negotiated release for?"

"Yes?"

"The senator had me call his wife too. She said she'd be glad to talk to you. She claims Santos saved her husband's life. She said he can be overbearing, but he's a workaholic. And, he knows his stuff."

She sighed with relief. This was Otto's way of conceding, and she was more relieved to have his support than she could have ever expressed to him.

———————

Josie quickly changed into jeans and a sweatshirt while Nick began setting up equipment in the dining room. When she was done, she walked into the room and found him typing on a laptop.

"We're monitoring the e-mail account the kidnappers used to send you the message."

"Don't they block their identity when they send the e-mail?"

"We can track the server from which the e-mail was sent. The problem is, the person or robo-account that sends the e-mail usually isn't associated with the kidnapping. We start small though and work our way up."

"You say *we*. You have other people working for you?"

"Absolutely. I need men on the ground running down information."

"So where do you go from here?" Josie held her breath, hoping for something to focus her energies on.

He turned from the computer to face her. "Keep in mind, I'm called a negotiator, but that's a little misleading. The majority of my time is spent tracking down information that will lead me to the victim." He looked at her and seemed to consider adding more, but turned back to his computer as he continued. "As I said, the money bothers me. I checked databases and several sources yesterday. The last two major ransoms anywhere near this amount were political. But they were in-country."

"You mean Mexico?" Josie leaned against the kitchen counter with her arms crossed, trying to see how this could relate to Dillon.

He nodded, facing her again.

She looked at him blankly. "I don't know what to say. Dillon isn't tied to any political party. I mean he's a Republican, but big deal. It's not like he's tied to any politicians."

"You?" He studied her expression.

"Me?" She laughed. "I'm even less political than he is. I hate politics, from the local to the national. Hate it all. And neither one of us are even remotely connected to politicians in Mexico."

"Let's go back to the money. I don't think I made this clear. I know you don't have nine million. But typically, the kidnappers plan on claiming ten, or at the most, twenty percent of the original ransom amount. So we're talking maybe only nine hundred thousand. A lot more doable."

She laughed again at the absurdity of the conversation. "Doable? I'm a cop in a speck of a town on the Mexican border. I don't have, and will never have, that kind of money. Ever."

He put a hand up. "I get it. What about your friend? Drench?"

"I can't ask him for that kind of money!"

"That's not my point. If the kidnappers see you associated with Drench?" He shrugged.

"Drench is obviously the wealthiest man in Artemis. Maybe in West Texas. But why use me? Why not kidnap his wife?" Her face reddened as she thought of his wife and how Drench didn't tell her about the money. She felt guilty for even mentioning her name.

"You're trying to think like a cop. Kidnapping negotiation is a completely different line of thinking. It isn't about right and wrong. It's not about justice. Not even about revenge. It's about the money. If they think you can lead them to Drench's millions, they choke you out until you deliver."

She stared at Nick, trying to understand what he was saying.

He leaned forward and spoke softly, his raspy voice a stark contrast to the silent house. "Josie. You're a pawn. Wrap your head around that. You're not a cop anymore. Life is seriously messed up, and the sooner you get your head around that reality, the sooner you start coping, making rational decisions."

She struggled to follow him. It felt as if the horizon line was off, as if her entire world had been knocked sideways. She rubbed her temples with her fingertips and stared at him. He was either talking all over the place, or she had lost the ability to focus.

Nick pushed his chair back and walked over to her. He stood directly in front of her and laid his hands on her shoulders, his eyes boring into hers. "I don't know what's going on right now any more than you do. I just want you to realize, your normal way of thinking won't cut it. It's difficult to change your perspective. But I want you to try. Okay?"

She held his stare for a long moment, feeling the intensity of it all, and it was almost more than she could take. He squeezed her shoulders, continuing to stare, then placed a hand on her cheek for a moment, just as quickly removing it, and walked out the front door.

As they drove to Otto's, Josie felt the road pass by her in a ribbon of gray, her head numb. Nick took a call from the head of the Department of Kidnapping and Ransom in Mexico, but did not elaborate once it ended. Josie wanted to grill him for information, but she felt stuck. And without Dillon, she didn't know where to turn for strength. She wondered at the effect that seeing this kind of human tragedy had on Nick.

She drove for quite some time before finally breaking the silence. "So, how does someone with a Bronx accent end up negotiating kidnappings in Mexico?"

He was quiet so long that Josie thought he wasn't going to answer. "I was born in South Texas. My parents were working class. My dad came to the U.S. through the Bracero program in 1963."

Nick looked over at Josie and she nodded, vaguely familiar with the long-ended program to allow Mexican laborers a day pass across the border.

"He was just a kid. But he eventually got his green card and legal residency. My mom was a loud-mouthed, tough-talking kid who lived in his neighborhood. He used to joke that he brought her along as protection. But the truth was they were both outsiders, second-class citizens, and it ate my dad up inside. He wanted his kids to succeed in this country, but then would feel threatened when we came too close to passing him up. He'd get angry and rant in his broken English, *I am the boss of everything!* It's funny thinking about it now, but as kids, that dictator rule was tough. We hated and respected and loved him like—"

Nick paused, lifting his hand in the air as if to indicate he was at a loss for words. He cracked the window and took a minute to continue. "I remember him sitting at the dinner table, wanting seconds of something at the other end. There were eight of us in this toolshed-sized house. He'd sit there, not saying a word, his eyes hard and black. The talk around the table would fade, heads turning one by one down to the head of the table as my mother tried to determine what he was lacking on his plate. We'd pass the potatoes, or whatever, and once he started forking the food back into his mouth, the talk would start again." Nick smiled and shook his head. "That's the effect he had on people. He was a real son of a bitch."

"So, you didn't get along with him growing up?"

"That's an understatement. But I watched him sit by my mother's deathbed for a month, whispering to her, stroking her hair, holding her hand. Praying. We all went to church as a family, except him. He always said we went for him, so he didn't have to. I didn't even know he knew how to pray. Still, the way he took care of my mother in her final month, that was enough for me."

"Did he encourage you to go into law enforcement?"

Nick laughed. "He didn't encourage. That just wasn't part of the culture I grew up in. I joined the military after high school because I didn't know what else to do. I wanted away from home. My brothers joined the family business. We were hired labor by that time, but we were a construction crew with a good name. My family was making decent money, but I wanted out."

"A good move?"

"The military was just a bigger version of my father. After that I worked as a city cop in New Jersey for eight years. By the time I hit thirty I knew I had to be my own boss. Then a friend from Texas was kidnapped, ransomed for fifteen hundred dollars. I negotiated a deal for his wife. That's how this all started."

They drove on in silence, Josie thinking about the events that could shape a person's life, some genetic, some chance, and she wondered if they all added up to a master plan, or just a dark path with no end in sight.

"What about you? How's an attractive young lady end up chief of police on the Mexican border?"

She smiled at his assessment of her and pondered his question for a moment, wondering how to sum up her past to a stranger. But, like Nick, she knew many of her adult decisions were a direct result of her father's influence. "I was eight when my dad died. At that age, your dad hasn't had time to screw you up or let you down like most of us do to those we care about. You know what I mean?"

Nick frowned and shifted in his seat to better face her. "I don't know. I think my dad shaped me into the person I am, but I guess I never thought that he screwed any of us up. He was always black-and-white. He was good and he was bad, to the extreme, but I wouldn't say he screwed us up."

"No, I don't mean it that way." She struggled to find the words that would explain what her father had meant to her as a child. "I didn't have any concept of him as being anything but brave and honorable. When he died, in my eyes, he was a hero. It sounds trite, but that's it. He was a cop. When he got out of his cop car at the end of a shift, wearing his uniform, hand on the butt of his gun as he slammed the car door, I would run outside to meet him. The neighborhood people looked at him different, like from a distance, but in a good way. They'd drink a beer with him on the weekend and treat him like any other guy. But when he was a cop, he was different. And he was my dad."

"He's the reason you became a cop?"

She nodded. "Our next-door neighbor was a son of a bitch. A hard-edged drinker who was pissed at the world. He would take on anybody on any topic and win, by sheer force of will. But when Dad was in uniform, Mike would raise a hand and wave from a distance. He wouldn't even talk to Dad until after he'd changed." Josie grinned at the memory. "Maybe that respect for law is gone now, I don't know. Too many cop shows on TV. But I have this vision of my dad that will never die. And I wanted to be that person."

Josie finally pulled into Otto's driveway and stared out the front window of the car. They remained silent for a minute, both still caught in their pasts. She felt his eyes on her as she shut the engine off.

"I've been doing this a lot of years," he finally said, his voice quiet. "I've worked with people who crumble with the first ransom demand, others who never drop a tear, and everybody in between. I have a good sense for how a person will handle this kind of ordeal."

She looked at him, understanding that he was offering her something, and she realized how desperately she wanted his advice and his strength. Mostly she needed him to give her hope. She wanted him to convince her that he would bring Dillon home safely. That Dillon would survive, get his life back, and that he wouldn't be forever damaged by what he experienced.

"You have the grit to make it through this with your soul in one piece," he said. "But you'll have to trust me."

She nodded.

"Here's what you need to understand. I've seen people at their breaking point, when they think they can't take any more. I'm here to tell you right now . . ." He paused and the intensity of his stare was unnerving. "You can always take more. Always. You listen to me, you do what I say, and you'll make it through this."

Nick held her gaze a moment longer, then turned from her and opened the door. By the time she took it all in, he was already making his way toward Otto's house. She wanted to call after him, tell him to come back. He had said nothing about Dillon. He'd not said that Dillon would make it through this, only her.

NINETEEN

Even though their time together was brief, there were life lessons that Josie learned from her dad, things that he taught her before he was killed. He had been good at math, something she struggled with, especially "story" problems. She could still remember sitting at the table one evening, in tears as she stared at the endless words floating on the assignment page: trains traveling a certain distance at certain speeds with so many stops and breaks and the question of how long it all would take. Her dad had sat down with her and said, "Break it down, Josie." He'd taken her pencil and rewritten the problems on a sheet of notebook paper. Then he had her underline each piece of relevant information, splitting the paragraph into separate pieces that she had to plug into an equation. He'd worked through a half-dozen problems with her, and once she'd begun to understand the process, he'd stood from the table and ruffled her hair. "It's how you fix a car, or build a house. It's how I solve a crime when I'm on the job," he had explained. "You examine all the details, you break them apart, and then you figure out how they all fit back together again. You solve the puzzle." As a cop, she thought often of this moment.

Josie stared into the plate of roast meat and potatoes as conversation among Delores, Otto, Hec, and Nick hummed around her. Like her childhood self, she felt overwhelmed with details. She felt like the puzzle was so jumbled that she couldn't ever pull it all together.

"Josie? Can you help me in the kitchen a minute?"

Josie looked up and saw Delores smiling at her from down the table. Josie scooted her chair back, placed her napkin beside her plate, and followed Delores through the swinging door to the kitchen.

Delores asked Josie to cut the pie on the worktable. She absently picked up the knife, slicing through the warm apples. Delores set down dessert plates beside the pie and turned to face her.

"Josie," she said, hands folded at her chest. "I'm worried about you. I know you're a tough one. I can't even imagine what you must be going through right now. But you have people who care about you. We want to help, but you have to let us. You see?"

Josie felt the lump rise in her throat, unable to reply. Delores's eyes were a watery blue, her face wrinkled and powdered. She squeezed Josie's arm and then began carrying plates of pie into the dining room.

———————

Hec acted as any eighteen-year-old boy might, eating two helpings of everything, including pie and ice cream, and laughing at the stories Otto told about his days as a farm boy in Poland, as if he wasn't caught in the crosshairs of one of the most deadly organizations in Mexico.

After dinner Delores ushered everyone into the living room so she could clean up, refusing offers of help. The Podowski living room was small, packed with a brocade couch and love seat, Delores's rocking chair, and a recliner that Otto settled into from long-standing habit. Nick took the love seat for himself, and Josie and Hec sat on opposite ends of the couch. Each time Josie came to Otto's house she was struck by the warmth that permeated the home, from the meals to the handmade pillows on the couches and the family photos hanging on the living room walls.

Once they were all settled and quiet, Hec became anxious, sitting with both hands tucked between his thighs as if trying to keep them still. He knew what was coming next.

"I hope you've enjoyed the evening, Hec," Otto started. "I want to be clear; everyone in this room wants the best for you. There's no one here looking to trick you or trying to set you up to get information about your dad. We're here because we believe the Medrano cartel is camped out behind your house, openly spying on you." Otto paused. "Is that true?"

"Yes." He didn't hesitate.

"Have they made contact with you?"

"Yes."

It felt as if the air were being sucked out of the room with a vacuum. The room was completely still. Josie was afraid to speak, afraid someone might spook Hec before he shared what else he knew.

"Will you tell us what happened?" Otto asked.

Hec took a deep breath and kept his attention fixed on Otto. "They came to my house. To the trailer. One guy knocked on the door and said he wanted to see one of the cars. That was before I knew anyone was down by the river. I walked outside and they put a gun to my head." Hec pointed to his temple as if he was holding a gun. "Then two guys got on each arm and walked me down to the river. They beat me up pretty good and threw me in a boat. Took me over to Mexico for a week."

"This was before Dillon was kidnapped?" Otto asked.

He nodded.

"They kept you for a *week*?" Josie asked, trying to keep the shock from her voice.

Hec nodded. "Five days. Nobody even knew. When they brought me back home, nobody knew I was gone. Buck almost died. I keep a five-gallon bucket full of water for him. It's a good thing, too. It was all gone. He had no food for five days. He almost starved to death."

Josie looked at Otto, certain he felt the same gut-wrenching guilt she felt, as if they should have known. They should have done something earlier. Legally, Hec was an adult, able to care for himself, but emotionally, after what he had been through? Josie knew many adults who would have already cracked after that kind of pressure.

"Why did they take you?" Otto asked.

He shrugged. "They want my dad. They kept asking me about him, but when Dad left he wouldn't tell me anything. He said if I knew they would beat it out of me. And he was right. That's why they let me go. 'Cause I didn't know anything."

Josie saw Nick shift in his seat, and she could tell he had a problem with that last statement.

"Why else, Hec?" Nick asked. "Why else did they let you go?"

Hec looked down and ran his hands back and forth over his blue jeans, his body rigid as he relived the details of his captivity. "When they shoved me out of the boat, back at the yard, they said I wasn't allowed to leave until my dad came back. They think he'll come back for me. I'm in prison, is what they called it."

"And if you leave the yard, like you did tonight?" Nick asked.

Hec frowned, confirming what they all knew. "They said they'd kill me."

"This has to stop, Hec. You can't go back to the trailer. You can't live like this," Josie said, trying in vain to keep the emotion from her voice.

His eyes widened. "I have to go back. They'll kill my dad. If I don't follow the rules, they'll kill him."

"Do they know where he is now?" she asked.

He gave her a frustrated look. "No. But if they find him they'll kill him!"

Otto changed tactics. "Okay, it's obvious your dad had a business relationship with the Medranos. Is that correct?"

He nodded.

"Is that who took you to Mexico and kept you for a week?"

"Yes."

"You have to help us understand here, Hec. A woman is dead.

Dillon Reese has been missing for several days, and they won't ship him back like they did you. They want nine million dollars before they'll return him home."

Hec nodded again, his hands clasped between his thighs again.

"So far, the only thing that connects Dillon Reese to the Medrano cartel is your dad," Josie said. "Help us understand what's going on here. You can help us save his life."

He nodded again and licked his lips, clearly nervous.

"Hec," Otto said. "You aren't going to get into trouble for what you tell us. I give you my word. And, it can't hurt your dad. At this point, the only hope he has is if the police intervene. If the Medranos get to him first, what do you think will happen?"

"Okay. I know. I see what you're saying. I'll tell you. Everything, I swear it."

Josie watched Nick slide his cell phone from his pants pocket as if checking for a text. He then looked up and caught Josie's eye. *He's taping*, she thought. They wouldn't be able to use it as evidence, but at least they'd catch the details.

"So, you know Medrano has drug rings in Houston and Atlanta?" Hec said.

Hec made eye contact with the three officers, who just stared back at him, shocked that he would know that kind of detail. The location of a particular cartel's drug rings wasn't common knowledge. *What a way to begin*, thought Josie.

"They have a lot of cash to ship across the border, from the U.S. to Mexico. Like, bills I mean. Fives and tens and twenty-dollar bills." Hec looked at them as if they ought to be catching on at this point. "Because the people that buy the drugs pay with small bills, right? So they're making millions of dollars selling drugs, but the money is coming in small bills. See what I mean?" Hec blinked and glanced around the room as if to communicate that was the revelation.

They nodded again, and Josie noticed a grin forming on Nick's face.

"I should have seen this coming," Nick said. "It's a lucrative business in Mexico. Cartels can't take suitcases full of cash into banks and deposit the money. Not like back in the eighties, in the *Miami Vice* days."

He looked at Hec. "You mind if I fill in some details here?"

Hec nodded again and relaxed somewhat, apparently glad for the help.

"In Florida, the Colombian drug dealers would take suitcases filled with millions in small bills into the banks for deposit. When the feds realized and intervened, the banking industry made a rule that any cash deposit of more than ten thousand dollars has to be reported to U.S. authorities. It's called a Currency Transaction Report, or CTR."

Just then Delores walked into the living room and Otto motioned for her to have a seat in her rocker. She must have sensed the tension because she said nothing as she sat down.

"So, explain to us what this has to do with your dad," Nick continued. "I thought he was shipping stolen cars to Mexico."

Hec's eyes were wide and bright. He was nodding his head yes, as if to physically give himself the courage to say the words. He finally said, "Dad's a transporter for Medrano. The feds knew Dad was shipping the cars, and they kept trying to prove he was shipping drugs, too. But he wasn't." Hec looked at each of them. "He was shipping cash."

Josie shook her head in amazement. "And he used the bodies of the junked cars. How much cash could he ship in the body of a car?"

"Dad could pack two million easy. Usually three."

Nick Santos laughed out loud and put his palm on his forehead. "Son of a bitch."

Josie looked at Delores, who didn't even seem to notice the swearing. She seemed as intrigued as the rest of them.

And then it all fell into place for Josie, like tumblers clicking as a key turned in a lock. The color drained from her face. "When your dad left, did he take off with a large shipment of money?"

Hec grew still, and he closed his mouth in a tight line. He had to know what was coming.

"Jesus, Hec. Your dad stole from the Medranos?" she asked.

He said nothing, just stared at her.

As Josie turned to Otto, she saw he was thinking the same thing she was. "They set me up, Otto. The cartel kidnapped Dillon so that I would find their goddamned money."

TWENTY

Josie pushed herself up from the couch, shaking with anger. She couldn't speak, afraid the wrong words would come out. She stood for a moment, feeling their eyes on her, Hec's terrified silence. She walked across the living room and out into the cold night, hoping to find something to still the chaotic thoughts spinning through her head.

As she walked down the driveway, furious with Hector, she heard the front door close and dreaded Otto, or worse yet, Delores. She couldn't handle their calm, sensible, rational demeanors. Not now.

She heard footsteps in the gravel, walking quickly behind her, and knew at once it wasn't one of the Podowskis. Nick said nothing as he fell in step beside her. They walked in silence down the road, her heartbeat slowing, her breathing finally returning to normal. She realized that he would say nothing. He got it. He was there and that was enough.

Hec sat awkwardly waiting for someone to make the next move. Nick had followed Josie, and Otto stared at the door like he didn't know what to do about any of it. Delores spoke first. "Come on, Hec. Let's get you a bag packed. Otto'll get the car ready."

Both Otto and Hec looked up at Delores in surprise.

"What do you mean pack a bag?" Hec asked.

"Well, you obviously can't go back to that salvage yard. It's just not safe. Those men have already beaten you once."

His eyes widened. "But she said she'd take me back tonight. Whenever I wanted. Josie said she'd walk back with me."

"Do you want to give them another opportunity? Because if your dad doesn't come back like they want, don't think they're just going to give up. They'll come back for you again!" Delores said.

Otto rubbed both hands over his face like he was scrubbing away dirt. His eyes felt like sandpaper. He feared his wife was about to offer Mina's old bedroom. As much as he wanted to help the kid, he refused to put Delores in danger.

"Hector. Delores is right. I know the plan was to take you back, but can't you see what a bad idea it is for you to stay there?"

"But what about my dog? I can't leave him there."

"We'll go get him. We'll take care of him until you're able to return home with him," Delores said.

Otto shot her a look, and she shot him one back. He could see there would be no discussion. Rottweiler or not, they would be taking in the dog.

"Do you know Manny? Owns Manny's Motel downtown?" Otto asked.

Hector nodded. "Yeah. He comes out to the yard. He fixes up old Mustangs. Buys parts from us."

Otto sighed. "Excellent. Then you know what a good man he is. We can get you a room at Manny's. You won't pay a dime. You can eat your meals at the Hot Tamale."

Hector was thinking, his expression bordering on panic. "But I have things I need. How will I go back to the trailer? I don't have my truck."

"We'll take you first thing in the morning. You'll need to leave your truck for now. With the lights on timers tonight they won't even notice you're missing. Tomorrow morning, we'll pack you up and get you out of there until this is over." Otto glanced at his wife. "I'll call Manny now and set it up."

———•—•———

Driving home from Otto's, Josie remained quiet, the anger inside her over the cartel's manipulation still too hot to touch. When they arrived at her house Nick excused himself to the spare bedroom. Josie listened to the bedroom door shut and opened the kitchen cabinet for the bottle of bourbon. She unscrewed the cap and smelled the musky sweetness. The anticipation of escape made her hands tremble and relief welled up inside her chest. She poured a glass of the warm amber liquid and drank, shuddering at the first gulp. She felt nauseous almost instantly, and with the second gulp she had to push past her gag reflex. Standing at the kitchen sink, she forced half a glass, shutting her eyes to hold back the tears. When she opened them again Nick was standing in the doorway, watching her.

"That shit's not the answer. I guess you know that," he said.

"What's the answer then? Somebody needs to start giving me some answers pretty damn quick."

"I need you alert."

She drained the glass and slammed it onto the counter. "Alert? What good does alert do when you're a pawn?" She laughed, her voice filled with hate. "You called it. I'll give you that."

"I want to sit down tonight and start on a plan, especially given Hec's information."

"Christina is dead. An innocent bystander. Dillon is enduring god only knows what."

His cautious observation of her made her even angrier. She wanted him to agree with her, to support her fury.

"You know what this means? The message I thought Dillon was sending me? Wrecked? He was forced to say that. Those sadistic bastards planted that information on the tape so that I would hear it, so I would start digging into Wally Follet's business."

"That's typically the way it goes, Josie. The hostage doesn't always get to make up his own plea. He reads from a script."

She shrugged, ignoring him. "It's not like the Medranos could file a police report to get their money back from Follet, right? The cartel can't come barging into the U.S. hunting down a U.S. citizen. So, they set up a foolproof plan. A life in exchange for their cash. And they used a cop to accomplish it. Someone who would investigate, find that bastard Follet and bring him in." She stared at Nick without really seeing him. "Unbelievable." She threw her hands in the air.

He walked over to the counter, picked up the liter of bourbon and twisted on its cap, then slid it across the counter, away from her. "So, what? You shut down? You drink yourself into a corner? Here's what people like you don't get. You're nothing special. This shit happens every day. You think a five-hundred-dollar ransom is any easier for some poverty-stricken wife to handle than a nine-million-dollar ransom is for you? Her husband or son or father is still gone. I've stood in kitchens just like yours, all over Mexico. And in every one of those kitchens the anger and the grief and the pain is so strong I can reach out and touch it. It's thick. You don't drink yourself into a corner, you prepare and you fight back."

He moved to the dining room, taking a seat at the table as he waited for his laptop to power up.

Josie went to her bedroom and sat on the edge of the bed, staring at the floor, still reeling from Nick's words. She finally stood and locked herself into the bathroom. She turned the water on as hot as it would go and let the tub fill up. She peeled off her jeans and threw her sweatshirt into the corner. She stepped closer to the long mirror hanging on the back of the door, staring at her face, at her bloodshot eyes. The black circles under her eyes had darkened since she'd last examined them. She ran her fingers over the thin skin and pressed away the tears in the corners of her eyes.

As she sank into the bathwater, her skin burned from the heat. Closing her eyes, she allowed her thoughts to roam, but they quickly turned to images of Dillon slashed, lying in a pool of blood, not able to comprehend the evil that had been forced on him. She thought about Nick's words: prepare and fight back. It's what she'd been trying to do, but it wasn't enough. What could Dillon do to help himself now? He was an orderly, competent, kind man. But now he would need hatred to sustain himself. Hope was too thin an emotion, too easily lost. She inhaled the steam from the hot water and forced the images of Dillon to fade, imagining herself sinking into black water surrounded by nothing.

Located across the street from the courthouse square in downtown Artemis, Manny's Motel was a six-room establishment with the doors to each room facing the street. The office was located in the center, where a neon green ROOMS FOR RENT sign hung crooked in the front window.

Otto parked his truck in front and Hec grabbed the small suitcase Delores had packed him. She had wanted to come, but Otto had refused. She was already more involved than he was comfortable with.

"Sorry about the slippers. I didn't think you fellas would mind," Manny said as he met Otto and Hec at the front office.

"Slippers are a given. We appreciate you taking us in," Otto said.

Manny pointed toward the door. "To your left. I put you in room six, right next to my apartment."

Manny followed them down the walkway, unlocked door number six, and ushered them inside. He handed Hec the room key, which bore a yellow smiley face sticker on one side.

"You bang on the wall and I'll come straight over. If you need anything? A trip to the grocery or the drug store? All you do is ask and I'll make a run for you. I'm a bored old man with too much time on my hands. Let me do some good for a change."

Hec thanked him and set the suitcase on the bed. He looked around the room, seeming lost. Manny patted him on the back and left.

"This will end, Hec," Otto assured him. "I can't give you a time or date, but you'll get your life back."

Hec looked at the floor and scuffed at the carpet with his toe. "I don't know what my life might be like anymore. I don't know what'll happen with the business. My dad told me we'd sell the yard this year and move somewhere different. We were going to start over again."

Otto wondered how much Hec knew about the missing money, a question that had been nagging him since Hec had spilled the story after dinner. They assumed he was a nice kid who'd been duped by his father, but at eighteen he was an adult, mature enough to potentially have been involved. He could serve time just like his dad. Otto sat down on the wooden chair in front of the writing desk and studied Hec, sizing up the kid's ability to take another conversation. Hec sat down on the edge of the bed. He looked thin and scared and Otto felt a pang of sorrow for the mess Hec was in, but the details were critical.

"I'd like to finish talking about the Medranos and their involvement with your dad if you're up to it."

He nodded. "I didn't mean to keep information. I just didn't know what to do. They said they'd kill my dad."

Otto shook his head. "Chief Gray isn't angry with you, Hec. She understands the terrible place you're in. She's angry that the cartel is using both you and her to get what they want. None of this is your fault, just like it's not hers."

Hec stared at his blue jeans, rubbing at the seams with his thumbs.

"Something doesn't make sense to me, Hec. What happens when the money goes to Mexico? The Mexicans have laws in place for depositing cash too. How is it any different there than here?"

"There's a guy they call the transporter, who we ship the money to in Mexico. Then guys called runners deposit the money into a bunch of different banks. I guess he has a bunch of accounts set up. I don't know what happens to the money after that. I've just listened to my dad on the phone with him."

Otto assumed the money was then wired overseas to a safe account. At that point the money would have been laundered and would be ready to come back to the cartel clean and untraceable, ready for new business.

"Do you know how much your dad makes on a shipment?"

"The transporter pays my dad five thousand for every one million in small bills that he stashes inside the cars and ships to Mexico. He then pays the runners, gets his cut, and the rest goes back to the Medranos." He looked at Otto for quite a while, and appeared to be deciding whether to offer more information.

"Help us understand this, Hec. We need you," Otto prodded him.

"Dad thought he was keeping it a secret from me. He tried to keep me out of it, but I'm not stupid. I knew he was shipping something in those cars, even at the beginning. Then he started shipping more often, every two weeks. I kept telling him that he needed to stop. We needed to sell out and leave before he got caught." Hec looked at Otto, incredulous at his dad's stupidity. "Then he started shipping stolen cars! Why would he do that? He made ten to fifteen thousand dollars every two weeks. We weren't even spending the money. I don't even know what the money went toward, but it's like he thought it wasn't enough."

Otto said, "Then the feds showed up asking questions. They thought your dad was selling drugs but they couldn't prove it. Instead, they got him on the stolen cars."

Hec nodded.

"But the feds don't realize the bigger scam. That your dad is shipping cash for the Medranos."

"Dad got a call from two different car dealers in Texas, telling him that the feds were asking questions about the stolen cars. I told him then, just stop. We don't need that much money. Our business was fine the way it was. Then, he heard they were going to indict him and he freaked out."

"So, when your dad heard about the indictment, he took a load that was intended for shipment and left town?"

"He took nine million dollars in cash. It's stuffed into three suitcases. I begged him not to do it. He didn't care. He tried to get me to come with him, but I said no. I didn't want that money. But now things have gotten so screwed up."

"Has he contacted you?"

Hec shook his head, no, but Otto could tell that he was lying.

The kid's face was like a road map. He couldn't lie to save his life. Probably why his dad hadn't told him anything when he left.

"That's all I know. I don't know if he's coming back. I don't know where the money is. I just know that everyone wants my dad dead."

TWENTY-ONE

At 7:00 A.M., Josie stopped by the office to check in with Brian Moore, the night dispatcher. She informed him she was headed to Marfa to meet with Jimmy Dare, a Border Patrol agent and long-time friend. At the corner gas station she grabbed a black coffee and filled up for the fifty-mile drive through desert country. She had left early to take the back roads, following River Road north out of Artemis to Ruidosa, a ghost town along the Rio Grande, and then turning right onto Pinto Canyon Road. This was one of her favorite drives in all of West Texas; it was scenic and isolated.

The first few miles were a dusty gravel road that meandered through ranch land, but the farther north she traveled the tighter the curves became, zigzagging a rugged path up into the Chinati Mountains. Coming around a bend she saw a small herd of javelina racing across the road and hit the brakes hard, her back tires spinning out in the loose gravel. Josie stopped the jeep and watched them scurry around a patch of mesquite and prickly pear cactus, each perched on dainty hooved feet that looked as if they couldn't possibly hold the weight of their large bodies and heads. She rolled down her window to let the cool air into the jeep, already warming in the bright morning sunlight. When they sensed she meant them no harm, the javelina came out into the open again, foraging in the dirt and around the bushes for food.

She finally hit pavement again for the last thirty miles into Marfa, where the headquarters for the Big Bend Border Patrol Sector was located. The sector covered over 135,000 square miles of Texas and Oklahoma, the largest area of any sector on the southwest border. The Big Bend Sector was responsible for over 510 miles of border along the Rio Grande River, almost a quarter of the country's border with Mexico.

As she pulled into the small headquarters parking lot, Josie spotted Jimmy standing and talking to a state trooper in a marked black-and-white car. She pulled in several spaces away to give Jimmy time to finish his conversation, and she radioed her location. Jimmy noticed her jeep shortly after and walked over.

She got out of her car and he approached with his hand extended, a look of concern on his usually smiling face. "I am sorry as hell to hear about what happened. Any leads on the kidnapping?" Jimmy wore the customary dark green Border Patrol uniform and a gun belt with a .40 caliber pistol and several clips hanging from the side.

"You won't even believe it. That's why I'm here."

"Absolutely. Let's get out of the heat. It's supposed to be upper eighties by this afternoon. We're about to skip spring and head right into summer."

As they walked into the building Josie said, "Congratulations on the promotion. Supervisory patrol agent?"

He shrugged like it was no big deal but gave her a wide smile. "Hell, it's just more paperwork. I don't know what I was thinking."

Trimly built, with a strong, capable bearing, Jimmy was one of the friendliest officers she knew, but he could turn aggressive in a heartbeat. He had worked with her almost two years ago when they had apprehended several vehicles crossing the Rio carrying enough ammunition and explosives to blow up the entire town. She had a great deal of respect for his abilities and knew his knowledge of the cartel situation along the Tex-Mex border would be especially helpful.

Josie followed Jimmy into his office and sat across the desk from him. It was a small, brightly lit room lined with bookshelves filled with various colored binders. His desk was neatly organized, and he picked up a pen that lay on a blank legal pad for note-taking.

"I was set up, Jimmy." Her throat constricted, and she looked away from him. She took a deep breath, angry at her emotional reaction.

Jimmy stood suddenly from behind his desk. "Where the hell are my manners? Let me get us both a coffee. Black?"

She nodded and he left the office. She closed her eyes, breathing deeply, taking the images of Dillon and filing them away for later. *Compartmentalize,* she told herself.

A few minutes later, Jimmy sat a cup in front of her and resumed his seat. "It's pretty strong, but I've had worse." He looked at her expectantly as she took a sip.

"Thanks, Jimmy. I'm just so pissed off right now. I've got this crazy, out-of-control anger that I've never had in my life."

"Tell me what's going on."

She stared down into the steaming coffee in the Styrofoam cup, and forced herself to consider Dillon as she would any other victim. She took a deep breath and exhaled, finally looking up at Jimmy.

"You know the ransom demand for Dillon is nine million dollars?"

"Yes."

"And they demanded fifty thousand by yesterday evening or they said Dillon would lose an arm."

He nodded.

"Okay. I'm working with a kidnapping negotiator who had prepared me. He said paying the kidnapper's first demand would be a huge mistake. It basically tells them that I have money. He also told me they would slash Dillon so that there was blood, enough that Dillon would cry out in pain."

Jimmy winced, having no doubt where the conversation was headed.

"I received a video clip from the kidnappers via email. They slit his arm open. He screamed out as the negotiator said he would. The intent was obviously to get me to take them seriously."

Jimmy's expression hardened, and he began to jot notes on the legal pad. "As if you weren't taking it seriously enough as it was."

"Here's the kicker though. On that same video, Dillon asked why I didn't send the money. He said his life was wrecked."

Jimmy glanced up.

"I thought he was sending me a clue with that wording. We found out that one of Dillon's clients is Wally Follet. He's been indicted for selling wrecked and stolen cars across the border. The Mexicans buy them, fix them up, and resell them with a clean title."

"Yeah, I know the case. We're pretty sure he's transporting drugs, but we can't pin him on it."

"It's not drugs. He's transporting cash. Millions of dollars in small bills that the cartel can't deposit in the U.S. because of banking regulations. So Wally hides the money in the frames of old junk cars and ships it across the border. Then a transporter for the Medranos—"

Jimmy finished the sentence for her. "Uses runners to deposit the money in banks throughout Mexico. Son of a bitch." He shook his head, his expression incredulous. "Wally Follet got himself mixed up with the Medranos."

"What can you tell me about the Medranos and money laundering?"

"It's not just the Medrano cartel. You ever hear of the Black Market Peso Exchange?"

Josie frowned. "The term's familiar, but that's about it."

Jimmy grinned. "It's ingenious. When people think of the cartels they think of drugs and guns. But there's a money side too, a totally separate business."

Jimmy pushed his legal pad across the desk, toward Josie. He drew a diagonal line across the paper and labeled one side *U.S.* and the other *Mexico*.

"It started with the Columbians, but it's widely used in Mexico now, too. Basically, there's all this cash that something has to be done with. In the early days, the cash was actually a problem. So some entrepreneur figured out how he could turn the cash into a money-making scheme. It's basically laundering drug money and then putting it back into the economy."

She nodded toward the pad. "Okay. Go ahead."

Jimmy pointed to Mexico with the tip of his pen. "The drugs are manufactured here. Smuggled into the U.S. and farmed out to big-time dealers in key distribution sites like L.A. and Houston. Those dealers get paid a cut to ship out the drugs to small-time, Joe Blow dealers all over the U.S." He tapped his pen on random places on the U.S. side. "The dope gets parceled out, eventually sold on the street in return for cash. Tens and twenties. Maybe fifties and hundreds. So what happens to the cash?"

"Joe Blow takes his cut and trades the rest in for more drugs."

"Exactly. Meanwhile, millions of dollars of cash are flowing through the system, back up to our big-time dealers. They sure as hell can't deposit that money in a U.S. bank. So our big-time dealers contract with someone locally to ship the cash to Mexico, just like you're saying Wally Follet is doing. The money gets converted into pesos, then bought by U.S. businesses at a cheap exchange rate. Clean money, almost impossible to trace."

Josie considered Jimmy's explanation. "That's a lot of different people dealing with a lot of money."

"Exactly. That's why the cartels rule with guns and murder. Too many people step out of line and the cartels lose their empire. But they don't allow that to happen."

"Evidently, Wally Follet figured out how to make it happen," she said. "His son admitted that his dad took nine million dollars in cash and left town. That's how I got involved. The Medranos kidnapped Dillon and put a nine-million-dollar ransom on his life so that I'd go hunt down Wally Follet and deliver him in exchange."

Jimmy's expression changed, as if he was finally understanding the magnitude of what she was saying.

"So what happens when someone like Wally Follet screws over the Medranos?" she asked.

Jimmy frowned deeply and sipped his coffee, looking at Josie as if trying to censor his words. He finally said, "The Medranos can't afford to let Wally go unpunished. If it's that easy to steal several million dollars from them, then the Medranos appear weak. This is a major breach in their system and they have to settle the score. Wally's a dead man."

———————

After the ride back, Josie walked into the office and found Otto on the phone.

She sat down at her desk and opened the notes she'd been keeping on the case. She began typing up her thoughts on her conversation with Jimmy, and then stopped to scroll back to her original ideas about Christina Handley's murder. She had written that Otto believed her murder was tied to the kidnappers, but Josie had a line of question marks after that statement.

Otto hung up and turned his chair to face Josie. "What's the word?"

Josie rubbed at her bottom lip, staring at Otto and sorting through her thoughts. "I met with Jimmy Dare this morning." After Josie quickly summarized her conversation with Jimmy, she gave her own analysis. "Here's my issue. The cartel would have never taken such a bad shot and left Christina's death to chance. Someone not only took a bad shot, but they also took the time to rifle through her purse, find the keys, turn out the lights, and lock the door on their way out. That's not the work of the Medranos."

"Who else makes sense? Who else had the motivation to kill her?"

"Let's talk about that. The feds don't know that Wally was working directly for the Medranos in a money-laundering scheme, right? They suspect he's involved in a drug- or gun-running ring, but Hardner said they couldn't find evidence. What if Wally went to the office the night Dillon was kidnapped to get the records before the feds could get to them? Hec said that his dad had been tipped off about the indictment. Maybe he believed those records could implicate him and Hec somehow."

"So he calls Christina and gets her to meet him at the office that night. He gets the records and shoots her because she knows too much," Otto continued her line of thought for her. "But how does he know to go that night? He just happens to show up the night Dillon was kidnapped?"

"Maybe. Or, maybe Hec is lying. Maybe Hec is in contact with his dad. He could have called him, told him about the kidnapping. Wally could have thought things were going to speed up with his indictment. He'd want to get in the office immediately and get the records."

Otto squinted at Josie as if he were trying to see it all more clearly. "But how would Hec have known about the kidnapping? Christina was shot just a few hours after Dillon was taken."

"Maybe the Medranos told Hec about the kidnapping. Maybe they came by the trailer again to rough him up, increase the pressure on Hec to find his dad. If your dad doesn't bring back our money, this is what's going to happen to you."

Otto tilted his head, conceding the point.

Josie pushed her chair away from her desk in frustration. "I think it's time to pressure Hector. I have a gut feeling that he knows more than he's telling us. He's scared and he's got the cops telling him one thing, his dad probably telling him another, and the cartel threatening to kill him."

"Agreed."

Josie glanced at her watch; it was just a little before noon. "I'm going to run home and talk to Nick. Ask him to go with me. I still don't think Hec understands just how bad the Medranos are. I want him to understand what a cartel kidnapping means."

Twenty minutes later Josie pulled into her driveway and shut off the jeep. The sun shone directly overhead, heating up the desert, an indication that summer was just around the corner. She kept her sunglasses on and scanned the area. Chester was nowhere in sight, most likely asleep on Dell's front porch, where he could be shaded from the heat of the day. She pressed her thumb against the quarter-sized fingerprint reader and then pushed the code into the keypad next to her front door, still slightly awed at the quiet clicks of the door opening for her entrance.

She found Nick sitting at the dining room table with a cell phone clamped between his ear and his shoulder, typing something into his computer.

He gestured with his elbow toward the empty seat across from him and Josie sat down. He spoke in Spanish for several minutes on the phone before hanging up. His eyes were wide and unblinking. He sat back in his seat and studied her for a moment. "Look, about what I said to you last night. I was too harsh, and I'm sorry."

"You have a lead?" she asked, pointing toward the computer, unwilling to rehash the night before.

He seemed to consider continuing with the apology, but finally nodded once and dropped it. He said, "I went to visit Hec first thing this morning at the motel. He talked me through every detail he could think of about his beating and the house he stayed in while they kept him in Mexico." He paused and gave Josie a cautious look. "My team has been collecting information about a neighborhood in Piedra Labrada. It's too early to tell, but it sounds like it may be the same area where Hec was held. There's a chance."

Josie's eyes widened and he lifted both hands up as if stopping her from moving forward. "Look. I just said, it's a chance. It's a lead at this point. Nothing more. It's way too early for hope."

She nodded.

"You obviously didn't come here looking for an apology from me. So what's up?"

"What kind of lead? From where?"

His face softened. "I shouldn't have told you that. You don't share every lead with a family during an investigation, right?"

She said nothing.

"I don't share information until I find something tangible, something I know won't fall apart. Otherwise, I'd spend all my time soothing the family's fears and insecurities rather than focusing on the job at hand." He seemed to notice the anger beginning to form in her expression and he stood from his chair. "Damn it." He opened the refrigerator and pulled out a jug of orange juice that he had evidently bought that day and took a swig from the jug. He finally turned to face her again. "Look. I am sorry for last night, for losing my patience with you. It was unprofessional. I'm struggling to separate the cop from the victim." He looked around the room as if trying to figure out how to explain his approach. "You're like the coach's kid. I expect more of you than other victims, just because you're a cop."

Josie watched him put away the orange juice and thought about his reasoning for not filling her in on developing leads. She knew he was handling it the right way. He turned and leaned against the refrigerator, crossing his arms over his chest. He wore a black T-shirt and dark jeans, and a line of sweat had formed across his forehead.

"An informant dropped in on a working-class area in Piedra Labrada about three months ago," he said, giving in. "He claimed there's a safe house there that may be tied to the Medranos."

Josie kept her face impassive, willing her heart to beat steadily in her chest.

"We don't even have a street, Josie, so don't get too excited. For now, that's all I know. I'll keep you posted," he said.

She nodded, not wanting to leave the conversation, but she was certain that Nick would provide nothing more. "I want to put some pressure on Hec. We've been nice, we've given him ample time to come clean with us. But I've run out of patience."

Nick raised an eyebrow at her.

She lifted her hand in response, smiling in spite of her irritation. "I get it. You were making a point with me last night. You'd obviously lost patience. The difference is, I'm not withholding information."

"True enough. But your attitude is everything. I can't have you off your game."

Josie ignored his comment. "I'd like you to come with me to talk to Hec. You're a negotiator. You know kidnappings, it's your job. And I could tell that Hec was impressed with you last night at Otto's. I watched him hang on every word you said. I'd like you to tell him what long-term kidnappings are like. As bad as it was, Hec was only abducted for a week. I don't know if he understands the urgency of getting Dillon back."

"I can scare the shit out of him if that's what you want."

"I just want him to know the truth. I want him to understand that his reluctance to tell us everything he knows could put Dillon—"

Nick nodded, understanding.

"Otto's picking Hec up at one o'clock. He's going to take him home to pack and get the dog. That should give us enough time to talk with him before Otto gets to the motel."

"Then we need to leave now. I'm going back to Mexico. I'm going to set up surveillance tonight." He paused. "You'll be all right here? By yourself?"

She considered him a moment. "Do you mean, do I plan on drinking myself into the ground tonight?"

He dropped his head and smiled. "All right. That's not what I meant, and I think you know that."

"I think I can handle a night on my own."

He gestured through the living room and toward the front door. "Then let's go beat up on poor Hector."

TWENTY-TWO

Night bled into day inside the hole. There was no schedule, no routine to track the hours and days, nothing but the low hum that buzzed inside his head. The water had stopped. The greasy tortillas had stopped. Hunger had taken the form of cramps that started in his stomach and traveled up his esophagus and into his throat, leaving him hunched into a ball, pressing his crossed arms into his gut. Intermittent convulsions from the cold were followed by numb periods when he could no longer discern his legs from the concrete beneath him. But the hum never left.

At some point Dillon woke and realized the cramps had subsided enough for him to get up off the floor. He forced himself into a sitting position, his spine scraping the concrete wall he leaned against. The black darkness swirled around him, causing rolling bouts of nausea. His lips were cracked and he could taste blood on his tongue. He realized he hadn't heard the bats for some time and wondered if they were dead: only a matter of time before he too would die from starvation. He had thoughts of scavenging for water, any kind of liquid around the edges of the room, but he had no light, no tools, and his strength was gone. He had never felt so hopeless.

Dillon was attempting to stretch his legs out in front of him when the hatch opened above. He cried out in pain from the blinding sunlight, his eyes clenched shut against the needles shooting through his pupils. He heard the rope ladder clank against the side of the hole. With his eyes shut he turned onto his hands and knees and used the wall as support to help him stand, the dizziness so intense that he feared he wouldn't be able to climb up the ladder. He'd been forcing himself to stand regularly, to stretch his muscles so that atrophy wouldn't prevent him from escaping if the time ever presented itself. He realized now that it was dehydration and physical weakness that would prevent his escape.

The men yelled in Spanish, but Dillon was confused and disoriented and couldn't make out the words. He pressed his back and palms against the wall just behind the ladder to steady himself and looked down, focusing on the shadows of the men above him. Their movement caused his stomach to seize up and he dry-heaved, his head pounding. Their shouts grew louder, more insistent, and he reached out for the ladder and began to climb, his muscles like gelatin.

Within two feet of the top, two men's arms dangled over the edge as they lay on their stomachs. Dillon obediently kept his head lowered so he couldn't see their faces. One of them slipped the pillowcase over his head and then each grabbed one of his arms. With no control of his arms and nothing to push against with his feet, Dillon scraped his body against the side of the hole as they hoisted him up and out of it. Once outside, Dillon kneeled, too weak to stand, too confused to process what was happening. Even with the bag over his head, the bright afternoon light caused him to clench his eyes shut in pain.

He heard an engine approach and two men pulled him to his feet. He could feel someone lifting one of his legs and was immensely relieved when he realized pants were being pulled over him, and then a drawstring cinched and tied at his waist. A shirt was pushed down over his head, and he gladly pushed his hands through the arms of a sweatshirt. The warmth of the clothing was like a gift and he found himself close to tears, wanting nothing more than to lie down on the ground, to let the sun warm his skin and soak into his bones.

Instead his arms were fastened behind his back with a plastic cord and he was shoved into the van. He lay on the metal floor and with every last bit of mental strength he could gather, prayed that he was going home.

About fifteen minutes later Dillon felt the van slow and pull into what seemed to be a short driveway. Dillon noted that they had not crossed the river. He was not going home.

———————

"This is a high-impact kidnapping. You know that term?" Nick asked.

Hec shrugged. He sat on the unmade bed in his motel room looking glum and tired. Josie sat in the desk chair across from the bed and Nick stood, pacing the room as he talked.

"There's no bargaining. No negotiating. The Medranos will trade the money your dad stole for Dillon Reese's life."

Hec said nothing.

Nick blew out air in frustration. "Okay. Let me draw you a picture here. The Medranos, they took you for a week, roughed you up, and let you go. Let's talk about long-term kidnappings." He pulled his cell phone out of his shirt pocket and swiped through several screens. "I want to show you a picture of a friend of mine. His name's Dave Mead."

Nick leaned forward and turned the screen around to show Hec.

"Nice-looking guy, right? Smiling, holding hands with his little girl. That's his wife next to him. Nice happy family." Nick took his phone back and swiped his thumb across the screen once and gave it back to Hec. "See that? That's Dave after seven months in a box thanks to the Medranos. Can't even recognize him, can you? That picture was taken by his wife a week after he was returned home. He walks with a permanent limp, still has nightmares that terrorize his whole family. The Medranos? Your dad's business partners? They kept Dave in a wooden box, shaped like a coffin, for seven months."

Hec dropped his head and stared at his tennis shoes.

Nick sat down beside Hec on the bed. He put his lips to Hec's ear. "And you know what the crazy thing is?"

Hec flinched at Nick's breath against his face.

"The crazy thing is, Dave considers himself lucky. For seven months he waited to die. Every single day. They kept him alive, just enough, to send gruesome pictures home to Dave's wife. Every day he waited for them to carry out their threats, or for his body to finally give up the fight." Nick stared at Hector's profile. "Seven months of dying."

Hec still said nothing.

"This is what Dillon is facing unless you help us find that money." Nick swiped at his phone several times, then glanced up at Josie, but she couldn't read his expression. Josie saw Hec close his eyes for a moment and grip the blanket on the edge of the bed. Nick tapped the screen and held it in front of Hec.

As soon as she heard background noise start, Josie knew exactly what Hec was watching. She had studied it herself a hundred times, watching Dillon's body, unaware of what was to come, his head completely covered.

Dillon screamed and the knife turned in her heart one more time, pushing a little deeper. The pain was as real as any physical trauma she'd ever endured. She watched teardrops darken the thighs of Hec's jeans.

"You have to help us save Dillon," she said, her voice barely above a whisper. "I think you've talked to your dad. You have to tell us everything you know. Even if it doesn't seem important, tell us."

Hec sniffed loudly and ran both hands under his nose, one after the other. He stood from the bed and walked to the back of the room, trying to put distance between himself and Josie.

"A man called me the night that Dillon was taken. He said he was a Medrano. He said they kidnapped Dillon and they would take me next if my dad didn't bring back the money."

"Why didn't you tell us that? We wasted days trying to figure out what happened, and you knew all along?" Josie asked.

"They said if I went to the police they'd kill me and they'd kill Dillon! I didn't know what else to do except hope my dad came home."

Josie lowered her voice. "Have you talked to your dad?"

Hec pressed his back against the wall and stared at her as if his world was falling apart. He nodded.

"Do the right thing," Nick said. "Tell us what you know."

"Dad called to check on me while I was in that house in Mexico. I swear, before then I hadn't talked to him. He called the phone at the trailer a bunch of times and thought I was just mad at him and wouldn't answer the phone. He called again the night I came back home. He was pretty upset." Hec's voice was soft, regretful.

Josie couldn't believe what she was hearing. Wally was upset, but not enough to come home and save his own son.

"Then for a while he was calling every day to check on me."

"For a while?" she asked.

He nodded. "Dad called the night they took Dillon and I told him what had happened, about Dillon and the man calling me. I haven't heard from my dad since then." Hec's tone of voice and expression were guarded. Josie couldn't tell if it was anger at his father he was feeling, or dread over the trouble he might be in with the police for withholding information.

"He never gave you a number to get ahold of him?" she asked.

"No."

"Did he give you any indication about where he's staying? Even what state he might be in?" Nick asked.

"He never told me where he was. I swear that's the truth. If I knew where he was I'd tell you."

"Do you have the last phone bill you got in the mail?" Josie asked.

"Yeah, back at the trailer. I already checked. The bill is for last month and doesn't include any of the dates from when Dad left."

The information was a huge break, and Josie didn't want to lose the momentum. She changed her line of questioning to throw him off. "Who else are you in business with?"

"I don't know. My dad takes care of that part."

"I'm not buying that. You're a smart kid. You're observant. You know who your dad works with."

He stared blankly at her.

"Come on, Hec. Enough." Josie was tired of dragging information out of him. She raised her voice. "Your phone records will be subpoenaed. I'll find out every phone call you or your dad made or received over the past year."

"The Conroys."

Josie felt a jolt of recognition at the name, but she kept a neutral expression. "What do they do, Hec?"

"They ship into Mexico."

"I thought your dad did that?" Josie snapped back.

"Dad gets the cars ready and fits the money into the car frames. The Conroys have the big haulers that ship the cars."

Josie and Nick got into the car and she faced him before turning the key. Her heart was pounding.

"Have we told you about the Santa Muerte necklace found at the office?"

He frowned. "No."

"It was found on the floor. The chain in one place, the pendant in another, as if ripped off in a struggle. When Otto was researching what Santa Muerte stands for he discovered there's a family in Artemis that worships her."

"Let me guess. The Conroys."

"Exactly." Josie started the car and pulled away from the motel. "We're getting closer."

She drove Nick back to her house so he could leave for Mexico. He was anxious to set up the surveillance for the night. She then headed back to the police department and found Otto standing by the courthouse entrance talking to Sheriff Martínez.

"You hanging in there, Josie?" Martínez asked. He stood with his hands perched on his gun belt, his barrel chest emphasizing the physical power that served him well as a cop.

"I actually have good news. Hector Follet finally let loose. He said his dad called him at home several times after the Medranos brought Hec back from Mexico. The night Dillon was kidnapped, the Medranos called Hec to threaten him again." Josie smirked.

"Hec said he told his dad about Dillon's kidnapping, and his dad hasn't called him since."

Otto leaned back and raised his eyebrows.

"And guess who ships the cars and cash to Mexico for Wally?" Without waiting for a response she said, "The Conroys."

"Son of a bitch."

"Exactly."

Martínez frowned. "Okay, give me the details."

"Remember Christina Handley was shot from the side, a bad shot from the front of the office?"

Martínez nodded.

"We didn't think the cartel would take that kind of shot. But, at the same time, who else would want Christina dead? Who else would have a motive for killing her?"

"Keep going," Martínez said.

"I think Hec told Wally that Dillon had been kidnapped. Wally lured Christina to the office because he didn't want himself, or his son, connected to the kidnapping."

"But he'd been tipped off about the indictment, right? Didn't Wally know about the subpoena for his records?" Martínez asked. "Why wouldn't he have taken the records before he left?"

"He didn't know about the subpoena. He found out about the indictment, panicked, took the money and ran. We didn't find Dillon's subpoena until after the kidnapping. Wally was long gone by then. When he left, his accounting records were the last of his worries."

Martínez nodded slowly, beginning to piece things together.

"But when Hec told his dad that Dillon had been kidnapped? Everything changed," she said. "All of a sudden, he had to worry the feds were going to figure out he was shipping cash for the Medranos. If the feds implicated Hec somehow, Hec could end up doing serious jail time."

"So Wally came home to get the records and to get his son," Martínez said.

"Exactly," Josie said. "He's already screwed his son's life up. Imagine if Wally had to watch his son do jail time over a part of the business that Hec didn't even agree with."

Otto squinted at Josie and rubbed his chin with his palm. "You think Wally grabbed the files, and then killed Christina to remove the witness," Otto said.

Josie nodded.

"Why wouldn't he just break in and steal the files?" Martínez asked.

"He wouldn't have had any idea where the files were. He needed Christina to find them," she said. "And remember the missing computers? I think Wally took them, too. He wouldn't have had any idea that we'd find files stored online."

Martínez tilted his head. "You think the files were important enough for Wally to risk coming back to town? He's hiding from the police and the Medranos. Pretty big risk."

"Hec said his dad was furious with him for not leaving town. I think Wally is a lousy dad, but I think he loves his son. I think he's worried Hec is going to take the fall for all of his bad decisions. He's probably still hoping Hec will leave town with him. Maybe coming back for Hec and the files was Wally trying to be a good father."

"That's some screwed-up logic," Martínez said. "Especially if he killed Christina as a result."

"How many criminals use rational logic?" she said.

"Touché."

"It gets better," Josie said.

Otto raised his eyebrows in reply.

"The Conroys ship the cars for Wally. He gets the wrecked cars and packs the cash into the frames. The Conroys do the shipping."

Martínez pointed at Josie in recognition. "The Conroys are the locals who follow Santa Muerte. That's the necklace we found beside Christina's desk."

"Exactly."

"After I talked with the Conroys about their involvement with the saint I checked Dillon's records. They're clients of his," Otto said. He turned to Josie. "You get the search warrant for Wally's phone records and get a tap on the phone line. Track down the judge for approval. Keep me posted. We need those phone records."

Josie nodded.

"I'll take Hec out to the trailer to pack up some things. We'll get his dog out of there." He rubbed his chin and looked at Josie. "Let's try to meet back here around four. We'll pay a second visit to the Conroys."

Back at the office, Josie secured the warrant and was promised the phone records by the next morning. As she and Otto were getting ready to leave, Agent Omstead called and said he was driving to Artemis from Houston that night to debrief. He asked to meet with them at 7:00 P.M. at the police department but would offer nothing else in terms of what information he might have.

Josie and Otto drove out to the Conroys' ranch at a little after five. The evening air felt charged with an electricity that left Josie on edge. A yellow cast saturated the sky and forecasters warned of a flash thunderstorm later that night. The monsoons in September had flooded West Texas, and now six months later they still hadn't had a drop of water. *Feast or famine,* Josie thought, watching the ribbon of dust flowing behind her in the rearview mirror.

She pulled onto Flatt Road as Otto described the Conroys based on his visit the previous day.

"We won't get a straight answer from Bea Conroy unless she thinks it will benefit her in some way."

"What's their cause? They second amenders, religious fanatics, or what?"

"The Conroys don't have a cause. They're just angry hilljacks," he said. "You watch your back though. I met one of the boys and his wife or girlfriend. Dave said there's two other brothers living there with their girlfriends and a passel of kids. And we're the enemy."

As they drove along the dirt lane to the Conroys' house, Josie noticed a car hauler parked just to the right of it. A large red metal pole barn was located twenty feet on the other side of the car hauler, its doors wide open. As they pulled up, she saw the outside of the barn was piled high on all sides with what looked to be mostly junk. Josie stopped the jeep in front of the barn and saw three men and a woman standing just inside the barn in what appeared to be a very unorganized mechanic's shop. Josie got out of the jeep and scanned the property for cars that might have been waiting for a haul, but she saw nothing. She wondered if the hauler was typically parked between the house and barn, or if they were getting it ready for a shipment.

They stepped into the barn and Otto introduced Josie to the woman in the group, Bea Conroy. She was wearing a pair of orange cotton shorts and a matching T-shirt that was at least two sizes too big even for her large frame. Josie offered a hand to Bea, but she just nodded and kept her arms crossed over her chest.

The men appeared to be in their thirties, all wearing oil-stained jeans and grimy T-shirts. They all scowled and made no move to greet Josie and Otto.

Otto stepped farther into the barn and extended a hand to a man standing on the left side of the group of men. He was the smallest of the three and appeared to be the youngest. "Good to see you again, Tim. This is Chief Josie Gray."

Tim put his hand out and awkwardly shook Otto's hand, glancing at the two men next to him as if for approval.

"Why don't you introduce us," Otto said.

He looked surprised to be put on the spot, but did as he was asked. He pointed to a bulky man in the middle with deep frown lines between his dark eyes and down the corners of his mouth. "This is my brother Daryl." Tim leaned forward and pointed down the line to a man on the end. "That's my brother Rich."

Rich had crazy eyes that put Josie on edge. He seemed like the kind of person who you feared might pull a gun out and start shooting just for the hell of it. His eyes darted around the room and he fidgeted from foot to foot. His hair was plastered to his head with sweat even though no one else in the barn appeared to be overheated. He had the telltale signs of a meth user: gaunt, pale, and anxious.

Bea spoke up first. "I done told you everything I know about the Santa Muerte. I don't know nothing about your necklace. You may as well turn on back for town." She sounded irritated at the intrusion.

Josie approached her but kept the three men on her left in her line of sight. "We're here to ask you a few questions about Wally Follet."

Mrs. Conroy glared at her and Josie noticed Daryl look directly at his mom. Tim's attention turned toward the house and he furrowed his eyebrows as if dreading what might come next. Josie turned and saw a skinny woman with a baby on her hip stomping her way over to the barn, her eyebrows bunched up with her puckered lips. She was angry, but Josie noted her focus was on one of the three men, not the police.

The woman brushed past Josie and Otto, and she walked up to Tim, who was shooting worried looks at his brothers.

"What the hell are you doing out here?" She shoved his chest with her empty hand and the baby started crying. "I told you I had to leave ten minutes ago. Get your ass inside and watch these kids so I can leave."

Tim took the baby from her and they both started toward the house.

"Excuse me, sir," Josie stepped in. "I'd like for you to stick around a minute. We have a few questions for you."

"He don't have time to stick around talking to you! You can talk to the rest of them." The woman was wide-eyed, as if she couldn't believe Josie's audacity.

"Ma'am, we're in the middle of a murder investigation."

"I don't give a good goddamned what you're doing. And you don't know what I'm going through either!"

"He'll be right in, right after we're done talking with him," she said.

The woman left with a flip of her head and an angry grunt. The baby stopped crying but puffed out her lip in protest. Tim absently patted the baby's back as his brothers glared at him in silence.

Otto had gotten nowhere with Bea, so Josie hoped the three men would offer more.

"I understand you're in partnership with Wally Follet?" She picked up where she had left off, looking at all three men in hopes one of them would take the lead.

Tim continued to pat the baby's back and looked down the line at his brothers but said nothing. Finally, Daryl, the largest of the three said, "Not partners. We just ship cars for him sometimes."

"How often do you ship for Wally?"

"We don't do nothing illegal," Mrs. Conroy said, her tone defensive. "We got permits and all the border boys know us. We're good legit business operators. They see us coming through the border line and pass us on through 'cause they know we got good clean shipments."

Josie knew enough about the border-crossing agents to know that was untrue but let it go. "How often?"

The woman shrugged. "Whenever he's got a load. Every few weeks."

"What do you ship?"

"Mostly wrecked cars. Drive 'em down to Del Rio and across the border. It's all above board, nothing illegal."

"Why didn't you tell Otto about your involvement with Wally when he was here before?" Josie asked.

"He never asked."

Josie turned and faced Tim to throw them all off. "What's inside the wrecked cars?"

His eyes widened and his mouth dropped open slightly. Josie looked to Daryl, who kept his poker face, and finally to Rich, who had been bouncing from foot to foot.

Josie repeated her question. "What's inside the frames of those wrecked cars, Tim? Answer me."

"I don't know what you mean. They're just cars."

Josie switched brothers. "Daryl. What gets packed inside the frames of those cars before you ship them?"

"I don't know what the hell Wally puts in there. All we do is drive the hauler."

"You do know. Wally packs those cars full of cash. Then you and Wally make a nice fat profit off that shipment for the Medrano cartel." She paused and looked at the three brothers, and then at Bea, who were all staring back at her, unflinching. "Problem is, Wally took off with a nine-million-dollar shipment and left you all high and dry." She jerked her thumb back behind her shoulder to indicate outside the barn. "That's why your hauler's empty."

No one moved. Even the baby remained quiet.

"We need access to Wally Follet," Josie said, her tone still hard and unflinching.

"Well, hell yes. We do too. Everybody wants Wally," Daryl said.

"Why do you want him?" she asked.

"Because he screwed us over!" he said.

"Because he stole the load of cash you were supposed to ship to the Medrano cartel. And now you don't get paid. Isn't that right?" Josie said.

Daryl pointed to the empty car hauler outside. "I don't know about no cash he's been shipping. But we missed two loads of cars now. We got no money coming in and we got eleven heads to feed. Wally screwed a whole lot of people over."

"Have you had contact from the Medranos?" Josie asked.

Silent stares from all of them. Josie looked at Otto, who nodded.

"Let me be clear. We have phone records that link you to the Medranos and to Wally Follet. Your best bet right now is to cooperate and give us whatever you can to help us find Wally."

Josie noticed Bea was motionless, watching her boys intently. Tim and Rich both looked to Daryl, who took some time before speaking up. "Our boss, one of the Medranos, called Mom and talked to her. They told her we was next." He sniffed deeply, trying to hold back the emotion from his voice. "If we don't find Wally, they'll take us one by one just like they did the accountant."

Josie looked to Bea, who stood with her arms crossed, her hands under her armpits, her expression now revealing the fear that she was undoubtedly living with from moment to moment. Josie noticed that Rich had stopped bouncing and now stood still, watching his mother for her reaction.

"What exactly did your boss say to you?"

Bea finally spoke up. "Emilio, my boss, he calls every day, asking where Wally is. Every day he calls and every day I say the same thing. We haven't heard from the son of a bitch. I keep calling Hec and the kid tells me nothing, says he don't know where his dad is.

Emilio says if the money isn't returned, that we pay. He says they'll kidnap my boys, one by one." She had the fierce protective look that Josie had seen in mothers young and old. "And I'll warn you right now. I'll put a bullet hole through that son of a bitch myself if I ever catch him."

TWENTY-THREE

Josie and Otto got back in the car and drove with the windows down, letting the damp evening air blow through the car. Fat raindrops hit the windshield for all of ten seconds, and then evaporated, the clouds taking the much-needed rain elsewhere.

Back at the office, they spent two hours meeting with Agent Omstead. Josie came clean about working with Nick Santos, and Omstead had smiled in response. He said they knew Santos was on the case and staying at her home. He explained the FBI couldn't use the private sector to circumvent the law to gain information. However, if Josie received key information from a negotiator, the FBI could certainly benefit from the intelligence. Omstead had said that Santos was well respected, and if he provided information that would benefit the case, they would use it. Josie had been surprised, but pleased with his response.

Josie also relayed the information about Wally's conversations with Hec: Hec telling Wally about Dillon's kidnapping the same night that it happened, the same night that Christina was murdered. Hector and Wally knew about the kidnapping and murder before the police. They discussed the phone records that had already been subpoenaed. They also explained that the Conroy family was working with Wally Follet to ship the cars directly to the Medranos. With the threat of arrest for obstructing a murder investigation Mrs. Conroy had finally given up the cell phone number for her boss, Emilio. Agent Omstead confirmed what they had learned. He had discovered that Emilio Medrano was one of the contacts for a money-laundering scheme being run out of Piedra Labrada. He took the phone number in hopes of tracing it back to an address in Mexico.

Shortly after Omstead left, Brian Moore buzzed Josie's office phone.

"The phone company faxed Wally's phone records that you requested from the warrant. I've already checked numbers for you. Wally placed a call to Christina Handley's cell phone at eight forty-five P.M."

Josie thanked Brian and turned her chair to face Otto. "You want to place a bet? I think we just identified Christina's killer."

"Now we just need to find him."

———

At nine thirty, once Otto had clocked off to drive Delores to Marfa to visit an ill friend, Josie texted Marta, who was sitting at the river again, this time within earshot of the men camped out behind Wally's Folly. The lights on timers in Hec's home seemed to have worked, as the two men along the river's edge had no idea they were watching an empty trailer, or at least didn't care.

Josie drove down River Road as the last light of the day slipped below the horizon. The pieces were in place. The connections were finally there. Wally Follet had been tipped off that he was being indicted by the United States government and subsequently stole nine million dollars from the Medrano cartel before slipping off into the dark. It didn't take long for the Medranos to figure out Wally was the culprit. He had disappeared and Josie was certain that the Conroys made it clear to the Medranos that Wally was the person who stole the money.

Four days after Wally and the nine million dollars had gone missing, the cartel abducted Hec and tried to beat the information out of him. Up until Hec was released by the Medranos and returned home, Hec had not had contact with his father, and Josie believed the boy still didn't know his whereabouts. After Hec failed to produce Wally, the Medranos kidnapped Dillon in order to get the police to find the money in exchange for Dillon's life. When the Medranos threatened to kidnap Hector like they had done to Dillon, Hec forwarded the information to his father. For a short period of time after Hec was returned home, Wally would call to check on him. Hec had told Josie that after he told his dad about the kidnapping, his dad quit calling.

Wally then convinced Christina Handley to meet him at Dillon's office. Josie knew this part was conjecture, but her thinking was that Wally was trying to save Hec from being indicted for their business practices. By refusing to leave town with his dad and the nine million dollars, Hec had left himself vulnerable to the feds' investigation. So Wally came back to steal the files and shot Christina in the process.

Josie was fairly certain Wally had not fled the country. He was in the area, waiting for the moment he could grab his son and leave town for good. Father and son living the good life as millionaires, somewhere up north, most likely the Canadian outback. It was the reason Hec wouldn't come all the way clean: he was protecting their getaway. The only part of her theory that she couldn't reconcile was how Wally could have left Hec to fend for himself with the Medranos. He had to have known that the Medranos would come for his son.

If she could find Wally and the money, the control would be hers. Without the money, she had nothing. The kidnappers hadn't communicated with her since sending the video, and the lack of contact terrified her. If the Medranos lost faith in her ability to recover their money, Dillon would be killed.

Josie resisted the urge to call Nick. He had promised to call her with anything significant, and told her not to call him unless his services were needed.

After a ten-minute scalding shower left her body slack but her mind still reeling, she dried off and dressed in jeans and a sweatshirt, too wound up to sleep. She made her way to the kitchen, staring into the refrigerator's shelves, which were either empty or filled with condiments.

She shut the refrigerator door and opened the cabinet to the left, considering the half-empty bottle of Old Crow as if it were her last resort. She needed sleep but she was too wired to shut down. Josie considered herself a stable person. It took a great deal to excite her, but for the past several days she'd felt as if she were buzzing on speed, unable to slow her thoughts or sleep more than an hour or two at a time. Her skin ached and was hot to the touch.

She kicked the cabinet door shut and opened the pantry door, pulling her Beretta out of the gun belt. She released the magazine, checked that it was fully loaded, then slapped it back up into the butt of the gun. She grabbed a box of ammunition off the shelf and tucked it into her sweatshirt pocket. She pulled her barn coat over her sweatshirt and kneeled down by the back door in the kitchen to lace up her hiking boots. Chester nuzzled her arm with his nose, excited for a walk.

Holding the gun in her right hand, she left Chester, whining and pawing at the back door, and walked out into the cool night. It was a walk she'd taken a hundred times, mostly to absorb the desert and forget whatever was troubling her. But hatred pushed through her body with a ferocity she didn't trust. She tried to focus on the blood that pulsed rhythmically at her temples, but as the light from the house faded behind her, the thoughts in her head turned black. At that moment, her ability to recognize good in the world had been obliterated.

Her nose was running from the cold, but she was hot inside the barn coat. She unzipped it and kept walking toward the mountains, stopping roughly two miles from the house. The stars lit up the dusty ground and cast deep shadows that mixed with the scrub and pine trees at the base of the black mountain before her.

Josie lifted her gun from her side and fired at a downed pine tree twenty feet from her. She shot ten bullets, then stopped, the ringing in her ears finally masking the storm blowing through her head. Sparks from the gun jumped into the night air. She walked five steps forward, raised the gun again, and emptied the final seven shots. She knelt in the dirt, released the magazine, and slipped the gun behind her bent knee so she could reload. Josie pulled the tray of bullets out of the box, her movements instinctive in the dark, and pushed sixteen bullets into the magazine. Feeling the flat side of the magazine with her left thumb, she then pushed it back into the gun and heard the click.

Josie stood, turned to her left, and fired another ten rounds into the downed tree, feeling the recoil up her arm into her chest, the impact satisfying. She imagined the Bishop standing in front of her, a large, imposing man with dark eyes. The bullet would exit her gun, and at the very moment she felt the release and power in her own body, he would feel it in his, straight into his heart. She would only come back to life when his ended. She closed her eyes, pulling the trigger slower now, imagining the penetration with each shot, his dead body hitting the ground.

Once her gun was empty, Josie knelt back on the ground and started the process again. Halfway through the reload she noticed headlights approaching from Dell's ranch. She cursed and shoved the ammunition box back into her sweatshirt pocket. She couldn't deal with Dell right now.

As the pickup approached she stood and waved her hands in the air slowly to catch his attention.

He pulled the truck to a stop and jumped out, his expression terrified. "What's going on out here?"

"Nothing is going on. And what if it was? What the hell are you doing driving up into the middle of a gunfight?"

He looked confused. "What are you talking about? What gunfight?"

Josie turned from him, the blood pounding inside her head.

"What are you doing out here?" he yelled. "Look at me!"

Josie turned and faced him. "It's none of your goddamned business what I'm doing! And, if you hear gunfire in the middle of the desert the last thing you do is drive your truck into the middle of it.

You understand that, right? You don't come out here and risk getting your head blown off in the middle of someone else's fight!"

He stood motionless, staring at her, his anxiety clear in the moonlight. "You can't operate like this. You can't go around shooting up the hillside in the middle of the night. You scared the hell out of me."

She closed her eyes. His judgment was too much. "Just go home, Dell. You don't want to be near me right now."

Her eyes remained closed and she hoped he would turn and leave. After several seconds she felt his hand lightly on her shoulder. She gritted her teeth, unprepared to receive sympathy or even human contact from anyone.

He placed his other hand on her shoulder and she said nothing. He finally stepped forward and wrapped his arms around her. She remained stiff, her back tight, her eyes closed.

He held her tighter and placed a hand behind her head, pulling her face into his shoulder. He whispered into her hair, "This is not your fault, Josie. None of it."

Josie stood rigid for a long while, until she finally let her guard begin to slip. She pressed her face farther into him, unable to speak, unable to put her rage into words.

"What happened to Dillon?" He paused and took a deep breath. "What happened to that young woman? That wasn't you. That evil had nothing to do with you. You can't transfer the blame. You're one of the good guys." He sighed into her hair and she felt his body tense from the physical touch that she knew was making him uncomfortable.

He ran his hand down the side of her hair, then pulled the loose hair tie out and threw it onto the ground. He stroked her hair, gently patting her back, and she felt her body settle, slowly, the anger receding.

She remained still, her arms at her sides, her eyes closed. "I don't believe in anyone. I don't feel anything but hate."

She felt his arms tighten around her.

"You're in a bad place. Stuck inside your head." He rested his forehead on top of her head and sighed heavily. "You can't stay there.

I spent too many years of my life stuck in that place. All that hate takes your strength. Leaves you nothing to fight with. It makes you see things that aren't there." He moved his hands up to her shoulders and she knew he was about to pull away.

He pushed her gently back and spoke quietly, but his voice was full of emotion. "I'd take heroin addiction over hate, Josie. It's easier to kick the habit."

"I don't have any control over it. It's like a poison that's become a part of me."

"When things get bad. When you feel like all the good is gone out of the world? That's when you take all that emotion inside of you, and focus it on destroying those sons of bitches." He squeezed her shoulders and shook her once and she looked up in surprise. "I'll be right there beside you."

She stared back and felt his words tighten something inside her.

Dell's expression was fierce. "Our government's run into the ground with laws that don't make sense. We're a country full of paralytics. If those laws are keeping you from doing what makes sense? What's obvious and right? Then dammit, you cross the river and you do what needs to be done."

She smiled slightly.

He pointed a finger at her chest. "We ignore the laws and we go take care of business."

Her expression grew serious. It was her impotence that was tearing up her insides. Some imaginary line drawn through the Rio Grande preventing her from doing what had to be done to get Dillon home.

He squeezed her shoulders and stepped back to look at her. "You with me?"

She nodded and felt a sense of confidence for the first time since the day she discovered Dillon had been kidnapped.

Dell patted her on the back and headed toward his truck. "Come on. I'll give you a ride home." He turned back and glanced at her. "You save those bullets."

TWENTY-FOUR

Josie pounded on the door of room 6 of Manny's Motel. Manny stuck his head out of his apartment next door and started to speak, but Josie motioned him back inside. He closed the door quietly and pulled his drapes shut.

Josie banged on the door harder and heard Hec yelling for her to wait a minute. He opened the door wearing a pair of jeans, his chest bare, and squinted into the bright morning sunlight. He had obviously just awoken. "What's wrong?"

Josie pushed her way past him and he followed her in, finding a place to stand by the bed. "This is what's wrong. I'm sick of playing games, Hec. I'm tired of treating you like a kid. Playing nice when you've been jacking us around for a week. Why the hell didn't you tell me about the Conroys? They know you well. Said they've talked with you several times since your dad left." Josie shoved Hec and he fell backward onto the bed behind him, a stunned expression on his face.

"Why wouldn't you just tell me about them? You're hiding something. Something you don't want the police to know that has to do with your dad."

"I'm not sure what else you want to know."

"Bullshit. Let's see if this piece of news helps you open up. Not only is your dad wanted by half of Texas for stealing nine million dollars, but now he's also wanted by the Artemis Police Department, for the murder of Christina Handley."

Hec's mouth dropped open. "No! That's not true!"

"We subpoenaed your dad's phone records, Hec. He called Christina Handley at eight forty-five. We have witnesses that say she was at the office shortly after that. Your dad stole the files, then shot Christina to keep her from talking."

"No! I swear! That's not what happened!"

Josie stared him down, her expression hard.

"He went there. To meet Christina. He just wanted to get the files, but he never shot her!"

"Then who did?"

"My dad said the Conroys are crazy. That I needed to keep my mouth shut. He says they're watching me. If they know I'm talking to you they'll kill me just like the other lady."

"You're saying the Conroys killed Christina?"

Hec began crying, his body shaking. He stood from the bed and punched the wall with his fist. He angrily wiped tears away from his face, blood staining his knuckles.

"Why, Hec? Why would the Conroys kill her?"

Hec sniffed and took several deep breaths to calm down. "I don't know. I swear it this time. My dad just says they're crazy and to stay away from them. He told me the lady got shot, but it wasn't him. He thought the Conroys would kill me before the cartel would. That's why he made me swear I wouldn't talk about the shipping. I wanted to tell you, I just couldn't."

Josie considered the situation. The cartel wanted her to learn about the illegal shipping so she could find their missing money; the Conroys wanted to keep it a secret to save their business with the Medranos; Hec was once again caught in the middle.

Hec looked exhausted but his face had changed. His eyes had lost the anxiety, the guilt he had been dragging around with him like a death sentence. *Confession is good for the soul,* thought Josie. She'd seen it in countless people. In the end, most people needed the punishment as a road to catharsis. Confess, take your knocks, and move on with your life.

He finally took a long breath and blew it out slowly, meeting Josie's stare head-on. "That's it. You know everything now. I swear it."

———•———

Josie left Hec and knocked on Manny's door. When he answered, she handed him a wad of bills from her pocket. "Go get him junk food, a sandwich and milk. Stuff for his room. If you've got anything he can read, that too. He's got to keep his head on straight, Manny. See what you can do. We just don't want him to take off on us."

Josie left and headed to the PD. She checked in with Lou, then found Otto upstairs pouring coffee.

"I just left Hec. He says Wally didn't kill Christina Handley. One of the Conroys did." She sat down in her chair and pressed her fingertips into her temples, rubbing in circles. "That's assuming we believe Hec's story. And, more importantly, that we believe the story Hec's dad told him."

Josie recapped her conversation. "I believe him, Otto. I think he finally came all the way clean. Maybe the Conroys went to Dillon's office for the same reason Wally was there. To steal their own records. They figured it was only a matter of time before they'd be indicted too."

"How do we know the necklace wasn't Wally's?" Otto said.

Josie gave him an exasperated look and he smiled. "Okay. A so-called Catholic saint. Probably not a necklace Wally would wear."

"Let's go back to the Conroys. Lay it on thick this time. See if we can shake something loose."

"Agreed. Let's call the prosecutor, keep him in the loop," Otto said.

He picked up his office phone, dialed, and small-talked for a moment with the prosecutor's secretary before being put on hold.

Tyler Holder was the newly elected prosecutor for Arroyo County. A lucrative private practice in Houston and a short stint as legal counsel for the Houston Oilers had allowed him to follow his new bride to her hometown of Artemis. He had made a name for himself as a former big-city attorney, and then quickly worked his way through the Artemis political machine with a term on the school board, a term on the county council, and finally as the prosecutor. He'd been in office for three months and appeared to be serious about his campaign promise to uphold the letter of the law, as opposed to the politically motivated former prosecutor whom Josie had found reprehensible. The political games the former prosecutor played had won him a few supporters, but the general public had caught on and voted him out in a landslide defeat. Josie had high hopes for Holder. At forty years old, he was young for the job, but he appeared to want the office for the right reasons.

Otto finally connected with Holder and asked him if he could meet with him and Josie about the kidnapping case. An hour later, Josie and Otto were sitting in Holder's office, presenting their case against the Conroys, hoping for support in the event they needed a warrant later.

"So, you're basing your case against this family on the story concocted by Hector Follet, whose father admittedly was at Mr. Reese's office the night Christina was shot? Doesn't it make more sense that Wally killed her?" Holder asked.

"I believe Hector," Josie said. After she said it, she realized how ridiculous her comment must have sounded to the prosecutor.

"The kid wants to keep his father from being a murderer. He may even believe his own story, but it just doesn't make sense to me that the Conroys miraculously showed up at the office the same time Wally did." Holder looked from Josie to Otto. "Do you buy into this theory too?"

Otto nodded. "I do."

"Was Dillon also the Conroys' accountant?" Holder asked.

"Yes," Josie said. "I think they ran their money through Dillon to make the business transactions seem more legitimate. After the kidnapping, they had to know that everyone associated with Wally was going to be under suspicion. His business had just been indicted."

Holder held a hand up, waving in the air as if only halfway conceding.

"Maybe the Conroys found out about the kidnapping and assumed Wally would go to the office."

Otto broke in. "It makes sense that the Medranos would have contacted the Conroys about the kidnapping the same way they did Hec, the night they took Dillon. The Medranos don't care who finds their money. My guess is they put pressure on anyone who they thought might find Wally and recover their cash."

"Bea Conroy could have sent one of her boys to watch the office hoping to find Wally and get the money back to the Medranos before their business fell apart. And Christina got in the middle of the fight," Josie said.

"Go put pressure on them," Holder said. "I hope like hell you find something."

After leaving the prosecutor's office, Josie and Otto went back to the police department to plan their visit to the Conroys. They decided Josie should talk to Bea, who clearly had little respect for men. They drove separately, hoping the arrival of two police cars might signal a bigger presence and cause the Conroy boys to back off.

The barn doors were closed and only one car was visible on the property, a red beat-up Chevy Malibu parked haphazardly in front of the house, as if someone had been in too big of a hurry to park straight. *Or,* Josie thought, *more likely they were too lazy to take the time to park right.*

Bea answered the door wearing a red T-shirt that looked like a souvenir from New Orleans, with giant white letters that proclaimed THE BIG EASY. Bea looked beyond the two officers, presumably searching for additional police.

"Ought to save the taxpayers some money and share your rides," she said.

"Where's the rest of your family, Mrs. Conroy?" Josie glanced around the property.

"Gone."

"We have some questions for you. May we come inside?" Josie asked.

"Suit yourself." Bea stepped away from the door. She crossed her arms over her chest and watched as the officers entered her living room. Josie looked around the messy room and thought Otto had described it perfectly.

Otto pointed toward the kitchen. "Mind if we sit down to talk? This might take a few minutes."

"For crying out loud." Bea turned and shuffled into the kitchen, ranting about the police not having anything better to do but harass people who were doing nothing wrong.

In the kitchen, Otto introduced Josie to Bea's husband, Leroy Conroy. He nodded his head at Josie but said nothing.

"Let's talk some more about your business with Wally Follet, and your connection with the Medrano cartel," said Josie.

"No law against doing business with either one of them."

"Why have you been calling Hector so often? We examined Follet's phone records and saw that you placed fifteen phone calls in a three-day period."

Bea laughed, loud and abrupt. "You really got to ask that?"

"So, you think Wally will come back?" Josie asked.

"Not anymore. He's long gone."

"But you call every day asking Hec where he is?"

"Well, hell yes! He destroyed our business."

"How do you know he's long gone? Did you see him leave town?" Josie asked.

Bea hesitated, sensing a trap. "Nobody's seen him. That's all."

"Did you see him the day he showed up at Dillon Reese's office? To meet Christina Handley?" Josie asked.

The look of panic on Bea's face as she realized the police were on to her family was all Josie needed to confirm her suspicions. Now, they needed proof. Josie glanced across the table at Leroy, who was staring, unblinking, at his wife. Bea suddenly got up and walked to the kitchen sink, turned on the water, and washed her hands.

"Don't know what you're talking about," she said.

"You do," Josie said. "You and Hector both received phone calls from the kidnappers. You admitted yourself that the Medranos said they were going to take your boys, one by one, if you didn't find Wally and the money. You went to the office because you were hoping Wally would come back to town to clean out the files. Not only had Wally ruined your business connection to the Medranos, but you were probably going to get pulled into his federal indictment."

"You don't know that!" She turned from the sink, her hands dripping water.

"We have a witness who saw you at the office. The game's up."

Josie avoided eye contact with Otto. He knew there was no witness.

Bea turned slowly to the stove and pulled a dish towel off the oven handle. She dried her hands, staring at them. Josie couldn't tell if she was buying time, caught up in her own thoughts, or too stunned to respond. Whatever the case, this was not the same fiery woman Josie had just met at the door.

"You went to the office to catch Wally. Christina Handley was caught in the cross fire," Josie said.

The kitchen door opened and alarmed all of them. Daryl walked inside followed by a woman neither Josie nor Otto had seen before. The couple stopped almost instantly when they saw the expressions of the people gathered around the kitchen table.

"Get outside, Daryl. We're talking," Bea said.

"What's going on here?" He shoved his elbows out like a middle school kid getting ready to pick a fight, but his mother wouldn't stand for it.

"I said get out," she yelled. Her eyes were bright and filled with a sorrow that surprised Josie.

Otto caught Josie's attention and put his hand up as if placing a phone to his ear. She nodded.

As soon as the door closed Bea turned to Josie. "I was there, but it was Wally that killed that girl. I watched that bastard do it." Bea watched Otto leave the kitchen and walk back through the living room. "Where's he going?"

"He's going to call the prosecutor. Then he's going to call the Arroyo County judge to get a search warrant for your house. We'll be looking for the missing computers and the gun that killed Christina Handley," Josie stated plainly. She watched Bea's expression turn to fear. Her husband put his head in his hands. The only sound in the kitchen was the *kisk* of the oxygen tank.

When Otto walked back into the kitchen with the judge's verbal approval for a search warrant, he found Josie, Bea, and Leroy sitting at the table staring at each other intently. Josie looked up, but Otto couldn't read her expression.

"Was it granted?" she asked.

Otto nodded. "We have verbal approval. A deputy is on the way with a signed copy."

Josie turned back to Bea. "So, here's the deal. We can spend the next two or three hours turning every drawer and closet and cubbyhole in your house and barn upside down and inside out, or you can come clean. Give us the gun. Give up the computers. Tell us what happened before you have a house full of police officers digging through your possessions."

Bea stared at Leroy for a long moment, the tortured look of a woman realizing her future had just dissolved.

Bea stood slowly from her chair and Josie got up as well. Bea swatted at the air, as if irritated by Josie's hovering.

"Come on. I'll show you."

They heard an engine that sounded like a pickup truck minus the mufflers spin gravel outside of the house.

Bea sighed heavily. "I don't have the strength for them boys right now."

Josie walked toward the door and by the time she reached it, Rich was opening the door, his eyes wild.

"What the hell are you doing in my house?" His voice was loud and threatening.

Josie put a hand up, palm out, to stop him from moving any farther into the kitchen. "Stop. You need to go back outside. We have a search warrant. You won't be allowed into the house until the search is complete."

"What the—"

"That's enough. Get your ass outside and keep your brothers out too. This ain't your concern," Bea said.

"What are you talking about? Use your head, Mom. They can't be in here without our lawyer!"

"Just shut up and get outside. It's over with."

Dumbfounded, Rich looked at Josie as if she might explain this turn of events to him. She motioned him back from the door and shut it. Otto put ten fingers in the air. Ten minutes before backup.

Josie followed Bea down the hallway and into a bedroom. Decorated in rose-and-beige-colored curtains and comforters, with lace doilies on the night tables and a blanket chest at the end of the bed, the room was soft and feminine. The wooden floors were covered in hooked rugs. *Bea's hideaway from the commotion of her family,* Josie thought.

Bea walked to an oak dresser with a mirror that ran the length of it. She held on to the top of the dresser for support and bent down to the bottom row of drawers. Josie walked up behind her and put a hand out to stop her from opening the drawer.

"Is the gun located in this drawer?"

Bea nodded but avoided looking at Josie.

"I'll get it out myself. We need to preserve the fingerprints."

Bea waved a hand and backed away. Josie noticed Otto standing in the hallway. He held up a plastic evidence bag. She nodded and pulled on the latex gloves she had ready in her back pocket.

"You have to take me out of here with handcuffs on? In front of the boys?"

Josie bent over to open the drawer and struggled to keep her voice level, the image of Christina's body clearly imprinted in her mind. "You murdered a woman."

Bea started to speak, but only a moan came out of her mouth.

Josie avoided looking at her and slipped a pen into the trigger guard to lift the gun out of the drawer and place it into the baggie. "The computers? The files?" she asked.

Bea pointed to the bedroom closet. Josie found them stuffed into the back next to a laundry basket.

She then read Bea Conroy her Miranda warning. Josie wasn't surprised when Bea refused an attorney. The woman was worn out, physically and mentally. Still, Josie took the opportunity to question her before the attorneys were inevitably brought into play. She decided to keep the handcuffs off at this point, to keep her more relaxed, more inclined to open up.

"You are under arrest for first-degree murder. You have a chance to tell the truth without lawyers and judges and jurors getting involved. You can tell your story like it really happened."

There were times when Josie manipulated a suspect through her words and felt the sickening connection with a person as they shared intimate details of their life. It was like bargaining with the devil. All she wanted was to throw the person in a cell and lock the door, but when a criminal was desperate or resigned, it was the bargaining that often paid big dividends at the end of an investigation.

"I don't give a hang about a lawyer. Those good-for-nothing boys of mine can earn their own keep. Send me off to a women's jail and let somebody else cook and clean."

Josie wondered at Bea's change in attitude toward her family. Was this her attempt to begin the separation she knew was coming? Josie led Bea back into the kitchen and they sat back down at the table across from Leroy.

They heard sirens approaching, and Otto stepped outside to organize the group of officers descending on the property. Until further investigation, Bea would be the only member of the family brought up on murder charges.

"When did you know that Wally had taken off with the load of cash?" Josie asked.

"First we knew something was wrong was from Hec. Daryl called Wally to set up the time to pick up the cars. There's no changing the date. We been shipping cars for three years now. Never one time missed a shipment. Daryl comes to me out in the machine shop. Says, 'Mother, we got issues. Hec says Wally's gone. Cars aren't loaded. Money's gone.' My jaw nearly hit the dirt. 'The money's gone'?" She shook her head and stared at Josie for a moment. "You don't steal nine million dollars from the Medranos, I don't care who you are! Especially if you're a dumb shit like Wally Follet!"

"What did you do once you realized he had taken the money?"

"I had to call Emilio and tell him the money's gone. Then the Medranos showed up at Wally's place and roughed the kid up, took him over to Mexico. Hec don't know nothing. Then they come banging on our door. We don't know nothing. Seven days of hell, phone calls and threats. Wally just vanished."

"Mr. Reese was your accountant, correct?"

"We're an honest business. Mr. Reese pays the taxes, keeps the books in order. We ship cars for other people, other than the Medranos, but we got eleven people living in that house. Medrano helped us make a decent living. We'd still be working it today if that dumb shit Wally hadn't tried to sell stolen cars. Once the feds got involved it all crashed. Wally got word they were coming after him with an indictment and an arrest warrant. He took off with the money."

"How did you end up at Dillon's office the night he was kidnapped?" Josie asked.

Bea glanced at her husband. "When we found out about the kidnapping, Leroy told me, we got to get our records out of that office before they connect us to Wally. Once the feds figured out Reese was kidnapped, they'd be digging through everybody's records. And if the feds figured out the shipping connection, our business was screwed. We got too much invested to lose the business." She looked across the table at her husband, her expression pained. "Can you imagine those dumbass boys trying to run this family?"

Josie noted that Bea was still describing the family business as an honest business, and yet they still needed to get the records from Dillon's office to keep from being indicted. Josie let the contradiction go. It made little difference at this point.

"How did you end up at Dillon's office at the same time Wally was there?"

"Leroy. He figured Wally would go for the records, what with the indictment and then the kidnapping. Sure enough. Leroy sent me to check on things. Told me to take the gun with me for protection. Wally was there all right."

Josie looked at Leroy, who continued to stare at his wife, his eyes wide and expectant. Bea was no longer referring to her son Daryl as the person giving orders. Josie wondered if Bea was implicating her husband to save her son. Josie had never heard Leroy utter a word, but she had no doubt the truth would come out later.

"What time did you go to the office?"

"I got there about eight and sat a block over, parked on the street where I could see the front of the office and the back lot. Christina showed up about nine and opened up the office. I figure, score one for me. I can at least get our records out of there. The front door was unlocked. I walked in and asked her to give me everything for our business. She says no. I say, 'I'm the customer, I paid, give me the files.' I start yelling at her and who comes in the front door but Wally Follet."

Bea stopped talking and rubbed her fingers along the vinyl tablecloth, her attention diverted.

"What did you say when he entered the office?"

"I can't believe my eyes. I start yelling, 'Where the hell is the money?' Christina keeps trying to leave and Wally keeps pushing her back down in the seat. I told Wally, 'My boys are outside.' I said, 'You're a dead man if you don't return the money tonight.'"

"Is that true? Were your boys outside?" Josie asked.

"They didn't know nothing about me going to the office."

"How did Christina get shot?"

"It was just an accident. It all happened so quick. Wally was standing behind Christina. He took off all the sudden, making a run for the back door, and I raise my gun to shoot the bastard, just stop him in his tracks is all. But the girl pushes off in her chair, rolls it away from Wally at the same time he turns to run. I raise my gun and shoot and it hits her right in the chest. I was aiming at Wally. That's exactly what happened. I never meant to hurt her."

"What were you going to do with her once she heard the story about the money?"

She stared dumbly at Josie. "I don't know. We never got that far."

"What did you do after you shot Christina?"

The threads of Bea's life had unraveled all around her. Her face was slack, and her cheeks had taken on a chalky pallor that matched her husband's. She stared at him for some time, but he didn't move, just stared back.

"After I shot her, I sat down on the floor," Bea said. "She just sat there limp in that chair and I knew I'd killed her. By the time I went out back to find Wally, he was long gone."

She then admitted, "That necklace your cop buddy was asking about? Santa Muerte? That was mine. Hell of a lot a good she did me."

TWENTY-FIVE

By noon, Bea Conroy was booked in the Arroyo County jail. Three state troopers Otto requested had arrived at the house to assist and ensure that the Conroy boys and their lawyer stayed at a distance while Josie and Otto searched the rest of the house and processed the evidence. At seven o'clock that evening, Josie finally made it back to the office to finish the preliminary paperwork while Otto walked down the street to the Hot Tamale to get them dinner. He arrived thirty minutes later with a feast: two monster burritos loaded with sauce and sour cream, tacos, Spanish rice, chips and guacamole, and sopapilla for dessert. Otto sampled the sugary fried flatbread as they spread the food out on the conference table.

Having skipped lunch, they were both extra hungry. They didn't bother speaking as they enjoyed the quiet office, cold drinks, and satisfying food.

After they finished eating, Otto said, "Nina wouldn't take money. She said this was her thank-you for a job well done."

Josie frowned.

"This was big, Josie. Celebrate the success. When Dillon arrives home, he'll at least know that Christina's murderer is in jail."

"Wally's still missing. And I doubt Dillon even knows about Christina. He'll just have one more trauma to deal with. And he's not home, Otto." For a minute, she thought she would throw up her dinner. She'd been so hungry those few minutes she hadn't even been thinking about Dillon, but now once again the same images threatened to descend upon her.

Otto looked bereft. He reached out to pat Josie's hand but she pulled it back.

Silently, they cleaned up the trash from dinner and sat back down at the table. Josie ran the palm of her hand along the smooth wood in front of her and thought about the connections, all of the separate pieces that needed to be assembled to form the larger picture. She looked up at Otto. "I keep thinking about Hec and how he's been caught in the middle. He had the Medranos watching. We were watching him. Who else wanted Hec?"

Otto thought for a second. "His dad."

Josie grinned, warming to the idea.

"So you're saying Wally was watching Hec like everyone else appeared to be doing."

"Exactly. Remember Hec saying that his dad quit calling him after he found out Dillon had been kidnapped?"

Otto frowned and nodded.

"We checked the phone records. Hec's not lying. So why would his dad suddenly quit calling when things are getting worse for Hec, not better?"

Otto had continued nodding his head, understanding where Josie was headed. "He quit calling because he's here."

"And where's everyone else been camped out watching Hec?"

Otto winked at her and grinned. "Down by the river."

She looked at her watch. "Got any camo pants?"

Fifteen minutes later Marta arrived at the police department from the jail, where she had been working with the sheriff to book Bea Conroy on murder charges. She pulled out a chair and sat down with Josie and Otto at the conference table to describe her hiding spot on the Rio.

"Both nights I was sitting on the east side of Wally's Folly, facing the river. Last night I got closer. I got settled into the woods, then after sundown I moved my way toward their camp, a few feet at a time." She looked at Otto. "My plan was to see if you could get me a deputy to drive an unmarked car into the lot tonight. I wanted to see how the men by the river reacted."

"Why's that?" Otto asked.

"They're either not real bright, or they're convinced what they're doing is a waste of time. They haven't caught on to the timed lights in the trailer yet. No one has entered or exited the trailer in two days, but they don't seem to notice. I'd like to see how they react to a visitor."

"Here's what I'm thinking," Josie said. "Wally quit contacting Hec by phone, but I believe he did so because he's found another way to keep tabs on him. With Dillon kidnapped, and the Medranos threatening Hec that they'll kidnap him next, I think Wally has come back to get his son. I think he's camping out down there, surveying the situation with the Medranos and with us. He's waiting to make his move, he just doesn't realize Hec isn't there yet."

Marta nodded. "It makes sense, Josie."

"I think we scout along the river, on either side of the salvage yard, just far enough away that Wally would be protected from view by the Medranos."

Marta narrowed her eyes at Josie, her expression suddenly skeptical. "I've been up and down the river to the east. The Rio Camp and Kayak is a half mile downriver that way. They've got half a dozen kids. I can't imagine Wally thinking that area would be safe to hide out."

"What about to the west?"

"Thick woods and scrub brush. No houses for several miles. That's a possibility."

"How far downriver from the salvage yard do we start?" Otto asked.

"I'd say a quarter mile at the most. It's pretty dense woods, and the river's choked with downed trees and salt cedar. It'll be tough walking," Marta said.

Wrapped up in Otto's barn coat, Delores stood on the back porch of their ranch home watching the goats wander toward the barnyard for the evening feeding. A turkey tetrazzini casserole was in the oven, ready to serve as soon as Otto arrived home. She was thinking what a fine life she had. She'd married her high school sweetheart and loved him still after all these years; they had a good daughter married to an equally good man, good friends, and a church family who rounded out their life. On evenings like this, looking out across the land that she and Otto loved so much, she wondered what she had done to deserve such bounty.

The distant ring of the phone brought her out of her reverie and she rushed into the kitchen to grab it. "Hello?" she called.

"I've bad news. I won't make it for dinner. Will you save me a plate in the oven?"

"Of course I will. What's happening?"

"We think Wally Follet is holed up down along the river. If this turns into what we hope, it may be morning before I make it home."

Delores hung up with Otto and took the casserole out of the oven, disappointed that he wouldn't be home, but certainly not angry. She had never understood a police officer's wife fussing over her husband missing dinner. It wasn't as if he had a choice. Dinner or not, the job had to be done. She set the teakettle to boil and placed the hot baking dish on the stove to cool. She stole small bites out of the corners of the dish, hungry but preferring to wait for Otto in case he made it home. She would have a biscuit with peanut butter later if she got too hungry.

Once the kettle's whistling started she placed foil on the casserole to prevent herself from taking any more, and she poured a cup of hot water over a bag of chamomile tea. Leaning against the kitchen sink, she stared out the window at the bloodred sunset, the color so violent it looked as if the desert had caught fire. She thought it was a fitting sundown for the work Otto hoped to accomplish that night. The horror that had been unleashed on so many people came down to nothing more than one man's greed. A very, very stupid man. They almost always were, criminals, though they often were surprised to find it out.

Delores sipped and thought about her friend Maggie's daughter, Sheila. Why were some women so drawn to men with no conscience, or drive, or even compassion? And, why on earth, when they discovered these men for who they were, did these women continue to pursue them? An idea suddenly came to her, and with it a quandary. She knew full well that Otto's conversations with her about police work were confidential, and in all their years of marriage she had never betrayed a confidence, never to impress or even to straighten out a stray bit of gossip with her girlfriends. But this case was different. Otto was in the woods, occupied, and she thought she might be able to help in other ways.

<hr>

It was the transition time between sunset and moonrise, when the dying light along the river made the colors of the day fade and objects morphed into shapes that the mind couldn't identify at first glance. They had decided to make use of the remaining daylight, hoping it would increase their chances of spotting a disguised campsite. Josie was in the lead, walking slowly along the river, dodging the debris that had collected through years of disuse, while trying to remain quiet and unnoticed. Marta followed behind her, watching both sides of the river closely as Josie scouted the path along the river's edge. They had chosen to stay within a few feet of the river, where their way was less encumbered and quieter. Both were dressed in black jackets, black SWAT pants, and boots. Otto set up a perimeter along the road in case Wally got spooked and took off before they could reach him. The road was a straight shot for several miles, so unless Wally braved the Medranos on the Mexican side of the river, Josie felt sure that if he was here, they would find him.

Delores needed Sheila to open up and share information she would most certainly not want to discuss. Maggie was too angry with Sheila to offer much help, and instead would probably only alienate her daughter even further, so Delores opted to keep Maggie in the dark about her plan.

Sheila lived in a duplex across from the county jail, and as Delores drove past the jail, she felt an incredible wave of both guilt and excitement sweep over her. She felt quite certain that Otto was going to be angry with her for getting involved, but if she was right, he would surely forgive her.

Delores rang the doorbell and a moment later Sheila answered with the flustered look of someone obviously not anticipating visitors.

"Sheila! It's so good to see you!"

Sheila looked around Delores to the driveway, most likely expecting to see her mother there. Delores knew her through Maggie, but certainly not well enough to stop by unannounced for a chat.

Sheila seemed to realize something was expected of her and she stepped back, pushing the screen door open so Delores could enter. She was in her late thirties with long curly hair that looked as if it needed to be cut and conditioned. She was thin with sallow skin and suspicious eyes, although Delores conceded that the girl was right to have been suspicious about her visit. She wore cut-off jean shorts and a skintight tank top. Delores wondered how this woman was related to, let alone the daughter of, sweet-natured Maggie.

"Come on in. It's good to see you." Sheila stood awkwardly at the door as Delores sat down on the lone couch in the small living room. "Is Mom outside?"

"No, no. No, this is just me. Just coming here with a favor to ask, really. I'm hoping you might be able to help out with something."

Sheila pulled a chair from the kitchen table and dragged it into the living room. She sat and faced Delores.

"Is there something you want to tell me?" she finally asked.

Delores sighed. "Well, yes, and I don't know how to do this. I'm breaking a confidence coming here. Do you suppose I could tell you something and swear you to secrecy? Even from your mother?"

Sheila made a face. "We're not exactly sharing secrets anymore, Delores. But, yes, I can keep a secret."

Delores placed her hands on her knees, resigning herself to get on with it. "Okay. As you know, Wally Follet is in quite a bit of trouble."

Sheila smirked as if preparing for a lecture she'd heard a hundred times before.

"Can I ask if you're still dating him?"

Sheila laughed slightly, obviously taken aback. "Not that it's anyone's business, but yes, I am."

"I just really can't get into everything, but the police believe he is directly connected to Dillon Reese's kidnapping."

Sheila's eyebrows raised and Delores felt instant gratification.

"When he went into hiding it was because he found out he was in big trouble with the government. You know that, right?"

Sheila tipped her head to the side.

"Do you know that he stole a lot of money?"

Sheila's face blushed a deep red. "How do you know that?"

"If you tell Wally that we know this, it will put my husband in terrible danger. Not to mention what it could do to Dillon Reese. Do you understand?"

Sheila went still and Delores knew her intuition had been right. Sheila finally nodded.

"He stole millions of dollars from the Medranos, Sheila. They kidnapped Dillon Reese, an innocent man in all of this, in order to force Josie Gray to recover the money. I know you love him, but Wally's done very bad things. Christina Handley died because of what he did. Do you realize that?"

Tears had begun to run down Sheila's cheeks, and her eyes squinted shut, as if she wasn't able to face Delores. "He told me he had to take a bunch of money but he wouldn't say why. I kept asking. I knew it sounded wrong, but he told me he'd explain everything once he got Hec back. I really thought he was a good man. People just never gave him a chance. They don't understand that Wally has a good side."

Delores stood and walked quickly into the kitchen. She brought back a chair and sat next to Sheila, who was sobbing now. "This isn't about a fight between you and your mother. Or even about whether Wally is a good or a bad person. The police have to find him. If they don't get that money back, Dillon Reese will be killed." Delores felt the hitch in her own voice, even saying the words.

"He's hiding, here in Artemis, but I don't know where for sure."

"How do you contact him?"

Sheila wiped tears from her face and struggled to catch her breath. Delores got up and grabbed a tissue box from the bathroom. Sheila finally calmed down enough to speak.

"He calls me, maybe once every few days. He just says he's nearby. That he's waiting until he can get Hec and get him out of town to safety."

"Is he camping by the river?"

Sheila gave her a pained expression and groaned. "He made me swear I wouldn't tell anyone."

"Come on, Sheila. A man's life could be saved. Where along the river?" Delores insisted.

"I don't know exactly. He's staying in an old barn where he can keep watch over Hec. That's all I know."

Delores grabbed both of Sheila's hands in her own and waited until the young woman made eye contact with her. "Promise me that you won't contact him. That you won't tell him we had this conversation. Even if he calls you tonight. Promise me that?"

Sheila nodded. "I do. I promise. He's gone too far. I didn't know all of this. I really didn't."

Delores squeezed her hands. "You did the right thing. You may have just saved a life tonight. Maybe even Wally's."

———•———

Once Delores was back in her car she found her cell phone in her purse and turned it on. She hardly ever used it, but Otto had convinced her to keep it with her as a safety precaution. He answered on the first ring.

"Delores?"

"Otto, I'm sorry to call. It's about Wally. Have you found him?"

"No. What's going on?"

"I talked to Sheila, Maggie's daughter?"

"Yes, I know her."

"She's dating Wally. Drove Maggie just about crazy. They won't even speak about it."

"Delores, what did she tell you?"

"She says he's staying in an old barn by the river."

"You're a saint. Sit tight. I'll call when I know something."

Delores could hear the pride in Otto's voice at the information she had just provided, and she knew she had made the right choice.

———•———

Ten minutes later Josie and Marta appeared on the road, dark shadows against the night. They had found nothing and came back to check in. Otto filled them in on his conversation with Delores.

"There's a barn back behind the Camp and Kayak. I saw it, but the roof's caved in. If he's staying there he can't see the yard. He'd have to move down during the night. But it would provide good cover," said Marta.

They got into Otto's jeep and drove to the Rankins' house and parked in the tree-lined driveway. Marta knocked on the door and Lisa answered in sweatpants and a T-shirt, her hair in a ponytail. Marta came quickly to the point of their visit.

"Has anyone been in the barn over the past month? Any of your kids play out there?" Marta asked.

"No, that thing needs to be bulldozed. We just haven't dealt with it. The kids are forbidden to go near it. It's old and already partially caved in."

"We believe Wally Follet may be hiding out there so he can keep an eye on Hector."

"On our property?" Lisa asked, shuddering. She made a noise of disgust. "I hope you find him, lock him up, and throw away the key."

"I just want to make sure you're all safe and accounted for. Are you and the kids all inside right now?"

"Yes, we're all inside." She furrowed her brow in worry.

"I want you to lock the doors and stay inside and away from the windows until you hear from us."

"Should we leave?"

"No, precautions are in order, though. Keep the kids inside. We're going to check the barn out. We'll let you know."

Shortly after they left, they noticed lights in the house being turned off.

The Rankins' property was a long strip of land sandwiched between the road and the river. It was only about a hundred yards deep, but a half mile long. The house and a quarter mile of man-made beach were open to the river. To the left of the beach area a small grove of trees and dense scrub brush blocked the river from view. A dilapidated wooden hay barn about twice the size of the house sat in front of the trees. It was located far enough down the road from the house that Wally could easily hide inside it. The outside walls were caving inward, but it was intact enough that some-one could enter it and take cover in the center.

It was decided that Josie and Marta would check the barn first, while Otto remained by the road with a clear view in case of an attempted escape. They had all agreed that Wally wouldn't cross the water; they were fairly certain that he had already scoped out Medrano's men, situated just over the other side. If Wally wasn't in the barn, they would try to find the route that he most likely took from the barn to the river when he observed the Medranos and Hec.

Josie and Marta checked their firearms and extra duty revolvers and then put the department headsets on and checked the signal. They carried their Berettas at the ready position and walked quietly forward in a crouch, taking each step almost in tandem. They reached the barn and circled it slowly at a distance of twenty feet, searching for all of the entrance/exit points. There was only one traditional tractor entrance into the barn, and it was now partially obstructed by a section of the caved aluminum roof. When the back half of the barn had caved inward, the roof had fallen into a heap.

Once they had finished circling the building, Josie waved Marta over, behind the cover of a tree. It was completely dark now, but the stars were providing enough light that a careful observer could see them moving.

Josie whispered, "We'll split and each take an entrance. Be careful though. It's dark now, and he may be ready to head out."

Marta nodded.

"If he has any sense he'll have an escape route. He'll take off on foot."

"He won't go south," Marta said. "He'll choose the police over the cartel."

"We have Otto to the north; you take the east entrance where the roof has caved. I'll take the west." Josie paused and put her hand on Marta's coat sleeve. "We're trained to clear buildings, to clear rooms. We can't bust into a caved-in barn and clear it. These old barns have storage areas and stalls that may have caved in. We'll have boards scattered with no clear floor plan. We'll just have to take it slow."

"You're sure we don't want backup?"

Josie shook her head. "What happens if the state or the feds get involved? We lose him and we lose access to the cartel's money. And all hope of brokering a deal to save Dillon. We need to move quick and quiet to keep the cartel's men unaware."

Marta nodded.

"Don't enter until your eyes have adjusted, then it's at a crouch, one step at a time. You clear the west side and we meet at the tractor entrance on my side. If you see signs he's staying in the barn, you tap me on the headset. I'll do the same. Your headset dialed in?"

Marta checked and nodded.

Josie pressed the button on her headset box that connected her to Otto, who was monitoring their conversation. She filled him in on the plan and he said he was ready.

"Gunfire as an absolute last resort, Marta. I suspect if Medranos' men heard gunfire they would come, assuming it had to do with Wally. We can't draw the cartel up here or we'll all be dead."

She nodded.

"You okay?"
"Let's do this."

Josie watched Marta slip behind the west side of the barn, and then Josie made it to the east side, peering between the slats in the boards as she walked along the outside of the structure. Ten feet down the side of the barn she spotted a pinprick of light coming from inside. She stopped and watched. The light wavered slightly, losing and gaining intensity. Josie signaled Marta, her voice barely above a whisper.

"You see light?"

"Nothing."

"Give me a minute. Don't move in yet," Josie said.

She walked another five feet to a wider gap between two boards. Near the ground, one board was torn away from the building, leaving enough room for a rabbit to gain entrance, but not a human. Josie slowly lowered herself to the ground to get a better view of inside and smelled the moldy hay from long-ago-stabled horses. She could tell that she was looking into one of the old horse stalls. About five feet behind the stall there appeared to be a room, maybe a tack room or storage area, but it was hard to tell in the dark. In between the gaps of the boards Josie could see light. Someone was inside the small room, using a flashlight.

Josie stood again and moved several feet back to signal Marta. She whispered, "He's inside a small tack room, maybe six by six feet. I can see the beam from a flashlight moving around."

"I have access to the barn," Marta said, her voice barely loud enough to register in the headset. "Fallen boards are everywhere, on top of old tractor parts and junk. But I won't have access to that room from this side without making noise."

"You stay there in case he bolts. I'm going in for him now. Otto. I'm going in."

"Clear."

Josie reached the entrance and once she was inside, she waited several minutes, adjusting to the inside of the barn with no starlight.

The flashlight beam was clearly visible now. There was no door on the tack room, just a doorway. From her angle she could only see about two feet into the room. She was standing eight feet from the entrance and to the left. From the movement of the flashlight beam, it looked as if Wally was sitting in the back of the small room. The light appeared focused down and toward the ground in the back of the room, possibly from a headlamp. She took a deep breath to steady herself. If he saw her and made a loud commotion, they were in trouble. She didn't have the backup in place to handle a cartel contingency, and she had placed her entire department in grave danger. The thought made her uneasy, but it was a calculated risk with the possibility of a huge payoff.

She stepped forward. The floor was dirt, and the barn still carried the pungent smell of horse manure, old decaying wooden boards, and oily tractor parts. She walked silently around the side of the tack room to peer between the vertical boards. In the dark barn, Wally couldn't see her. She was more concerned with the sound of stepping on or knocking into something that she couldn't see.

Wally was sitting low in a folding camping chair. His flashlight was a headlamp that was now focused on his lap where he appeared to have taken a gun apart, probably to clean it. She calculated it would take her two long steps to reach him in the chair. The floor to the right of the chair appeared to be clear, and she intended to roll him out of the chair and onto the ground, where she could keep him quiet.

Josie couldn't enter the room and announce herself as police protocol dictated, but she was well beyond protocol at that point. Doing so would give Wally time to respond, to make noise. She stood just outside the entrance to the tack room, took a long breath, and in one fluid motion entered the room, reached him in two strides, and pointed her gun directly at his chest. He lifted his head, his eyes wide and terrified, the headlamp pointing directly into Josie's eyes. Before he had time to react she jumped on top of him, collapsing the cheap camping chair, both of them landing on the ground. Metal gun parts clattered to the dirt floor as she rolled Wally facedown and sat on his back, clamping her hand over his mouth.

Josie whispered into the headset. "I'm in. All clear."

The headlamp had fallen off and was facing up. She flipped it so that the light couldn't be seen by anyone outside. The takedown had caused very little noise, and Wally was breathing hard from his nose, but not attempting to twist free or make noise. Josie figured he didn't want the cartel's attention either.

She leaned forward on his back, and with her right hand she positioned her Beretta directly in front of his eyes and whispered, "See this?" She rubbed the tip of her forefinger lightly across the safety. "It's off. I'm going to take my hand off your mouth, and if you make so much as a sound I will knock you out cold. If you attempt to escape I will shoot you dead and leave you here for the cartel to clean up your remains. Nod your head if you understand."

He nodded his head, the dirt underneath him scratching his face.

Josie removed her hand and wiped it on her pants. Without another word she pulled his arms behind his back and handcuffed him. Marta was suddenly on her knees beside them. She helped Josie roll him over, onto his back, then pull him to sit upright. Josie crouched beside him, her gun just above his head. She whispered, "Remember, I will knock you out cold if you so much as breathe hard."

He nodded his understanding.

"Where's the money, Wally? And don't jack me around. I will not play games," Josie said.

Wally tipped his head toward the corner of the room. With the headlamp facing the floor the room was barely lit, but she could see a piece of aluminum that appeared to have been pulled from the roof and propped up in the corner. Josie nodded at Marta, who stood and moved the metal. Behind it stood three large black suitcases.

For the first time in her life, Josie recognized her heart as an organ with a shape. It knocked against her chest cavity, the soft thud pushing fear up into her throat. Those three black suitcases could hold the key to Dillon's safety.

Wally was now in a sitting position, his hands cuffed behind his back, his legs straight out in front of him. Kneeling beside him, Josie leaned forward and placed her mouth just above his ear.

"Tell me exactly what is inside those suitcases."

"Nine million."

Josie knocked her gun onto the side of his head and he flinched, shutting his eyes. "Not so loud."

"It's all there, minus a few thousand. Other than that, count it. It's there."

Marta slowly unzipped a corner of the suitcase and they held their breath in paranoia at the sound of the zipper, imagining the Medrano cartel outside the barn, waiting with their arsenal for Josie to find their money, ready to claim what was rightfully theirs.

TWENTY-SIX

The drive to the Arroyo County Jail was excruciating. Josie, Marta, and Otto had only taken one vehicle to the river to avoid drawing extra attention. Now, nine million dollars held in three suitcases was piled so high in the back of Josie's jeep that she could barely see out the back. As each car passed in the opposite direction, Josie couldn't help but think about the fact that she was carrying some of the most sought-after cargo in the world at that moment, cargo that would get each of them killed if certain people knew they had it. From the silence and the icy tension running through the jeep, she could tell Otto and Marta both felt the same. To add to this edge, the smell emanating from Wally Follet, who sat handcuffed and breathing heavily in the back seat with Otto, was revolting. Hovering above the smell of the cigarette smoke that permeated his filthy clothing was the smell of a body that had not been washed in many days. Otto asked Josie to roll both windows down in the back, preferring the cold night air to Wally's odor.

Josie wondered what Wally Follet was thinking. On one hand, his arrest and turning over the cash had just ended half of his issues; he hadn't won, but the battle with the Medranos was at least over. But what happened when he made the transition to prison? Josie had little doubt that the long arm of the Medranos could reach him behind bars. It happened every day.

Sheriff Martínez met Josie outside of the loading bay behind the prison. They had agreed Wally's arrest would remain confidential until the money was in federal custody. That kind of money brought incredible danger not only to the jail but also to the citizens of Artemis. Josie realized she was turning over the cash that might ensure Dillon's freedom, but there was no other choice. The money could never be given to the Medranos, but they didn't need to know that.

Booked on a host of charges from the federal government, Wally was then led down the hallway to a bathing area used for new prisoners.

While Martínez processed Wally, Josie called Agent Omstead.

"We got him. Wally's in custody and we have the nine million dollars at the Arroyo County Jail."

"You have Wally *and* the money?" He laughed, obviously shocked by the news. "Nice work, Chief Gray."

Josie smiled at his response. She explained the takedown, and the fact they now had nine million dollars of cartel money in their custody. He told Josie how impressed he was with their police work, and it was no surprise when he said they would have an agent to Artemis within an hour to seize the money.

Josie stood with Otto outside the interview room to discuss what came next. Otto was the lead, but he had no trouble giving the interrogation to Josie. "You deserve this one. Go in there and nail that bastard."

Josie entered the room and shook hands with Wally's attorney, Charlie Givens. Wally had accepted the offer of a public defender. Charlie was sixty years old and had retired several years ago, but then a year later had come back to work after his wife was diagnosed with cancer and money became an issue. Charlie was a genuinely nice person, and Josie wondered occasionally how he handled representing such lowlifes for all these years.

Charlie said he had just been informed they would be escorting Wally to the interview room shortly. Josie took the opportunity to explain the charges and the need to question Wally immediately.

"I feel confident he has information that could help us bring Dillon back home," she said. "I understand your need to protect your client, but anything you can do to help us speed this along could be critical to Dillon's survival."

Charlie leaned back in his chair and considered Josie for a moment. He was wearing a tan suit, white shirt, and a yellow-and-navy-colored paisley tie. His silver hair was neatly combed to the side and Josie could smell his aftershave. Charlie was a country gentleman and he was one of Josie's favorite attorneys to work with.

"Contrary to what television tells you, all attorneys are not sons of bitches out to set vicious criminals free and screw over grandmas and small children. I will do everything in my power to ensure you get the information you need without further jeopardizing my client. How's that for a compromise?"

Josie smiled, stood from her chair, and reached across the table to shake his hand. "That'll work. I appreciate your cooperation."

Five minutes later, Wally Follet entered the interview room wearing an orange inmate jumpsuit with his ankles shackled and his hands in plastic cuffs. His uncombed black hair was still damp from the shower, but he was clean and the stench was now gone. Heavyset with a large frame, he looked nothing like his lanky son. He had thick hair that sat on his head like a cap, and deep-set wrinkles that ran vertical lines down either side of his chin and gave him a constant deep frown.

Josie ran through the formalities of the interview, and then Charlie ran through his set of instructions. Wally stared at the table as if completely tuned out.

Josie had a written list of questions she intended to ask. She did not need a hostile conversation with Wally Follet. She needed information. But the image and sounds of Dillon's arm being slashed pressed into her thoughts, and she couldn't stick to her list.

"Explain to me why you sat on nine million dollars knowing that your son had been abducted and terrorized by a group of mercenaries? Knowing that your accountant was kidnapped? Knowing that Bea Conroy murdered Christina Handley while you stood back and watched? Can you help me understand any of this? Because right now I am royally pissed off."

Charlie interrupted her, his tone stern. "Chief Gray."

Josie continued, her face red with anger, unable to stop herself. "I would like nothing better than to see you rot like spoiled meat in a federal pen for the rest of your life. Better yet, let the cartel mete out your punishment. You were willing to allow the cartel to beat your son to a pulp while you hid like a coward."

Charlie raised his hand and called her name again, clearly annoyed with her approach. He turned his attention to Wally. "Mr. Follet, you don't need to answer any of those questions. They were inflammatory and inappropriate." Looking at Josie again, he said, "Let's stick to the facts here. Harassing Mr. Follet won't serve any of us at this point."

Charlie was a nice guy, but he was a professional who wouldn't allow his client to be badgered, no matter what kind of lowlife the defendant might be.

Josie clasped her hands in front of her on the table and clenched her jaw. She stared at Wally, who stared back, his eyes devoid of emotion, his expression flat.

"Okay. I'll be completely honest," she started again. "My concern isn't you or your money. It isn't even about the charges. My concern is finding a way to bring Dillon Reese home. Tonight. I want you to make that happen. You started this mess, you need to clean it up."

Wally appeared to be sizing her up, staring at her with suspicion. "I been watching everybody else watching out for me. I been down at the river. I heard things."

"And?"

"I been listening to those river rats talk for days."

"What did you hear that pertained to the kidnapping?"

He rubbed his chin and tilted his head as if giving her question careful consideration. "You cut me a deal? I can lead you to Dillon Reese."

Charlie's eyebrows rose and he stood at the same time Josie did, ready to stop her.

She put both hands on the table and leaned in toward Wally. "Listen, you miserable piece of shit. Your greed killed a woman and led to two kidnappings. One of them was your own son!"

Wally turned calmly to Charlie. "I think we're done here. This lady don't want my help."

She banged both her fists on the table, and then pointed a finger directly at him. "The FBI and a kidnapping negotiator are observing the neighborhood where we believe Dillon Reese is stashed at this very moment. If they find him tonight, and you go to trial, and you *will* go to trial, and the jury hears that you withheld information from the police? Information that could have led to the kidnappers? Information that could have saved a man's life?" Josie paused, lowering her voice. "The judge and jury will eat you alive. And I will enjoy every second of your miserable meltdown."

Over the next several seconds, Josie watched the volley of meaningful looks that occurred between attorney and client. Wally looked anxiously to Charlie, expecting his attorney to save him from the smartass cop. Charlie frowned. Wally's expression turned to worry. Charlie pursed his lips, and in Wally's expression Josie could detect his realization that it was over. How many times had she seen that scene play out through the years? It was the beginning of the end for Wally Follet.

"I believe, Mr. Follet, that it would be in your best interests to cooperate. Holding back information at this point will not serve you well in court," Charlie said.

Wally didn't hesitate. In the end, he was a con man who knew when to lie and when to cut his losses and tell the truth.

"By the way they talked, it had to be Piedra Labrada. He's in a house. They keep talking about Espinoza Street. I don't know where that is, but there can't be two streets with that name in a town the size of Piedra."

"Is it a residential neighborhood? A family home?" Josie asked.

"I don't know."

"How many people are in the house?"

"I don't know."

"Give me something, Wally. Anything to help us identify that house."

Wally stared at the table. "I know they said the bedroom windows were boarded up."

Josie watched him with a lump in her throat. If he could narrow down the house for Nick, she could be going after Dillon that night. He could be coming home.

"Think about that house. What else did they say?"

He looked up at her, his eyes expectant. "I remember them talking about an old camper trailer. One of them talked about using it. Taking it somewhere south."

Josie glanced at Charlie, who gave her a nod, a sign of encouragement. She stood and walked out into the room next door, where Otto sat in front of a computer monitor watching the interview by a live feed. He put his fist in the air when she sat down in the chair next to him. "Excellent, Josie. This is it. I can feel it."

She said nothing, but her pulse was racing. She took her phone out of her shirt pocket and called Nick. When he answered she asked if they had narrowed down the safe house they were searching for.

"I've got four guys watching a three-block neighborhood. It's a big area, so we need more time."

Josie summarized Wally's arrest and her conversation with him in the interrogation room. "I got a street and a description." She took a breath to steady her voice. "Wally claims the guys along the river described a house on Espinoza Street."

Nick made a noise on the other end, obviously excited. "That's one of the streets we're watching. Street number?"

"He didn't know, but he said there are bedroom windows that are boarded up, and there's an old camper parked behind the house. That's all I've got."

"That's enough. I'll let you know if we find it."

———

Josie returned to the interrogation room with two Styrofoam cups of black coffee. Wally took one and Charlie declined, so Josie set the other in front of her. She'd had a surge of energy after talking with Nick, and was ready to push Wally for more. She asked him to describe the last two weeks of his life, which were spent similar to how she'd predicted. Wally had been tipped off by two different U.S. car dealers that the feds were ready to indict him for racketeering and selling stolen property over an international border. Wally knew they had him, and that he would do time, but that wasn't his worry.

"I didn't run from the feds," he said. "I ran from Medrano."

Wally then went on to explain that the investigation would have eventually led the feds to discover his involvement with the Medrano cartel, and when it did, his business would be destroyed. He said he'd been shipping cars with the Medranos for three years, and he knew them well enough to know he would have to leave the country forever if he stole their money, especially that amount. There was an implicit understanding when conducting business with the Medranos that mistakes are not made. If they are, you pay with your life. Wally claimed everyone doing business with the Medranos thought they were being careful. Some other schmuck might screw up, but not them. The risk was always worth the profit.

"So you run from Medrano by stealing millions from them?" Josie asked, her tone incredulous.

"Why not?" Wally said. "If I stayed, the feds would arrest me. The Medranos would never let me get to trial though. They wouldn't let their business get hacked around in a U.S. courtroom. I'd be dead before I ever made it to trial. So why not take the money and run? At least I had a chance."

"You don't think you'd have stood a better chance making it out alive if you'd left without taking their nine million dollars?" Josie asked.

"You ever heard of a *dead man walking*? The Medranos were going to kill me whether I took the money or not. Not much to think about. At least with the money I stood a chance of making it somewhere safe. You think I couldn't buy a fake identity with a million dollars? That could hide me a hell of a lot better than the witness protection joke."

"So why are you still here? In Artemis?"

Wally leaned his head back and stared at the ceiling a moment. When he looked back at Josie his eyes had welled up. "I tried to get Hector to come with me. He wouldn't. The kid wouldn't lift a loaf of bread if his life depended on it. The kid's got an ulcer as it is. He drove me crazy over it all. Tried to get me to turn myself in. He didn't get the danger we was in. And I couldn't force him. He wouldn't leave that damned dog. I finally took off."

Josie glanced at Charlie, who was listening intently, jotting notes on his legal pad.

"I took the money and drove north. I got as far as Idaho and started worrying what might happen to Hec. Then I called the trailer a couple days in a row. Got no answer." Wally shook his head and pressed his forefinger and thumb into his eyes. He sat for several minutes, gritting back tears. "Come to find out, I finally get ahold of Hec and find out the bastards took him."

He looked at Josie as if still shocked at the way the Medranos had treated his son. Josie said nothing and he finally continued.

"So I came back to get him. I brought the money with me 'cause I didn't have anywhere else to hide it."

"Why not do what the Medranos wanted? Exchange the money for Dillon, and Hec is out of danger?" she asked.

Wally laughed. "How stupid you think I am? There's no even trade with them. I might give them the money, but you think Dillon goes free? You might be that naïve, but not me."

"What was your plan then?"

"I hid out in the barn, biding my time. I knew they wouldn't kill Hec. If they did, they'd know I'd never come back. I figured they'd use Hec as bait, and that's exactly what they did. I called and called and Hec wouldn't pick up the phone in the trailer. When he finally answered the phone, he said he'd been taken by the Medranos and they wanted their money back. So I came back to watch and wait. I knew I'd get my chance. They'd take off and I'd get up to the trailer and take my boy. We'd leave this filthy town for good. But then you showed up and took him."

"And you couldn't exactly drive into Artemis to retrieve your son."

Josie sipped at the cup of coffee and decided to change her line of questioning. "I don't understand why you bothered with your records. You admitted you're screwed. Why care about your business records at this point?"

Wally's expression changed, his face growing more animated. "I got indicted for selling stolen cars, not shipping cash for the Medranos. When Dillon Reese got kidnapped I figured the feds would eventually figure me out. My boy's got nothing to do with this business, not with the Medranos or the stolen cars or any of it. I didn't want him to get busted just because of me."

Josie frowned and said nothing, hoping he would continue.

Wally scooted his chair up to the table and folded his hands in front of him. Josie wondered if he was trying to appear earnest. "Those feds were after me hot and heavy, and I figured they'd take my boy as a consolation if they could link him to me in some way. I couldn't risk it."

"But you said you were coming back to get Hec. Why would the records matter if you were both leaving?"

"He'd already told me no before. But he's my only kid. I had to try to make it right." Wally made a dismissive face. "At least if I had the records it would slow things down."

"So do the right thing for Dillon. He's being held in Mexico, because of your decisions. You get that, right?" she said.

He looked angry, then frustrated, and Josie wondered if it was actually a reaction caused by guilt. "I know I did this to him. I screwed over everybody. It wasn't like I sat down and planned all this out. I'm sorry about what's happened. But I told you what I know. That's it. A house on Espinoza Street. The Medranos got him locked up, waiting on the money. And they got no idea where the money is. But when they find out you got me, and you got the money?" He shook his head. "They don't bargain. They find out you're not giving the money back? They just kill him."

———

As soon as the paperwork was completed and Wally was escorted to his cell, Otto and Josie walked outside into the cold night. She was thinking about her conversation with Dell the night before. What had he told her? *You cross that river and you do what needs to be done.*

Josie stopped under the outdoor light on the jail's front entrance and faced Otto. His face was in shadow, his expression unreadable. He may have been lead investigator, but it no longer mattered. She had a clear plan in her mind. "I'm going to Piedra Labrada. I'm going to be there when Nick moves in on that house."

Otto nodded slowly. "I expected as much. But we go together. I won't let you do this alone."

"Not a chance. You have Delores. You have—"

"This isn't about Delores. Why do you do that? Why do you devalue your own life because you don't have a family?"

Josie was surprised at his tone. He was angry, his voice loud in the otherwise silent parking lot. "I get the importance of you being there, but let's be smart," he said. "You don't barge into an investigation in a foreign country without some thought. Call Nick. Get an update before we go any further."

Taking in his rigid posture and fists, Josie felt a terrible sense of guilt for dragging him in this far. Still, she nodded and called Nick and was relieved when he answered.

"Tell me what's happening," she said.

"We found the house, Josie. The bedroom windows are boarded up. Sergio is here. He talked to one of the neighbors, who said the lights are on in the kitchen all the time, curtains pulled tight in the kitchen and living room. The neighbors say they've never seen a female enter or leave. Just men looking around before they enter the house. The neighbors said no one on the block makes eye contact with anyone who parks in that driveway. No one will confirm that it's the Medranos, but I'm sure of it." Nick paused. "If it isn't Dillon in that house, there's someone else being held."

"Otto and I are on our way now."

She was surprised when he didn't protest. "Sergio can meet you at the border crossing. He'll get you through the checkpoint, then you ride with him. No guns. Bring your badges. We'll get you weapons when you arrive."

"I've got pictures of the money on my cell phone. Proof, if it comes to that."

"Okay. I'm pulling the team together now."

She hung up and kept her phone out, staring down at it. "We

should call the mayor. Or the prosecutor at the very least, to let them know our plans."

"You're right. We should."

She hesitated and looked up at him and he pursed his lips.

"We both know the prosecutor's answer. And the mayor's," she said.

"Which is why we won't tell them."

"We could lose our jobs. Law enforcement officers crossing the border illegally? Mayor Moss would love to see me fry over this one," she said.

"They won't fire me at this point in my career. Drench wouldn't allow it. They could force a resignation, but I'd still get my retirement. You, though . . ."

"Otto. If I don't do everything in my power to bring Dillon home?" She shrugged. "The mayor can go to hell."

TWENTY-SEVEN

When Josie and Otto arrived at the border crossing, Sergio was standing at the gatehouse with a guard who waved them through to a parking lot. Josie locked the jeep and she and Otto got into Sergio's marked Federales police car. He took off with sirens and lights and sped through the city streets of Ojinaga, then drove a state road thirty minutes back toward Artemis's sister city, Piedra Labrada, a town of roughly five thousand people. Sergio took the opportunity to fill them in on the progress that had been made.

"After Nick left you yesterday evening, I met with him at the police station. He had already contacted me several days ago about his belief that Dillon was being held close to Artemis but still in Mexico. The neighborhood where we believe Dillon is located is peppered with cartel activity. Many poor people, barely hanging on. There's allegiances to the Medranos. People know if they protect the cartel, they get protected in return, maybe even rewarded with a job. Maybe money to send their kids to a private school."

"Where is Nick's team located?"

"We've set up a command post at an empty house a half block from where we believe Dillon is being held. Nick is getting a floor plan based on other houses in the neighborhood. We meet at one A.M.

to plan for the rest of the night." He glanced at the clock on the car radio. "We should be there right on time."

Once they arrived in Piedra Labrada, they drove through several blocks of small one-story homes.

"Is this the old St. Agnes district?" Otto asked.

"That's it. But the Catholic school burned down in the seventies," Sergio said. "It used to be middle-class families, but most moved out when the Medranos moved in. The families who still live here want out, but no one's buying."

Most of the homes they drove by were lit up brightly against the cold night. Josie wondered what kind of hell lay behind some of those doors.

He pulled into the driveway of a home that looked dark from the outside. "This was an empty house. The owners just left it. The windows were already boarded up. Good for us. Gives a measure of privacy." He shut off the car and turned to Josie. "Nick has two men positioned on the street, observing the safe house. If anything happens we'll know."

They entered the command post through a side entrance that led into a small kitchen, lit by a fluorescent light fixture typically seen in outdoor garages. A long, narrow table had been set up using sawhorses and a board, and several folding chairs were positioned around it. Josie could see Nick talking on his cell phone in a darkened living room situated next to the kitchen. The living room was littered with scattered boxes and odds and ends that made it look as if the home had been deserted in a hurry.

A policeman in a Federales uniform walked into the kitchen from the living room. Sergio introduced him as Marcos Alonzas. He was a middle-aged man whose uniform sagged on him as if he'd recently lost a great deal of weight. He nodded, smiling, but when Josie tried to ask him a question he gave her a quizzical look and shook his head no. Sergio explained he knew very little English. This was a big concern. The officers' inability to clearly communicate with each other put them all at a significant disadvantage. As the commander in charge, Nick would be the primary source of communication, but he couldn't be in all places at once. If shots were fired from multiple locations, it would be critical for the officers to communicate the position and actions of the shooters to each other. Their lives could depend on it. Josie and Otto both knew rudimentary Spanish, enough to get by on traffic stops, but not enough to communicate in a high-stress situation. Marcos smiled warily and nodded at Josie, worry also evident in his eyes.

Nick entered the room looking wired. He went straight to the makeshift table, where a brown paper grocery bag had been cut open and laid flat. Someone had drawn a floor plan and planted an X in a small room at the back right corner of the house. The visual made the hair on Josie's arms stand up.

"Have you confirmed Dillon is in the house?" she asked.

"The road name that you received from Wally, Espinoza Street, combined with local intel I received, supports that the Medranos are holding someone in that house. But it may not be Dillon. There's no way to know until we go in." Nick leaned over the floor plan and pointed. "The window on the front door of the house is boarded up. There are blackout curtains on the living room windows that allow a sliver of light to escape at almost all hours. Same thing in the kitchen. Neighbors say the lights are on throughout the night. We believe there are currently three men inside."

Nick ran his finger down a hallway and tapped it on two rooms at the back of the house. "These are small rooms, probably bedrooms, maybe eight by eight. Somebody did a hatchet job nailing up boards on their windows. They're nailed on from the outside. There's a window in the back that allows access into what we'll call the back bedroom. It's next to the kitchen. There's another window on the side of the house with access to what we'll call the corner bedroom." Nick tapped his finger on the X. "I believe Dillon is located in this back bedroom."

"Did your men see anyone inside the rooms?" Josie asked.

"We've not been able to get that close." Nick looked at Josie for a moment. "I want you to be prepared. I can't guarantee it's Dillon inside that house, but we need to move now. Kidnappers move victims frequently and with no pattern. Whoever it is could be gone by tomorrow."

Nick leaned over the crudely drawn floor plan and discussed its orientation toward the street: the alley behind it and the houses on both sides. A thick red line in the back wall of the house represented the back door leading into the kitchen, and the same line in the front of the house represented the front door leading into the living room.

"We approach this like a police raid. I have six men here tonight, all former SWAT team members, American military trained. Four men are located at key intersections around the neighborhood. If the Medranos are alerted to what's happening tonight, those men will be our first line of defense if the Medranos attempt to converge on the safe house. I'll get everyone set up with tactical headsets. You'll hear all communication, but orders come from me. I'll remain in the truck monitoring your progress, giving orders." Nick drew an X in front of both doors and said his other two men would enter the house first. "Tom and Juan will be here shortly. They're getting the other four team members set up at their observation points. Tom will enter the back door, followed by Sergio as backup. Juan will enter the front door with Marcos as backup. Josie and Otto, you'll be located outside the two bedrooms. If you can see into the room through cracks in the boards and can remove boards with little noise, do it. Just remember there may be a guard in the room. Don't tip off the guard before we're stationed or we're all screwed. As soon as you get the signal from me that we're going in, you get the window open."

Josie took a long breath and exhaled slowly, trying to calm her racing heart. Walking into a house in a foreign country with so many unknowns, including the firepower, was extremely dangerous. But knowing that Dillon's life depended on their actions complicated everything for her. She couldn't allow her fears for Dillon to cloud her judgment.

Nick continued. "Best-case scenario, my men move inside the house, take the guards hostage, and Sergio and Marcos move in for Dillon. Worst case is gunfire, which will alert the neighbors and certainly draw the Medranos. If there are multiple guards, they may try to escape out the back windows. Josie and Otto, you'll be there to make sure that doesn't happen. You'll also have a protected vantage point to shoot inside the bedrooms if it comes to that."

He looked at both Josie and Otto, who nodded. "The man inside that house is worth nine million dollars to those guards. If they lose him, they die. They will not give him up out of fear, they will fight to the death. You understand?"

Sergio had been quietly interpreting for Marcos, who nodded at Nick to indicate he understood.

Nick's expression was grave, his eyes dark and aggressive. "To capture these men alive would be a coup for the police. The chance to gather intelligence for a small-town department would send a clear message to the Medranos. However, the chance that the night ends in no casualties is not good. My men are dressed in riot gear, properly armed, and prepared to take the guards by surprise. If your safety is compromised, shoot to kill."

Nick outfitted each of them with SWAT gear and headsets. Josie and Otto were both provided metal crowbars to pry off the window boards.

Then one of Nick's team members carried in a chest and opened it to reveal six AR15 assault rifles. Nick introduced the man as Tom, the team's ammunitions expert. He was tall with a dark complexion and eyes as black as his short-cropped hair. Josie guessed he was of Middle Eastern descent. Tom quickly distributed the weapons and two extra magazines to each officer. Tom explained the mechanisms behind the gun, how to safely load, unload, and switch to safety. Josie would have felt more comfortable with her Beretta, but she'd not been allowed to carry it across the border. A major positive was that the AR15s had been outfitted with lasers and night scopes. What had originally seemed like an exorbitant cost for Nick's negotiator's fees now seemed legitimate.

———

Thirty minutes later, Nick's two team members, Tom and Juan, cleared the area and set up their position at either door. Once they were stationed, Josie and Otto followed Sergio and Marcos outside and jogged across the dark street, noticing how eerily silent it was. Josie hoped the Medrano cartel had not been tipped off they were coming. They continued down an alley that ran behind the row of houses and stopped behind the stash house.

There were no outside lights on the house, or on either of the neighboring houses, but the sky was clear and the moon and stars lit the area enough to navigate the yard. Light also streamed around the edges of the boards nailed onto the back window and through the curtain covering the window on the back door. Nick said he'd be in a black, armored Chevy Suburban, positioned half a block away, ready to move in front of the house and dispatch as soon as the team members were inside. Keeping the laser sights off to better maintain their secure position, each of the officers quickly acclimated to the night sights on their weapons. Josie watched as Sergio stepped up to the back door, turned, and waved Otto and Josie into place.

They ran to the window on the back of the house and attached their guns to the three-point hitch on their gun belts. The hitch was specifically designed to hold the AR15. Through the cracks between the wood, they could see a small portion of the floor but nothing else. They ran around to the side of the house, attempting to see into the corner bedroom, but the boards were too close together. Nick signaled in the headsets that Tom and Juan were inside.

Hearing no noise from the team members inside, Josie slipped her crowbar under the bottom piece of wood on the side window and tried to pry it up quietly, but the nails squeaked as they were pulled out of the plank. She paused a moment to listen for movement or a reaction inside. Hearing nothing, she and Otto pulled the board off slowly, as quietly as they could, and peered into the bedroom. It was filled with boxes and trash bags and piles of what looked to be old computer equipment.

Seeing no movement, they ran again to the back of the house, where Josie worked at the bottom board. The nails were tighter and required her to jerk on the crowbar to get the nails to budge. She could feel Otto beside her, his body as tense as her own. When the board gave way they saw a man sitting in a tattered recliner to the right of the closed bedroom door, his head tipped back in sleep. An automatic weapon lay across his thighs, his hands resting on the gun. Suddenly all hell broke loose at the front of the house and the man leaped up from his chair and faced the bedroom door, fumbling with his gun.

Josie and Otto pried off the next board as quickly as they could while the gunfire inside disguised the noise. With the boards off the window, the guard finally noticed movement outside and jerked his head in their direction. They saw him turn his body toward them, and as he lifted his gun to begin firing, Josie and Otto moved from the window and ran several feet down the side of the wall to keep from getting showered with glass. A hail of bullets shattered the glass, and Josie felt shards bouncing off the back of her SWAT uniform as she crouched down to the ground.

When he stopped shooting, Josie peered in through the left corner of the window, trying to find Dillon, but saw only the man, jamming a fresh magazine into his weapon. Otto looked from the right side of the same window and lifted his thumb up.

"He's on the floor, on the wall to the left of the door from where I stand," he said.

The guard began shooting out the window again, but Josie and Otto were both out of the line of fire.

Josie moved ten feet down the back side of the house, scouting for other attackers outside the home as she moved. She spoke into the headset. "I have a visual. Dillon Reese is in the back bedroom. As you enter the room he's on your right, sitting on the floor. Condition unknown. Shooter is left of the door."

Josie struggled to hear Nick confirm over the hammering of bullets inside the home.

The gunfire inside came to an abrupt stop. Nick responded, "Two cartel guards down in the kitchen. Juan is down. Repeat, Juan is down. He's being removed from the scene by Marcos. Tom and Sergio are inside. One guard barricaded in the back bedroom. Josie, your position again?"

She pressed the mic button and spoke into the headset, repeating what she had said earlier during the gunfire, and then stated her own and Otto's location. "Visual contact has been made in the back bedroom. A guard is in the room, last seen to the right of the door. Guard is heavily armed."

Gunfire started again and continued for a full minute before stopping. After thirty seconds of complete silence, Nick's voice sounded on the headset. "Third guard down. Tom and Sergio unharmed. Juan has been removed from the house. Critical but he's alive. Josie?"

Before she could answer, the last guard inside the home yelled something in Spanish that she couldn't interpret. Standing to the left of the window she yelled back, "In English."

To her surprise he yelled back in perfect English. "I want out! I'm coming out with the prisoner. If you try to shoot me I will kill him! Back away from the house or I'll kill him!"

Josie could hear the desperation in his voice. Otto ducked below the window and came to stand by Josie. "The guard's moved. He's pulled Dillon up to a standing position, although he's barely standing upright. Dillon won't have the strength to run if given the chance."

Josie turned her head away from the window, pressed the mic button, and spoke quietly to Nick. "Let me negotiate with the last guard. He doesn't know about the remaining officers, correct?"

"Correct."

"I'll tell him everyone is dead. I'll tell him I've got the money. He can trade me for Dillon," she said.

"You can't do that."

"He's holding Dillon with a gun to his head. Let me talk to him. Otto will follow me as backup. I'll go inside, offer to throw my gun into the room, then enter in exchange for Dillon. He takes me as hostage. We'll have Sergio and Tom in the kitchen. They'll get Dillon to the truck when he comes out of the bedroom. Otto will take cover in the empty bedroom and shoot if he gets a clear shot as we come down the hallway."

There was nothing on the headset. Surprisingly, Otto gave her a thumbs-up sign. It was a solid plan and would provide the best chance to bring Dillon home alive. She stood a much better chance at surviving as a hostage than Dillon. She had the money, or she at least had pictures of it on her cell phone.

"Let's do it," Nick said. "Time is critical. We're six minutes into the first shots. Someone has tipped off the rest of the Medranos by now. You have five minutes to make the trade or we come in again with guns. We have no choice." She listened through the headset as Nick called the other two officers off and told them to back into the kitchen in silence.

Josie pressed the mic again. "Juan?"

"He'll make it," Nick said.

Josie looked at Otto for support and took a deep breath. She yelled through the window. "This is Josie Gray. I have the money. I'm coming into the house now to make the trade."

She heard nothing in return. She felt certain he would negotiate to recover the money instead of admitting to Medrano that he'd been part of the disaster that was unfolding.

Otto followed Josie through the back door. The kitchen was filthy with dishes and trash, and smelled like rotting garbage and spent ammunition. Two bare mattresses lay in the middle of the living room floor and guns were piled on top of a large crate sitting next to it. Two bodies lay on the floor just inside the living room. Josie's eyes traced the blood-streaked path from the living room to the hallway where the bedrooms were located. She figured that the man must have been dragged into the living room to clear the way. It was obvious this place had been used as a safe house for a long time.

Sergio and Marcos gave a thumbs-up from the living room and motioned them down the hallway. The doors to both bedrooms were closed. Otto slipped quietly past the first bedroom where Dillon was being held and slowly opened the door to the corner bedroom. Once he had cleared the space he turned off the light and pointed a finger at Josie, letting her know he was in position.

Josie was betting the last Medrano guard wouldn't remain in the bedroom with her; he'd leave as soon as Dillon was exchanged. At this point, he probably wanted out of there as desperately as everyone else. As the remaining member of a job that had gone completely wrong, he would face certain death if he didn't come up with a solution. Josie knew that having her in custody and her promise of nine million dollars were his last hope.

Josie nodded to Otto and reached the bedroom. "I am standing in the hallway now," she called out. "Two of my officers are dead. Your guards are dead. It's you and me. I have the nine million dollars. I have a picture as proof. This is your chance to get out of here alive. You let Dillon Reese go and I give you the location of the money. All of it."

After a short pause, he called out to her. "Open the door, empty your gun. I trade you for him. You drive me to the money. If I make it safe, so do you. Anyone tries to take me out, you go with me."

Josie slowly turned the door handle and pushed the door open with her toe. "You shoot me? You will never find the money. I have it all in three suitcases. I have photographs as proof with me."

"Let me see you."

Josie tried to still the shaking hands that held her gun. She realized at that moment that both her own life and Dillon's life depended on the decisions she would make over the next few minutes. She stepped inside the room, her gun pointed toward the floor. Standing to the left of the door, the man held Dillon in a chokehold, his pistol pointed directly into Dillon's temple.

Josie's breath caught as she saw Dillon. His eyes lifted to hers and registered her presence but his face remained slack. His eyes were gaunt and ringed with black circles. He wore a sweatshirt and sweatpants that were too short and baggy for his malnourished body. He appeared extremely weak and Josie worried he couldn't walk on his own. She noticed his shoulder was saturated with blood.

She forced her attention on the guard. She had only glimpsed the man through the window as he was shooting at them. He seemed smaller now, his expression both terrified and full of hatred. He wore a filthy white T-shirt and khaki pants. With dark hair, light pockmarked skin, and wide-set green eyes, he seemed to be of mixed heritage, maybe Mexican-American given his perfect English. He was about a foot shorter than Dillon and appeared to be struggling to hold him upright in a chokehold around Dillon's neck. Dillon's knees were buckled and it looked as if he might faint from weakness and fall to the floor at any moment.

The man said, "Lay your gun on the ground and kick it to me." His voice trembled and sweat dripped down his cheeks. His terror increased her confidence.

Holding her left hand in the air she slowly bent down and did as instructed, laying her gun on the floor, her eyes never leaving the guard's.

"Now, come forward with your hands raised. I need to make sure you don't have another gun," he said.

She walked slowly into the room and raised her hands. Every move she made was calculated to position herself to overpower him, to grab his weapon. With Dillon's neck held awkwardly in the crook of one arm, the guard used the back of the hand that was holding the pistol to pat her waist and the front and back of her pants, then her groin. As he did so, he let the barrel of his pistol drop away from her. She noticed movement outside the window on the side of the house, and then a red dot appeared in the dark that she recognized as a laser. She could only hope the gun was held by a police officer and not a Medrano approaching from the rear of the house. Forced to make a split-second change to the plan, Josie calmly said, "You have an AR15 sighted on your head. If you lift your gun, your head will be blown away. Stay very, very still."

"You're lying," he said, but remained motionless, his hand now poised over her foot.

Dillon moaned, struggling to keep from dropping to the floor. Josie made eye contact with him. He was bent at the waist, his face turned up and toward her. She mouthed the words: *Don't move.* His unblinking eyes never changed their expression.

"The red laser is trained on your temple," she said to the Medrano guard. "There is a clear shot from the window. If you drop your weapon now and kneel down on the floor, you live. If you stand, or if you move that gun, you will be shot."

"You're lying!" He yelled the words now, his tone furious at the position he found himself in. But he still didn't move.

"Do you think I would have entered this room without backup? The moment you lift that gun in my direction you will die."

Josie had lost sight of the red laser dot and prayed the shooter was still in the window. If the guard called her bluff she was defenseless.

"Let go of the hostage."

He tried to stand quickly, but the weight of Dillon slowed him down, and as he maneuvered to turn and lift the pistol toward the window, two shots were fired and he fell to the floor, dragging Dillon with him.

Terrified that Dillon had been shot as well, she dropped to her knees, still not sure who had fired the shots. Dillon was lying on his side, the guard lying facedown across his legs. Josie shoved the man off and gently rolled Dillon over, looking into his eyes. He blinked at her but didn't speak.

She leaned toward him, blinking back tears. "Are you okay?" she whispered.

He nodded. She kissed his forehead and then heard Otto talking outside of the window, his voice barely audible over the ringing in her ears.

"All clear. Shooter down. You are clear to enter the room."

At that same moment, Sergio entered the room with his gun drawn, his expression desperate.

"He wasn't shot, but he's in shock," Josie said, not taking her eyes off Dillon. Tears fell down her face and she knew that she had to stop, to try and distance herself from the emotion. She stood, still keeping her eyes locked on Dillon's. "You're okay. You're going home," she said, choking back tears.

Josie heard Nick on the headset. "Get out of there. One of the team members said two pickups circled the neighborhood twice. We need out immediately."

Josie and Sergio pulled Dillon to his feet. They moved out into the hallway, where they were met by Tom, who opened the front door for them and helped to get Dillon outside. Nick had pulled the Suburban into the yard, just outside the door. They quickly loaded Dillon into the back and Josie climbed in behind him. Otto got into the front passenger seat and the rest of the team left in Sergio's police car. Nick said Sergio would drive Juan to the hospital for a gunshot wound to his thigh.

As they drove away, the houses on Espinoza Street stayed silent. It was a neighborhood that had experienced violence in the past. No one dared to step outside; doors were locked, cars parked, windows dark, their occupants lying in wait for the retribution that was sure to come.

TWENTY-EIGHT

While Nick drove the Suburban, he communicated with his other team members via his headset. From the seat next to him, Otto talked on his cell phone to Vie Blessings, Artemis's Trauma Center nurse, about Dillon's condition and their estimated time of arrival. In the backseat, Dillon had slumped against Josie without speaking. She wrapped one arm around his back and felt his spine sticking out from his frail body. Otto passed back a bottle of water. Josie gently pushed Dillon up and pressed the bottle to his lips, her hand trembling.

"Can you drink some? We need to get water into you," she said.

"I can't believe you're here." He struggled to talk, his voice cracking, barely able to speak. He drank from the bottle, dripping the water down his chin. After several sips he leaned back against the seat, turning his head to Josie, his eyes only half open. "When I saw you in the window, I thought I was dreaming it. I thought I'd never see you again."

And with those words, she finally let the emotion of the night soak into her body like the ground taking in a long-coveted rain. She cried openly, pulling him into her chest and crying into his hair as she held his back. She was overwhelmed by the love she felt, a love that she knew could carry them through the horror that would shadow their lives for many months to come.

———·——

Ten minutes later, they drove over an illegal makeshift bridge that Josie assumed Nick's team members had set up earlier in the day. Back on U.S. soil, she felt immense relief. She hadn't known for sure they would make it to safety until she heard the Rio rushing under her feet. There was no conversation in the car. The tension and exhaustion were palpable. They all knew Dillon's health was in critical condition.

When Nick pulled up to the emergency room entrance Vie and two EMTs were ready with a stretcher. They loaded Dillon up and whisked him away as Josie followed. Once they had reached an examination room, Vie stepped in front of Josie and put a hand out to stop her.

"Stay out here, Josie. We have a job to do. We'll take good care of him. The doctor will come get you as soon as we know something."

Josie stood in the hallway and watched the doors swing shut. She felt her body physically pushing to follow Vie, wanting to stand guard over Dillon. She wanted to see with her own eyes that he was going to survive. She felt a hand on her shoulder and turned to see Otto smiling kindly at her.

"You did good work tonight." He put his arms out and wrapped Josie in a hug.

"He's going to make it, Josie. Delores has called the preacher and they've got the prayer chain going. Dillon's in good hands."

Josie nodded, wishing she had his same faith.

Otto pointed behind him toward the emergency room door. "Nick is staying in the Suburban. He'll stand guard tonight at the hospital. If Dillon is cleared to go home tonight, he plans to take him to your house, given your new security system. He'll follow you if Dillon is moved."

Josie followed Otto into the waiting room and was shocked to find Mayor Steve Moss walking through the entrance. His face was unreadable. She wondered if he was here to place her into custody for crossing the border illegally. Instead, he walked up to her with his hand outstretched. He clasped her hands with both of his. "Excellent work, Chief Gray. Excellent."

She looked in confusion at Otto, who nodded slightly.

"Chief Gray saved a life tonight," Otto said. "And confiscated nine million dollars of drug cartel money in the process."

"Well done." The mayor patted her on the back again. "I just wanted to stop by and tell you in person. I've got an interview with WKIX at the city office first thing in the morning, but I'll catch up with you tomorrow." He walked out, his cowboy boots clicking across the shiny floor, the thick scent of his Polo cologne remaining behind.

She looked at Otto after the mayor left. "What the hell just happened?"

"On the drive to the hospital I texted Mooo to give him the basics. Thought he should hear it from us first. No surprise he's already turned it into a media event."

An hour later the emergency room physician came out to talk with Josie. By that time, Delores had arrived to wait with them. They all stood as the doctor approached Josie.

"At first glance I have good news," he said. "Dillon is severely dehydrated, but he's responding well to fluids. My biggest concern is kidney failure from the water loss. We'll keep him at least overnight. He's receiving fluids through an IV, and I've ordered a full line of blood work."

"He's so thin," she said. "I hadn't expected that after just a week."

"It's the dehydration. Seventy-five percent of the body's weight is from water. He's probably lost fifteen pounds just from the lack of it. The symptoms of shock and the physical weakness are from the dehydration as well."

"Can I stay with him? Stay in the room?" Josie asked.

"That would be fine. We can roll you in a bed if you'd like."

"The chair's okay. Can I talk to him yet?"

"He needs sleep, time for his body to recuperate. You can see him, but he won't be able to talk due to the sedative." The doctor put a hand out and gently squeezed Josie's arm. "I'll be back at seven tomorrow morning. By then, I'll have a better idea what kind of care Dillon may need."

After promises to keep Otto and Delores informed, Josie finally ushered them to the exit. Otto said he would drive her jeep to the emergency room parking lot and leave the keys with the nurse so that she could get home in the morning. Josie gave Otto and Delores hugs and they left. Josie knew they were worried about Dillon, and most likely her too, but her mind was beyond offering assurances that everything would be fine. She was too exhausted for assurances. She needed physical proof. She needed to see Dillon.

She entered the patient room, and closed the door behind her quietly. Dillon was lying flat on his back, his head facing up. He looked as if he hadn't moved since they rolled him into the building. The lights were off in the room except for the soft white glow of a bedside lamp that allowed the nurses to check the IV drip and read his chart. Josie approached the bed tentatively. She hadn't talked to anyone about her fears for Dillon: at this point she was more worried about his emotional health than his physical health. He had experienced extended trauma that most people never encountered in a lifetime. For seven days, he endured abuses that he might never be able to talk about. And if he did want to talk, she had no idea how she'd respond. She had no training or background or even understanding of PTSD. She realized, as much as she wanted him awake, she was also terrified of what she might find.

She stood by his bed for a long time, staring at his face, at his pale skin and rough beard. He'd been so meticulous with his appearance; she'd never seen more than a day's growth of stubble on his face. His hair was dirty. She wanted to take him home, draw a steamy bath, and soak him, gently wash away the memories, if only for a moment. Then she would feed him dinner. She'd find good recipes, fix his favorite lasagna and cheesecake. She reached out her hand and laid it across his forehead, then brushed it down his cheek. She leaned farther over the bed and placed both her hands on his shoulders, then ran them slowly down his arms, and then his chest, feeling his body under the covers, reassuring herself he would be fine. He was just thin, but he was okay.

Dillon's eyelids moved and she could see he was struggling to open his eyes. She knew he needed sleep, but at that moment she desperately wanted for him to see her and realize he was back at home. When he finally opened his eyes and saw her he gave her a sleepy, drugged smile, then closed his eyes again in exhaustion. He shifted in bed, slightly onto his side, and lifted his arm with the IV attached, just an inch, but enough for Josie to realize what he wanted. With his eyes still closed he slowly whispered, "Come here. Beside me."

Josie placed her shoes under the chair next to the bed and slipped under the covers, pressing her back into his chest. Gently, she reached back and laid her arm over his side. His legs curled up into her, and she felt his face on the top of her head, breathing in her scent.

"I love you," she whispered, but his body had once again given in to sleep.

TWENTY-NINE

Walking across the parking lot of the emergency room at seven thirty the next morning, Josie realized she had missed daylight savings. The past week had not revolved around schedules or eight-hour workdays, and she only now recognized that she was experiencing the sunrise an hour later. From the ground to the sky there was a psychedelic color scheme: orange at the horizon line fading up into magenta and then streaks of deep violet across the sky. The colors were broken by strips of cirrus clouds that reflected a white light so bright it hurt her eyes. She followed the lay of the land, the dark silhouettes of rocky outcroppings and the awkward angles of cactus that tripped across the desert.

Josie had lived in the Midwest and spent time out East, but the desert solitude always felt like home. It was the West Texas mix of isolated heartache and profound beauty that had settled into her bones, and she knew she could never leave this place. She thought sometimes that the desert resonated more profoundly inside her than did the people in her life. Moments like this made her wonder at her own psyche. Did other people feel this way about their homestead, the family ranch, life at sea?

The doctor had checked Dillon first thing that morning and

provided excellent news. Test results indicated Dillon's kidneys were fine, and the doctor agreed to release him to Josie's care later that afternoon. He had been clear that the physical wounds would heal quickly, but the psychological trauma would need long-term attention. He had promised to look into finding a mental health professional who could offer the kind of care Dillon would need.

Josie had to tie up a few loose ends at work and take a shower at home before she needed to be back at the hospital. She drove downtown to Manny's and knocked on room 6. A minute later, Hector answered the door, dressed in jeans and a T-shirt, his hair still wet from a shower. He didn't look surprised to see her. He stood back from the door.

"Come on in."

Hector walked over to the bed and pulled the comforter up to cover the bedsheets. He sat down on the edge of the bed and Josie took the chair across from him.

"Otto called me a little while ago and said I could go see my dad this morning before they take him away."

"Did he explain what happened yesterday?"

Hector nodded, his face clouded with an emotion that Josie couldn't interpret. She said nothing, giving him time to say what he needed.

"He told me about you finding my dad in the barn, and about the money in the suitcases. He said you found Mr. Reese and he was in pretty bad shape." Hec stared at his hands, grasped together on his lap, his thumbs pressed tight against each other. He finally looked up at Josie, his expression full of regret. "I never meant to hurt anybody. It seemed like no matter what I did somebody was going to get hurt, either my dad or Mr. Reese. Then that lady was killed."

Josie noticed he didn't mention the danger and stress he had been under and she felt a wave of sympathy overcome her.

"None of what happened goes back on you, Hec. I'll tell you the same thing Nick told me. We're not the bad guys in this. Other people did bad things and we got caught in the middle."

"I should have told you sooner."

Josie put a hand up and recognized the familiarity of Hec's statement. *If I had checked on Dillon sooner.* It was like a mantra and it would be for a long, long time. "I'm not saying you didn't make mistakes. I made them too. But you were motivated by what you thought had to be done to save your dad. What matters is that you came clean in the end."

Hector considered her. Josie knew he would be turning over decisions he made in his own mind for years to come. So many things in his life had changed over the past month.

"You understand that you can't go back to the salvage yard without police protection? We don't know how the Medranos will react to all of this."

"Otto's taking me to see my dad this morning. Then we're going to get my truck. I'm going out to Otto's to see Buck. Delores said I could stay at their place." He grinned at Josie, obviously taken in by Delores's kindness. "I think I'll stay here for a while though, until I figure out a plan."

Josie stopped when she reached the door to go. "You have a lot of people backing you up. We want to see things go right for you. It's too soon right now, but just know we'll help you get on your feet. You won't have to do it alone."

As Josie walked into the Artemis PD, Lou looked up from her computer.

"You look like hell," she said.

"It's good to see you too."

"Seriously. You need some sleep." Lou smiled slowly. "Congratulations on last night. I'm sure happy you got Dillon back."

Josie nodded her thanks. "Just checking in. I'm on my way home. I'm bringing Dillon home this afternoon. I won't be back in until tomorrow unless you have any issues."

"You got two minutes?" Lou asked.

"Sure."

"Come over here then and pull up a seat."

Josie walked around the counter and sat in a spare chair beside Lou's computer.

"I went online and copied this so you could take a look. The mayor made morning news in Houston and San Antonio."

Josie rolled her eyes and sighed. "Do I really need to see this?"

Lou frowned. "I think you do."

Lou clicked Play and for the next two minutes Josie watched the puffed-up mayor nod and frown and offer self-deprecating comments as he took full credit for seizing nine million dollars in drug cartel money. When the clip was done, Josie sat back in her seat and faced Lou, stunned at the performance.

Lou laughed at Josie. "You ever hear that old expression, you can't coach stupid?"

Josie left Lou and walked down the street to the mayor's office. Helen stood from behind her desk and came at Josie with her arms extended. Josie accepted the hug, smelling the sweet scent of baby powder and oranges. Helen wrapped her tight, patting her back until Josie finally pulled away.

"I am so happy for you. Everything turned out just the way we all knew it would."

"Thanks, Helen. I appreciate it. Is the mayor available?"

"You go right on back. He just got back from the courthouse. Big excitement for little Artemis today!"

The mayor's door was open, and Josie found him standing in the middle of his office, apparently staring at a painting of Lyndon Johnson that hung behind his desk. Josie knocked and he turned, glanced at her absently, and motioned her in. He made no move toward his desk and instead turned back toward the painting. Josie stood beside Moss, who pointed a finger at it. "Our most famous Texan. Served as representative, senator, vice president, and president. Ever hear of the Johnson treatment?" Moss glanced at Josie and grinned. She had no idea what he meant. And he didn't care. "One day, you'll hear of the Moss treatment, mark my words."

"I'm sure I will," she said.

Moss finally walked around his desk and sat. He scrutinized Josie with narrowed eyes. "You feeling okay?"

"I'm headed home to get cleaned up. I spent the night at the hospital."

He looked relieved. "Good. Did you see the news this morning? It'll get picked up by CNN by this afternoon. Damn good interview."

"That's why I stopped by. I understand it's good press for you, for Artemis, but you have to remember who you're dealing with."

"I'm not an idiot. I know exactly who I'm dealing with. We sent a very clear message to the bastards this morning."

Josie cocked her head. "You did. That's my point. You basically told the Medranos that you single-handedly stole nine million dollars of their hard-earned money."

The anger was instant and fierce. "How dare you come in here and insult me. I am the mayor of this city. It was my police force who—"

Josie held her hands up, supplicating. "I'm not disagreeing with anything you said. I'm trying to get you to see it the way the cartel will see it. If they think this whole thing is on you?" She shrugged. "That's a lot of money for them to lose. And they want it back. That's all I'm saying."

The mayor stared at Josie and she could see he was searching for a suitable comeback. Before he could come up with one she took a deep breath and finished what she came for.

"It's a good reason to stay off the back roads from Marfa. I'd say let Roxanne find her own way home at night. You keep your doors locked." She raised her eyebrows. "You know, I could give you the name of my security company. Have your wife call me, and I'll give her the phone number."

Josie left the mayor fuming. She'd hit a nerve. There *is* such a thing as bad press, and the mayor had just opened up his own deadly line of it.

The drive home was a blur. As she approached her home, she noticed Nick carrying a large bag out to his SUV and then walking back inside her house.

She hadn't thought Nick would leave so soon. While she wanted a return to normal life, she also realized how much she had come to view Nick as a safety net. She had not been able to keep Dillon safe; that was the hard reality she'd had to face over the past few days. So what now? How could she establish the kind of procedures and routines that would allow her, and hopefully one day Dillon, to feel a sense of security?

The front door was open and she walked into the house to find Nick packing up his computer equipment in the dining room. He stopped when she walked into the room.

"How's Dillon?" he asked.

Josie nodded and sat down across from him at the table. "The doctor said his kidneys are functioning properly. They hope to release him this afternoon."

"Will he stay at his place?"

"I'd feel better with him here," she said. "At least until we get word on how the Medranos are reacting."

"That's a good idea. I've got feelers out everywhere. I'm leaving today, but I'm not off the case. There's quite a bit of follow-up intel gathering. I'll be in touch. Daily for a while."

Josie hesitated.

"What's going on?" he said.

She struggled to make sense of her thoughts. "We've got Dillon home. He's safe and already recovering physically. The money is in our custody. Wally and Bea Conroy are behind bars. And I still feel like nothing has been resolved."

"It hasn't. That's the bitch of it. It's the worst part of the job for me. I finish a case and know nothing is resolved. It's never over. The kidnappings continue. The cartels get bigger, their networks spread around the continent. Around the world."

Josie shut her eyes and leaned her head back against the dining room chair. "So this feeling never leaves you?"

"Josie."

She opened her eyes and looked straight into his.

"I only got so many years of doing this job before I hit the brick wall. I know that. My life is this job. I can't bring a woman into this kind of hell. So I got a few more years and then I retire. Try to live a normal life for a while. Settle down. But you already have a normal life. Don't you see that?"

She smiled with no humor. She couldn't see how any of this could be considered a normal life.

"You have someone to love and he loves you back. That's a life. Learn to separate your cop life from your personal life. Get Dillon counseling, and go with him. Figure out how the two of you can push through this nightmare and come out on the other side."

His cell phone rang and he answered it, talking on his headset while he packed up his remaining bag. He briefly pushed the headset away from his mouth and shook Josie's hand, said he'd be in touch, and walked out to his car, resuming his conversation with the person on the other end. He had avoided the good-bye, the awkward exchange of emotion, and in a moment of clarity, Josie saw the parallels between her own life and Nick's. He would never retire. The job was his safety net: it kept him from having to figure out how to lead a normal life, a messy life with kids and a wife, a family that loved him. Dillon had been trying to provide that life for Josie; he had been patiently leading her to it with love and compassion, but she had never seen that kind of a life as a real possibility until now.

Nick backed out and paused before he put the car into drive, catching Josie's eye for a beat too long, then drove away to the next family in desperate need of his help.